WORLDS APART

"Yes, I should call you by your title, for there is no use in my imagining any deeper intimacy between us. Mr. Carlyle did me the favor of pointing out the difference between our worlds. I have no place in yours, none at all."

Nathaniel was silent, searching for words to explain that which was not clear even to him.

"You do not know what you want with me, do you?" she snapped.

"I cannot categorize you, if that is what you are asking," he said, still searching for his own understanding, for an explanation he could give himself for why he could not stand the thought of breaking off their acquaintance. "But God knows I want you."

"For what, Nathaniel? Am I a friend to have a meal with, or a woman to seduce with a silver bracelet? What do you want from me?" she cried.

He grasped her face between his hands and slid his fingers into her bound hair, abandoning the effort at the thought for that which his body already knew to be true. "This," he said, and bending down he captured her lips with his own. She resisted for only a moment.

Other *Love Spell* books by Lisa Cach:
THE CHANGELING BRIDE

Bewitching The Baron

Lisa Cach

LOVE SPELL BOOKS NEW YORK CITY

To Rebecca.

LOVE SPELL®

March 2000
Published by

Dorchester Publishing Co., Inc.
276 Fifth Avenue
New York, NY 10001

ISBN 0-505-52368-X

Printed in the United States of America.

Bewitching The Baron

Prologue

Yorkshire, 1722

The air was grey and frosty. Death, sliding its way inside through the crack beneath the door, crept stealthily down the hall and into the bedrooms. It had already caressed the faces of two in this house, draining the warmth from their lifeless flesh, and now had returned to wrap itself around the one remaining member of the family.

Valerian Bright did not feel its cold touch as it slid under the covers at the foot of her bed, stealing up her body, searching for weakness. She was deep in battle with her fever, fighting with the strength for which she had been named. She did not know that her parents lay dead in their room, did not hear the voice of her neighbor Mrs. Beatty, who prayed quietly at her bedside: prayed for Valerian's recovery, for the souls of her parents, and prayed most fervently of all that her own family would be safe from the fever.

The gloom of twilight slowly grew, a deep charcoal that expanded from the corners of the room. Mrs. Beatty lit candles against it and stirred the fire, listening to the crackling of the burning wood that was so incongruously cheerful in a house of death.

Mrs. Beatty heard the front door open and footsteps on the wooden floor, and she traced the paths and owners in her mind. It was her husband and the village undertaker, come to take away the bodies.

She went to the bed and looked down at Valerian. The girl was gaunt from her illness, her black hair lank, her cheeks flushed crimson. Mrs. Beatty pressed her own cool fingers to the child's forehead, and she brushed back a wisp of sweat-dampened hair stuck to Valerian's fevered cheek. "So young," she whispered. Even if the girl survived, she would be orphaned. There was an aunt somewhere in Cumbria, but Mrs. Beatty had been unable as yet to contact her.

Down the hall, the front door opened again, creaking loudly on its hinges. Mrs. Beatty turned her head, her face still, listening. The men were yet in the next room, voices and footsteps muffled by the wall.

A cold wind rushed through the bedroom, and then the front door slammed, hard, the force of it sending vibrations through the walls and floors of the house. A gentle warmth began to heat the room, and the chill that had been present throughout the long day finally dispersed.

Footsteps, loud and purposeful, approached from down the hallway.

Deep in her fever, Valerian saw strange images. Her mind wove stories from them as time flowed on around her, unnoticed. She hardly knew that she continued to exist at all. As she weakened, the confusion of the dreams gave way. The images faded and darkened, until a night fell upon her mind.

Ahead of her appeared a distant glow, and she moved toward it, slowly at first, then rushing soundlessly through a vast distance, the luminescence growing brighter and stronger. All at once she was in it, surrounded by it, and warmth infused her. Her parents were with her, and caught her up in their arms.

After an eternal moment they set her down, and her father spoke.

"Valerian, my dearest. You cannot stay here."

"You are not yet finished with your life," her mother said. "You have much to do, and a gift to share with others."

"You must go back," her father said.

For a moment she understood. The path of her life lay before her in perfect clarity. She felt the power of her gift flowing through her, as rich as blood. But then something was pulling her away, dragging her from her parents, from warmth and understanding. She fell from them, back through the empty black space, and awoke to the heaviness of her body, hot and weak and damp under a layer of blankets.

She heard the subdued voices of women and opened her eyes, squinting against the dim light.

"Mother?" she whispered, her throat hoarse.

There were quick footsteps, a firm hand taking her own, and then a face, familiar and not familiar. The woman had black hair streaked with lightning bolts of white at the temples, a face weathered by sun and wind. The line of her nose, the curve of her brows were as Valerian's mother's but the eyes themselves were deep green, not the light blue that Valerian had inherited from Emmeline Bright.

Valerian frowned, concentrating, the seemingly familiar

face confusing her. An answer finally came, forming on her lips as she thought it. "Aunt Theresa?"

"Yes, my sweet. I shall take care of you now. Your mother asked me to."

"They said I had to stay," she complained softly.

"I know they did." Theresa kissed her brow as tears spilled down Valerian's cheek. "I know. Sleep now, child. Sleep."

Chapter One

Cumbria, 1737

"Grey skies over Greyfriars. How appropriate. And exactly how I remember the godforsaken place." Nathaniel Warrington, the new Baron Ravenall, surveyed with distaste the thatched roofs of the small village coming into sight, thin streamers of smoke rising from the stone chimneys and blending with the heavy sky.

"It looks welcoming enough to me, if it means we have almost reached Raven Hall and I can get off this bleedin' horse," Paul Carlyle grumbled, shifting his posterior on the smooth leather of the saddle. "I do not know when I last spent such an eternity on horseback. My arse is not used to such cruel treatment, I am telling you. And I need a drink. Is there an inn in this midden heap of a town?"

"Last I remember, but that was over fifteen years ago, and it looked ready to fall apart then."

"Inns never fall apart. They slowly sink and their beams

go askew, but they never fall apart. Burn, sometimes. You do not think it has burned down, do you?"

"How the hell should I know? I told you, I have not been here for years."

"Maybe there is something to drink at the hall. Your old Uncle Georgie had a cellar, right?"

Nathaniel gritted his teeth. Paul's company had been entertaining for the first fifty miles, bearable for the next forty, and then had slowly deteriorated into intolerable. In as foul a temper as he had himself been upon leaving London, he had somehow thought that Paul would lighten his mood. *Quelle erreur.* What a mistake.

Paul had certainly had his own reasons to accompany him into this uncivilized hinterland, not the least of which was the sword-wielding husband of a certain plump lady in the city. Which reminded Nathaniel:

"Your battle wound acting up?" he inquired with saccharine sweetness.

"Shut your mouth!"

"Such rudeness, my friend."

"I would like to see how cheery you would be, if it were your ass with the slash."

"*I* would never be caught in flagrante delicto with a man's wife, and most certainly would not have scrambled bare-assed through a window if I had."

"Made a bloomin' big white target for him, I did," Paul said, his mouth twisting. "He aimed for the moon, and got it."

The miserable trip was almost at its end, and although unlike Paul he was in excellent physical health, Nathaniel too would be happy to get off the roads and out of the saddle. Despite their retinue of armed footmen, they had twice been accosted by highwaymen, and had left more than one thieving body dead along the roadside to be collected later by his comrades. It wore on one's nerves, travel did.

"You should be safe from the temptations of wedded female flesh at Raven Hall," Nathaniel said. "I hardly remember a clean face, much less a pretty one."

"Thank God for that. Maybe it will not be so bad for you, your exile here. It should be an effortless endeavor to remain in your family's good graces. Nothing to distract you from upright and moral behavior. Be a proper young baron, pillar of the community, eating beef and pudding, and growing fat with gouty joints."

"Good God, man, you do not need to make it sound worse than it already is."

"Rrrrawk!" came a harsh cry from off to the side of the muddy road. Nathaniel pulled his mount to a halt, Paul and the footmen behind following suit. His eyes lit on the source of the noise, an immense black raven perched on a tree branch, its black head hunched down into its glossy feathers, one eye turned to examine him.

The men stared at the unusually large and curious bird, and then Paul burst out laughing. "He has come to welcome you home, Baron Ravenall. If I were a more superstitious man, I would say it was an omen." He lowered his voice dramatically. "The ravens of Raven Hall shall claim your soul, and you shall never see London again."

Annoyed by his friend, and subtly disturbed by the knowing look in the bird's eye, Nathaniel nudged his mount to where he could reach the end of the branch where the raven sat, and jerked on the limb.

"Rrrawww!" the bird protested, wings spreading and flapping as he sought to hold tight to the branch. Nathaniel shook the branch again, harder, and at last the raven gave up, dropping toward the ground before his yard-wide wingspan caught the air, and he beat his way up, passing close enough that Nathaniel could feel the rush of air on his cheek.

"Eee-diot!" the raven screeched, and flapped his way off toward town.

Stunned, Nathaniel watched it go, his jaw slack. "Did that bird just call me an idiot?"

When no answer came, he turned to look at Paul and the others. One and all, their eyes were round, their jaws agape.

"You heard it?"

Paul finally spoke. "I am suddenly not so eager to see this ancestral hall of yours."

Nathaniel shrugged, trying to shake off the eerie occurrence. "The bird called me as he saw me. If I were not a fool, I would not be here now." And there was truth to that statement. It was an unexamined sense of guilt over his recent actions that had made him willing to submit to the punishment exacted by his disappointed family: exile to the remote estate he had recently inherited from his maternal great-uncle.

Damn the raven. It had probably only sounded like it had spoken, and it had been their own imaginations that had given meaning to the cawing. Ravens did not speak.

Valerian lifted the hot compress from the back of Sally's neck and examined the boil, gently testing the surface with her fingertip.

"Will you be lancing it?" Sally asked with a tremor in her voice, tilting her head so she could see Valerian's face. She was sitting on a stool outside the front door of her small cottage, where the daylight allowed Valerian to better see the boil.

"I think that might be best. It will heal more quickly, and you will not be in such pain, what with your collar rubbing against it all the time."

Sally stared down at her hands clasped tightly between her knees and nodded, a few strands of lank brown hair falling against her cheek, shielding her face.

Valerian tucked a few of the strands back behind Sally's ear, her other hand resting lightly on the woman's shoulder. "You will barely feel it," she reassured her. "It will not take but a minute to do, and I will put something on it that will help it to heal quickly."

"I have been through worse."

Valerian silently agreed with that. Sally had three sons living, and had given birth to four other children. The woman knew something about pain. Lancing the boil would hardly compare, but Valerian had come to expect people to dread any form of medical care. Most put off any treatment at all until their condition grew so terrible that they were forced to it.

She dipped her rag back into the small kettle of steaming water at her feet, then gently pressed it once again against the inflammation, drawing the infection to the surface. She took out her small case of knives and made a selection, then paused. Best to give Sally something else upon which to concentrate. She dug into her basket and pulled out a small wooden carving of a bird with two shiny black stones as eyes.

"Here, hold this."

Sally looked up from under her brows, then down at the carving Valerian had thrust into her hands. She chuckled softly. "It looks like Oscar."

"It does rather, does it not? It is more than a mere carving, though. Hold it tightly in your hands, and let only the eye show. Now, I want you to stare into that eye. Concentrate on it. Think only of the bird in your hand, and the eye watching you."

As Sally obeyed, Valerian finished preparing. She heard and sensed movement nearby in the lane, but ignored it as the usual activity of village life. She was as intent on her task as Sally was on the carved bird. "See only the eye, you are aware of nothing but the eye," she murmured, and with a swift, short stroke she lanced the boil. Sally did not even flinch.

"The eye is watching you, watching over you, protecting you," Valerian continued softly, and proceeded with draining the boil, using scraps of clean cloth to catch the discharge. When she was finished, she took a small pot of salve from her basket and began to dress the wound.

Now that the worst of it was over and little concentration required, her senses shouted that she was being watched, and she turned. Her breath caught at sight of the mounted figures, who had paused to observe her. They were a mass of rich cloth riding high on fine horses, and for a moment she could not distinguish one from the other. She had never seen such a collection on the muddy street of Greyfriars.

"By God, Nathaniel, I declare that was by far the most revolting scene I have ever witnessed. I am of a mind to leave you to your fate. Derogatory birds from hell, bursting pustules—what further pleasures await?"

Valerian narrowed her eyes at the speaker, a slender young man, perhaps a couple of years older than herself, with blond eyebrows. A wig of curls hid his hair, but his features were fine, with a thin straight nose. Her diagnostic eye took in the pained manner in which he sat his horse, favoring one buttock.

"If you find my activities so repulsive, sir, then I shall be most happy to leave the care of that sore on your buttocks to your own hand."

The blond man's eyes widened, and he shifted in his saddle, but it was his companion who answered her.

"My apologies for my friend. It has been a long journey, and as you correctly surmised, his hindquarters are not in their usual state of youthful health."

Valerian examined this new speaker, taking in the

breadth of his shoulders and his relaxed attitude in the saddle. His brows were dark brown, and a faint shadow of whiskers darkened his jaw. She could not see the color of his eyes, but they stared at her from a strong, symmetrical face that wore an expression of condescending amusement. He was a handsome man, but his air of entitlement annoyed her.

"Who are they?" Sally whispered behind her.

Valerian turned her head, frowning. Sally still clasped the carving, but obviously Valerian's altercation with the strangers had broken the entrancement. Sally's eyes were bright with a mix of nervousness and curiosity.

"A very good question," the dark man said in his lightly mocking tone before Valerian could answer. "I must apologize again, this time for having failed to introduce myself. I am Nathaniel Warrington, the new Baron Ravenall, and this rude man is my friend, Paul Carlyle. Presently sans title, but if he lives long enough, he may yet see the day when he inherits one."

Valerian gave Paul one of her notorious smiles, the smile that showed her slightly long, pointed canines, and made her look, she had been told, like a wolf salivating for the kill. The smile clearly expressed her doubt that Paul would live to see his inheritance. She was rewarded by his shudder.

"Welcome to Greyfriars, Baron Ravenall," Valerian then said, turning to the man who, apparently, had every right to act entitled in the town he now owned. "Your great-uncle is mourned by us all. He was a good, fair man, and is sorely missed." She tilted her head, and her voice took on a musing quality. "We have all been wondering if his successor would prove his equal."

His eyes narrowed, sensing the challenge. "Are you the healer or midwife here, Miss . . . ?"

"Bright. Valerian Bright. My aunt and I share that honor."

"Miss Bright. Will you do me the kindness of coming to Raven Hall tomorrow, to tend to my friend's wound? I know that a healer would not hold the ill-tempered words of a suffering man against him."

She opened her mouth to refuse, then shut it again, and gave a bare nod. He was right: She would not let personal aversion stop her from helping anyone. Which was rather a pity in this case, she thought.

"Splendid. I shall expect you at noon." With a nod to her, he nudged his horse, and the whole troupe continued down the street, turning at the crossroads onto the road that lead to Raven Hall.

Valerian watched them go with her lips pressed tightly together.

"What did you do that for?" Paul wailed, once they were out of earshot. "I am not going to let her touch me. Did you see the way she smiled at me? Did you see those teeth?"

"They did look remarkably healthy. Do not tell me she frightened you, a poor country girl like that?" Nathaniel mocked.

"Damn right she did. Probably a witch. Probably will poison me as soon as look at me."

"A week away from London, and already you fall prey to the superstitions of country folk. Really, Paul, I am surprised. Where is the harm in having her check your wound?"

"Do not tell me it was concern for my bodily person that made you do that. Why did you ask her to come?"

"She looked like she knew what she was doing, and you were less than complimentary of her skills. It would be good to make it up to her. I do not wish to alienate my people my first day amongst them."

Paul narrowed his eyes at him. "Is that all there is to it?"

Nathaniel affected a look of surprised innocence.

"Certainly. What else do you expect? I would not ask her to come purely for the entertainment of watching her prod your hairy backside with her sharp little knives. I have no desire for revenge on you for the last fifty miles of whinging and complaining, and your ceaseless yowling for ale."

"God knows I do not compare to the bright ray of sunshine that you have been this past fortnight. I have been blinded by your good humor on many an occasion, truly I have."

"Careful now," Nathaniel said. "You shall sour your stomach with that bile."

They rode a bit in silence, then Paul spoke again. "I worried that you might have had something else in mind with her."

Nathaniel felt a spurt of resentment, and did not resist the urge to goad his friend. "She did have a clean face, after all. When she is finished with you, perhaps I shall impress her with the baronial armature, eh? Give her a taste of the master's rod. After all, no one in London will ever hear of it, or care if they did."

Paul stared at him, aghast. "You cannot mean it, after all that has happened! And not with *her*, surely not. A muddy-toed peasant girl?"

Nathaniel kept his expression bland. "I believe she was wearing shoes."

"Nate—"

Nathaniel gave an exasperated sigh. "I am but jesting with you, Paul. For God's sake, I of all people know better than to involve myself with the likes of her."

Nathaniel could feel his friend staring at him for a long moment, sifting his words for truth. "Well," Paul said at last. "So you should."

Nathaniel chose not to answer, having neither the energy nor the heart for the argument, especially as Paul's suspicions were not entirely off the mark. In his mind's eye he saw Miss Bright's curved figure as she bent to her disagreeable task over the woman's neck. He saw her red lips, pulled back in that grimace of a smile that she'd used to terrify Paul. And those eyes, bright enough to pierce him from a distance, looked startlingly light set amidst her thick black lashes. She had not shown him a hint of subservience, not even the required curtsy.

Yes, she had caught his attention, there was no question of that, but he would have to be a fool to seek anything more from her than her doctoring skills. He would like to think he had learned his lesson about entanglements with those of the lower classes.

A breeze rustled through the woods along the lane, and somewhere a branch snapped. Nathaniel scanned the waving leaves, light green with new spring growth, and saw only trees. Ahead loomed the grey stone wall that fronted the estate, and just as they reached the gate, with its twin stone sculptures of ravens on either side, he thought he heard a rough voice calling from the forest.

"Eee-diot," it said.

Idiot, indeed.

Chapter Two

Valerian kept to the grassy verge to the left of the footpath that wound through the hills to home. Her shoes were in her basket, now that she was beyond the filth of the street of Greyfriars. The grass was cool and slightly damp beneath her callused soles, and welcome after the sweaty confines of the leather. The hem of her dull purple skirt was just high enough to keep from the damp ground. She hummed under her breath, swinging her basket, and tried to regain her usual sense of calm, so rudely disturbed by the baron.

Halfway home she took the left fork in the path, following it to the low hill with the standing stones, from which the small bay that emptied onto the Irish Sea could be seen, and the hump of the Isle of Man in the distance. The skies had cleared somewhat, and the sun had begun its descent and was low enough to cast a yellow light upon the water and through the green vegetation of the hills. She stood silent, soaking in the tranquil beauty, but the peaceful oneness she usually felt here eluded her today. Nathaniel Warrington's mocking features imposed themselves before her mind's eye.

"Arrogant peacock," she muttered sourly, and went to examine the goods that had been left on the Giving Stone.

"The Giving Stone" was what she and her aunt, and the villagers as well, called the fallen stone on the north side of the circle. No one knew who had built the circle, raising the huge slabs of granite in two concentric rings, but it and hundreds of others like it dotted the countryside, along with the mounded cairns of long-buried Britons. This circle was far from complete, several of the stones having disappeared into the fences and foundations of farms, or having been buried in fits of paranoia.

The fallen stone was the place where those Valerian and her aunt had helped with their healing or their water-divining left their payment. It was considered harmful to the healing or magical process—not to mention extremely bad manners—to pay a healer directly, and so the villagers followed the age-old custom of anonymous donations, left a discreet interval after seeking and receiving aid. Of course, in a small village such as Greyfriars, it was not hard to determine which offering had come from whom.

Valerian smiled to herself. The crocks of honey, butter, and preserves, those had most likely been from Mrs. Hubert, who lived with her husband and brood of children on a farm a couple miles from Greyfriars. Aunt Theresa had given her a tonic for her colicky baby, and ointment for rashes. She had also suggested that the tonic might do the digestion of Farmer Hubert a bit of good, a suggestion for which Mrs. Hubert was apparently grateful, judging by the generosity of her gift.

The bodice laces were probably from Gwendolyn, the miller's fifteen-year-old daughter, who had come seeking advice for winning the heart of her beloved Eddie. Eddie was the smith's oldest son, nineteen years old, and Gwendolyn had been overcome by the passions aroused from viewing his muscled arms and chest at work, gleaming with sweat in the light of the forge.

Valerian had worked quietly in the background, crushing herbs under her pestle, as Aunt Theresa gave the girl both honest advice and warnings on the consequences of unbridled passion. Gwen had gone away without the love potion she had requested, but with a steely determined eye, much unexpected in a girl known for her vivacious frivolity. If he was not careful, Eddie would soon find himself with a wife.

Valerian gathered the offerings into her basket and descended the hill, regaining the path toward home. It was mostly women and children she and her aunt helped; the men usually sought out the services of the surgeon in the next town. Only in emergencies would she or her aunt be called in to help with an injury, even though she was certain she and Aunt Theresa did a better job than the surgeon.

Perhaps that was the reason Baron Ravenall kept intruding so rudely into her thoughts. She should be the last person he would ask to care for his friend. Why had he insisted she come to Raven Hall? It was baffling. Perhaps he had been impressed by her treatment of Sally's boil.

She shifted the basket to her other hand. It was heavy now, and bumped against her leg as she walked. The path led through a cool, dark grove of trees in the dell between two hills, then emerged into a sloping meadow. A rocky stream tumbled its way through the meadow to the bay and thence the ocean, a wedge of which shimmered between the hills. The path crossed the stream via a narrow footbridge, then finally ended before the cottage that had been Valerian's home since her parents died and Aunt Theresa had come and taken her away from the Yorkshire village of her birth.

The distinctive sound of a spade working the dirt came from the far side of the cottage, and Valerian followed it around the corner to the kitchen garden. The formidable figure of her aunt, tall and somewhat stocky with muscle and middle age, was bent toward the ground, one hand pulling at the remains of the weed that the spade had unearthed.

"I am back," Valerian called to her.

Theresa Harrow straightened up, one hand going to the small of her back, massaging the muscles there. "Did everything go well? No problems?"

"None that you mean." It was not just the healing that her aunt was asking about. There were certain dangers around being perceived as a healer or white witch, however inaccurately, even now that it was no longer legal to persecute witches.

Theresa tossed the weed onto the wilted pile at the edge of the garden and came to join her. "What happened?"

Valerian shrugged uncomfortably. "I met the new baron, Nathaniel Warrington. He rode through town and stopped to watch me lance Sally's boil."

Theresa leant the spade against the side of the house, and she dusted her hands on her homespun apron. "Let us have some tea, shall we, and you can tell me all about it."

Over a cup of soothing peppermint tea, Valerian told her all that had transpired, and of the command to come tend to Paul Carlyle's derriere.

"A good sign, I must say," Theresa laughed. "He hardly seems likely to encourage our good neighbors to hang us if he is requesting your assistance for his friend."

Valerian shrugged one shoulder, uncertain. "I think it more likely he is unaware of how things are in villages. He did not strike me as a man who would be aware of our concerns, or particularly care even if he were."

"Neither did George Bradlaugh show much interest in the workings of the town."

"But he cared enough about what happened to you."

"Poor old fool." Theresa's lips curled in a fond smile. She rubbed her thumb along the rim of her heavy mug, musing, Valerian knew, on the former baron's romantic tendencies. "I do not think we can count on this Warrington fellow to think me the stars and the moon. He sounds a trifle young for me." She raised her eyebrows at her niece.

"Aunt Theresa, the man would as soon adore a pig as a poor village girl. And even if he did take notice of me in that way, which he would not, I would not return the interest."

"It sounds to me as if he has taken notice of you already."

Valerian's cheeks pinkened slightly. "I do not think so."

"And most certainly, he has made an impression of a certain strength on you, has he not? All this complaining—I think the lady doth protest too much."

"Oh, really, Aunt Theresa!" Valerian cried, cheeks flaming to scarlet.

"Perhaps you wish he had taken even more notice of you, hmm? But at any rate," Theresa continued before Valerian could protest yet again, "you know how important it is that we remain in his good graces. The town will follow his lead in their treatment of us. If the baron shows disapproval, it will be more than our lives are worth the next time some farmer has a cow die on him, or his wife miscarries."

Valerian turned her eyes away, staring out the open door at the twilight settling over the meadow. The fluttery shape of a bat crossed her field of vision, chasing insects. "I know."

In those two words were fifteen years of awareness that

she and her aunt were outsiders, for all that the townsfolk and farm wives sought their aid. They were respected for their knowledge, and both despised and feared for suspicion of whence that knowledge had come. That fear, while keeping them somewhat safe in their isolation, could turn destructive with a change in the wind. The witch hunts of the past century were long over, the witch laws recently repealed, but the countryfolk found more truth in their own beliefs than in the letter of the law. She who was a healer and midwife today might tomorrow be denounced as a poisoner in league with Satan.

It was not a fate to wish on anyone, much less oneself. If being nice to the baron would do anything to prevent it, nice she would be.

Chapter Three

"You are not going to wear that, are you?"

Valerian turned from the small silver mirror at her aunt's critical tone. "What is wrong with it?"

"Really, Valerian."

Theresa's exasperation spoke for itself. Valerian tightened her lips for a moment in defiance, then loosened them as she gave in, and she began to yank at the laces of her work-a-day bodice.

"I know, I know, my foolish pride," Valerian muttered, removing the bodice and pulling on her best black one over her chemise. It had elbow-length sleeves, and was both stiff and tight enough to provide support for her breasts. It was her best more by virtue of newness and quality of material than because of any decoration, although with the purple laces that matched her skirt it had a certain attractiveness to it. "I did not want him to think I had dressed up for him."

"Come here, let me fix your hair."

Valerian flounced down onto a stool with an exaggerated sigh. Theresa pulled a few wisps of hair from her braid to frame her face, then squinted at her critically. "You need something more."

The cottage had a high roof, steeply peaked, and thatched with heather. In the dark recesses above their heads hung line after line of drying plant matter, from herbs to flowers to lengths of root. The cottage forever smelled of a combination of wood smoke and sweet dry greenery, punctuated with touches of scents both more spicy and more noxious. Theresa dragged out their ladder, and she quickly retrieved a spray of dried purple statice from where it had been hiding in the shadows above.

Ignoring her niece's fierce frown, she twisted the papery flowers into Valerian's braid. "There. It goes against human nature to think a witch would wear flowers in her hair."

"More likely he will think I am trying to attract his attention."

"And so what if he does? If he thinks you like him, he will be more inclined to be kindly disposed towards you. The last thing we want to do is antagonize the man."

"I do not want him to take it as an invitation."

Theresa shrugged. "I know you will be careful. And it might not be so bad, if you decided he was not so disagreeable. . . ."

"Aunt Theresa!"

"Hush, child. I am not trying to sell you into prostitution to secure our safety. But you are twenty-seven years old, and you have never had a sweetheart. They are all afraid of you. If the baron shows an interest, I see nothing wrong with experiencing a little of what life has to offer."

Valerian pulled out from beneath her aunt's hands and quickly gathered up her things, her movements jerky.

"When I do decide it is time to 'experience' things, it will *not* be with the baron. The very idea repulses me."

Valerian hurried out of the house, eager to escape her aunt's knowing smile. Sometimes becoming a hermit and living in a cave sounded like a very good idea.

The path she would take to Raven Hall was no more than a deer path through the hills and woodland. Raven Hall was between her own home and the town of Greyfriars, and the path she normally took to town made a wide circuit of the estate. Today she took the shortcut that would lead directly into the Raven Hall orchard, and thence to the gardens and the house.

Once out in the late morning sunshine her mood lifted, and she managed to forget for a bit her aunt's lewd suggestions. Her eyes scanned the greenery to either side of the path, taking in the first shoots of plants that had lain dormant through the winter. What should have been a ten-minute walk stretched to twenty, then thirty minutes as she repeatedly left the path to examine bits of flora, her mind cataloging locations and stages of growth. It was only when the path spilled her out into the edge of the apple orchard that she recalled with a start where she was headed and for what purpose.

A glance at the sun told her that she might be late, and she hoped that the baron was not too punctilious. Mr. Carlyle, on the other hand, was probably thanking God for each minute of her absence. She hurried through the orchard, caught in a false blizzard of color as the breeze brushed through the blossom-laden trees, the silky pink-white petals catching in her hair and dress, floating about her in a springtime snowstorm.

It was this vision of unexpected, almost magical loveliness that met Nathaniel's eye when he reached the end of the gardens. Having grown impatient with waiting for Valerian in the house, he had come out to the gardens to walk and distract himself, and to silently chastise himself for caring whether she came or not.

He stood motionless, frozen with surprise and wonder as she seemed to float towards him through the natural gallery of arching trees. He knew the exact moment that she noticed him, for she stopped and stared, her eyes wide, her full lips slightly parted. They stood, eyes locked, for an endless moment, and then the wrath of hell descended on his head.

There was a scraping rush of wind and feathers, and then a great flapping blackness blinded him. He felt cruel claws digging through his hair, accompanied by a harsh and grating series of screams. He batted wildly at the demon, and was stabbed cruelly in the hand for his efforts, the creature's hoarse and fiery cries of "Finders keepers!" barely penetrating his consciousness as he sought to rid himself of his assailant. Suddenly the weight of the creature lifted, and his hands touched his bare head, his hat gone, his hair snarled by the claws of the beast.

"Oscar! You bad bird! Bad bad bad!" he heard Valerian scolding, and dazed, he looked around and saw an enormous raven sitting on his hat some ten feet away, its beak ripping gleefully at the gilt braiding that lined his tricorn. The raven stopped long enough to tilt its head and eye the healer, then squawked out, "Finders keepers!" once more and resumed its destruction of what had once been a fine piece of haberdashery.

"Oscar!" Valerian hollered, clearly outraged. The bird hunched its head into its wings, and sat protectively over the hat. Valerian strode forward and yanked the hat away from the bird, who flapped his wings angrily and cawed in protest, then launched himself at her head.

Nathaniel lunged, pulling her out of harm's way, his hat

crushed between them as he sought to shield her from the satanic bird. The raven circled them once, then flapped his way to the top of an apple tree, landing with enough force to shake loose blossoms.

"Let go of me!" Valerian protested, startled. Her face was pressed into his chest. She struggled to free herself, to no avail. She had not realized he was such a big man.

"He is watching us," the baron murmured into her hair. His arms all but squeezed the breath out of her, and he began to walk backwards, dragging her with him away from the apple tree where Oscar perched, grumpily observing them.

"Ees muh et, oo ee-ee-ut!" she said into his brocade vest, tasting metal as a silver button found its way into her mouth.

"What?"

He loosened his hold on her head enough for her to gain some breathing room, and she spit out the button and repeated what she had said. "He is my pet, you idiot!"

She saw now that his eyes were dark hazel, lined with black lashes, his brows slanting dangerously under a loose shock of deep auburn hair as he made sense of what she said. "You lay claim to that evil creature?"

"He is not evil. Mischievous and greedy maybe, but not evil."

His arms around her loosened further, and she pushed herself free, then tried to beat some shape back into his tricorn. "Sorry about your hat. He likes shiny things." She held it out to him, and he stared blankly at the mangled blue fabric and dangling gold trim before reaching out to take it.

"Do not give it another thought," he said politely, and she could see his face begin to change as he drew on the same mask of arrogance he had worn in Greyfriars.

"Here, let me properly introduce you," she offered,

remembering Theresa's cautions against offending him. "Oscar!" she called, and then whistled once, a short, high note.

Oscar launched himself from his branch and swooped gracefully down to where they stood, landing smoothly upon Valerian's shoulder and leaning his head against her hair, camouflaging himself against the glossy locks that matched his own feathers.

"Oscar, this is the new baron. You remember his great-uncle, do you not? The old baron?"

"Eee-diot!" Oscar squawked.

"No, 'Baron,' " Valerian corrected, biting the inside of her lip to keep from smiling.

"Eee—"

"No! He is the baron, Oscar. Baron." Valerian chanced a peek at the baron's face, and was gratified to see that there was open interest there, the mocking, arrogant mask at least temporarily at bay.

"Baron!" Oscar repeated. "Baron Ravenall!"

The baron's eyebrows shot up in surprise, and Valerian explained. "He learns phrases, not just words. Give him the first half of a phrase he knows, and he will add the ending himself."

"Remarkable! I once heard a parrot speak, but never a raven. How ever did you teach him?"

Valerian smiled at his childlike interest. His eyes were sparkling, and she could feel the curiosity coming off him in waves, with no trace of anger. He seemed to have forgotten the mangled tricorn as well as his air of superiority. "I caught him when he was still a baby. It was then mostly a matter of repeating words and phrases until he could say them himself. Something like teaching a child to speak, I should imagine. He is quite intelligent, although his manners leave something to be desired."

The baron raised his hand, as if to touch the bird, and

Valerian noticed for the first time that he was bleeding. She grabbed his large hand in both of hers, turning it to examine the small gash. "Did Oscar do this to you?"

"What? Oh, it is nothing." He was still staring, mesmerized, at the bird on her shoulder.

"I will clean it for you, and bandage it." She turned her head towards her pet. "And as for you, Oscar," she scolded in a deeply disapproving tone, "You have been a very naughty bird. You ought to be ashamed of yourself."

Oscar buried his head in her hair, and began to make the loud wails of a baby with colic. "Waaa aaa aaa aa, waaa. . . ."

"That is right, you naughty raven. You should cry. Did you see what you did to his hand? Did you?"

The wails grew louder and more lifelike, and the baron began to protest, "Really, is that necessary? It is just a scratch, no harm done, really. . . ."

Valerian tried to keep from smiling, and stroked Oscar's back. "There now, he forgives you, which is more than you deserve." Oscar's head emerged from her hair, and the crying stopped. The bird's eyes were as beady and dry as ever. "Go on now," Valerian told the bird. "Leave me to my work."

"Baron Ravenall!" Oscar said, looking at Nathaniel, then bobbed once, as if bowing, and leapt into the air. They watched him go, and then Valerian picked up her basket.

"I suppose I should see to your hand now, and to my other patient as well," she said briskly. She found it was herself who wanted to retreat behind a facade of politeness, now that the distraction of Oscar was gone. She was reluctantly finding his interest in Oscar, and his silly attempt to protect her, rather charming, and the one thing she did not want was to be charmed.

Despite Aunt Theresa's sentiments on the subject, she did not believe that this man could ever have any interest in her. Aunt Theresa claimed that the reason she had never had a suitor was that all the men were afraid of her, but she knew the truth. She had no suitors because no one wanted her. So, it was better not to let herself become interested in men she could never have. It saved a lot of heartache.

Her tone appeared to recall him to himself, and he offered her his arm. No man had ever done that for her. Embarrassed, made nervous by the unfamiliar gesture, her instinct was to reject it. She fumbled with her basket, pretending to check its contents until his arm dropped back to his side. She glanced at his face, and saw that he was watching her carefully.

"May I carry your basket for you?" he asked.

"No, thank you. I always carry it myself." She clutched the handle tightly, scared of exchanging its worn familiarity for the baron's arm.

One dark eyebrow quirked upwards at her refusal, and she had the uncomfortable suspicion that he knew he was making her nervous. He probably thought her funny, the ignorant little country virgin. The thought stiffened her backbone.

"You know, I met your pet yesterday just south of town," the baron said as they began to walk back towards the house, through the formal gardens. "He called me an idiot then, too. Paul thought him an omen that I would never leave Raven Hall."

"There would be a surfeit of males in Greyfriars if that were the case. Oscar calls all men idiots."

"Indeed?"

"He is a most perceptive bird."

The baron snorted. "And was it chance alone that I met a raven upon my arrival, or would you agree with Paul that the sighting augured an attachment that I would soon develop?"

She did not understand the suggestion she sensed in

his tone, and chose to ignore it. "I would have found it far more peculiar if you had seen no ravens whatsoever, than that Oscar or another sought you out, in your bright clothes. We do not see much similar here." She thought his rich clothing made him look something like a flower against the soft greens of the garden.

"No, I do not suppose you would." His tone was coolly casual.

Valerian set her jaw. No doubt he thought her hopelessly provincial, living her life in a small town in the back of beyond. "Besides which, the ravens were here long before the town or the hall. It is not as if the hall bears its name for no reason. And come to think of it, why would God bother to send *you* an omen in the first place?"

It was out before she knew what she was saying, and she grimaced, appalled at her bad behavior. This was not the way to stay in his good graces, not to mention being inexcusably rude. She peeked up at him from under her brows, her mouth twisted in distress. Supercilious hazel eyes met hers, and then the mask slipped and he laughed.

"Why indeed? You are perfectly right. It would be sheer arrogance to assume God had any interest in the likes of me." He paused, and the next words were so soft and darkly said, she almost missed them. "No doubt if there is a god, he has already given me up for lost."

Before she could comment on that, they had reached the bottom of the stone steps to the terrace that overlooked the garden, and the baron had his hand on the small of her back, pushing her forward. She could feel the warmth and strength of his wide palm through her clothing, and stepped quickly up the stairs to avoid the sensation.

She had been to Raven Hall many times, for the old baron had had a fondness for both Aunt Theresa and drink. His indulgence in the latter had resulted in a need for frequent visits from the former, although Valerian suspected that he'd exaggerated his illnesses in the hopes of luring Theresa to his home. Many times Theresa went alone, but just as often she would bring Valerian, who would receive permission to borrow books from the library and to explore the house while the baron received his treatment. In the end it was his heart that failed him, despite Theresa's foxglove teas, which had perhaps given him a few more years than he would have had otherwise.

She was pleased to see that the drawing room had not been changed since the baron's death: heavy, ornately carved wooden furniture with deeply colored upholstery was scattered about the room, mismatched with the delicate harpsichord that stood near the windows so that its music stand caught more light. A fire blazed on the hearth, sending a cheery glow into the somewhat medieval-looking room, with its stone floors and scattered woolen carpets.

It was a friendly room, with arched, leaded glass windows left over from the days when the hall had been an abbey. They faced west, and more than once Valerian had amused herself with her own creations on the harpsichord, then turned to sit and watch the colors of the setting sun in the skies above.

The old baron had never seemed to mind her presence, and she felt a familiar pang of loss at the thought of him. While he had been no hero, and had had his share of human frailties, he had exuded a vague goodwill toward everyone, and his tolerance and occasional generosity had set the easygoing atmosphere of the village. These past few months of waiting for the arrival of the new baron had sent a thread of anxiety running through Greyfriars, as if the inhabitants were children suddenly orphaned and awaiting the arrival of an unknown uncle to take charge.

"Let me take care of your hand," she said, setting her basket on a table.

The baron pulled out an expensive-looking handkerchief and dabbed at the blood. "It is hardly worth the bother."

"Better safe than sorry." She took his large hand in both of hers, tilting the back of it into the light from the windows. It was indeed little more than a scratch, and she tried to concentrate on that rather than the texture of the skin beneath her fingers. Her hands looked delicate and white against the brawn of his own, her capable fingers fragile. His was not a soft hand, for all that she might have expected an aristocrat's to be so. She wondered how he spent his time, to put the calluses there.

"I will put a little ointment on it. Wash it frequently, and do not let a scab or any crust form. It will heal more quickly and cleanly without them." He was silent as she worked, and a tension grew within her as she felt his eyes on her. She could hear her heart loud in her ears, and each rustle of her own movement seemed magnified under his scrutiny.

She finished with relief and released his hand, and then they both heard faint footsteps from behind the blackened oak door that led to the front hall.

The baron strode through the room to the door that was arched at the top like the windows, and stuck his head through. "Paul! Good, I do not need to send someone to hunt you down. Your healer is here."

Valerian heard incoherent protestations from the other side of the door, and could only make out a few words. "Poison" and "teeth" she definitely heard. She made her way to where the baron stood, and pushed the door all the way open. A very worried Paul Carlyle stood on the other side, his brow wrinkled in distress. He grimaced when he saw her, then caught himself and tried to cover his anxiety.

"Good afternoon, Mr. Carlyle," Valerian said softly, trying her best to look harmless. It was never easy to work with a frightened patient, and if she had known she would be examining his buttocks today, she would never have bared her teeth at him yesterday.

"Miss Bright." He swallowed, then continued. "Nate here—the baron, I mean—exaggerated things to you, I am afraid. I had my wound treated before leaving London, and there is really nothing further that needs to be done. It is healing quite nicely on its own. Sorry he dragged you all the way out here for nothing."

The baron opened his mouth to speak, but Valerian cut him off with a glance, then took one of Paul's trembling, moist hands in her own, and began to softly stroke the back of it. Startled, Paul stared at his own hand as if it belonged to someone else, but did not pull away.

Valerian led him into the drawing room, and over to a couch, where with a gentle tug she got him to sit down. In a soft, measured voice she asked him questions about his general health, his eating and drinking, what exercise he got, and gradually lulled him into relaxing, stroking his hand all the while. He brought up his wound on his own, in reference to riding, and explained the details of the damage done.

"If you had stitches put in over two weeks ago, do you not think it would be a good idea to have them taken out now?" she asked gently.

"I have been meaning to have my man do it."

"I would not like to see them become infected, or to have your skin stick to them. A skilled hand takes only a moment to remove them."

Paul stared at his hand, where it still rested in Valerian's, then met her eyes. Helpless submission was written there, and she gave his hand a squeeze. "A few quick tugs, and it will be over."

Seeing his friend's easy capitulation, Nathaniel found himself a seat and sat back to enjoy the show, intrigued already by the way Valerian had soothed Paul into compliance. He vividly recalled the fuss Paul had made about having the cut treated by the surgeon, and the constant complaining, flinching, and cursing while the stitches were put in place.

In contrast, here Paul was, awkwardly but willingly pulling down his breeches and lying on the couch, meek and vulnerable, allowing this woman he had sworn was a witch to approach his bare buttocks with a small, sharp pair of scissors.

Miss Bright was an unusual young woman, there was no question. And a lovely one, too. Nathaniel examined her figure as she worked. She lacked the corset-grown slenderness of the women of his circle, it was true, but he could not find fault with that. She looked strong and healthy, and he recalled those moments he had held her in his arms during Oscar's attack, smelling the slightly smoky, lavender scent of her, and feeling the softness of her curves even as he was surprised by the vigor of her struggles to escape him. He was reminded of trying to hold an unwilling, well-fed barn cat as a boy, and the combination of silky softness and strength as the cat twisted free of his hold.

Valerian's back was to him as she bent over her work, and his eyes settled on the curve where waist flared into hip, imagining his hands holding her steady as he took her from behind, her skirts rucked up about her hips. As if feeling his eyes, she turned and stared at him, her bright blue eyes questioning. He smiled slightly, impersonally, and turned his attention back to Paul's buttocks and the strip of wounded pink flesh.

Valerian finished her work, dabbing an ointment onto the healing wound to control the infection she saw there. She had felt the baron's eyes on her, and when she turned she caught that he was paying far closer attention to her hindquarters than to those of his friend. She shrugged off his examination as the idle interest every man showed in a woman, as instinctual as a dog sniffing grass.

She gave an internal sigh. She knew more than enough about the birds and the bees in theory. It was a pity she would never have a chance to put her knowledge into practice.

Chapter Four

The smithy rang with the clang of metal on metal, the roar of the forge a wild backdrop to the heavy blows of Jeremiah's oversized hammer. The skin on Valerian's face felt hot and dry from the heat of the shop, and her fingers tingled uncomfortably at the change from the chilly damp air outside.

The blacksmith's son Eddie did a final inspection of the clamming shovel Aunt Theresa had brought in last week to be repaired: rust, salt water, and rot had broken the marriage between handle and blade. Valerian watched the play of muscles on Eddie's arms where they emerged from the rolled sleeves of his shirt, wondering if Gwen had yet found a way to claim them for her own. They truly were magnificent arms, she had to admit, and his chest was equally well-developed. Her eyes ran over his body in a way they never had before, trying to fit what she saw displayed in the scorching smithy to what might lie under the cool silks and brocades of Nathaniel Warrington.

It had been nearly a week since her visit to Raven Hall, and she had not seen the baron again. Their meeting had ended on a most uncordial note when the baron had offered her coinage for her services.

Tight-lipped and deeply affronted, she had refused his offer politely at first, then with growing hostility as he tried to press payment upon her. She had gathered her things and quickly left, her offended pride not allowing her to consider his point of view until she was in sight of home.

Of course he had offered her money. He was used to dealing with doctors in the city, who would be fools if they did not demand payment for their services. He could not have known that he was insulting her. Even such rational thought, however, did not completely erase the humiliation she had felt at being offered the small stack of coins.

"Miss Bright?" Eddie's troubled voice finally pulled her from her thoughts, and she colored as she looked up at his scarlet face and realized that for some time she had been staring at his crotch.

"Ah . . . Is it is ready then?" she asked, gesturing to the shovel.

"I fixed it myself. Is there anything else you will be needing?"

"No, no, that is all, thank you." She took the shovel, her hand brushing his accidentally, and she briefly met his startled eyes. She tucked the shovel under her arm and fairly dashed from the smithy, bumping into Gwen a few steps outside the door.

"Miss Bright! Good day to you," the girl said, surprised. "Would you know if Eddie is inside?"

Valerian glanced back over Gwen's shoulder, to where Eddie had appeared in the shop's doorway, watching her with interest. "Turn around, and you will see him yourself," she answered, and patted the girl's shoulder before turning and walking as fast as she could from the scene.

What on earth had come over her? For the past week she felt as if her thoughts had not been her own. They had a distressing tendency to wander to the baron—"Nate," as Mr. Carlyle had called him.

A black fluttering at the corner of her eye warned of Oscar's approach. He landed with a clench of claws, a heavy and welcome weight on her shoulder.

"Valerian Bright!" came an angry female voice.

Valerian hunched her head down into her shoulders, in a gesture borrowed from Oscar. No, not Charmaine. Not today. And good lord, not with Alice Torrance trailing along behind.

"Do you know what that horrid creature of yours has been doing?"

Valerian turned to face the irate countenance of her cousin. Charmaine was at least ten years older than herself and they had not been kind years. Her face bore the striking structure that marked the females of their line, but a lifetime of dissatisfaction had worn unpleasant grooves into its surface, her lips thin and white in a perpetual expression of discontent.

Charmaine did not like being the daughter of one supposed witch, Theresa, and the cousin to another. She had never wished to pick up the broom of family tradition, so to speak, and whatever unusual qualities she may herself have possessed were deeply buried beneath her quest for normalcy. Her husband was the town cobbler.

"Good day to you, Charmaine, Mrs. Torrance," Valerian said, acknowledging the innkeeper's wife. "Has Oscar been causing trouble?"

"And when does he not?" Charmaine asked. " 'Tis the second time this week he has pulled my laundry to the ground. If I did not know better, I would think he had been sent on purpose to aggravate me."

"I am terribly sorry about your laundry," Valerian apologized, genuinely contrite on behalf of Oscar. She could not wish extra laundry chores on anyone, not even Charmaine. "If I knew how to break him of his bad habits, I would."

"Someday someone is going to shoot that bird," Mrs. Torrance put in.

Valerian narrowed her eyes at the woman. "I would be quite upset by that," she said, her voice filled with unspoken threats. "I do hope no one is so foolish as to try it."

Mrs. Torrance tucked in her chin, taken aback by the fierce tone. "You ought to keep him away from town, is all," she temporized.

"Is Howard well?" Valerian asked Charmaine, seeking to change the subject. Mrs. Torrance loved to stir up trouble, and she was best ignored.

"Yes, fine. Gone to Yarborough for supplies for the shop," Charmaine said absently of her husband, and then she lowered her tone, her eyes turning bright and hungry. "You have met the baron, I hear."

"Baron Ravenall!" Oscar squawked joyfully, then buried his head in Valerian's hair.

"Yes, we met." Charmaine and Mrs. Torrance were the last people with whom she wished to discuss the man.

"I saw him from a distance. He is young. Good-looking." Charmaine eyed her cousin's body in a manner that made Valerian acutely aware of her own breasts and belly. "I also hear he invited you to the hall, and you went. Alone."

"To tend Mr. Carlyle's injury, yes."

"And?"

"There is not much to say. I did my job, and I left."

Charmaine stared at her for a long moment. "He has been asking about you, you know."

A flush crept up Valerian's cheeks, her cool composure suddenly in danger. "What? Who has?" She was aware of Mrs. Torrance listening closely, a smug smile on her lips.

"The baron, silly girl. Or so I hear. He even asked Alice about you, at the inn." Charmaine nodded towards Mrs. Torrance.

The temptation to ask for details was nearly overwhelming, but that Valerian would not do, not with this pair. "Well, I hope he heard nothing ill."

"Pity he did not come to me. But perhaps he does not know that you and I are family."

"I cannot imagine the genealogies of the townsfolk are of any interest to him."

"It would be better for him if he knew we were not all witless farmers. It might save him making mistakes in his treatment of us."

Valerian did not want to think about what Charmaine was implying, or what scandalous scenarios she may have been speculating upon with Mrs. Torrance. "I must be going. I apologize again about the laundry, Charmaine. Good day."

Charmaine nodded, wishing her good day in return, but Valerian felt both women's eyes on her, following her down the street. She wondered if others were watching her, too. Did the whole town think she had thrown herself at the baron, simply because she had gone to the hall alone?

She heaved a sigh. Her reputation was bad enough, without having harlotry added to the list of her sins.

She hefted the clamming shovel up onto her left shoulder, Oscar bobbing happily on her right as she walked down the street, her mind chewing over why the baron might be asking about her.

She hardly noticed when Oscar left her shoulder, and her feet had already taken her halfway home and up the path to the Giving Stone before a sense of something wrong pulled her from her reverie. She was in the midst of an imaginary conversation with the baron, explaining to him why she had no interest in furthering their acquaintance, when Oscar's squawks of "Eee-diot! Eee-diot!" finally caught her attention.

Heart beating wildly, she quickened her pace. She came around the last hillock and saw him, sitting with arrogant languor upon the Giving Stone, legs stretched out and crossed before him. His horse cropped at grass just outside the stone circle. She stopped where she was, observing him as he frowned up at Oscar, now perched atop one of the few remaining upright stones. As if sensing her presence, or perhaps assuming that Oscar's arrival heralded her own, he turned and saw her.

The frown smoothed out and he smiled, then stood and gestured negligently towards Oscar, who was now pacing the top of a stone slab like a soldier on watch. "I begin to wonder if that bird does not bear me a certain amount of ill will. Or perhaps he warns me to beware my own foolish impulses."

"What are you doing here?" It came out harsher than she had intended, her breast a welter of conflicting emotions: eagerness, embarrassment, distrust.

His smile, suspiciously smooth to begin with, only deepened. "Why, to see you, of course." Valerian stared at him, not sure how to react to this peculiar statement. "And to apologize," he continued. "I had not realized I would be offending you by offering coinage for your services. I assure you, I was quite unaware of this custom of leaving gifts, else I never would have tried to pay you."

"Apparently whoever you asked neglected to tell you that it is to be left anonymously."

"Is that so?" He sounded entirely unconcerned. "I shall keep that in mind for the future."

Propping the shovel against the rock, Valerian came forward to see what, if anything, was on the stone.

"It is not much of a way to make a living," the baron said, "if today's income is any measure."

The stone was devoid of offerings, which was no great surprise. There was only so much illness to be tended, so many requests for water-divining in the countryside. "Aunt Theresa and I take care of ourselves quite well, thank you."

He moved closer to her. "So I hear, although it does sound like a lonely sort of life. Does not a young woman like yourself dream of pretty things? Fancy dresses, parties, baubles for your ears and throat? Of the city, and perhaps a young man to escort you from ball to ball, and to lead you out onto the dance floor?"

She looked up at him, into his hazel eyes. He was focused entirely upon her, and a blush heated her cheeks under his scrutiny. She looked away. "I have plenty to keep me occupied. I have no need of such frivolities. What good would jewels and silks do me in Greyfriars, but earn the envy and hatred of others?"

He did not answer her, and the silence vibrated between them, growing in heat and intensity. She saw him lift his hand, and could not move as he reached toward her and lightly ran the back of one finger down her cheek.

No man had ever touched her like that, and the shock of it rooted her in place. She knew she should move away, but she stood motionless instead, caught in the surprise of the sensation. Her lips parted as he moved his hand to the back of her neck and delved his fingers into the hair at her nape, gently massaging.

The fine hairs on her skin rose as he bent his head down beside hers. She felt his warm breath on her ear, then the moist heat of his lips as he kissed her lobe, then took it into his mouth. Quicksilver ran through her nerves, her muscles contracting in pleasure. The intensity of it startled her back to herself, and she jerked away from him, her hand going up to cover her ear.

"Stop that!" she cried.

"Are you certain you want me to?" He sounded disappointed.

"I am not accustomed to being accosted by men," she said, her eyes wide in fright at the newness of it. Indeed, she could hardly believe he had even wanted to accost her.

"I do not suppose you are. You have them all too cowed to attempt it, with that ferocious smile of yours. I do believe it is their loss."

"It is certainly not going to be your gain," she snapped, backing away.

The deviltry in his eyes slowly disappeared, retreating behind an apparent indifference. "You had me so distracted, I almost forgot," he said. For all the emotion he now showed, they could have been discussing the weather all along. This whole encounter was leaving her feeling distinctly out of her depth.

She watched warily as he withdrew a delicate silver bracelet from a vest pocket. He held one end between his fingers, letting the filigreed chain dangle, the links catching and reflecting the clouded sunlight. "I thought it would suit you."

Despite herself Valerian reached out and touched the bracelet, letting it lie across her fingers. The workmanship was exquisite, the silver shaped into interlocking ovals with flowers in their centers. It was a well-chosen piece for an herbalist, but there was no way on earth either pride or propriety would allow her to accept it.

She withdrew her hand and looked up at the baron, a

slight tightening around her eyes and mouth the only hint of the emotions that roiled within her. "Is this what you believe to be fair trade for ten minutes plucking stitches out of a man's arse?"

"There was also the slight injury to my hand, and the soothing of Paul's nerves."

"It is too much, and you either are ignorant of that fact, and can be forgiven, or you know it and cannot. Jewelry is a gift a man gives to his lover. What would they say in town if I wore it? And what makes you think I would be the type of woman who would accept such an extravagant gift?"

"It is hardly extravagant. I will not be reduced to eating cabbages for a month for having given it to you. Do not wear it in town if the thought distresses you. Keep it for your own pleasure."

"You, sir, lack the understanding of a sheep, and I want nothing more to do with you." She picked up her shovel and marched back down the path, inarticulate with offended pride.

If he did not understand, how could she explain to him? If he overpaid her for her services, then he was paying her either out of charity or ulterior, dishonorable motives. Either way, it discounted the work she did as not worth a fair trade. The people of Greyfriars, who worked hard for what they had, understood that as a matter of course. It was a timely reminder that this London aristocrat came from a different world, and she would be wise to avoid him.

And besides, what did he think he could buy with that trinket, pretty though it was? This must be a game he played with her, for his own amusement. There were no London ladies here to pursue, so he must think she would do until more attractive prey came along. She recalled his mouth on her ear, and blushed in shame at how still she had stood for him, enjoying it.

Hoof beats caught her ear, and she cast a glance over her shoulder. He was coming down the path, mounted on his horse. She stepped to the side to make room for him to pass her, but he stopped when he reached her, and slid gracefully from the horse's back.

She kept walking, forcing him to lead the horse by the reins. He made as if to grab her arm, and she swung the shovel around in a defensive gesture, letting him know that he had better think twice about trying it.

"Valerian—"

She flicked her eyes at him in warning.

"Miss Bright. I do apologize. I have offended you once again. Life is . . . somewhat different in London, among those of my set. Can you possibly give me a second chance? I will be staying at Raven Hall indefinitely, and I see I have much to learn about the ways of the country. Could you not find within yourself the patience to tutor an outsider?"

He looked soulfully at her, imploringly. Valerian wondered if he practiced the look in a mirror, perhaps modeling it after a favorite spaniel. "I do not see why I should, as I have a suspicion that your purposes in asking me to do so are purely selfish."

"I can hardly blame you for seeing me in such a light. Do you truly believe there is not a shred of hope for one such as myself? I cannot think that you feel there is no hint of decency to be found in my character."

That is *exactly* what she thought, she wanted to say. "Stop looking at me like that. No, I do not believe there is anyone who is entirely evil. Permanently, irrevocably damaged, perhaps, but not that there is a complete dearth of good."

"You will give me another chance?"

"No. Go away."

He was silent, keeping pace with her. After some minutes during which she tried to ignore him, he spoke again. "I think I would like to meet your Aunt Theresa. I have heard a good deal about her during my short time here."

Valerian stopped short, shoved the blade of the shovel into the ground, put her hands on her hips, and glared at him. "Why are you doing this? I cannot be so interesting as to be worth the bother. Are you bored already, is that it? You are like a little boy, tormenting a helpless animal for his idle amusement."

"You, my dear, are anything but helpless."

Valerian gave a disgusted grunt of futility and tossed her hands in the air. "Fine. Do as you please. Follow me home, harass my aunt, make a general nuisance of yourself."

He grinned at her. "You almost sound pleased."

"Argh!" She glared at him a moment, then gestured towards the shovel. "At least you can make yourself useful and carry that."

He gave her an elegant bow, one stockinged leg forward. "At your service, Mademoiselle." He plucked the shovel out of the ground and propped it against his shoulder. It looked like a toy rifle against that broad shelf. He made a "lead on" motion with his hand, and inclined his head.

Valerian tightened her lips, and without another word resumed walking down the path. He kept pace at her side, and every inch of her skin felt alive with awareness of his presence. Her mind wanted to flit back to when he had his wet mouth on her ear, but she clamped down on the traitorous thought. She wished he had gone away after she rejected the bracelet. She wished he had gone away after the first time she saw him.

* * *

Nathaniel smiled to himself, glancing occasionally at Valerian's head of dark curls beside him. She came to just above his shoulder, and looked extremely cross, putting a little marching stomp into each footstep. He had badly bungled this encounter, but although he was presently in her bad graces, he suspected that she was already on her way to forgiving him.

Although, perhaps, she would be best off if she did not. He had privately sworn not to involve himself with her, but obviously he could not trust himself. Ten minutes alone together, and he had been unable to keep his hands off her. It had sounded so sad, her lonely insistence that she did not need frivolities, that he had felt impelled to reach out and touch her. And then, when he had felt the silk of her cheek, and seen the way his touch affected her. . . .

Of course, if his intention was to behave, he should not be following her home, but he was enjoying himself too much to leave her just yet. He had spent a week learning about her from others as he tried to figure out how he had managed to offend her, and none of the information he had gathered seemed to bear any relation to the woman he saw before him.

Most everyone in Greyfriars was afraid of her and her aunt. Yes, there had been those who thought well of her, but even they could not hide their nervousness in speaking of her. His curiosity was piqued, and the mystery was a welcome distraction from his own troubles. This was no ordinary village girl. No ordinary healer, either. There was something special about her, beyond her lovely face, something that begged him to intrude upon her life.

Content for the moment to let her stew in silence, he followed her lead down the path and through pockets of woodland, always staying a little closer to her than was strictly polite. The set of her shoulders revealed her tension, and he was pleased she could not ignore him.

They emerged from the woods into the meadow, and he stopped a moment to take in the bucolic scene. He had seen enough of the countryside to know that dirt and malnutrition were the norm for most countryfolk, with nary a picturesque scene where man had laid his hand. This meadow, though, with the footbridge over the stream, and with the thatched cottage, freshly white-washed, was a marked exception to that rule. The meadow felt magically enchanted, removed from the world, and the cottage not at all the dingy little "witch's hovel" he had imagined after his talks with the villagers.

He tied his horse to the limb of a tree and followed Valerian to the cottage. She called out for her aunt, who appeared in the open doorway, drying her hands on a stained work apron. The woman cut a formidable figure, the impression made all the stronger by her aura of calm, omniscient confidence.

With an undisguised look of distaste on her face, Valerian made the required introductions. Nathaniel leaned the shovel against the side of the house, then bowed over Theresa's hand. A bitter green scent tickled his nose, and he wondered what she had been doing. Mixing potions, perhaps?

"Let me offer my condolences, my lord, on the death of your great-uncle," Theresa said as he straightened. Her eyes met his own, and in that moment he felt her perception reach down to his very soul. "I know that he would be pleased that you are here now, looking after Raven Hall and Greyfriars. He was quite fond of you. I know he had great hopes for the kind of man you would turn out to be."

Nathaniel was struck by the irrational certainty that this woman knew of the disgraces in his recent past. "Thank you, Mrs. Storrow," he finally managed to say, unbalanced. "I in turn have heard a good many things about both you and your niece since my arrival. It does sound as though between you, you keep the local population in good health."

"Good health and good spirits, I like to think. Come, let me fix you some tea. Valerian? Do bring out the biscuits from yesterday."

He followed them into the cottage, the heels of his boots sounding hollowly on the wooden planks of the floor, loud in contrast with the silent movements of the women.

He had but once or twice been in the homes of the lower classes, and so the interior of the cottage surprised him with its open space, having never been divided into rooms. There was a large canopied bed to one side, the draperies half open, and a loft with a well polished ladder leading up to it. The rest of the space was dominated by an enormous worktable, black with age, looking as if Merlin himself could have prepared his elixirs upon it. The large fireplace was surrounded and occupied by an astonishing assortment of kettles, pots, bottles, bowls, and items whose use he could only guess.

Overlying all was the combined scent of wood smoke and the vast assortment of herbs that hung in mysterious clusters above his head. The cottage was plainly as much workshop as it was home, and he wondered at the uses the women knew for all those herbs, and how effective their cures were.

Theresa indicated he should sit on the bench at the clear end of the table nearest the fire. Valerian was busy taking dark brown biscuits from a jar and arranging them on a plate. Theresa began making the tea. They both appeared to ignore him as they went about their business, which gave him a further chance to gawk at the assorted collections on the shelves lining the walls.

The lighting was dim—the day was overcast, and the windows not overlarge to begin with. The daylight that reached inside was augmented by the orange flickerings of the fire, the light of its flames caught and refracted from dozens of intriguing sources. Dark humps revealed themselves as carvings of animals, their jet eyes shining in the firelight, watching from their aeries on the shelves. White shapes became bones as his eyes adjusted, the skull of a sheep juxtaposed with that of a man. There were pewter dishes and candlesticks, leather-bound books, several shelves packed with opaque jars, and baskets heaped with unidentifiable sundries.

A flutter and swoosh announced the arrival of Oscar, who landed gracefully upon a perch attached to the mantel. "Poor hungry bird!" he cried.

"Nonsense, Oscar," Valerian chided, and set the plate of biscuits on the table. "You have been out foraging all day."

"He is a shameless beggar," Theresa said, pouring tea into a set of delicate china cups, incongruous in this practical household. She sat down across from him. Valerian dawdled for a moment, petting Oscar, then sat on the stool at the end of the table.

For a brief moment he saw himself as if from the outside, sitting in this peculiar cottage with two eccentric women, a talking raven on the mantel. He could almost believe that a sort of magic inhabited this cottage in the meadow, and that these two women were witches, as the townsfolk more than half suspected.

"Now then," Theresa said, "I am sure you have heard countless rumors about us, so if you have questions, feel free to ask them." Her green eyes met his with friendly mischief.

Surprised again by the sense that she read his thoughts, he glanced at Valerian and saw her lips quirk before she hid them behind the rim of her teacup, taking a sip. He smiled at her and followed suit, in the hopes of buying time to compose a suitable query for her aunt.

The moment the liquid hit his tongue he jerked, and spluttered the stuff back into the cup. "Good God!" he cried. "What is this stuff?" He squinted at the liquid, trying to make out the color, too startled by the unidentifiable taste to apologize for the gross faux pas he had just committed.

"It is Valerian's own blend," Theresa said, laughter in her voice.

He looked at Valerian, and saw her frowning at him, a biscuit almost to her lips. He gave her a strained smile, gathered his courage and his manners, and took another sip. After letting the hot liquid sit in his mouth for a moment he decided that it was not quite as awful as at first taste, as long as he did not try to think of it as tea.

"Rosehips, lemon balm, orange, and a few other things," Valerian finally explained.

"Delightful," he murmured, setting down the cup.

"Biscuit?" Valerian asked, holding out the plate.

"Pooooor hungry bird," Oscar wailed from the mantel.

Nathaniel took one of the dark biscuits and chomped off a bite. An explosion of peppery spices filled his mouth, and his eyes widened. The hard little cookie was enough to make his eyes water.

"Spice biscuit," Valerian said.

He coughed as a crumb of the potent pastry lodged in his throat, and quickly took a sip of tea, thankful now for its harmless fruitiness. "So I gathered."

"You know, we are not actually witches," Valerian said. "We do not poison people."

A startled bark of laughter escaped his throat. "I never thought you were."

"Your friend Mr. Carlyle did," Valerian said.

"Paul is a man with a mind better suited to the imagination than to reason. No, I share the view of the courts of

England on the the existence of witches," he said, a bit relieved to have something to say off the topic of the fare. "Hysteria and ignorance cause the simple to believe they exist, and those who believe themselves to be witches are either deluded or charlatans. If deluded, they are to be pitied. If charlatans, then they deserve to be prosecuted, as the law allows."

"I am pleased to hear that you hold such a sensible view," Theresa said.

"But are you so certain that witches do not exist?" Valerian asked, looking at him from the corner of her eyes with the slyness of a fox. "What seems farfetched in London becomes easier to believe when there are no city walls between you and the night."

"You may as well ask if I believe in ghosts and fairies, or the fortune-telling of gypsies."

"A man of pure reason," Valerian said, and he heard the hint of mockery in her voice.

"How else are we to know the world? Superstition is but a pap to quiet ignorant minds, fearful of what they cannot understand. While it comforts, to hold the comfort is also to reject the search for truth."

Valerian rolled her eyes at him, and he was suddenly aware of how pompous that had sounded.

"And do you view God with the same detachment?" Theresa asked.

He had not expected that their conversation would so quickly take such a serious turn, and wondered what reason they had for it. "I do not know if there is a place in science for God and religion," he said more carefully. "For many it is a habit more than a faith."

"And just more superstition, I suppose," Valerian said. "But have you never felt that all the science and reason in the world could not help you, could not succor you in your need? That there must be something more than this physical world, something that had the power to save you or to damn you?"

He considered his words before he answered. "I have felt my limitations, and seen my follies, but ultimately I do not think it is for any being but myself to save me or to damn me. Any crisis of faith has been in myself, never in science. I do believe that one day men will find in science the answers many now find in God."

Valerian smiled. "So perhaps you are of a mind with Pope, then: 'All our knowledge is, ourselves to know.' "

"You read Alexander Pope's work?" he asked, amazed, but the moment he saw her reaction, he knew he had made a mistake much worse than that with the tea. Anger sparked in her eyes, where only exasperation and a hint of teasing had been before.

"It would appear that I do. Imagine that. Wherever did the little country lass learn to read?"

"Valerian—" Theresa warned.

"Do not worry yourself, Aunt Theresa. He fancies himself too far above me to be offended by my utterances. He pays no heed to what I say."

Nathaniel grimaced, reminded that he had followed her home despite her protestations. "I meant no offense."

When Valerian remained silent, Theresa spoke. "You are welcome to stay for supper if you so desire."

Nathaniel suddenly realized that the light had grown dimmer as they had talked, and that he was no doubt keeping the two women from their meal and chores. He stood and gave a short bow. "My thanks for the tea and biscuits, and for the delightful conversation. I fear I must be going. Paul will no doubt think I have been carried away by succubi if I do not make an appearance soon."

"It has been a pleasure, my lord," Theresa said. "I do hope that you will feel free to visit us. If ever you need a guide for the surrounding countryside, Valerian knows every hillock and stream."

Nathaniel caught the glare that Valerian sent to her aunt. "I will keep that in mind." He headed for the door, aware of a subtle change within himself in his attitude towards these women. They were not to be taken lightly, that much was clear. He was beginning to get a sense of why the villagers would be wary of them. They might not be witches, but both aunt and niece shared an intelligence and force of personality that could be intimidating when they chose.

Not that he would describe himself as intimidated, of course. A better description would be . . . challenged. It had been years since he had had an intellectually demanding discussion with anyone. Who would have thought he would have it here?

Almost as an afterthought, he turned to Theresa. "The greenhouses at Raven Hall are half empty. If it would be of help to you, please do use them for whatever plants might require them."

"Thank you, my lord. I will do that. Valerian, show the baron the path that leads to his orchards. It will save him no end of time."

Nathaniel fetched his horse while Valerian waited, then she led him to a narrow break in the wall of woodland around the meadow.

"Stay to the most trodden path," she explained brusquely. "You will come out at the back of your orchards."

"You have no wish to guide me?"

"No, I do not. I will give you credit for sufficient wit to find your own way home."

"Most generous of you."

"I thought so."

He smiled at her, then took her hand in both of his own,

not allowing her to pull away. "Give me another chance, Miss Bright. I would hate to think that I had irrevocably botched any chance at friendship between us."

"Friendship?"

"There is much that we could learn from each other." He raised her hand and gave her knuckles the barest whisper of a kiss. "Your servant, Mademoiselle." He mounted, gave her frowning face one last look, then rode through the break in the foliage.

The darkening woods were heavy with shadows, the rustlings and snappings of the forest making the horse's ears twitch. He thought about Valerian and her aunt as he rode through the deepening dark, considering their intensity on the subjects of superstition and religion. It occurred to him that they might consider their own safety in this village to rest on his good will, and had been testing the depth of his tolerance and convictions.

By the time he reached his orchards, all he had concluded was that nothing was as simple as it looked with those two. He would not agree with Paul that they were witches, but it was quite obvious they were women.

That alone could baffle the most intelligent of men.

Chapter Five

A river of pain shot through Theresa's gut and she grimaced, grinding her teeth to keep from groaning out loud. She pressed her hand to her belly and leaned against the high windowsill, fastening her eyes on the early morning vista of the meadow and trying to stifle the pain.

Bit by bit it eased, and she exhaled in relief. Her fingers searched her flesh, prodding until she found the small lump that was daily growing larger in her abdomen. It was an irregular mass, firm to her touch, and if she was not mistaken it had already spawned an offspring. The second lump was no larger than the tip of her finger, and nestled in the vulnerable flesh under her left arm.

She took another sip of her tea, knowing that its mild analgesic effect would mask only a fraction of the pain. To take a strong enough painkiller would be to render herself senseless, and she was not ready to do that. Not yet. And neither was she ready for Valerian to know what was happening. Fortunately, Valerian had attributed her recent weight loss to grief over the death of the old baron.

"Silly bird!" Valerian grumbled up in the loft. "Do not just look at it. Eat it! That beak is good for something other than talking."

"Oscar is a superior bird," Oscar croaked back.

"You are not too good to pick through garbage."

"What is going on up there?" Theresa called.

Valerian's head appeared over the edge of the loft, her heavy braid sliding over her chemise-clad shoulder and flopping down, hanging like a rope. "Good morning, Aunt. It is the maggots again. They keep falling out of the thatch, and Oscar, the useless creature, refuses to eat them."

"You could always dispose of them yourself."

Valerian screwed her face up in disgust. " 'Tis bad enough to have them dropping on me as I sleep, the fat little things. I keep thinking one will fall into my hair, or crawl in my ear. I can smell it, too, whatever it is that died up there."

"You are welcome to share my bed until they are gone. The canopy will keep you safe from the mortal threat of falling worms." She tried to keep her face serious, a losing battle.

"You would not laugh if they were falling on *your* head. No thank you, I will face the beasts. You know I can never sleep that close to your snoring."

"Rude girl."

Valerian snorted, and her head disappeared, the end of her braid flipping up over the edge of the loft a half-second later. Theresa smiled, enjoying her niece's company. Her own daughter Charmaine had always been serious and self-conscious, and unable to outgrow her embarrassment over her mother. Being an outsider had been too painful for her, and she had found relief only by rejecting her family and becoming a villager heart and soul. Theresa understood that, even as it hurt her.

She eased herself down into one of the chairs by the fire, quietly cherishing the mundane routines of the morning, and Valerian's voice as she continued to chide Oscar for his fastidiousness.

"What type of scavenger are you, anyway? Will not eat worms. I have never heard of such a thing."

How long had it taken her to discover that it was the small moments that made up a life, and not the big ones? Theresa's mind wandered back to the days when she had moved in different social circles, and had encounters with men whose rank would put the baron to shame.

An image of herself flashed to mind, dancing with a young nobleman, in a room filled with silks and satins, and the heat of candles and bodies. It was strange to think how important appearances had been to her then. Strange, too, how all the passions from that time had faded into nothing. It was as if someone else had lived that life.

Valerian climbed down the ladder from the loft, enjoying the pressure of the smooth rungs on her bare arches. She was dressed in her oldest clothes, the skirts not even reaching her ankles, the waist having been let out several times. The edges of her bodice were frayed.

"Are you certain you do not want to come with me today?" she asked her aunt.

"Yes, my poor plants have been under Daniel's care long enough. It is time I went and checked how many he has killed."

"What would you have done, if the baron had not offered his greenhouses?"

"Asked, I suppose. Or perhaps kept using them anyway. I do not think he would have minded. We are lucky in the character of Nathaniel Warrington, you know."

"I find it hard to be enthusiastic about the man."

Theresa smiled. "That is because you are attracted to him."

"I have always been impressed by your imagination, Aunt Theresa. You do say the most ridiculous things."

"Not imagination, my dear. Perception."

Valerian was silent a moment, hesitant. "You do not . . . have any sense about him and me, do you?" She felt her cheeks flush.

Theresa sat back and closed her eyes, her limbs visibly relaxing. Valerian waited, heart beating nervously. She had plenty of time to regret asking, and to wonder what had prompted her to, before Theresa let out her breath in a long sigh and opened her eyes.

"What?"

"You know how this goes," Theresa warned. "I sense possibilities. I get a feel for what is happening now, and in the immediate future. Not everything I sense will happen—it is tendencies I sense, not facts."

"I know, I know." She came and sat on a low stool beside her aunt, her fingers twining about each other. She bent her head down and examined her nails, scraping at a hangnail, trying to hide her eagerness to hear what her aunt had seen.

"I sense men attracted to you. The baron, and others. They are coming toward you, and there is turmoil as well. Trouble."

"No doubt caused by the baron," she said.

"I did not say that. I do not know." Theresa sighed. "Men chasing women. They are like children chasing butterflies. They do not mean to harm what they catch, but often they do."

"It must be the baron. No one else ever approaches me."

"You know this is why I do not do this for people," Theresa said, sounding mildly annoyed. "They always see what they want to. They do not listen, just as you do not now. I did not say the baron would do you any harm."

"I knew I should stay away from him," Valerian muttered.

Theresa threw her hands in the air. "Go dig your clams. I have plants to tend. They are much better listeners than infatuated young women."

Valerian had a quick breakfast of oatmeal hasty pudding, kissed Theresa on the cheek, went out to the shed behind the cottage to get the clamming shovel, and dumped an old pair of shoes caked with dried mud into a bucket. She would put the shoes on when she reached the rocky edge of the shore. Even her thick calluses were not proof against barnacles.

The morning sky was a rich turquoise, dotted with cumulus clouds that promised a day of gentle sunshine. The tide would be at its lowest point for the month in about an hour and a half, and she knew she would not be the only clam digger down on the bay today.

She tried to push any thoughts of the baron out of her mind. He was a scoundrel in aristocrat's clothing, and if she knew what was good for herself, she would not have anything more to do with him.

The walk down the narrow, overgrown path from the meadow took her twenty minutes, winding between hills and through wind-brushed pockets of trees. The walk back up would not be half so pleasant, she knew, lugging a bucketful of clams and tired from the digging. Oscar flew off ahead, eager to scavenge, leaving her to her own unsettled thoughts and the breezy quiet of the walk.

The path ended at the shore, dumping her out onto a bank of rounded stones and driftwood. The main path from Greyfriars ended a half-mile to the south, across a shallow stream that emptied into the bay, its waters carving a channel through the sandy mud. She saw figures in the distance, dotting the shining expanse of muddy sand, and smiled, breathing deeply. The air smelled of rotting eggs and salt water, the familiar scent of the uncovered seabed.

She sat on a pale piece of driftwood and slipped on her shoes. They felt stiff and crusty on her feet, the mud flaking and falling off in scales. It was a relief to start walking and wade through a saltwater puddle, and to feel the cold squish of the water in her shoes, softening them.

The seabed was a mix of sand and mud, fairly firm in places, slippery and soft enough to sink into several inches in others. She poked the ground in front of her with her shovel every few steps, testing for quicksand. She had been out here many times before, and knew there were several places, fed by underground water, that it formed.

The mud suddenly quivered beneath her, and her foot sank past the ankle into liquefied sand and mud. With her free foot she calmly took a step backwards, and pointing the toe of the buried foot, slowly pulled it out, watching in mild fascination as the vibrations of her movement kept the mud liquid. Once she was free, the ground resumed its firm appearance. With her knowledge of how to escape, the treacherous sands had long ago lost their power to scare her.

She made a wide circle around the area, and continued on, finding a nice stretch of mud perforated with the holes denoting buried clams. She set to digging, feeling a vague sense of community with the other clam-diggers, for all that they were some distance away and gave her no greeting.

Eddie the blacksmith's son and his two best friends were slouched behind a pile of driftwood, enjoying a jug of purloined liquor. Johnnie, whose father owned the inn, had filled the jug over the course of two weeks with splashes of whichever alcohol was at hand as he served, and whatever dregs were left in the cups. His father kept an eagle's eye on his inventory, and knew too well the temptations of drink for a young man. He did not trust his son with a key to the cellar.

"Gawd, Johnnie, this is a hellish mixture you have made," Stinky Samuelson declared, gasping, as he passed the jug to Eddie. Stinky's real name was largely forgotten, his present moniker being the result of a sad fact of his existence: If something around had a foul stench, sooner or later Stinky would manage to fall into it.

"I think I got more whiskey this time," Johnnie said, and belched.

"Not so much wine," Eddie agreed. They were all feeling quite pleased with themselves. Ale was a regular part of their diets, but not one of their parents would approve of the luxury, waste, and ill effects of their sons drinking anything stronger.

With three-quarters of the jug gone, they were feeling cross-eyed and bold when Eddie lurched upright, bent over the log they leaned against, and vomited onto the rocks on the other side. When he raised his head and looked out over the bay in an effort to clear his head, he blearily made out Valerian digging her clams. "Now there is good female flesh wasted."

Stinky and Johnnie crawled to their friend and poked their heads up above the log. Good female flesh was always worth a look.

"Who?" Johnnie asked.

" 'Er," Eddie grunted, pointing with his chin. He propped his elbows on the log and tried to hold his head steady with his hands.

"Miss Bright?" Johnnie asked disbelievingly.

"Have you ever really looked at her? *Really* looked at her?" Eddie asked Johnnie.

"Why would I want to?"

"Ssshe is beautiful," Eddie answered.

Johnnie was not buying it. "Not beautiful. But maybe she would be kind of pretty, if she were not . . . you know."

Eddie belched, and wrinkled his nose at the taste of vomit, exhaling through his mouth. "What? You think she is going to turn into a badger and bite off your pecker the next time you take a piss in the woods?"

Johnnie colored. "You would not make such fun, if you had heard the things I have!"

"Aaaa, what things? A bunch of gossip. You have been washing too many dishes with your mother, Johnnie-boy."

"My mum says there is plenty that goes on out at that cottage that we are better off knowing nothing of."

"All I know is she has not ever done anything to me," Eddie said.

"Well, I do not see you courting her, and you are the one lusting after her."

Eddie shrugged. "Too old. But I tell you, she came into the smithy yesterday. I had not ever really looked at her. Was afraid to, I guess. She never seemed quite . . . I dunno. Friendly. Seemed like she would as soon whack you with a stick as talk to you."

His friends nodded.

"But yesterday she was different. I caught her looking at me. You know. Looking at me like she wanted me."

"Miss Bright?" Stinky asked incredulously.

"I think I could have had her right then and there if I had said anything."

"I think your da's been using your head for an anvil," Stinky said.

"She was staring at me, her eyes all over my body. It was like I could feel them on me. And her face got all soft. She was pretty. And she has nice titties."

"Do not let Gwen hear you say that," Johnnie warned.

Eddie scrunched his face. "Gwen."

"I thought you liked her?" Stinky asked.

"Sometimes she seems like such a child."

"Oh," Stinky said, rolling his eyes. "I understand. She won't let you touch her, will she?"

Eddie rolled a shoulder in reply, and his friends hooted.

"So now Miss Bright," Johnnie said, taking a swig from the jug. "To teach Gwen a lesson."

"*I* did not start it with her. *She* was the one looking at me."

"Sure. We believe you," Stinky said. "Right, Johnnie? No question but she is lusting after him, making love potions to pour in his drink. Miss Bright! Hoo hoo!" The two of them rolled onto their backs, laughing, punching each other in high humor.

Eddie glared at them. "You do not believe me?"

"Aww, sure we do. Why, I bet if you went out there right now she would not be able to keep her hands off you," Johnnie said, laughing. "She would have you down in the mud before you knew what hit you, stripping off your clothes, moaning for you, Eddieeee, Eddieeee, take me, Eddie, take me. . . ."

Eddie's face went crimson. "Shut up! She would, I tell you! She looked at my crotch like she was drooling for it!"

"Eddieeee. . . ." Johnnie crooned.

"Touch my titties, Eddie, my lovely titties," Stinky said, holding his palms up to his chest and making squeezing motions.

"Want me to prove it to you?" Eddie hollered at them.

They stopped their teasing to look at him in hopeful glee.

Valerian tossed another clam in the bucket with a wet "plurp," then straightened up to stretch the muscles in her back. She peered into her bucket. Her clams were ajar, siphoning salt water in and out. She would give them clean water before leaving, so they could wash the sand out of their own bellies.

Movement caught her eye, and she squinted against the glare of the sun. Who was that coming toward her? The figure slipped, arms windmilling, then righted itself and continued toward her, feet moving gingerly on the uncertain ground, arms held out for balance.

As he came closer she recognized Eddie, and pursed her lips in concern. What did he want? This did not have anything to do with yesterday's encounter, did it? She saw two other figures stumbling around closer to shore, but did not have a chance to identify them before Eddie was upon her.

"Good morning," he said, stopping beside her bucket.

She caught the stench of alcohol and vomit. " 'Morning."

His eyes shifted down to her bodice, lingered, then found their way back to her face. She frowned disapprovingly at him.

"Uhhh . . . Digging clams, are you?"

"Yes." She paused, waiting. "Is there something I can do for you, Eddie?"

"No, no. . . . just saying hello." His eyes searched her face, skittered away over her shoulder, to the bucket, and finally alit on the shovel. "So! Is the shovel working well for you, then?"

"You did an excellent repair . . ." Valerian trailed off as she noticed the two figures, vaguely recognizable now as Stinky and Johnnie, horsing around and shoving each other as they wended an irregular route toward her and Eddie. They were wandering near the place she had encountered the quicksand. It was not dangerous, as long as you kept your head about you. If Eddie was any indication, though, they none of them were particularly rich on wits today. They had probably been stealing liquor from the inn again.

Valerian waved her hands in the air, and shouted at the two young men. "Johnnie, Stinky, stop! Go back!"

Eddie looked over his shoulder. Seeing his friends, he

nodded at them, and waved. Valerian grabbed his shoulders and tried to turn him all the way around. "Send them back, or they will get caught in the quicksand!"

Eddie grinned stupidly, and he tried to shoo his friends back with his hands. After a few flicks of his hands, he turned back to Valerian. He swooped forward and wrapped her in a bear hug, knocking foreheads with her, then planting a sloppy wet kiss on the side of her mouth.

Valerian let out a sound like a stepped-on mouse. She tasted alcohol and bile in his saliva, the fumes filling her nose. His arms were warm and strong, his chest hard against her breasts, but all she felt was repulsion as his lips crept like slugs over her mouth, leaving a slimy trail, and she struggled to break free.

A terrified howl echoed across the mud, breaking Eddie's amorous concentration. He loosened his hold on her, and she squirmed out of his grip.

A hundred yards away, Stinky was flailing madly in a welter of quicksand, and Johnnie, shouting ineffectually, was trying to reach him. Valerian took in what had happened in a moment, grabbed her shovel, and began to run as best she could over the slippery mud.

By the time Valerian reached them, with Eddie bringing up the rear, Stinky was up to his shoulders and wild-eyed with terror. Johnnie was weeping, lying in the mud, still trying to reach his friend.

Valerian tested the ground, then lay flat at the edge of the quicksand. She pushed the spade end of the shovel out to Stinky. Johnnie screamed.

"Stop her, Eddie! She is trying to kill him!"

Eddie jerked, and made a move to obey, but then Stinky's hand lashed out of the liquefied sand and grabbed the metal blade. Eddie threw himself to the mud next to Valerian, his longer, much stronger arm reaching out and taking the handle of the shovel.

Stinky practically climbed up the shovel in his desperation, and Eddie pulled him to the edge of the quagmire with his powerful blacksmith's arms. When he was close enough, Valerian grabbed one of Stinky's arms and helped haul him out of the muck.

"I told you to go back," she chided, both angry at his foolishness and relieved he was all right.

Stinky lay gasping, covered in mud, staring wildly at Valerian and Eddie. Other clammers had heard the commotion and finally reached them, gathering round, voices raised in excited questions that the three young men tried to answer all at once, suddenly realizing they were the center of attention.

The press of bodies and the jabbering of voices made her uncomfortable, and reminded her that many could have seen Eddie kiss her. People would blame her for that somehow, and part of her felt they would be right to do so, after the way she had looked at Eddie yesterday. She did not want to hear their accusations.

She slipped out of the group and went back to get her bucket of clams. As she headed back to shore she made a wide detour around the milling group, but then remembered the shovel. She hesitated a moment, then continued toward the dry sand. Doubtless someone would leave the shovel for her at the Giving Stone, she told herself. She would rather trust that to happen than have to explain to anyone her part in what had just occurred.

At the top of the beach she stopped to slip off her shoes. The front of her clothes were soaked through, and were heavy and cold against her skin. Looking down the beach, she could see Stinky being led away, concerned arms around his shoulders, and suddenly she wished someone were there to comfort her.

She watched disconsolately as the last of the group drifted away, leaving her shovel lying in the mud. Then one of the women, Gwen judging by the color of her hair, turned back and got it, then did a quick little jog to rejoin the others.

Most likely someone had seen Eddie kiss her, and sooner or later that news would get back to Gwen. She sent a prayer heavenward that Gwen would not hear of it, but that had about as much chance of happening as she herself did of waking tomorrow as a duchess. She might as well go ahead and count Gwen on the list of people who hated her and wished her dead.

In the Raven Hall greenhouse, Theresa snipped away dead leaves and tested moistures with her finger. The air was warm and humid, scented with that unique hothouse combination of dirt and foliage. She usually enjoyed coming here, but today her mind was uneasy.

Her psychic abilities, such as they were, were impressionistic and vague, and did not reach beyond the near future. She sometimes thought that the immediate past and the near future somehow became jumbled with that moment of time that was the present, and that it was that confused mix of events that she was somehow able to hear better than most others.

What her psychic ears were hearing was change and turmoil, and Valerian was at or near the center of it. Or maybe it just felt that way, as the girl was so important to Theresa's own life. She had faith in Valerian, and believed she would come out all right in the end. She just wished she could *know* it, for certain. And she wished, too, that she could be certain of the role the baron would play in the coming tempest.

Unaware that she had even sensed his approach, she set down her shears and looked toward the glass doorway. A moment later the baron appeared. He was bareheaded, and his clothes were more subdued than yesterday's finery. He probably did not realize that these simpler clothes made his masculinity all the more apparent and appealing.

"Good day, Mrs. Storrow. I saw Daniel out in the gardens. He told me you were here."

Theresa inclined her head. "Good day. I was hoping that I might see you during my visit."

"Indeed?"

"To thank you again for the offer of your greenhouse, among other things."

Nathaniel looked around, as if seeing the place for the first time. He noticed the shears on the table in front of Theresa, and the vigorous growth of plants that were not seedlings. "You have been using it for years." It was more statement than question.

"Your uncle was good enough to show the same generosity that you have."

Theresa led the way through an archway, into the more decorative part of the greenhouse. The glass roof was high enough to allow for the growth of a few scraggly orange trees. A bench sat near a raised bed filled with the spiky fronds of pineapple plants. The fruit, the size of a large fist, was a delicacy that few had ever tasted.

Theresa sat, relieved to get off her feet. She was tiring more quickly these days. The baron remained standing, idly examining the sickly leaves of the orange tree.

"You will have to pardon me for being a forward and presumptuous old woman. I find I no longer have the patience to wade through niceties when there are issues of deeper interest I could be discussing."

"I do not know whether to be alarmed or intrigued by that, if it is a prelude to what you are about to say."

Theresa gave him a small smile. "You do not have to worry that I am going to lecture you about Valerian, and your intentions towards her," she said. And truly, his attraction to her niece was more a source of happiness for her than of worry, not that he would understand that. "What I would like to know most is why you came to Greyfriars."

"Surely that is obvious."

Theresa waved that answer aside. "Your uncle's death, the inheritance. That is the excuse. You need not have come here yourself. Indeed, I do not believe you would have unless there were another reason."

"Whatever my reason may have been, I do not see how it concerns you," he said stiffly, and she knew she had touched a nerve.

"Oh, come now. Do you think your private life has no effect on the lives of the inhabitants of the town you now own? This is not like London, where actions have no consequences other than causing tongues to wag a little faster. Like it or not, you are the patriarch of this village now. I would like to know what type of father figure you will be." She allowed her voice to soften. "I have no intention of judging you. Tell me what brought you here. Whatever it is you have done, I assure you I have heard worse. Or done it, as the case may be."

His eyes searched hers, and she could feel him approaching the possibility, and then backing away again before he spoke. "I admit there is a certain temptation to the idea of confessing all to a virtual stranger, but I see no reason to indulge it."

She tried a different tack. "I suppose I would be correct in assuming that you do not intend to stay here, that you think you will return to London as soon as you are able, as soon as this . . . exile?" she raised her brows in question, then continued—"is finished."

He gave a short laugh, but she could hear the discomfort in it. "I suppose that you claim to tell fortunes as well as read minds."

Theresa slapped her hands on her knees and stood, seeing that he was not ready to tell her anything and was only growing more defensive. "Well, no matter."

What she had wanted to know was if he could be counted upon to control the mood of the village, to protect Valerian from any harm that might be done her after she herself was gone. His past behavior, and the honor or dishonor of it, would be her best indication of how he would act in the future.

Valerian would be more vulnerable alone in Greyfriars than she was now, with Theresa standing guard. The two of them together, with old George Bradlaugh in the background, had been able to avoid any major trouble from the villagers and farmers. Valerian alone, with the questionable support of a baron whose interest in her was mainly lascivious and who might soon depart, was a different story.

She smiled wryly at him. "Whether I can see it or not, I still cannot control the future, much as I would like. I will trust that you will make the right decisions if ever called upon to do so."

He frowned at her, clearly puzzled. "I am not at all certain of your meaning. Of what decisions do you speak, and of what future?"

But she would not answer, preferring to let him puzzle it out for himself, and hoping that in the process he might learn something of his own character. "As I told you yesterday, your uncle always had great hopes for the man you could become. I would like to think he was not mistaken."

And on that note, she ended the conversation.

Chapter Six

Paul Carlyle stopped and bent to tug at his stocking. The blasted thing had slipped loose of its garter more times than he could count, twisting and sagging around his calf, in very real danger of dropping round his ankle in a puddle of wrinkled cloth. He wrangled it back in place, straightened, mopped his brow with his sodden kerchief, and stepped directly into a half-dried patty of cow manure.

Dark curses spilled from his mouth. The country. Who needed the country? Flies and dirt and filth, that is what the country was. He stomped over to the edge of the road and scrubbed his shoe in the grass.

It had been a mistake to walk instead of ride. On horseback, his head a safe eight or nine feet from the ground, he might have been able to maintain a few illusions about the bucolic scene around him. His imagination, however, had gotten the better of him, and he had pictured himself a country squire, taking a brisk walk down to the village for a cool tankard of ale at the inn, sharing jokes with his fellow man and sharing in the general spirit of bonhomie.

A trickle of sweat crept from under his wig, making a trail down the side of his damp forehead. Midges hovered in a cloud, attracted to his moist skin. He swatted at them, to no effect. His skin had the itchy feeling that insects had somehow found their way inside his clothing.

Of course, the whole miserable walk might not have been so bad if Nathaniel, Lord Gloomy Baron himself, had agreed to come along, but ever since that ghastly affair in London his friend had been changing. Gone was the exuberant rake, full of deviltry. In his place was an increasingly subdued man, burying himself in books and aimless solitary rides. The only time his eyes lit with interest was when anyone mentioned that witch.

Paul still could not believe he had let the woman pluck the stitches from his arse. When she had taken his hand, he had been too shocked to protest, and her soothing voice and the way she kept stroking his hand had cast some manner of spell on him, rendering him helpless. He had thought her an angel of mercy at the time, but now that he had his senses back he recalled that evil snarl she had given him at their first meeting.

Nathaniel ought to be careful. It seemed she was already casting an enchantment over him, and the devil only knew what the price would be.

The first home on the edge of town came into view, and Paul picked up his pace. A week and a half was too long to be cooped up with a morose friend and no outside entertainment. Old George Bradlaugh had had a well-stocked cellar, but half the fun of drinking was the company one kept. He needed friends! Laughter! Conversation! Or at least a barmaid to ogle.

The inn was not hard to find. It was much like every other inn in the country, right down to the nonsensical name, "The Drunken Raven." He wondered if the witch's hell-bird, or one of its ancestors, had had anything to do with that. The wooden sign above the door was of a black bird, beak wide in an insane caw, lurching drunkenly across a painted field. Paul sincerely hoped he would be in a similar state upon leaving.

He pushed open the door with the grating creak of rusted hinges, and stepped down into the dark interior. There was no one in the main room, the tables empty but for a dusting of crumbs and rings of sticky ale. He heard the clanking of dishes from a door behind the bar, and after a moment's hesitation, went and stuck his head through to the kitchen area. A middle-aged woman, her hair tucked up inside a mobcap, was putting away heavy crockery bowls. He cleared his throat.

The woman started, bowls clattering in her hand. She turned quickly. "Sir! You startled me!"

"My apologies, mistress. Is the inn not open for business?"

"It is open. 'Tis only that the regulars have already been and gone. Low tide today, you see."

"Ah." He gave a knowing nod, having no idea what she was talking about. To ask a question, however, was to invite an explanation, and all he cared about at this moment was a tankard of ale.

"You looked parched, sir, if I may say so. What will you be having?"

He gave his order, and at her invitation went to settle in a dim, cool corner of the room. He did not relish drinking alone, but ale alone was better than no ale at all, and he would be damned if he would undertake the walk back to the hall without it.

The woman returned with his tankard, and set it before him with a thud that sloshed a few precious drops over the rim. "So. You must be Mr. Carlyle, from up at the hall?"

He took a grateful sip of the ale, regarding her from under his brows. Her round brown eyes gleamed with an avarice for gossip. He set down his tankard, and sucked the bit of foam off his upper lip. "One and the same."

"I am Alice Torrance. My husband and I own the inn." She gave him a little smile, and began to twist her apron in her hands, blinking at him in a gross pretense of coquetry. "Would you mind, sir, if I asked a question of you?"

Paul was about to evade the request, then thought better of it. Perhaps he could pump her for information about the healer, and save Nate from getting himself into trouble. He gestured to the chair opposite, and after a brief hesitation she dropped down into it, then leaned forward over the table, the ruffled edge of her mobcap quivering eagerly.

"There is a rumor flying about." She looked at him meaningfully. "Concerning Baron Ravenall. Do you know whereof I speak?"

A dozen unsavory possibilities flashed through his mind, not least of which was what had happened so recently in London. "I am afraid not."

She wet her lips, and cast a glance to the side, as if checking for eavesdroppers. She leaned a bit farther forward, her hands clasped before her on the table. " 'Tis being said that when the baron rode through the gates to the hall, one of the stone ravens spoke, telling him that he would never see London again."

Paul's eyes went as round as hers, and he had to bite his cheek to keep from laughing. That threat, those had been his own words. One of the footmen must have embroidered the tale and passed it on. " 'Tis God's own truth that he heard those words," Paul said, lowering his voice to match her sinister tone, and leaning forward until his nose was but inches from her own. "And I have been worried ever since about what it might mean."

"Do not say you think it foretells his death!" Mrs.

Torrance gasped, a wild excitement in her eyes. "We have only just lost the last baron. We cannot have this one dying as well!"

"Danger lurks in every shadow. . . ." Paul said darkly, enjoying this bit of mischief.

"Oh, aye, and here more than elsewhere." Her eyes narrowed. "He may already be in harm's way."

Paul's humor deadened at that, and he frowned at her. "What do you mean?"

Mrs. Torrance's lips puckered in distaste. "I do not wish to spread tales, sir, but . . . the girl he has been asking about, Miss Bright. She is not as harmless as she sometimes seems." She nodded slowly, as if agreeing with herself. "He would do well to be careful of her."

"Causes trouble, does she? Perhaps . . . dabbles in the dark arts?"

Mrs. Torrance began to look nervous, and lowered her voice to a near whisper, although there was no one there to hear. "Nothing that you could swear to in a court of law. But one hears things."

"Go on."

She crouched down a bit in her seat. "There are some as say that bird of hers is a demon in disguise, sent by the devil himself. At night it takes a man's shape and shares her bed with her, where they engage in all manner of perversions. And Mrs. Frowdy says as how she went into her barn and found a hedgehog suckling at her best cow's teat, and she knew as how it was either Miss Bright or her aunt, come to collect the payment she had been late in giving."

"Are you saying she and her aunt are witches?"

"Shhh!" Mrs. Torrance hushed him with both palms flapping the air. "I did not say that."

"But you said—"

"Witch or no, she and her aunt have done favors for most of the people of this town, and I would not want to be the one accusing them. We have a business here that depends upon the good will of the village."

"Especially as such an accusation of witchcraft is now illegal."

She rapped the table with her knuckles, then pointed at his face. "The laws of the city are not necessarily those of the country. There are those of us who do not want the devil's whores in our midst."

She left him to his own musings after that, and he could not help but picture the wicked Valerian Bright cavorting naked in the woods, dancing madly round a bonfire, a pot of boiling blood sitting in the flames.

He was debating a second tankard when the door opened, and a pair of village men came sauntering in, the broken-wind stench of the mud still on them.

"Hey there, Alice, how about something to cool the throats of the fearless hunters?"

Mrs. Torrance appeared from in back and gave a snort. "Fearless hunters! And that will be the day. What, did a big clam take a jump at you? Bite you on the arse, did it?"

"Aye, and I wrestled it to the ground, almost losing my arm to its great chomping jaws."

"Get on with you!" Mrs. Torrance cheerily replied, waving a towel at him.

Other villagers straggled in, and before long the inn was a babble of voices. Mr. Torrance appeared to tend the kegs, and Paul heard Mrs. Torrance calling angrily for some unfortunate Johnnie, who was apparently shirking his duties.

A roar went up in the already noisy crowd when a trio of young men stumbled through the door. There was a good deal of laughter, backslapping, and sheepish grinning. Paul sat with a half-smile on his face, wishing he knew what was so funny. Eventually he found someone to tell him.

"They were like flies after honey," the man laughed,

when he finished his long and undoubtedly embellished tale. "Only, Eddie got there first and laid one on her. The others were too slow. Aah! You should have seen Stinky when they hauled him out of that muck! Damned if I have ever seen the boy so scared."

As the man speaking was Stinky's father, Paul thought the fellow was showing remarkably good humor about his son's unfortunate accident. The man also seemed to have no worries about Miss Bright's sorcerous tendencies.

"All I cannot understand," Stinky Sr. continued, "is what possessed the fools to go after Miss Bright in the first place."

Paul thought of Nathaniel's growing interest in the girl. Could his friend's attraction be the result of the same witchcraft that had undoubtedly drawn the young men? "I wonder that myself."

No one was home when Valerian returned to the house. She did not know that she would have wanted to talk about what had happened, but it would have been nice to have Aunt Theresa there, if only so she would not feel quite so alone.

She put the bucket of clams in the shed, where they would stay cool until the evening, and left her shoes in a corner. Some of the mud on her clothes had already dried and was crumbling off. She considered dunking herself in the stream—a basin of water and a cloth would not suffice with this much filth—but that sounded too miserably cold to do on such a depressing day.

She went into the quiet house and gathered clean clothes and soap into a basket, then left and crossed the meadow to an almost invisible break in the greenery. Mud scaled and sloughed off her feet and ankles as she walked through the woods, and her skin was a bare dusty grey by the time she began to climb a narrow, rocky path up into the hills.

Oscar fluttered down out of the sky, landing heavily on her shoulder. "Where have you been? Faithless bird." She did not turn her head to look at him, an omission she quickly regretted when she felt something wet and slimy stuffed under her bodice shoulder.

"Ugh! Oscar!" She reached under the cloth on her shoulder, bumping Oscar aside, and pulled a jelly-like strip of clam out of her bodice. "Ehhh!" She flung the soggy clam onto the ground. Oscar leapt down to fetch it, then turned his head and eyed her accusingly.

"Do not look at me like that. It is no use caching your goodies on my person. They will not be there tomorrow when you try to retrieve them." As if in understanding, Oscar hopped further into the brush, and emerged moments later without his molluscan treasure.

"You are a peculiar sort of raven, you know that?"

Her destination was a narrow rift in the steep rocky slope of a hill, hidden in shadows some distance from the path. She had been just thirteen, living with Aunt Theresa for a year when she discovered it, a year of wandering the hills as she sought, in the unpeopled countryside, solace from the death of her parents.

Oscar recognized the place and flew off. He had been inside the mouth of the cave only once, and had never shown any inclination to return.

Valerian scanned the hillside once to be sure there was no one about, then slipped through the opening. She had told Aunt Theresa about her discovery, but had kept it secret from the town. If any of the townsfolk had ever known about it, they had long since forgotten. She always felt a twinge of guilt for guarding her secret place so jealously, but was adept at assuaging that guilt with the argument that she needed the cave's comforts more than the villagers.

A small iron lamp, of the same style that had been used

for hundreds of years with oil as fuel, sat in a niche in the rough wall along with flints for lighting it. Even these few steps into the cave the temperature had dropped noticeably, sending a chill over her skin. She lit the lamp, its flickerings barely reaching into the dark passage ahead. She could have found her way without the light, but even she was not immune to the imaginings a dark cave could arouse. A light, however small, was a comfort.

The passage slanted and twisted, the ceiling rising and falling, and there were several places where she had to climb over boulders. The sound of rushing water grew louder as she progressed, reaching her ears through fissures that led to a subterranean river. She had never seen the river, and where it went was one of the mysteries of her world.

The air in the passage gradually grew warmer and more humid, and soon she had reached her destination, the chamber with the pool. The chamber was about ten feet across, and the ceiling high enough that she did not feel claustrophobic. The water, steaming with geothermal heat and filled with minerals that gave it an unpleasant flavor, entered through a rift surrounded by a stone face that was carved into a rock. The water poured out through the mouth, and had eaten away the lower half of the carving. The face had round, pupil-less eyes, and hair that radiated outward like the rays of the sun.

She had been more than a little afraid of it when she had first discovered the face, but when she had sketched the carving for Aunt Theresa, her aunt had explained that it had most likely been left there by the Romans, centuries earlier.

Those long-vanished Romans had bricked in a small dam at the opposite end of the pool, preventing the water from rushing away through a dark chute of stone. That dark, empty drainage maw was the one part of the chamber Valerian could have lived without. The water that overflowed the dam ran into and down that passage with an eerie echoing rumble that she imagined was precisely the sound a cave-dwelling ogre would make devouring children.

She lit the three other lamps ranged along the near side of the pool, then stripped and slid into the warm water. It was hot enough to make her chilled fingers and toes burn, and she savored the pain of it as long as she could, then lifted both feet and hands out of the water, gradually letting them sink back in as her body adjusted to the heat.

She closed her eyes and let her mind drift free. The heat relaxed her muscles, and she leant her head against the edge of the pool, the rest of her body submerged. She imagined she could feel the remnants of mud lifting and floating away.

Eddie's image and his unwelcome embrace flashed into her mind and replayed itself in horrid detail. She could feel his touch, and a shudder of revulsion shook her. She pushed the images and sensations away, and she tried to replace them with thoughts of her carvings, the wooden animals she made. Eddie came back. His lips slimed over hers, his tongue oozing between her lips, rich with whiskey and vomit. She brought Oscar to mind. Clams. What to do tomorrow. Anything but Eddie, but he and his thick tongue kept creeping back into her mind.

She thought of the baron and mentally plastered his face over Eddie's, making it his arms that held her, exchanging Eddie's scent for the baron's clean one. The revulsion subsided, and a warmth tingled through her. She imagined him leaning down to kiss her, careful and erotic in his assault as he had been by the Giving Stone, and a shiver ran through her. She slid her hands up over her breasts, thinking of how it would feel to have his hands on her bare skin.

A part of herself rebelled against the fantasy. She did not

want the baron invading such an intimate part of her mind, living in the erotic scenarios that were her deepest secrets. He had no right to be there.

The rest of her only cared that the images felt good and had the power to erase Eddie.

She slid her hand down to the soft hair between her legs, cupping herself. She let the edge of her finger press between the fold, and rubbed gently. She imagined it was the baron touching her, stroking her softly as he kissed her.

What would he look like, devoid of those rich garments? Would there be hair on his chest, or would his skin be smooth and silky? And what would it feel like to hold his manhood in her palm, to lead him inside her . . . Her fingers changed their movement, and she imagined his strong hips between her thighs, her legs held wide, and the penetration she had never felt except in erotic dreams. Her muscles tensed, and then the contracting waves of her relief washed through her.

Her eyes opened to the dim cave, the shadows dancing on the wall, and the water gurgling through the mouth of the stone face. Her fantasy lover had departed with the spent desire, and she was left feeling empty and alone.

Maybe Aunt Theresa was right, and she should think about taking what the baron apparently had in mind to offer. Sex with a real person surely would not be so lonesome as this. Surely she could not be so sad afterward if there were a warm body next to her, to touch and lie against and have hold her.

Other women her age were getting married and starting families, having spent ten or more years working at crafts or in service, saving money for just such a future. She had some money of her own saved, and had a craft that would provide additional income to her family, but there would never be a man who wanted to marry her.

It was hard enough to accept that she would never marry,

but it was even worse to think that she might go her whole life without ever experiencing what it was to lie with a man. The baron would never want to marry her, and his interest in her might pass in less than a week, but he did seem to want her now. Perhaps he would be her only chance to know what it was to join with a man.

She submerged herself completely in the water, as if hiding from the thought.

Chapter Seven

Valerian sat on an old rug in front of the cottage, the meadow grasses around her bright with new growth. Several of her father's medical texts were piled around her, and she squinted in frustration at the one that lay open in her lap. It was not telling her what she needed to know.

It had been three days since the Eddie and Stinky disaster, and she had stayed close to home. Charmaine had visited with loud complaints about Valerian's behavior, and let them know that the whole town was gossiping about Eddie's amorous advances on the tidal flat. Any hopes Valerian had that the kiss had gone unnoticed were thoroughly dashed. She told herself she was staying home to avoid adding fuel to the gossip fire. The truth, which she could barely admit to herself, was that she was too cowardly to face anyone just yet.

So, she had stayed close to home, and had more time to spend with her aunt than she had had for a couple months. By the second day she realized that all was not well.

Although she hid it well, Aunt Theresa was tiring easily and appeared to be in pain. Valerian could hardly believe she had been so blind as not to notice it sooner. Aunt Theresa must be trying very hard indeed to keep it from her, which was an alarming fact in itself. There would be no reason to hide it, if it were only a minor ailment.

Her father's medical books, despite their wealth of information, could offer her no firm diagnosis for her aunt based on the few symptoms Valerian was aware of. It would help considerably if she could examine her aunt.

Valerian sighed and closed the book, staring out across the meadow at the distant wedge of blue water between the hills. Before he had died, her father had taught her the eyesight-saving trick of interrupting her reading by focusing on a distant object. She smiled, remembering the Latin lessons in his study that had taken so very much squinting, puzzled perusal on her part. Her father, a doctor, had seen no reason not to teach his daughter to understand the medicine of science, just as her mother taught her the medicine of herbal tradition and women.

She slid the heavy tome off her lap and reached for the anatomy book, giving up for the moment on diagnosing her aunt. The anatomy book was her favorite of them all, with the detailed drawings depicting bones, muscles, the circulatory system, and all the internal organs. When she was small the images had held a repulsive fascination for her. The repulsion had since faded, and she now viewed the workings of the human body with intellectual fascination.

She flipped to the page depicting the male sexual organs, casting a glance over her shoulder to check that Aunt Theresa was still inside. Not that there was anything to be secretive about: Aunt Theresa would be the first to encourage her prurient interests.

She was tracing the route of the urinary tract with her fingertip when a shadow fell across the page. She dropped her hands over the page, and squinted back over her shoulder. At first all she could see was a backlit shape, and then, even as she realized who it was, he spoke.

"Doing research?" the baron asked.

Her face flooded with heat. She took her hands from the diagram, and with false calm turned the page, striving to appear unaffected by his presence while her insides quivered. "A healer must have knowledge of all the body's systems."

The baron went down on one knee beside her and lifted the heavy leather cover of the book in her lap, flipping through a couple pages, closer to her than he needed to be. "You read Latin?"

"Yes." She narrowed her eyes at him. "Probably better than you do." His nearness made the hairs on the back of her arms stand.

To her surprise he smiled widely, showing perfect teeth. "No doubt you do. Languages were never my strong suit. The maths and sciences were more my field, not that they have done me any good." He moved away and settled onto a corner of her rug, one leg stretched out to where it nearly touched her knees. "Where did you learn to read Latin? I cannot quite imagine any local priest deciding to teach you."

He was certainly making himself at home. Did all aristocrats assume they would be welcome, or was this arrogance peculiar to him? "My father taught me," she admitted grudgingly. This man had no right to know her personal history. "He was a doctor, and saw no reason not to teach me what he knew."

"He is dead?"

"Both he and my mother. When I was twelve."

He was quiet a moment, his eyes gentle. "I am sorry. That must have been very hard." He sounded sincere, and she softened a bit.

"It was a long time ago. I still miss them, but it does not hurt so much anymore. Mostly I wish that they could see me now, and see that I turned out all right. I know that sounds selfish." She did not know why she was revealing so much personal information. Maybe it was because of the way he was looking at her: as if she were an interesting human being, worthy of being listened to. No one but Aunt Theresa ever looked at her that way.

"Selfish how?" he asked.

"Selfish that I wish they could see me, but I give no thought to the lives they still had to live, the years that were taken from them."

"Not selfish," he said, crooking a smile at her. "I imagine that is how fortunate children think of their parents, as having existed only for them."

"Perhaps. Aunt Theresa came and got me after they died, and I have been living with her ever since. She continued the education that my parents began."

"So you come from a family with a tradition of healing."

"You could say that. Some of my ancestresses were not particularly lucky in having followed such a calling, though. People who know no better have a way of confusing knowledge of herbs with witchcraft."

"You and your aunt seem to have led a peaceful life here in Greyfriars. Has no one ever accused you of being a witch?"

She shrugged. "There have been a few tense situations."

He tilted his head and looked at her, almost as if she were a painting he was trying to understand. "You have led a serious life, I think. I doubt there is your like to be found anywhere amongst the young ladies of London, for all their sophisticated appearance."

Valerian rubbed her palm along the worn dark purple of her skirt. She must look plain as a beggar to his eyes. "There would not be much point in my dressing in fancy clothes," she said, almost to herself. "There is no one here I need to impress."

"But would you dress to impress them, if there were such people? I doubt it. You act as if you are content to spend your time here, alone with your aunt, interacting with the townsfolk only when necessary."

"There have not been so many eager to befriend me."

"The young smith seems eager enough."

"So you heard about that." She grimaced, meeting his eyes for only a moment. "I do not know what got into him."

"The way I have heard it, you lured him and his friends out to you with your sorcerous ways, trapping the one you did not want in the mud."

She was incredulous with surprise for a moment, staring at him, then exploded. "Ridiculous! I did no such thing. The fools were drunk. Can I help it if they are too stupid to keep from falling into quicksand that a child knows how to avoid? They were imbeciles with a jug of pilfered liquor, and they did not need any help from me to behave like brainless goats."

He was laughing by the time her tirade wound down. "Calm yourself. I never thought you did want the boy. Maybe I could imagine you as a temptress, but never one who set her sights so low."

"I am afraid I do not understand you," she grumbled.

He took her hand, rubbing his thumb along the back of her knuckles. "I think you do."

She tugged her hand free, trying to ignore the delicious shiver his touch had aroused. "Why are you here? Did you need my aunt for something?"

"I have decided to take you up on your offer of a personal tour of the district."

"That was my aunt's offer, not mine."

"Do you refuse me?"

Valerian looked into his face, friendly with a hint of mischief. The arrogance of their first meeting was nowhere in evidence, and she hoped it had gone into permanent hiding. Did he really want to be shown around, or did he want an excuse to be with her? Whichever it was, she found she was not displeased at the thought of spending time alone with him. "No, I do not refuse you."

He helped her carry the books back into the cottage. Theresa was measuring drops of extract into a bottle when they came in.

"Good morning, Mrs. Storrow."

"Baron." She nodded a greeting, then turned to her niece. "Valerian dear, would you mind bringing this to Mrs. Frowdy? Young Toby is having fits again."

"I will be showing the baron the sights of the district, such as they are. It should be no problem to include the Frowdy farm."

Aunt Theresa looked terribly pleased at this news, and Valerian gave her a warning glare. She was rewarded with a knowing and rather encouraging wink.

Valerian wrapped the stoppered bottle in a cloth, and dropped it through the slit in her skirt into the pocket pouch that hung from her waist.

Back outside, the baron's mount was cropping grass.

"Do you want Aunt Theresa to keep an eye on your horse?" Valerian asked.

"Not necessary. We will be riding."

"I do not see two horses."

"No, Darby is most assuredly just one horse."

"My lord, surely you do not—"

"When we are in private, could you call me Nathaniel?"

Valerian stared at him, protests to riding double forgotten. "Why on earth would you want me to do that?"

"Humor me. Come now, let me hear you say it."

"I would not want people to assume we were so intimate."

"Who is to hear? And if they did, would not it be better for them to assume you were sharing your bed with me than with young Eddie?"

"More likely they would believe I was after you both."

"I will challenge to a duel the first man who suggests you are unfaithful," he said melodramatically, putting a hand to his sword.

Valerian could not help a smile. He was jesting, she knew, but it was nice to pretend a man might fight for her honor, albeit a dubious sort of honor in this instance. "I suppose 'twould be ungracious of me to refuse after such a declaration . . . Nathaniel."

"Music to my ears, my dear." He leered comically at her, but she thought she saw in his eyes a touch of true appreciation, underneath the levity.

He mounted Darby, then took his foot out of the stirrup and put down his hand. "Up we go."

There seemed no point in arguing. She could stand and complain that she did not want people to see her clinging to his back, and he would laugh off her protests. Truth be told, she wanted to ride. She had only rarely been on a horse, and the prospect of being carried to the Frowdy farm was far more enticing than that of walking the three miles.

She put her foot in the stirrup, and Nathaniel grasped her small hand in his own. He pulled her up in one swift movement, and she found herself behind him, astride the horse on a small cushion attached there for riding pillion. She arranged her skirts as best she could, tucking the cloth under her legs. Darby shifted his weight, and her arms quickly went around Nathaniel's waist.

"All set?"

"Set enough."

"You will have to tell me where to go."

She told him which path to take from the meadow, and with a soft click from him Darby started off. Valerian could feel the shifting muscles of the horse under her legs, and of Nathaniel from her arms around his waist. She rested her cheek against his back, watching scenery go by. She liked having this innocent excuse to touch him, even if her thoughts of him were not always so pure.

They traveled overland, leaving the path behind, and did not speak beyond the directions Valerian gave. Once or twice they passed people out tending flocks, and Valerian let her eyes pass over them, not acknowledging their presence. She wanted to pretend they would not notice her; at the same time that she wanted them to see that a nobleman had chosen her to ride with him.

They arrived at the Frowdy farm far sooner than Valerian had expected. A horse had definite advantages over walking. She straightened up, pushing away from his back, and tapped his shoulder.

"Let me down. I do not want Mrs. Frowdy to see me up here. 'Tis bad enough that you are with me."

Nathaniel reined in, and with his help she slid off Darby. Nathaniel followed suit, and walked beside her up the dirt track to the stone cottage.

A scrappy-looking dog barked his hoarse warning at their approach, drawing Mrs. Frowdy out of the house, a toddler peeping round her skirts.

"Good day," Valerian called.

"Good day, Miss Bright." Mrs. Frowdy stared at the baron, surprise and embarrassment pinkening her cheeks, and Valerian made the introductions. Mrs. Frowdy curtsyed, and looked considerably more flustered than Valerian had ever seen her.

"I have brought the tincture for Toby. How bad have the fits been?"

Mrs. Frowdy cast a self-conscious glance at the baron. "Not so bad."

Valerian gave Nathaniel a look that said this would go better if he made himself scarce, and she subtly shooed him with her hand. He raised an eyebrow at her. His curiosity obviously outweighed any impulse to accommodate her.

Valerian moved closer to Mrs. Frowdy and lowered her voice. "How bad?"

"It is not that they have been so bad," Mrs. Frowdy whispered back, darting glances over Valerian's shoulder at the baron. "But they have been too often for my liking. Once or twice a day it is happening. The poor little thing shakes something terrible, twitching and jerking."

Valerian nodded and handed her the bottle. "Give half a spoonful every morning. It is valerian, same as last time, only my aunt has strengthened the concentration."

"Will it stop the fits?"

"It should, especially if you can keep him from getting too upset by anything. If it does not stop them . . . Well, there are always other things we could try. If it does work, though, I can give you some plant starts, and teach you how to make the tincture yourself. I do not think this is something Toby will grow out of."

Mrs. Frowdy thanked her, and curtsyed again to the baron, who nodded in acknowledgment. The farm wife stood in the doorway and watched as Nathaniel remounted, and then in complete disregard to the concerns Valerian had expressed upon arriving, he put down his hand to help her onto the horse.

Valerian ground her teeth. She could not refuse his hand, hanging there in the air, with Mrs. Frowdy watching. He would make a fuss, and that would be even more of a spectacle. He probably *wanted* people to think he was bedding her. She mounted with ill grace behind him, giving him a hard pinch in the side as revenge.

When she turned to make her farewells to Mrs. Frowdy, it was plain from the woman's sparkling eyes that gossip would be flying by nightfall.

"I told you I did not want her to see us like this," Valerian hissed at the back of Nathaniel's neck as they headed down the road.

"Others have."

"But not Mrs. Frowdy."

"Is she a particular problem?"

"Let us say she is not always kindly disposed towards Aunt Theresa and me. She will make the worst of this."

"I disagree. She will no doubt conclude that you hold a special place in my heart, and be reluctant to speak against you. I do, after all, hold the deed to the farm she lives on."

The man had no understanding of how life in Greyfriars worked. "That will not stop her. She is devious. She would never speak openly against me: She is mistress of the innuendo. She spreads rumors, and gossips with the innkeeper's wife, which is as good as putting out a news sheet."

Nathaniel leaned to the side and craned over his shoulder to see her face. "I do not understand. If she causes you and your aunt such trouble, why do you go out of your way to help her? I understand treating the child, but why offer to teach the woman to make the medicine herself? Why deliver it to her, when she could come get it?"

"I cannot hold against her her failings," Valerian said, "although at times I confess I am hard-pressed to hold a charitable frame of mind. She does not mean to be so terrible. She fears us, and so she strikes out. What good would it serve to be petty in return? That would only increase her resentment, and then perhaps Toby would not get any medicine at all."

Nathaniel blinked at her, and turned to face front again. "You are kinder than I."

"Cruelty is a luxury I cannot afford."

They were silent, heading up into the hills. Valerian had to cling tightly to his waist, and scoot herself forward when she began to slip back over Darby's broad back.

"What was it you gave her?" Nathaniel finally asked, breaking the silence.

"Mrs. Frowdy? A tincture of valerian."

"Is that an herb of some sort, or a mixture named after yourself?"

Valerian laughed. "It is a plant. The roots make a strong sedative. My parents named me after it, as it is so useful in healing. The name means strength."

"It was a good choice for you."

Valerian smiled, her cheek against the warm cloth covering his back.

They came to the peak of a small mountain, and Valerian felt Nathaniel catch his breath. Stretched out below them was the ocean, and to the left the bay. Greyfriars, set back some way from the shore, was a short strip of thatched and slate roofs partially hidden by trees, with the river flowing by beyond, nothing more than a sparkling line at this distance. On the horizon in front of them, the Isle of Man was a mysterious shadow hunched in the sea.

Valerian dismounted, and staggered. Her legs felt like she still had a horse between them. She put her hands on her thighs to check that her legs were not indeed spread wide like they felt. Her skirt was damp with combined human and horse sweat where it had been beneath her legs.

"I want to show you something," she said as Nathaniel dismounted. The hill sloped down in front of them for a hundred yards, then dropped off in a cliff. She led Nathaniel down near the edge, then got down onto her belly, inching forward. He followed suit, leaving Darby to crop grass, and together they peered over the top of the cliff.

Powerful winds scaled the cliff and provided lift for dozens of ravens, swooping and hovering along the cliff face. Their nests clung to cracks and outcroppings, and to bits of brush growing from the stone. Far, far below, waves crashed upon jagged black rocks.

"This is where I got Oscar, when he was a baby still in pin feathers."

"Here?"

"I had come up here for the view, and was peering over the edge like we are now. As I watched, a chick in one nest tumbled out, bouncing halfway down the cliff. The nest was crowded, the other chicks larger, and I think they shoved him. I climbed down and rescued him, carrying him up tucked in my bodice."

His eyes were wide in amazement. "That was a terrible risk you took."

Valerian shrugged. "I was more concerned about Oscar than myself. It was not long after my parents had died, and I did not care much what happened to me. The only thing I was afraid of, really, was being attacked by the adult ravens while I was climbing. I thought they might make me lose my balance."

"They left you alone?"

"Yes. And I do not know why. Maybe they knew I would not harm their chicks, or maybe. . . ."

"What?" Nathaniel prompted, when she did not continue.

"Oh, a silly idea I had at the time." She had never told anyone this part of the story, and felt now how foolish it sounded, especially being told to this man who had seen so much more of the world than she had. "When I had regained the top of the cliff, with Oscar still alive, I imagined that the ravens had wanted me to have Oscar, so I would have something to live for."

"And did he give you that?"

She paused, remembering what those first few weeks

had been like. "In a way. He gave me someone else to think of, someone who needed me." And then there had been that other thing she had discovered when she held Oscar in her hands that day, the discovery that set her even further apart from the folk of the village.

"He distracted you from the guilt of surviving, when others had not."

Valerian turned to look at him, but his eyes were still on the ravens coasting the air currents below. "Yes, that was a part of it." She watched him, the wind ruffling his dark auburn hair, and saw the lines of some deep regret etch his face. "I think you know something of loss."

He gave a grunt of false humor. "I have some familiarity with the feeling. Or at least with the guilt part of it."

"Is this anything to do with the rumors that you left London after a terrible scandal?"

He finally turned to look at her, his hazel eyes meeting her own, and she read pain there. Their shoulders were touching. He leaned his head in close enough that their foreheads almost touched as well. "The rumors—whatever they may be—no doubt have as much truth to them as the ones that fly about you." He looked away again. "Only you are more innocent than tongues would say, while I am far less."

Valerian inched back from the edge and rolled onto her side, propping her head on her hand so she could watch him. "What did you do?"

"Your aunt asked me the same question, albeit not quite so bluntly. I did not answer her."

"You are going to answer me."

He laughed and drew away from the edge, sitting up. "And why is that?"

"Because you want me to know you." She did not know where the words came from, but she felt their truth as they left her mouth.

"If you truly knew me, you would lock yourself inside your cottage and never come out again. You would warn mothers to hide their daughters and tell fathers to fetch their swords." His tone was light, but the crooked smile had the barest hint of a quiver in it.

"Do not assume that I would judge you so harshly. I have been on the receiving end of such judgments too often to do that."

"You and your aunt both, mother confessors. Telling you will do nothing to change what happened."

"I never said it would. I did not mean that telling me would change the past, any more than praying will change God. The telling, and the praying, are to change yourself."

"Ah, but I am quite enjoying my shame and guilt. I richly deserve them, and am not so ready to give them up." He stood up, dusting off his breeches, and reached down a hand to her. "And it is much too lovely a day, and my companion far too beautiful, for hours spent morosely reviewing the low point of my life. Come, we shall return to Raven Hall for something to eat, and then I shall bring you home, chaste and pure, with all your illusions intact of me as a frightfully handsome, charming, and slightly mysterious man."

She snorted, taking his hand and letting him pull her to her feet. "I do not think I am the one with the illusions."

Chapter Eight

To Valerian's dismay, Paul was sitting hunched over a bowl of soup, slurping loudly, when they came into the dining room. He paused mid-slurp and dropped his spoon back into the bowl with a splash and a clatter, his eyes going from Nathaniel to her, and back again. "Nathaniel. What a surprise."

"Good afternoon, Paul," Nathaniel said cheerily. "Are you enjoying your private dining, or would you like a bit of female companionship to enliven your meal?"

Paul cast a disparaging eye at her. "I would have thought you would much rather have her to yourself. And God knows, she will do nothing for my appetite."

Whatever sense of well-being and comfort she had begun to feel in Nathaniel's company collapsed with brutal abruptness. She suddenly felt the difference in her and Nathaniel's stations, and that she did not belong at this table in her rough dress and stained leather shoes. It was as if she could feel each bit of grass and vegetation clinging to her clothes, and the inelegant picture she made with her braid hanging down her back, wisps of hair rubbed free.

"Surely you can forgive her for having seen you with your breeches down," Nathaniel cajoled, not taking his friend seriously.

Paul grunted in response, giving Nathaniel a look of disgust little kinder than that he had given her.

Valerian narrowed her eyes. Nathaniel might not be aware that his friend was serious, but she certainly was. "Lord Ravenall," she said formally, doing her best impression of a duchess, holding tight to her pride, "I am afraid I must decline your earlier offer of dinner. I will just slip down to the kitchen and beg a crust of bread before I go—I am much more comfortable down there than in these fine surroundings. Why, heaven only knows what a mess I might make of things!" She dropped a mock curtsy and swept away, her cheeks burning.

His hand on her arm swung her around before she had taken two steps, her skirts swaying with the force of his pull. She gave his hand a vicious slap without thinking, and he let go. Perhaps ladies did not hit. Their eyes met, and she saw the confusion there, and she almost relented. Then his eyes shifted to Paul, and she turned on her heel and stomped off down the corridor. She expected his hand or voice holding her back, but neither came. It was only Paul's mocking laugh that followed her down the hall.

The way down to the kitchen was familiar to her from her many visits to the manor with her aunt. Familiar as well were James and Judith, king and queen of the cooking domain. She had not meant it when she had said she would go beg in the kitchens, but it occurred to her that it was not such a bad idea. Far better company was to be had down there than above stairs. James and Judith had always been kind to her, whereas most of the other staff gave her a wide berth.

Her feet tapped their way down the stone stairs, which had depressions worn into their surfaces from two hundred years of servants rushing up and down with platters of food. At the moment all that rushed up was the combined scents of roasting meat, pastries, and spice; and the clattering noise of kitchen workers at their jobs.

She banked her anger for the moment, seeking distraction from the hurt in the company of others—others who did not think her too dirty and poor to sit at their table. Let Nathaniel pacify his friend for the insult of having brought her before him while he ate. Fine! It served her right for forgetting she had no place in their world.

She poked her head around the corner of the doorway, observing James as he rolled out pastry dough on the large center table, other kitchen servants dashing to and fro like bees around their hive. His belly was as big as ever, covered by a food-stained, once-white apron. His thin, grey-streaked hair was pulled back over his balding head and tied off with a sad and scraggly strip of twine. "Good day, James!" she called.

He looked up, and his face creased in a smile that was missing the left half of its teeth. "Valerian!"

He claimed he had lost the teeth fighting brigands on a road outside Yarborough, and that he had narrowly saved Judith from their rapacious hands, but the truth was he had walked into a wall while drunk. Given his fondness for his own sweets, Valerian was not surprised his teeth had been so loosely anchored as to tumble out upon impact. Hygiene had never been one of his strong points.

"It has been too long since you have been down to see Hairy and me," James said. "He misses you dreadfully, you know. He does not like anyone else."

Valerian laughed, and went over to the huge fireplace with its low-burning, wood-scented fire. A huge chunk of beef turned slowly on a spit, the juices dripping into a pan beneath. A belt attached to a small wheel on the spit was in turn attached to the axle of a three-foot exercise wheel mounted on the exterior stone of the fireplace.

The black and white spotted dog inside the creaking wheel, loping to nowhere with his tongue hanging out, was the infamous Hairy. The wheel wobbled on its axle, and Hairy tilted his scruffy head and twitched a floppy ear as Valerian approached.

"Hairy, you lovely dog, have you been good?" His ears perked and his brush-like tail wagged, and he ran a little faster in his spinning cage, the meat jerking on its spit at the increase in speed.

"Lovely! Har!" James said behind her, loading up a plate with cheese and bread. "I have never seen a sorrier example of the species. Bred in a stinking midden, he was, with the manners of a rabid rat. We will be making bow-wow mutton of him one of these days, just you wait and see."

Hairy cast a urine-yellow eye at his master and growled, his raised lip showing a broken canine tooth.

"Eat Hairy, indeed! 'Tis no wonder he bites you, if he must endure such threats and insults."

"He bites me for sausages. Are you hungry, Valerian girl? I would rather feed you than that mangy piece of flea-ridden cur. Or any of these other louts," he said, gesturing at his staff in general. Valerian noticed that several were taking the opportunity of his distraction to slip from the room for a break.

"I will eat only if you join me and tell me how you have been since I saw you last."

"You mean since the new baron came. Ha! Cannot fool me. You want to hear the dirt." James wrinkled his face in disgust at the plate he held, dumped the cheese and bread back where he got it, and started reloading the plate with tarts and roast beef. "Cheese and bread, paugh!" he grumbled. "Let *them* eat it, as do not work for their living." And then, louder, "So, I must bribe you with gossip to get you to eat my food. Seems a poor trade."

"Nonsense. You have the pleasure of my delightful company, which is worth any amount of gossip and pastry."

"Give me Hairy any day."

"Paul, what in God's name is the matter with you?"

"With *me*? Nothing, My Lord Baron, Sir! 'Tis your brain I wonder at."

"For bringing Miss Bright to my home for dinner? What do you have against her that you cannot treat her with even a modicum of civility, and this after she was kind enough to help tend your sorry ass?"

"I have nothing against her, except for the very real possibility that she is a witch and a poisoner, and has put you under her spell," Paul said, his voice rising.

"My God, Paul, you must be joking," Nathaniel said, genuinely astonished. "You do not believe that superstitious pap."

"Do I not? I have been spending time at the inn in town and have heard all manner of ills spoken of that girl. When I see my friend poised to repeat the very errors that drove him from London, why should I not question but that something unnatural is afoot?"

"Miss Bright is nothing like Laetitia."

"No. At least Laetitia was somewhat civilized and had a brother to defend her, for all the good it did either one of them. She also understood her place."

"And what place would Miss Bright's be?"

"Amongst her own kind, and well you know it. You cannot bring common girls home for dinner, having them think they have as much right to sit at this table as you or I. You would never dare such a thing in London."

"You think you are so superior to her that you cannot share a table?"

"I am not judging her as a person, Nathaniel," Paul said, lowering his voice and taking on a pedantic tone. "I am judging her as your society and mine would. What favor are you doing her by bringing her here and making her sit down to eat with you, waited on by those she knows as her equals? If we were anywhere but where we are, and I were anyone else, you would not have done it. Our peers would humiliate her, and her friends will hate her for the favors you show her."

"She has no friends. If anything, it will help her to have these petty-minded villagers know she is in my favor."

"And when you tire of her? What then?"

Nathaniel clamped his jaw tight, the heat of anger on his cheeks. "There will not be a repeat of Laetitia, do not worry yourself on that score." He pivoted on his heel and strode off down the hall.

He found the stairs down to the kitchen, his boot heels making a racket on the hard stone steps. He slowed when he heard Valerian's voice, and the answering laughter of a man. He had not quite believed her threat to go eat in the kitchen.

He came around the corner, observing her for a moment. She had a tart crust in hand, and was feeding it to the turn-spit dog. The cook—he could not recall his name—was eating one of the tarts himself, noisily sucking out the filling.

"My lord!" the cook gasped upon seeing him, inhaling a piece of fruit in the process. He coughed grotesquely, spitting bits of crust into the palm of his hand.

Valerian turned, and he saw the delight fade from her face at sight of him. For an instant he saw himself through her eyes, a finely dressed aristocrat with boorish friends, standing in the kitchen like a peacock in a hen coop, lording himself over the lowly, mundane birds. He felt out of place and unwanted, and then he saw the vulnerability in Valerian's eyes, and the rest did not matter.

He went to her side, ignoring the surreptitious glances of those still present in the kitchen, and the continued hacking of the cook. "Come," he said, his voice low enough to reach only her ears. "Let me take you into the garden where I can apologize for Paul."

She flashed him a look that said Paul was not the only one at fault. "And for my own behavior," he added. He bent his head closer to hers. "Do not—"

He was interrupted by a low growl, and he raised his head. The turn-spit dog, its face a mish-mash of black and white spots, was glaring at him with evil yellow eyes. He looked back at Valerian in time to see her smile at the beast's disfavor. He took her hand, and dragged her only half-resisting from the kitchen, away from the eager eyes and ears of the staff.

The moment they gained the garden she pulled her hand from his and kept walking, tramping down a gravel path. He followed a couple paces behind her until they were out of sight from the house, hidden behind hedges and shrubberies, and then stopped her with a hand on her shoulder.

"Do not touch me!" she snapped. "You have no right."

"Valerian, I am sorry. Sorry about the way Paul treated you, and sorry that I did not immediately defend you. He was wrong to have been so rude to you."

"And you were wrong to have asked me to eat with him. My lord."

"Valerian—"

"Yes, I should call you by your title, for there is no use in my imagining any deeper intimacy between us. Mr. Carlyle did me the favor of pointing out the difference between our worlds. I have no place in yours, none at all."

"There is no law against befriending one another. It is not as if we were being married, for God's sake."

"No, it is not, is it?" Her voice took on a false puzzled tone. "Just what are we to each other, Nathaniel? Do you want me as a mistress? A friend? You will have to explain it to me. I fear I have no experience with any of this."

He was silent, searching for words to explain that which was not clear even to him.

"You do not know what you want with me, do you?" she snapped.

"I cannot categorize you, if that is what you are asking," he said, still searching for his own understanding, for an explanation he could give himself for why he could not stand the thought of breaking off their acquaintance. "But God knows I want you."

"For what, Nathaniel? Am I a friend to have lunch with, or a woman to seduce with a silver bracelet? What do you want from me?" she cried.

He grasped her face between his hands and slid his fingers into her bound hair, abandoning the effort at thought for that which his body already knew to be true. "This," he said, and bending down he captured her lips with his own. She resisted for only a moment, then her mouth softened, and her hands came up to rest lightly, uncertainly on his chest. He deepened the kiss, moving against her mouth, dipping the tip of his tongue gently through her lips, allowing the intensity of his feelings to speak to her through his touch.

When he finally lifted his mouth he could feel her shaking, her hands tightly clenching the cloth of his jacket. "This is what I want," he said.

"I see," she whispered, her blue eyes enormous as she looked up at him. "This, and nothing more."

His heart protested at that. Nothing more? Yes, he wanted more. He wanted to climb behind those brilliant eyes of hers and learn the mind inside. He had jested that he was the mysterious one, but she was the true enigma. A beautiful, isolated woman, living a life of magic, conflict, and kindness. He could not name what he wanted from her—no, not wanted, but needed from her. He could not name it, but he knew it was there.

But he did not know how to say that, hardly knew how to think it, and knew only how to ask for that which was obvious and physical. "We can share this together," he said, feeling the inadequacy of it in his own heart.

"And that is all," she said softly.

He heard the question hidden in her statement, that asked if she was no more than a body to him. He knew she thought that the physical would satisfy him, as it had satisfied countless men who dallied with those beneath their station, and he could not bear it. He wanted her to know more of him than that, to understand that he wanted to protect her from himself at the same moment he wished to possess her.

"Shall I tell you why my family has banished me from London? You will understand better Paul's hostility."

She blinked at him, pulling back slightly at this apparent change in topic. "Yes, of course."

He led her to a stone bench, sitting beside her with her hands in his. "You may hate me when you have heard the whole sorry tale."

"I do not doubt I have already imagined and accepted worse."

He took a deep breath, and felt it shudder in his chest, dreading this baring of his soul. There was no one with whom he had shared the entire story, start to finish. "It was a year ago when it began. One of my friends had befriended a young lawyer, Lawrence Mowbray. He met him in a tavern, they got drunk together, they liked each other. Lawrence became somewhat of a regular with our group, no matter that his family was just barely respectable.

"Lawrence had a sister, Laetitia, seventeen. She was lovely, with pale blond hair and soft brown eyes. She looked innocent as a fawn. Underneath, she was anything but. She was a passionate young woman, with a will that would brook no opposition. She took a fancy to me, and maneuvered Lawrence into asking me to escort her to a party one of her friends was having.

"I confess I was only too happy to oblige. I knew she wanted to impress her friends with me, an older man, a member of the nobility. I enjoyed it." He snorted in disbelief at his own overweening pride. "And on the ride home from the party I found that she was not at all unwilling to express her gratitude in a tangible form. So I took what she offered. I debauched her." He paused, letting the phrase hang there in all its shame.

"And our liaison began. I thought I was clever, and careful, and while some suspected my intentions towards Laetitia were not honorable, there was no proof to the contrary. Lawrence, the foolish man, thought I was enamored of his sister, and even joked that we might someday be brothers-in-law. His friendship with our circle had given him false impressions of the possibility. He had no notion of what I did with his sister in private.

"Laetitia was largely unchaperoned, her mother dead and her father either working or drinking—and as she ran the house, what servants there were would not speak against her, for all that they might gossip amongst themselves. It was not difficult for her to arrange times when we could meet in private.

"She was less certain than her brother of the constancy of my affections. She would bring up the topic of marriage, indirectly, and watch for my response. However carefully I thought I answered, she would sense the truth that I had no intention of speaking for her, and she would fall into what I can only describe as a raging depression. After one such conversation, she cut her wrist with the glass from a broken mirror. On another, she tried to eat poison. If I had not been there, she might have died, or seriously harmed herself.

"Then she told me she was pregnant. I was appalled. I offered to pay for the care of the child, send him away to be raised in the country, but she would not hear of it. I was at a loss for what to do. She had worn me down with her hysterics, and I was beginning to hate her. But she carried my child, and if I abandoned her she might hurt not only herself, but the babe. I resigned myself to staying with her at least until the child was born, and then trying again to persuade her to some other goal than marriage to me.

"She hid the pregnancy up until the fifth month, when she miscarried.

"Well, there was no hiding that. Of course a doctor had to be called in. When Lawrence discovered what had happened, and who the father was, he demanded I marry Laetitia. I refused, and he challenged me to a duel. I could not refuse. What little honor I had left made it imperative I give the man the chance to avenge himself and his family.

"I had no intention of trying to kill Lawrence in the duel, or even wounding him. I chose swords, with the thought that he could beat out his fury on me, spill some of my blood, and we could both retire from the field.

"But I had underestimated his anger. He would not stop with a show of blood. He wanted me dead, and he fought for it. I confess I was not so noble as to stand still for my own slaughter. When a man comes at you with death in his eyes, you fight for your life, thoughts of honor and good intentions long forgotten. I have spent time in the army, and know that well." He paused, and stared into nothing, seeing again the blood on his sword.

"I killed him."

He was silent for a long moment, then looked at Valerian, and saw that she watched him, face expressionless, waiting for his next words.

"Laetitia still wanted me, even after that. I told her no, that I would see her well settled with a husband of her own rank, and offered to settle a sum on her. But she wanted me."

His voice went flat. "We were in a carriage, arguing over it as we always did, she was alternately weeping and yelling. The carriage slowed in traffic while crossing a bridge over the Thames. She opened the door and leapt out, then ran to the low wall and climbed up on the stones. She threatened to throw herself off.

"People turned to look, staring at the shrieking woman, but kept their distance. I went after her. She saw me coming, and put out her hand to stop me. I stopped, not wanting to force her into action. If she wanted to talk from ten feet apart, so be it.

"And then the wind caught at her skirts, billowing them against her legs, a great gust of wind that felt as if it had traveled the whole length of the river to reach her. I lunged for her, but I was too late. She fell.

"It took three days for her body to float to the surface and be retrieved. Her father never recovered from the shock."

He fell silent once again, and when he resumed his voice was more matter of fact. "By now, of course, everyone knew my part in the sorry affair. My friends knew, my relations knew, bare acquaintances on the street knew.

"My parents and grandparents, the uncles and aunts, they all came together. This was a scandal such as the family had not faced for decades. Laetitia may not have been of their circle, and they would have done all in their power to prevent a marriage, but she had been no street prostitute either. This was a disgrace that had cost two people their lives, and ruined the health of a third.

"My family banished me to Raven Hall, more than one of them having visited it in the past, and knowing how remote and, by their reckoning, desolate it was. I was not bound to obey—I have money of my own—but spending time in Cumbria seemed a small penance for what I had done."

He met her eyes and could read nothing in them. "It is as terrible as you imagined, is it not? You can understand now why Paul views you as such a threat. He does not want to watch me make the same mistakes twice."

"So where is the difference between what you did with Laetitia and what you wish to do with me? Why do you pursue me, when you know what havoc you wreaked on her family?"

How could he explain the difference, when it was so unformed a feeling that he could not describe it even to himself? Laetitia had been young and selfish, attractive to him through her beauty and his own vanity. He had never truly cared who she was inside. They had been shallow pleasures he had with her, pleasures of the body but not of the soul.

"I can give you honesty from the beginning," he said. It was not much, but it was all he could offer, and was more than he had given Laetitia.

"Does that honesty extend to my family? Will you tell my aunt what you wish to do with me, as you did not tell Laetitia's brother?"

"I think she already knows."

She was silent, eyes staring unfocused at a distant point. He waited, dreading what she might say. At last she returned his gaze. "Give me time to think."

He nodded once, curtly, although his heart cried out that he should not let her leave him, even for a moment. Let her decide while his arms were around her, while he kissed her weak with passion, and made clear thought impossible.

But still, her response had been almost more than he had hoped for. "As you wish."

Chapter Nine

"And to think I went to them for help. I can hardly believe myself," Gwen ranted. "The scheming witch. I probably gave her the idea. How old is she now? Too old. Too desperate. She is man-hungry, that is what she is, and all the time standing there like butter would not melt in her mouth, with her aunt telling me not to cheapen myself. A pair of whores, they are. Well, I will not let them have you, Eddie, you can count on it."

"Huh?" Eddie was drawn from his lewd thoughts by his name. Gwen had been yakking non-stop for the past mile, and he had long since ceased to listen. He shifted his grip on Valerian's clamming shovel, and wondered if Gwen would finally let him touch her breasts when this was through.

"At first I thought you preferred her to me, can you believe that?" Gwen angrily tore a handful of leaves from a branch crowding the path and ripped them into little bits as she tramped down the narrow trail, Eddie in tow. "But then I heard Mrs. Torrance talking with my mother. Strange things have been happening of late," Gwen intoned darkly. " 'Tis most likely the three of you were lured to her. She used the devil's own wiles, and drunk as you were you had no defenses. She made easy work of you three. Another reason not to drink so much, Eddie."

"Uh-huh," he grunted, his eyes on her backside.

"She needs to know that I am the one you want, and that I know what she is trying to do. She will not dare continue, if I threaten to expose her." Gwen stopped suddenly, and Eddie bumped into her. She turned around, her cheeks flushed, and leaned against his chest. "I am the one you want, right?"

Eddie looked down the top of her bodice at the valley between her breasts. His mouth went dry and he felt himself harden. "Yes, Gwen."

"They were lying to me, telling me not to give myself to you," she said, and rubbed against him. "They wanted you for themselves. But I know better now. Do you still want me, Eddie?" she pouted up at him.

"Yes! You know I do." He could hardly keep from grabbing her and grinding his hips against her soft body.

"Tonight, I will sneak out of the house—"

"Tonight?" He could hardly believe his good fortune.

"That is . . . if you will tell her to leave you alone. Tell her that I am the one you want, not her, the old hag, and that you know she put a spell on you. Then I will make myself yours, truly. Will you tell her, Eddie?"

In the quiet forest, with her pink lips wet and parted, her belly pressed up against his erection, he would say yes to anything. He could even begin to believe anything. "She has been sending spirits to me in my sleep," he told Gwen. "They fondle me." He would not add that he woke sticky with spent pleasure, vague images of plump thighs and breasts flitting through his mind.

Gwen smile up at him. "Would it not be better to have me fondle you?"

His eyes widened as she slipped her hand between them and rubbed her palm against the ridge in his breeches. His hips thrust against her hand, and he pulled her into his arms, pulling up the back of her skirts until he could hold the cool soft mound of her buttock. He moved his hand over the giving flesh, kneading it, then sliding his fingers down to where the tips could brush against the furry wet heat between her legs.

"You did not feel like this when you kissed her, did you?" Gwen breathed at him, still rubbing.

"God, no . . ."

Gwen pulled away from him, her skirt dropping back over her legs. "That just goes to show. You never really wanted her. 'Twas witchcraft."

He stood panting with frustrated desire. He wanted to finish what they had started. He would finish it with his own hand, if he had to. Her hand would be even better.

"Come on, then," she said briskly, turning and continuing down along the path. "Let us get this over with."

Hopelessly aroused, he followed.

Valerian saw nothing of her surroundings during her walk home, her mind a muddle of emotions and conflicting thoughts.

Common sense told her that the practical course would be to refuse any but the most cursory contact with the man. Her reputation, or what was left of it, would remain intact. She would retain her virginity, on the almost nonexistent chance that someone would one day want to marry her. If she rejected him, she would not risk caring for him, only to be abandoned at some later date.

Common sense had guided her through many difficulties. It was safe. It was practical. One seldom regretted using it. And it was boring.

She admitted it to herself: She was tired of being careful, and tired of denying her desires. A careful life was so difficult to maintain, so much work and worry. A rebellious light within her wanted to smash it to pieces, relieving herself of the burden of doing the right thing. She wanted to destroy it all in a glorious bonfire of misguided passion, and not spare a single thought for the future after the flames had died to ashes.

Nathaniel Warrington was the only man who had taken an interest in her. It did not seem possible that there would ever be another, or at least not another who was young and handsome. Maybe some fat old sheep farmer who had been alone in the hills for too long would want her, but she sure as God would not want him. This might very well be her only chance.

And then there was a small part of herself, that she could only barely stand to admit, that liked the idea of being the mistress of the baron, for the twisted prestige of it if nothing else. Let the townsfolk see that a nobleman wanted *her*, and not one of their own daughters.

It was with these ruminations in mind that she arrived home. She was halfway across the meadow before she noticed Gwen and Eddie waiting for her, sitting on the wooden bench against the front of the cottage. They stood as she approached.

"Good day, Gwendolyn, Edward. What brings you here?" They were neither of them people she wished to see, reminding her of that humiliating incident on the mudflats.

"Good day, Miss Bright." Gwen's voice was as stiff as Valerian's own. "We have brought your shovel back," Gwen said, gesturing to where the tool leaned against the cottage wall.

"Thank you. It is much appreciated."

"And Eddie has something he needs to say to you."

Valerian turned her attention to Eddie, who colored under her gaze. "I . . ." He looked at Gwen, swallowed, then stared past Valerian and spoke in a rush. "I want you to stop chasing after me. It is Gwen I want."

"What are you talking about? I never went after you. *You* were chasing *me*."

Eddie's lips moved silently, like those of a fish. His round eyes searched out Gwen for help.

" 'Tis not true, and you know it, Valerian Bright!" Gwen said hotly. "You cast a spell on him, luring him to you. Well, it will not work, and you cannot have him. He is mine, and he wants me, not some dried-up old hag."

"You are welcome to him!" Valerian snapped, Gwen's misguided anger sparking her own. Eddie's slimy kiss flashed revoltingly to mind. "And good luck to you. You will not be having much pleasure from him, I will tell you that!"

"Is that a threat? Are you cursing us?"

"Oh, for God's sake, get out of here, will you? Go!"

Gwen's face was livid, in stark contrast to that of Eddie's, which was pale with apparent fright. Gwen dragged him by the arm across the meadow.

For a moment, Valerian almost wished she really could curse the pair of them, or at least bean one on the head with a well-aimed rock. The most offensive part of it all was that they were convinced that she lusted after Eddie. As if she would want the empty-headed boy.

She stomped inside the cottage and busied herself chopping vegetables and making loud noises with the crockery. Idiots. She would like to see their faces if they heard she was spending her nights with the baron. She dumped onions and water into a pot, then hung it on the swinging iron arm over the fire. They would probably think she had cast a spell on him, too.

Her seething had calmed to a low simmer by the time Theresa came home, carrying a small bag of rare plants that only showed themselves at this time of year. They worked silently for a time, Theresa preparing the plants to be made into an infusion, Valerian slicing bread and preparing for supper. Her aunt's calm presence was soothing, and when the meal was half-eaten Valerian finally told her about Gwen and Eddie.

"I cannot decide whether to laugh or to worry," Theresa said when she had finished. "That girl's foolishness grows less charming by the day. It is not a pretty picture, what Eddie's life will be like if they do marry."

"They deserve each other."

"Have they hurt you so deeply that you must be uncharitable?"

Valerian poked at a remaining potato chunk on her pewter plate, examining her feelings before replying. "No, they have not hurt me. Offended my pride, perhaps. And it galls me that they had the power to do even that."

"They do not have that power, Valerian. Others can only offend you if you in some way agree with them. What would you have done if Gwen had said you were too ignorant to cure the rash on a baby's bottom?"

"As if she would know!" Valerian laughed.

"Right. You would laugh. You are confident of yourself in healing. But you are vulnerable in your relations with others, especially men. You have grown up being avoided by most of the townsfolk and ignored by the men your age. In part, you may believe that they were right to reject you."

"They are ignorant. I have always known that."

"I know you think that, and may almost believe it, but does not some part of you feel that they would not dislike you unless there was something to dislike? Is not the truth that the worst part about that encounter with Gwen and

Eddie was that Eddie was saying he had no interest in you?"

"But I do not want him."

"I know you do not. But it was nice to have the attention, was not it? To have someone act foolishly over you, and find you more attractive than Gwen, the closest thing to a beauty the town has. You believed him sincere, and now here he comes and says he did not mean it."

Protests came to her lips, and remained unspoken as she felt the hidden bite of truth, and then the hated sting of tears in her eyes. "How miserable and weak it all sounds."

"How human it all is."

"So how do I change it?"

"That is for you to decide."

In her loft that night, Valerian lay staring up into the darkness, listening to Theresa's snores and the rustling of small creatures in the thatch above her head. She thought about herself and about Nathaniel's desire for her. It seemed impossible that he would ever have feelings beyond lust for her. Was that the truth, or was it only her own insecurities? And even if he never loved her, would it not do her good to be adored, in whatever way he offered? Being wanted by one man for however short a time sounded infinitely better than being wanted by none.

She rolled onto her side, pulling her blankets down tight around her neck, her hands bunched in front of her throat. There were a hundred reasons not to become involved with Nathaniel Warrington. She closed her eyes, and felt the yearning of her skin for a loving touch. There were a hundred reasons, and she could not care about a single one.

Eddie crouched in the shadows outside Gwen's house, waiting for her to appear and make good on her promise. For months he had dreamt of this. For months he had known just what he would do to her. His waiting had gone on so long that he had abandoned hope of it ever being rewarded.

A half moon cast pale light across the dirt yard. A small shadow darted across the space, startling him. A cat, just a cat. He waited. A breeze picked up, rustling through leaves and making branches creak. Were those wings he heard in the air?

He did not like waiting in the dark like this. It gave him too much time to think about Miss Bright, and what she had said. He had felt his balls shrink and suck themselves up into his groin when she had cursed him. Gwen had said prayers against the witch all the way home, but he did not think that was enough. Had she not first cast her spell by staring at his crotch? Had she not visited him in his dreams, making a plaything of his flesh? And now she had cursed him, and he had felt his tool shrivel in response.

An owl swooped silently down, clear enough in the silvery light that he could see its talons snatch a small form from the ground. Owl, evil omen. Damn that Gwen, where was she?

You will not be having much pleasure from him, I will tell you that! That is what she had said. She had cursed him, he was sure of it. He put his hand down to cup himself, but could not find the familiar bulge. He whimpered, patting at his breeches. God in heaven, had she taken it completely?

A touch on his shoulder made him yelp, and then there was a small hand over his mouth.

"Eddie! Hush, you fool, you want to wake my father? Come, into the barn."

Gwen dragged him by the hand into the musty barn, with its warm scent of animals and the quiet sounds of their movements in the straw. She led him through the near blackness to an empty stall, where she pulled him down on top of her.

Gwen's eager wet mouth sought out his own, her hands running down his chest. He pushed her away, holding her hands captive in his own. "She has cursed me cock, Gwen," he whispered, his voice quavering.

"What?"

"It is gone. I cannot feel it."

He felt her stiffen beside him, and a silence full of evil possibilities built between them. "Have you looked for it?"

"I have not had the chance, but I cannot feel it."

She pulled her hands free of his, and reached for the fastenings at his hips. "Let me check."

He submitted, helping her to pull down his breeches. He felt her hands on his skin, and then they disappeared.

"Eddie, here it is right here," Gwen said, and he could hear the relief in her voice. It only frightened him the more.

"Where? I do not feel it, I tell you!"

She grabbed his hand and brought it down to his groin. "Here, feel it in my hand?"

"I feel your hand, nothing more. 'Tis gone, I tell you!" His voice rose. "She has stolen it. It is her revenge against me for throwing her aside!"

"Quiet! Eddie, come outside. We will look in the moonlight, and you will see it is there."

They made their way back through the barn and out into the yard. He dropped his breeches and turned into the light.

"There, you see it there, sitting nestled like a mouse in its hairy nest? It looks a bit small, but the cold does that, does it not? That is what my brothers say."

He looked, and an owl hooted from the trees.

"Jesus Christ preserve me, it was the owl took it. He swooped down and took a shadow from the ground, and it was after that I could not find it. I have lost me cock!"

"She has bewitched you. The Satan-loving whore! She has made it useless to you, invisible, though I see it clear as day."

"How am I going to take a piss?" he wailed.

"Who is out there?" a suspicious male voice called from the house.

"My father! Go, Eddie. I will meet you tomorrow, and we will think on this. There must be a way to break it."

"Gwen, is that you?" the voice asked.

"But how will I piss?"

"Quiet! Squat down like a girl, if you have to. Now go!"

Eddie went, sobs in his throat, his hand down the front of his breeches, cupping the hairy stretch of flesh where his manhood used to be.

Chapter Ten

"Darling, could you bring me up some apples from the cellar? I have the urge to make a tart."

Valerian looked up from her mending. "A tart? Is Charmaine coming today?"

Theresa frowned in concentration. "I do not know. I only know that I have a strong feeling that I should make a tart. An apple tart."

"Then she is no doubt on her way already." Theresa's gift often gave oblique messages such as this. Apple tart was Charmaine's favorite dish, and any time Theresa made one, Charmaine was certain to show up. Or perhaps the family's psychic abilities had not completely passed her cousin by, and Charmaine had inherited a sense for when and where tarts were baking. For all Valerian knew, the woman might spend her days roaming from house to house, partaking of tarts from here to Yarborough.

Valerian lifted the hatch in the wood floor and climbed down the ladder into the cellar. The air was cool and faintly damp, with the clean scent of the earth. She found the apples, withered from their long winter underground.

She climbed out again, and dropped the hatch into place. "You must have been frightened when you discovered you were pregnant with Charmaine, after all that had happened to you and Mother," she said, putting the apples on the work table.

"I do not know if 'frightened' is the right word. After all that had happened, having a child seemed more a blessing than a curse."

"Tell me about it, when you and Mother left London."

"You have heard the story a hundred times, Valerian. Why do you want to hear it again?"

She shrugged.

"Are you thinking your life might end up running along a parallel path?"

Valerian picked up a knife and chopped an apple in half, not looking at her aunt. "Not really. I like the story, is all."

"Hmm." Theresa did not sound convinced.

"Please, Aunt Theresa?" Valerian pleaded, looking up at her with her best innocent expression. "Start after Grandmother Grace was murdered."

"Murdered," Theresa intoned in her story-telling voice, finally giving in. "And set to burn. 'Twas a blessing they killed her first. Your mother, Emmeline, came and found me, still entangled in Thomas's arms, wearing nothing but a chemise."

"Thomas the viscount."

"Yes, Thomas the viscount. He had been pursuing me for months, from party to party, and I finally gave in. It was only for a few short hours, but what hours they were! But then, when he heard what Emmeline said, he became frightened."

"He had ignored the rumors until then," Valerian put in, the story as familiar to her as a childhood rhyme.

"I have often thought since then that the rumors excited him. Maybe they made me seem more appealing, more of a challenge. Who but the wildest dared to bed a girl whose mother was a suspected witch, who had foretold more than one death? I think he wanted to impress his friends with his bravery, or maybe he wanted to appear more wicked than he truly was."

"He abandoned you."

"Who is to say who abandoned whom? There was Emmeline, her eyes wild, begging me to flee with her. They would be after us next. I think poor Thomas was too shocked to think clearly. He gave me what gold he had on him, as well as his horse. I think it was that horse that saved us. We would have never made it on foot or by coach."

"You fled north."

"Yes, although not before slipping back to Mother's garden for the stash of gold. She had always feared something like this would happen. So we fled north, changed our names from Harrow to Storrow, and settled into a town as spinster sisters."

"And Mother met Father."

"It was acceptable to be female and a doctor's assistant. It is only unacceptable to act and think on your own. Your father was a different breed from most, though. He loved your mother for her wits as much as her beauty. He did not want her to practice any sort of medicine on her own, but to his credit it was out of fear for her safety that he felt that way."

"And then Charmaine."

"Yes. I discovered I was pregnant. One night with Thomas, and Charmaine was on her way. The town knew me as a spinster, not a widow, and I did not want to raise my child as a bastard. Neither did I want to ruin the life that Emmeline was hoping to build with Dr. Bright."

"And that is when you came here."

"Yes. I bought myself a wedding ring." Theresa waggled her hand in the air, showing the familiar gold band. "Came here, and claimed I was the widow of a fisherman by the name of Storrow, gone down with his boat in the North Sea, God rest his sainted soul." She put her hands together in an attitude of prayer, and rolled her eyes heavenward.

"I do not know that they completely believed me," she continued, dropping her hands back to the bowl where she mixed pastry for the tart. "But it was a good enough story. And then Baron Ravenall showed his favor for me, and whatever the townsfolk did or did not believe, they kept to themselves. With the baron's patronage, I felt safe enough to seek work as a healer and midwife, albeit amongst far simpler folk than those I was used to."

"Did you miss your former life, all the parties and gowns and Grandmother Grace's big house?"

"I did not much think on it. I could not think of London and my life there without thinking of what happened to my mother. I knew I could not go back, and there were new pleasures to be found here. The country has its own rewards, if one is of a mind to look."

"And Thomas?"

"I do not know what happened to him, or where he may be. I hope he has led a happy life. I am thankful that Charmaine has never asked for his full name."

"You do not think he would love her, were he to learn of her?"

"I do not know what he would do, but I can hardly imagine any good coming of it. Sometimes I think it has been of help to Charmaine, having him unknown but for his noble background. I think she enjoys seeing herself as the tragic offspring of a noble affair, and imagines that Thomas would have loved her if he had had the chance to know her. She can imagine the truth as she pleases, without threat of disappointment."

Theresa was just taking the tart from the brick oven when Charmaine arrived. The warm scent of apples and cinnamon mingled with the other smells of the cottage, creating a sense of welcome to which even Charmaine was not immune.

"Good morning, Mother. I see I chose a good day to visit."

"Any day would be a good day."

Valerian kept to the background as mother and daughter engaged in stilted small-talk. Charmaine's visits were few and far between, and Valerian knew that Aunt Theresa was pained by the distance between herself and her daughter.

Valerian watched her cousin, wondering what had prompted her to drop in like this. There was worry in Charmaine's eyes, which skipped around the cottage, rarely making contact with her mother's. She was pale, and the lines around her mouth had deepened. Valerian relaxed the habitual mental guard she wore around her cousin, and allowed herself to accept the fragments of subtle information Charmaine put out.

Her focus centered on Charmaine's posture, and the outline of her midriff. She was not surprised she had missed it the last time she and Charmaine had met—she had been too busy apologizing for Oscar and thinking about both Nathaniel and getting away from Charmaine to spare so much as a real look at her. But it was obvious now, despite the fact that Charmaine had always had a slightly stocky figure and wore loose dresses.

Charmaine was pregnant.

Valerian forgot her reserve and came to where Charmaine sat at the table. Hardly thinking, she lay her hand on Charmaine's belly.

"How long?" Valerian asked. "Four months?" She was beginning to get a sense of life within her cousin, flowing up into her hand.

What color there had been in Charmaine's face drained away. "So it is true. I was not sure for so long, and even now. . . . Am I not too old? I thought all chance had passed."

Valerian took her hand away. "Four months, maybe a little more."

"We have hoped for so long." Charmaine sniffed back a sob. "You are sure?"

Valerian nodded.

"I cannot believe I did not see it myself," Theresa exclaimed, coming forward and clasping her daughter's hands in hers. Theresa's cheeks flushed with pleasure, giving her a healthier look than she had had for weeks.

"Will you help me through this?" Charmaine asked her mother tentatively. "I would not trust anyone but you. I know I have not come to see you as much as—"

"I will do everything I can," Theresa interrupted. "And Valerian will help you, too. You know she is the more talented of us."

Charmaine spared a doubtful glance for her young cousin. "But you will be there for me?" she asked her mother, vulnerable in a way she had not been since a child.

"I will do all in my power."

Charmaine ate most of the tart, asking Theresa question upon question about childbearing. Valerian could not help but notice that Theresa hardly touched the tart on her own plate, just as she had not been eating her meals of late.

Charmaine finally left, and after Valerian had finished cleaning up she sat down across from Theresa, who was sitting silent and lost in thought.

"I do not know if I will be able to help her, when her time comes," Theresa finally said.

"I was wondering when you would admit to being ill."

"You knew?" Her eyebrows rose fractionally. "But of course you knew. How did I think I would hide it from you, of all people?"

"Will you let me examine you?"

" 'Twould be of no use. There is no help for this."

"You do not know that. Mayhap there is no medical treatment, but I could—"

"No, Valerian. I will not have you wasting your energies on what cannot be stopped."

"You do not know—"

"This I do know."

"You have seen it." It was a statement, and Valerian's voice was dead as she spoke it, knowing what it meant, and yet unwilling to accept it. "But it is not certain," she protested. "It is possibilities that you see, you have always said that."

"Sometimes there are no other possibilities. Sometimes all paths lead to the same end."

Valerian's throat closed. "I cannot lose you, too. Let me help you, you know I can help."

"No, child," Theresa said gently. "There is nothing that will not serve to merely prolong the inevitable, and I will not have you wasting your energies on that. And I must be frank with you, and say that as much as I want to stay, I do not know that I could stand to. Accept this, Valerian. I want you to take care of Charmaine when I cannot. She will need you."

"I refuse to believe there is nothing to be done." Even as she said it, she knew it was empty defiance. It was rare for Theresa to be certain, but when she was, whatever she saw came to pass.

"Come, feel it." Theresa gestured her over. Valerian knelt before her, and Theresa took her hand and pressed her fingertips into her abdomen.

Valerian felt the solid mass where none should be. She closed her eyes, letting her senses flow through the pads of her fingers. She visualized the tumor in its warm fleshy nest, and sensed the spreading seeds of its presence. Without direction to do so, she reached up to Theresa's armpit, feeling there the offspring of the tumor. She moved her hand again, to the nodes under her aunt's jaw. The more she felt, the deeper became her awareness of the illness. She sensed the traces all through Theresa's body, depriving her of nourishment and consuming her energies. She felt as well the distress of the tissues, and knew her aunt's pain must be severe.

Theresa took Valerian's hand in both of hers. "Enough."

Valerian sat back on her heels and opened her eyes. "Why did you try to hide it?"

"I did not want to worry you."

"Does it make it easier for me to know that you have been alone with this knowledge? How could you have not even allowed me to try to help, when it was early yet and something might have been done? If there is one thing above all others that you have taught me, it is the value of letting others know they are not alone with their pain."

"I am sorry," Theresa said, and Valerian saw the sheen of tears in her aunt's eyes, and knew they were for her rather than for Theresa's own self.

Valerian felt her lip tremble, her neck muscles clenched against emotion.

"I am sorry," Theresa repeated, and Valerian covered her face with her hands. She leant forward and buried herself in Theresa's lap. She sobbed deeply into the heavy cloth that smelled of green plants, Theresa's gentle stroking of her hair all the sweeter for the knowledge that it would soon not be there.

She did not know how long she wept. She sniffed back the last of her tears and turned her head to the side, resting her cheek on Theresa's thigh. Theresa brushed the hair back from her face, and they stayed that way for long moments.

Valerian broke the silence. "I am not sure that Charmaine's baby is healthy."

Theresa's fingers stilled in her hair. "Oh, no. . . ." she whispered.

"I do not know the extent. I do not think I wanted to know, so I stopped looking. I will not be enough to help her through that. She does not care for me, and will not turn to me for comfort."

Theresa did not answer, her silence an acknowledgment of this truth. When she closed her eyes the paths to the future stretched before her, and in all but the vaguest and least likely, great turmoil and a sense of growing danger surrounded her niece, and now her daughter, too.

She wished she did not have this gift of sight. It was hard enough to leave the two she loved dearest in the world. It was torture to know she would be abandoning them at a time they would need her more than they ever had.

Chapter Eleven

Valerian tossed and turned in her bed, her mind running beyond her control. Theresa's tumors, Charmaine's flawed baby, Gwen and Eddie, Nathaniel and his licentious offer—her mind spun round and round, refusing to give her rest. She could hear Theresa's snores from her bed below, and for a brief moment Valerian considered waking her to talk out her thoughts. But her aunt needed her rest, and Valerian did not want to burden her when she already had so much to worry about. It was Valerian's turn to be strong, to be the supportive one.

Only, when it was all over, who would be there to support *her*?

She sighed and let her limbs lie loosely. She stared into the dark above her. She tossed back the covers, kicking her feet free of the blankets in disgust. She could not lie here another moment.

Valerian crawled to the ladder and started down, then heard Oscar rustle his feathers.

"Biscuit!" he croaked out, his voice loud in the quiet cottage.

"Hush!" Valerian hissed. "No biscuits. Go back to sleep."

"Go for walk, walk."

"Oscar, quiet, you will wake Aunt Theresa." She heard him drop from his perch onto the boards of the loft, and then the scrabbling sounds of his claws on the wood. She reached her hand into the dark at the top of the ladder. Oscar found her fingers and tried to swallow one.

"Silly bird," Valerian whispered, dragging him off the loft. He hung by the grip of his throat around her finger, a favorite trick of his when he was feeling lonely or frightened, or did not want her to go. "Do you need comfort, too?"

At the bottom of the ladder she set him on the floor, and gently pried her finger from his grip. Once free, she grabbed her cloak and wrapped it around her, then lifted Oscar up onto her shoulder. He nuzzled into her hair, and she could not say she was sorry for his presence.

Pale moonlight seeped through the windows. Her dark-adjusted eyes picked out the grey shapes of furniture, and the dark shadows where the light did not reach. She walked on the balls of her bare feet to the door, and paused. Theresa's snores continued, undisturbed.

The door opened with a faint whining creak, revealing a silvered vista of meadow. Dark shapes shifted in the grass—deer, grazing on the new growth. They were far from the garden, and its hanging sachets of blood meal and human hair put there to keep them from devouring the herbs.

The deer raised their heads, and she knew they were watching her, scenting the air for danger. Then their heads lowered back to their grazing, a tacit acceptance of her presence.

Valerian walked out into the meadow, the grass cool and wet on her feet. The hem of her chemise dragged against the stalks. She wrapped her arms around her middle, holding herself in the chill air, and looked up at the moon, half-full in a clear sky shimmering with stars. There was a cold beauty to the scene—sky and stars, white moon and silvery meadow—but Valerian could not be comforted by it. She wanted warmth and closeness, not this sterile, distant light that told her only that she was alone.

She leant her head against Oscar, wishing there was more understanding to him than allowed by the mind of a bird.

She remembered the kiss Nathaniel had given her, and the sense of losing herself within his arms. He would not question her if she came to him: He would only welcome and accept.

She stood wondering if this was what she wanted, and could not answer. She knew she did not want to be alone in the night, and could not bear the thought of returning to her bed and the torture of her thoughts.

She went to the shed for a lantern and put on her mud shoes. She would go to him as she was, for she would not return to the cottage to dress and perhaps wake Theresa. She wanted a private escape, however temporary, from the considerations of real life. If she could not disappear into dreams during the night, then she would find oblivion in a different manner. Let the worries of daylight stay in the waking world.

The lantern cast a feeble, patterned light, illuminating the ground for only a few feet around her with its yellow glow. Her shadow flickered on her left, dancing a mad jig beside her on the grass. She did not often go out this late, and when she did it was almost always with a son or husband sent to fetch her for an ailing family member. Still, the forest even in its darkness did not scare her, for she knew it as well as she knew her home.

Oscar dug around in the folds of her hood, arranging the cloth to his satisfaction. She scratched the ridges over his eyes as she walked, and his head tilted forward in a trance of pleasure. The forest path was dark, the moon casting little light through the tangled branches overhead. Once a pair of pale green eyes caught and reflected the light from her lantern, then the creature turned and ran from her intrusion.

It was not until she was at the edge of Nathaniel's gardens that she paused to wonder how she should get into the hall if all had retired for the night. She would rather sit in the cold all night than pound upon the front door for admittance.

She blew out her lantern and left it under a bush, and emerged from the last row of shrubberies onto the open ground before the house.

George Bradlaugh, Nathaniel's uncle, had had his suite of rooms on the ground floor. She hoped that Nathaniel had taken them over, and would be there. She walked around the house, stumbling in the moonlight on deceptive shadows of ground. As she approached the windows to the suite, she was filled with a certainty that he was in there, and her heart raced with the first hint of nervousness.

The bushes under the window rustled and cracked as she shoved her way through them. The room was dark through the window but for the orange glow of the coals in the fire. She cupped her hands around her eyes to shut out the moonlight, and pressed her face to the glass. The reflective window so close was more than Oscar could resist. He rapped his beak against it, three times in quick succession.

Valerian jerked back, grabbing Oscar's beak. He wiggled free, and gave out a loud "Rawwwk" of affront.

"Hush, Oscar!" She hissed.

"Bad bird, bad bird," he squawked.

She turned back to the window. A pale figure stood faintly visible behind the glass. She caught her breath, frightened by the sudden apparition, her heart skipping a beat, and then she realized who it was. He opened the window, the casement pushing outward. She stared. Even in the moonlight she could see that he was naked.

"I would know that voice anywhere," he said.

"Eee-diot!" Oscar screeched, and leapt from Valerian's shoulder into the night.

She stood mute, at a loss for words, allowing anticipation and a queer, thrilling fear to overtake her thoughts. She would not falter from her path now that she was here, but did not know what to do next.

"Wait a moment. Let me throw something on." He disappeared into the dark room. Valerian stepped forward again, leaning through the window. She watched his faint movements as he wrapped a dressing gown around his body.

When he came back he paused for a moment, as if trying to read her face in the darkness, to be certain of her reason for appearing at his bedroom window. He must have seen enough to satisfy him, for he put his hands on either side of her face and held her there, and then his mouth came down on hers. She closed her eyes and let him kiss her, his lips hot on her chilled skin. Every trace of worry, every trace of grief was for a moment pushed aside by his touch.

She raised her hands to his neck, stroking the angles of tendons and muscles, then slid her fingers up into the hair at the base of his neck. His own arms moved down around her to clasp her closer to his chest, and he dragged her off her feet and over the low sill of the window.

"I thought you would never come to me," he said, breaking the kiss.

She put a fingertip to his lips. "I do not want to talk."

"I want you to be certain that you know what you are doing."

"Shhh. . . ." She did not want this talk of rational decisions. She did not come here to be logical. She pressed her hands against his bare chest, exposed by the vee of his robe. She pushed the robe open and pressed her lips softly against the warm flesh. She inhaled the scent of him, tinged with soap and his own scent.

She wanted him to ravish her, to take control and sweep all will away. She did not want to be herself, with her life, responsible and alone with her grief. She wanted to be overwhelmed, pushed outside herself. She kicked off her shoes, and untied the throat of her cloak, letting it fall to the floor.

"Please," she whispered.

He accepted the invitation, and untied the string that gathered closed the neck of her chemise, pushing the garment down her shoulders, following his hands with his lips. He moved across to her breasts, tugging the thin cloth over her hard nipples with his teeth, the roughness of his unshaven jaw on her skin. She stared wide-eyed at the top of his head, a welcome sense of unreality falling over her.

She came back to herself with a groan of pleasure when he raised his head to suck at her breast. She felt her nerves light a trail down to her groin, the wet heat of his lips and tongue kneading a response from her. His hands shoved her chemise down over her hips, and she felt it fall to the floor, lying over her feet.

She felt him shift as he shucked his own robe, and then his arms came around her and lifted her against him, his head still at her breast, one arm against her buttocks. She felt the hard ridge of his manhood, and quivered with pleasure when he rubbed himself against her, bringing her hidden flesh to the yearning beginnings of arousal.

He carried her to his bed, still warm from his sleep, and slid in beside her. He threw his leg over hers and propped himself up on an elbow, leaving one hand free to roam at will over her body. She closed her eyes, tracing in her mind the route his hand took, trailing lightly over her face, down over her breasts, swirling in gentle circles over her abdomen, then stroking solidly against the insides of her thighs, never quite touching their apex.

Valerian moaned softly, deep in her throat, and shifted her hips to draw his hand to her. His mouth found hers, distracting her with the intrusion of tongue, and then his fingers finally touched her. She could not concentrate on kissing him back, her whole body listening to each minute movement of his hand. A fingertip slid just inside her and she tensed at the unfamiliarity of it, feeling a virgin's fear. It moved in and out, the tip only, and then he took the wetness he found and moistened the folds that hid the nub of her desire, and she forgot the fears in the rush of luscious pleasure.

She pulled his face into her neck, leaving her mouth free. He chewed gently at the spot where her neck met shoulder, and against her thigh she felt the turgid length of his arousal. His finger dipped into her once again, pushing farther, and she lifted her hips against his hand even as her passage tightened against this unfamiliar entry.

"Relax," he said softly, and rubbed the heel of his hand against her mound.

She did her best to obey, and he slid his finger deeper within her, then began stroking her somewhere inside, she could not tell where, for the shimmering sensations he produced seemed to come from everywhere at once. With each stroke she only wanted more, and heard herself moaning softly in entreaty.

"Nathaniel," she pleaded.

He withdrew his hand, and nudged her thighs. She

opened them willingly to him, and he rolled over on top of her, forcing her legs wider with the width of his body. She felt him guide himself to her, and then a stretching as the broad tip of him entered her. His thumb played against her folds as he slid within her, but even that pleasure could not keep her from feeling the gritty discomfort of his entry. He moved slightly in and out, sliding deeper with each thrust. She wrapped her legs around his hips and pulled him home with one hard thrust, a cry of pain escaping her throat.

He lay still, his hips pressed against hers. She could feel the throb of his pulse where his flesh met the tight opening to her, as if his very heart were connected to her in this embrace. He began to move again, thrusting slowly and deeply, then more quickly. He propped both hands beside her, keeping the weight of his chest off her.

The pleasure she had felt earlier was lost with his entry, and she could not regain it. With each thrust home the breath was forced from her, and she listened through her pain to the sounds she made and to the wet slaps when their sweaty bodies met. The discomfort had not lessened, and she wished it were over. From some deep instinctual wellspring of knowing she clenched her interior muscles despite the pain, squeezing him when he thrust inside her, hoping to finish this.

His movements slowed and he groaned out her name, "Valerian . . ." He thrust once more, and then froze in his pose above her, his body jerking. She moved her hips slightly, and he grasped them with one hand, stilling her. "Do not," he gasped.

All at once the tension left his body, and he collapsed atop her, her legs still spread wide, knees raised above his thighs. She could feel her muscles trembling with weakness, but did not ask him to move.

It had been gritty and painful, but she had expected that for the first time. She liked the weight of him on her, the feel of his chest hair against her breasts. She stroked the back of his head, combing out the damp tendrils of hair with her fingers. There was something satisfying in having this large man lying weak as a baby upon her, brought to this state by her.

"I am crushing you," he said, and rolled off her, his half-turgid manhood stinging as it slid from her. He lay on his back, and pulled her against his side. She lay her head on his shoulder, and almost timidly laid her leg over his, still feeling weak. He held her there with one arm around her, his hand stroking her arm. She let her fingers play with the hair on his chest and rub softly against his flat nipple.

"It will be better next time, I promise you," he said quietly, and she thought she heard a trace of sheepishness in his voice.

"I knew it would hurt the first time. It was not as bad as I had expected."

He grunted at that, then pulled her closer and kissed her forehead. She lay within his arm, enjoying this new contact between naked bodies, so much warmer and smoother than she had imagined, her flesh giving way to his. There was comfort in feeling bare skin against skin.

A few minutes later his hold on her began to loosen, and then his arm dropped from around her shoulder. His breathing deepened, and she raised her head. "Nathaniel?" He gave no answer.

She put her head back down and tried to snuggle closer, but the comfort of his presence had lessened with his descent into sleep. Even naked next to him, she began to feel alone now. With each of his deep breaths, her sense of isolation grew, her sadness creeping back.

She was tempted to wake him, but if she did she might tell him about Aunt Theresa, and she did not know if that was something she wanted to do. Instead, she slid from the bed and found her chemise, dressing in the dark. She stood on one leg to put on her shoe, her muscles quivering like they had after riding Nathaniel's horse, feeling a soreness where he had been inside her.

She looked back at him, a faint shape in the bed. Her emotions were in too great a welter for her to know what she felt about him at this moment. She let the question pass, to be analyzed beyond recognition at some later time. She climbed through the window, dropped onto the ground, and retreated to the forest.

Chapter Twelve

Nathaniel awoke a few minutes after Valerian's departure. The half-smile on his lips faded as he realized he was alone in his bed. The sheets where Valerian had lain were still warm.

"Valerian?"

Silence was his answer. He threw back the covers and walked naked to check the chair by the fire. "Valerian?"

A draft from the window sent goose bumps up his arms. He went and leant out into the night, searching the shadowed landscape for some sign of her. He heard the rustling of leaves in the wind and saw the black silhouetted branches moving against the sky, but nothing more.

"Damn," he cursed under his breath. It was an unpleasant experience to have been left while sleeping, and a new one.

He closed the window and went back to his bed, punching up the pillows with unnecessary vigor. The action did little to make up for the absence of Valerian's warm and plush body between his sheets.

Tomorrow he would find the little she-devil and make her explain herself, and then he would give her the proper bedding he would have bestowed if she had stayed. He had not been surprised to find she was a virgin, and had intended to love her more gently, but the feel of her body finally beneath him had driven him beyond restraint. *It was not as bad as I had expected,* she had said. He snorted in disgust.

As he lay in the dark, unable to sleep for thoughts of how poorly he had acquitted himself, it occurred to him to wonder what had made her come to him. He considered asking her when next they met, but then thought better of it. *Best not to look a gift horse in the mouth,* as they say.

At breakfast he was still mulling over that question when a bleary-eyed Paul came in and collapsed into a chair across the table.

"Late night?" Nathaniel asked.

Paul grunted and scrubbed at his eyes. "Late enough. If I were not such a good friend to you I certainly would not have dragged myself out of bed."

Nathaniel cocked an eyebrow. "And how, pray tell, does your lovely countenance at my breakfast table prove your friendship? I can think of far more cheering sights."

"I think you should be warned. Your black-haired healer is a cock snatcher."

"I beg your pardon?"

"She turned into an owl and snatched Eddie the blacksmith's cock."

He laughed: It was too ludicrous, even for Paul. "Did she hang from his crotch, wings flapping against his legs as she chewed it off? And I suppose she took it home and roasted it with a bit of pepper for her supper."

"I would not laugh if I were you. You may be next. Has she shown signs of coveting your manhood?"

"I do not know that that is any of your affair," Nathaniel said primly.

Paul leant forward, his arms on the table, his red eyes glazed and intent. "This is a serious matter. The boy is a wreck. He will show no one the wound, and but huddles in a corner of the smithy. He says the iron around him will ward off further attacks."

"Well, she has what she wants. Why would she come back? Unless he has another hidden in his breeches."

Paul thumped his hand upon the table. "There is no reasoning with you! If she would steal the cock of this man, what will stop her from doing it to you? You are playing with fire, Nathaniel. I would not see you burned."

"I thought you said it was an owl I should beware of," Nathaniel said, considering the possibility that despite the early hour his friend might be drunk.

Paul narrowed his eyes. "If she comes to your bed, search her body for witch marks and signs of the devil."

"Like hooves, perhaps, where her feet should be?"

"Look for moles, Nathaniel, where she suckles her familiars. Prick her with a pin, and see if she bleeds the red blood of a mortal."

" 'Tis not a pin with which any sane man would wish to prick her." He did not add that there was a small smear upon his sheets to prove she bled as red a blood as himself.

"God's foot, Nathaniel, will you not take this seriously?"

He finally lost his good humor. "Take seriously the superstitious conjectures of a drunken imagination? Why should I? What I do take seriously, and indeed am most concerned about, is how quickly you have slipped from being a man of reason to one indiscernible in thought from the ignorant, dung-brained villagers with whom you drink. *That* does concern me most sincerely. There are no witches, Paul, and you are a fool to believe there are."

"If you will not listen to me on behalf of yourself, then at least be aware that the townsfolk grow increasingly distrustful of her."

He went cold at that. "Explain."

"The mood is turning against her and her aunt."

They were neither of them too young to remember the gruesome ends that women found guilty of witchcraft had met in the not-so-distant past. "They will not harm her," Nathaniel stated, his voice filled with both menace and determination.

"I have heard no plans to do so," Paul admitted. His tone became softer. "Do not listen to me about Valerian's nature, if you will not, but at least pay attention to the threat of scandal. What will your family say if they hear you are caught up with a local witch, whether she is one or not? Will they be pleased to hear you have the citizenry of your town set entirely against you? They will hardly think you have mended your ways."

"I will set this out for you a final time, Paul. One: My family will hear nothing of what I do in this piddling backwater. Two: They do not care for the gossip of farmers. Three: Valerian is not the manipulator that Laetitia was, if that is what you are trying to imply, and there is no family that will be brought to ruin because of any involvement I may choose to have with her. And four: I do not have to explain myself to you."

"And you would not have, unless you knew I was right."

They glared at each other for a long minute, and then Nathaniel sighed. "We are neither of us going to convince the other."

Paul gave a crooked smile. "Which is not to say that we

will stop trying." He rubbed his temples. "Agh. This has done nothing for my head."

"You enjoy spending your time at that inn. I think you fancy you would have been happier born the son of a sheepherder."

"Maybe. Then I would not have had the job of protecting the good name of such a pig-headed friend."

"I am sure you would have found yourself a similar companion to attempt to correct. You seem unable to stay out of affairs that do not concern you."

"Aunt Theresa, are you certain you are up to this?"

"I will not be treated as an invalid. I am not on my death bed yet, you know."

"But it is such a miserable morning."

Theresa fastened her cloak at her throat, and lifted the hood of the woolen garment up over her head. "And it is not likely to get any less so for us standing here discussing it." She paused, and reached out to cup Valerian's cheek in her hand. "Do not worry so, child. It will do nothing to hasten my end, and you know I could never be confined indoors, just as you could not."

"I know." Valerian bit her lip, restraining herself from saying more. She wanted to wrap her aunt in blankets and hold her until she was well again.

"I understand how difficult it is to sit by and do nothing," Theresa said, "But that is what I ask of you. You will be doing me the greatest of favors by allowing me to follow the course I choose."

"You want me to pretend that nothing is wrong, that nothing has changed?"

"For a little while yet, in action if not in thought. Soon enough there will be no pretending possible."

Valerian lifted her own hood over her hair and followed Theresa out the door into the drizzling rain. The cloud-heavy sky cast little light over the dripping trees and meadow.

Oscar flew on ahead, giving them a raucous caw as he flapped past, and then the two walked in silence, their footsteps squishing in the muddy path. After a time the quiet became an invitation to speak.

"I went to my hot spring this morning, before you awoke," Valerian said hesitantly.

"I thought you might have."

A silence stretched again, and Valerian felt an intuitive certainty that her aunt knew how she had spent her night. "It was not entirely how I had expected."

"The water?" Aunt Theresa asked innocently.

Valerian could not see her face, as her aunt walked in front of her, but she thought she heard a smile. "No."

"The cave, then?"

"You already know, you awful woman."

Theresa cast a glance over her shoulder and blinked at her in a grotesque mockery of naïveté. "I do not know to what you are referring, young lady."

"Do not try to play the innocent with me. I have never encountered a woman with a less chaste mind."

Theresa laughed. "Dearest, we are all wantons at heart. It simply takes some of us longer to realize it." She put her arm around Valerian, and walked beside her. "I do hope he was not a disappointment."

"I am not at all certain I want to discuss the particulars," Valerian grumbled.

"Come now. Who else can you tell? Did you take the Queen Anne's lace seeds afterward?"

"Yes, after the hot spring." The chewed spoonful of seeds would keep her from getting pregnant. "I sometimes wonder what Mother would have thought if she heard our conversations. She was so much more restrained."

"She was not always so, or at least not to such a degree.

Our mother's murder had a sobering effect on her, and she had certain ideas of what a village doctor's wife should be like. When at long last you came along, she thought to give you a different life than the one she had led as a young woman. She may have been happiest if you never knew that your grandmother made her living as a kept woman, but it is in our blood to follow such a path."

"Charmaine has not."

"Charmaine has contorted her natural passions into a most uncomfortable form."

"I do not see how you can argue that it is in my blood to be a man's mistress, just as it is in my blood to be a healer."

"When at least four generations of women before you have followed that course, it does not seem so unlikely that you will as well. It seems to be one of the family talents, and it is no shameful thing. Your grandmother was a woman of importance because of her choice of lovers."

"Not so important she could not be killed."

"Yes, well, one must be careful when one also has gifts of a more spiritual nature. Now tell me, how was your encounter with the manly baron different than you expected?"

She sighed, and gave in to Theresa's curiosity. "It was not different so much as it was not as important as I thought it would be. I mean the act itself. Given the fuss that is made of it, I expected something more dramatic emotionally. I thought I would feel like a different person afterward."

"You mean you are still the same Valerian, after allowing a man to know your body? I do not believe it!"

"Stop it. You know what I mean."

Theresa squeezed her shoulder. "Of course I do. I have sometimes thought that the true loss of innocence is not when a maidenhead is broken, but when a woman realizes she cannot change who she is inside by putting a man in there with her. There is something frightening when he pulls out of you and you discover you are as alone in your body as you ever were."

"Do you suppose married women feel the same?"

"It is one of the truths of life that no words or ceremonies can blend two people into one."

"What about love? Can that do it?"

"Love. Now that is a tricky one. Love casts the illusion that two people are one, but it is the nature of illusions to be false. Eventually, if you are fortunate and wise, you are glad to break the illusion and remain as yourself."

Valerian did not answer. The idea of not being alone in her own skin appealed to her, and she could not understand how the wise choice could be separateness.

When they reached Greyfriars they parted company. Theresa needed to tell Charmaine about her own illness, having decided in the night that it would be unfair to keep it from her. About Valerian's sense that the baby might not be well, however, she would say nothing.

Valerian herself headed for Sally's home. The boil she had lanced had healed quickly, but she wanted to check on the children and bring Sally a fresh supply of St. John's wort. The woman had suffered from melancholia for years, and the herb was showing signs of helping to lighten her mood, as well as helping to impair her fertility and give her body a needed rest from childbearing.

She felt the eyes of passersby on her as she walked down the street, stronger than usual. Gwen's father, the miller, actually stopped and stared at her as she went by.

She was frowning when she reached Sally's home. She called in to her through the open shutters, and Sally quickly came to the door. Her eyes were wide and searched the street nervously from behind their curtain of stringy bangs. "Inside!" Sally whispered urgently, and all but yanked Valerian into the dark little house.

"What is it, Sally?" Valerian asked. The small room reeked of old cooking fat, all but obscuring the fresh scent of wood shavings from the attached carpentry shop out back where Sally's husband worked.

Sally pulled her to the wooden shepherd's chair by the fire, the best seat in the house. The baby sat under the table, gnawing the head of a wooden figure carved by his father.

"What is going on?" Valerian repeated. "People were staring at me like I had grown another head."

"What dealings have you had with Eddie?" Sally asked.

Valerian rolled her eyes. "Not *that!* I thought surely it must be over by now. Are people still talking about that kiss he gave me?"

Sally waved away her words. "After that."

"Sally, tell me what has happened. Do not make me guess."

Sally dropped onto the low stool beside Valerian. Her face looked paler than usual in the grey light from the window, her lips colorless. "Eddie has had a spell cast upon him."

"A spell? What nonsense. Who would have put a spell on Eddie?" Even as she spoke, the answer came clear. "Oh, no."

"He says you did it, or he did say that. He is not saying much of anything now, but Gwen is going about spreading the tale of how you cursed him, that you said that she would get no joy from him as a husband. That same night an owl came and snatched Eddie's cock."

"An owl?"

"Swooped down and snipped it off."

"How would an owl even get to it through his pants? Or was he not wearing pants?"

Sally stared blankly at her, and then some of the tension slipped from her shoulders, and she smiled. "I did not think you had done it."

Valerian felt a quiver of alarm. If Sally could have seriously doubted her, then what must the others be thinking? "You thought it possible I might have."

Sally looked away, her head slightly bowed. "You have never shown me anything but kindness. I did not want to think you would do such a thing, however provoked."

"But you thought that I had the power to cast such a spell."

"We all know that you and Mrs. Storrow command more than earthly powers. How else could you heal so many when even the surgeons cannot? And Mrs. Storrow, she sees into the truth of one's soul."

"It is not witchcraft, Sally. It is knowledge and perception, that is all." She could see in Sally's eyes that she was not believed, as well she should not be. Both she and Theresa did call on powers most others could not, though there was nothing demonic about it. "I do not cast spells."

Sally did not answer.

"Where is he?" Valerian asked. "I want to see him."

"At the smithy. Surely you do not mean to go over there?"

"Indeed I do. I intend to put a stop to this nonsense." Valerian stood, and Sally scrambled to her feet, her eyes wide and anxious.

"You cannot go over there, it might be dangerous."

"Oh, yes I can. What are they going to do? Throw rocks at me?" she said with false bravado, for in truth she was frightened by this turn of events; but the best thing would be to stop this before it went any further. She took the little jar of Saint John's wort from her basket and put it on the table. "For the melancholia," she said, then hoisted the basket over her arm. "We will just see what is missing from Eddie's breeches."

She marched out into the rain and headed down the street. She was vaguely aware of the attention of those few people out and about, but her mind was focused on the smithy and what she would find. She did not pay attention when they stopped to watch her pass, and then turned to follow her.

A man leaving the smithy stumbled out of her way when she stomped up to the door, then stood and stared as she pushed her way inside.

The heat hit her face with a blast, making her eyes sting. She blinked them clear and scanned the interior for Eddie. The rhythmic beating of metal on metal ceased, and Eddie's father, Jeremiah, approached. He was a large man, black-haired and bearded, wearing a leather apron over his work clothes. A heavy hammer dangled from one of his huge fists, and his fingers were black with grime. He looked a living embodiment of Hephaestus, angry god of fire and forge.

"Good day, Mr. O'Connor. I have come to see Eddie," Valerian said firmly. Her heart beat rapidly in her chest, and she could feel nervous sweat under her arms.

The burly smith adjusted his grip on his hammer and said nothing. Valerian could see his uncertainty. She knew him as a kind man who made decisions by the promptings of his conscience, but he was clearly in conflict at this moment.

"I would not be here in the middle of the day if I intended to harm him," Valerian said.

O'Connor's eyes flicked to something behind her. She half-turned, and saw the crowd that had gathered at the door, their faces both guarded and eager.

She turned back to the smith and spoke softly. "You know me, Mr. O'Connor. Have I ever done you or your family any harm? Have I ever done *anyone* in this village any damage?"

She could see his internal battle rage a moment longer,

and then he relented, gesturing with his hammer to the back of the smithy. "He is back there, in the corner. Will not come out."

Valerian nodded and slipped past the smith, winding her way through the equipment and piles of metal to the far corner. Eddie sat on the floor, arms around his knees, crooning to himself. He had not shaved, his chin was stubbled with irregular patches of hair, and his face and clothes were smudged with soot.

Valerian sank onto her knees and set down her basket. "Eddie?"

His glazed eyes blinked at her voice, then focused on her. Horror crept over his features. His hands dropped to the earthen floor, and he scrambled against the dirt, trying to shove himself farther away from her, his efforts voided by the wall at his back.

"Eddie, stop it." Valerian ordered. "I am not going to hurt you." She reached out a hand and placed it on his knee. He stilled. She locked his eyes with her own and concentrated on her breathing, bringing it down to normal and calming herself, then sent that calmness to him through her hand and her gaze. She felt her palm grow warm, and imagined the heat spreading up his leg to his heart. Within a few minutes his breathing was matched to hers, and some of the color had returned to his face.

"Tell me what scared you," she said softly, and she sent her senses searching through his body for any injury.

"You said she would have no pleasure of me," he said flatly. "And then the owl came, and I could not feel me self." He looked down at his breeches. "And when I look, I cannot see it."

"Can others see it?" She could sense no wound upon him, only hunger and exhaustion.

"Gwen says she can, but I cannot. The owl took it from me."

"The owl took nothing from you," she said calmly, putting the force of her will behind the statement. "Everything is where it has always been. You are whole and healthy."

"I have not lost it?"

Valerian could see the thought swimming in his mind. The lack of sleep and food had confused his thinking beyond his normal impressionability. A dim acceptance of her words began to form in his eyes. He saw her as enough of an authority on this topic to believe her, the calm she had sent through her hand allowing him to accept her words.

"Witch!" Gwen's voice screeched from behind her. "Get away from him, you cock-stealing whore of Satan!"

Valerian began to turn, and Gwen struck her on the shoulder. She lost her balance and slid off her knees onto her hip, her hands on the ground to catch herself. She saw the blur of motion and something black in Gwen's hand, then felt the sharp blow as the girl stuck her forehead. A searing pain followed a moment later and she fell to the floor, blood running down into her eyes.

"Feel for your cock now, Eddie!" Gwen crowed triumphantly. "I have scored her above her breath. If 'twas she who put the spell upon you, you will have your cock back."

Valerian put her fingers to the gash on her forehead, stunned by the attack. No one had ever struck her before. There was an old superstition that drawing a witch's blood from above her breath—her nose and mouth—would break a spell, but she could hardly believe someone had used it against her.

"It is back, I feel it!" Eddie cried out.

The gathering of villagers drew an awed breath, then erupted into a confusion of angry words and crowded forward to the corner where the three young people crouched.

Valerian's forehead throbbed, and the blood was making it hard to see. The press of bodies and the tone of the crowd unnerved her as she had never been unnerved before. They did not sound in the mood to listen to reason, not when Gwen's attack had to their eyes broken the spell. No matter that he was free of his delusion moments before Gwen hit her with . . . with what?

Valerian found the black object on the ground, and picked it up. It was a scrap of iron, and one edge was wet with her blood. She dropped it and began to scoot away towards the large sliding shed doors at the rear of the shop.

Someone noticed her movement, and eyes turned from Eddie and Gwen to herself. She wiped blood out of her eyes and felt a chill in her flesh as the malevolence in the faces above her became clear.

"Do not come near me," she warned in a voice made high by fear, and shakily she stood, backing away to the shed doors. She could only presume that a wariness of her evil powers held the crowd as she fumbled one of the doors open.

"Do not let her escape!" a voice cried. Valerian's eyes flew to the speaker, Mrs. Torrance from the inn. "She will be after your own children next," the woman said. "Christ will protect you from her evil." She came lurching through the crowd, and her forward motion freed the villagers from their own inertia.

Valerian turned and fled through the doors, lifting her skirts to keep them from hindering her. She slipped and almost fell in the mud in back of the shop, then gained her footing and ran around the building to the cobbled main street of the town.

Some of the crowd had come back out through the front door of the smithy, and they shouted when they saw her. There was no place to hide here on their own ground. All she could do was run. She heard more shouts behind her and put all her strength into her legs, sprinting down the center of the street.

She cast a glance over her shoulder, and saw that two men were bearing down, their long legs and light clothing giving them every advantage over her. She whimpered low in her throat and faced forward again just in time to see two mounted riders emerge from the side street right before her. She could not deflect her path in time, and ran with a thud into the side of the nearest horse, startling both it and its rider.

She and the horse danced out of each other's way, Valerian pushing against the warm body of the mount and the leg of the rider, desperate to escape prancing hooves and buffeting horseflesh.

Nathaniel fought to control his mount, simultaneously taking in the chaos that he and Paul had ridden into. He would know Valerian's black hair in any crowd, and but for it might not have recognized her terrified face, covered with blood, as she was jostled between the horses.

He bent down to seize her, pulling her bodily up onto his mount. Beside him, Paul unsheathed his sword with a distinctive ringing sound that was a clear warning to all who approached. Whatever Paul's thoughts on Valerian, Nathaniel knew that he could count on his loyalty as a friend.

Valerian briefly continued to struggle, then looked up into his face, and when he saw recognition register, she wrapped her arms around him and buried her face in his chest. Fury roiled within him that anyone had dared to harm her, and that she had been chased down the street like an animal.

"Halt!" he shouted to the villagers in the voice he had used as an army officer.

The approaching mob, that had slowed when the riders appeared, now stopped completely.

"What has happened here?" he demanded. "Who did this to Miss Bright?"

The crowd shifted, and he easily read the emotions of the villagers. They looked like a group of unrepentant children, not sorry for their actions, but certainly considering the welfare of their own skins now that authority had arrived. He felt loathing for them swell within him.

"Speak, goddamn you!"

Several flinched, and heads turned towards Gwen, who was just now bringing up the rear of the group. Nathaniel locked eyes with her.

"You. Come up here."

Gwen gave a defiant toss of her head and strode forward, the villagers parting before her.

"Your name, girl."

"Gwendolyn Miller, my lord."

He did not like the tone of her voice. "What part have you in this affair?"

"I have done nothing wrong, my lord."

"As I act as magistrate of this district, I will be the one deciding that. Unless you think you are better suited to the task?"

"No, my lord." A little of her confidence slipped, and she shifted her eyes away from him.

"You are the girl involved with young Eddie, are you not?"

Her blue eyes flew back to him, surprised that he knew anything of her. "Yes, my lord."

"And you are the one who has been spreading tales that Miss Bright casts spells and sends owls after young men." He could not keep the disgust from his voice, and indeed did not even try. "You say she stole Eddie's privates. Tell me, what do you think she did with it once she had it? Do you suppose she tanned it and mounted it on the wall above the mantel?"

A nervous chuckle escaped from a few of the men in the mob.

"She did not steal it physically," Gwen protested. " 'Twas the spirit of it she stole. I held it in my very hand, and yet he could not feel my touch, no matter how I rubbed it."

There was a burst of laughter this time, except from Gwen's father. He pushed his way through to his daughter, turned her to face him and gave her a resounding slap across the face. "I for one would like to know what my daughter was doing holding a man like that," he said, then slapped her again.

"Father!" she pleaded, her hands on her cheeks, and tears starting in her eyes. "I did nothing wrong. I was checking him for injury."

"Miller," Nathaniel interrupted. "If I may continue?"

The barrel-chested man nodded and stepped back, keeping his eyes on his disgraced daughter. It was apparent to all that Gwen had not heard the last of this from her father.

Nathaniel whispered to Valerian. "Lift your head. Turn to them." He felt her arms tighten around him, and with his own hands coaxed her to unbury her face from his jacket and turn.

Some of the women gasped, and more than one man looked away. The wound to her forehead, though not large, had bled profusely. Valerian's face was coated in crimson, her light blue eyes all the more startling in contrast. Gwen herself grimaced.

"Are you the one responsible for this?" Nathaniel asked Gwen.

Gwen chewed her lip, then, prodded by her father and knowing half the town was witness to what she had done, nodded. "But it broke the spell!" she immediately protested. "He could feel it again as soon as I scored her. That proves she cast the spell."

"There is no such thing as witchcraft. It is clear to me that Eddie had at least one motivation for claiming he could not feel his manhood." He paused, and there was an answering wave of laughter in the group. "And it is also clear that there was never any physical harm done to him, by your own word. The only person I see who has been injured is Miss Bright."

"Gwen will see a proper punishment from me," the miller said, gripping his daughter's arm.

Nathaniel narrowed his eyes at the pair. Gwen had harmed someone he cared about. He had the power to wreak his own vengeance upon her, and he would use it. "Certainly you may impose whatever punishment you wish for your daughter's private misbehaviors. This, however, has been a public affair, and as such should be dealt with in a public manner. Are there stocks in this village?" he asked the crowd.

"Aye, in front of the market square," Mr. Torrance, the innkeeper, said. He cocked his head back towards the ten-by-ten-foot roofed area with open sides where goods were sold on Saturdays. "But they have not been used in years. The hinges are all but rusted off."

"Then perhaps young Eddie can make new ones." Nathaniel allowed himself a moment of pleasure at the irony of this arrangement. "The stocks will be repaired, and Gwen will spend one day in them, sunrise to sundown."

Gwen gasped in outrage. "The stocks!"

An excited babble immediately erupted from the villagers. Nathaniel was distracted from the uproar by a fist rapping on his chest. Valerian was glaring up at him through her blood and disheveled hair.

"You cannot put her in the stocks!" she protested. "She should never have attacked me, but she thought she was helping Eddie. Let her father deal with her."

Nathaniel barely listened to her words. The blood on her face was too vivid, too glaring a reminder that a wrong had been done. Perhaps the stocks were too kind.

"Are you listening to me?" Valerian asked. "She is a misguided girl. Do this, and the village will not thank you for it."

"What do I care whether they thank me?" Nathaniel asked. The idea was ludicrous. "You need your wound tended. I will take you to your aunt."

"Nathaniel, do not do this. She is being punished enough with this humiliation right here."

He touched the skin near her wound, where the blood still seeped out. He showed Valerian the brilliant stains upon his fingers. "The longer I look at you, the more certain I become that the girl should be whipped."

Paul interrupted quietly. "Then perhaps we should get her cleaned up."

Nathaniel returned his attention to the crowd. "Gwendolyn Miller will spend Wednesday in the stocks, as a reminder to herself and the village that witchcraft does not exist, and that persecution of a woman for that reason is forbidden by the laws of England. Now go home, the lot of you!"

The group slowly broke up. Mr. Miller nodded to Nathaniel and pulled his forelock, then jerked Gwen's arm to make her curtsy. He whispered something to her that made her cheeks flush.

"Thank you, milord," Gwen mumbled, her face scarlet. She pulled free of her father and stalked away.

"Paul, will you make sure the blacksmith's son knows about the hinges? I do not see him here."

Paul sheathed his sword. The look he gave Nathaniel was filled with unspoken comment, but Nathaniel knew he would not contradict him here in the middle of the street.

"I will take you to your aunt." Nathaniel nudged his horse.

"She is visiting her daughter." Valerian gave him directions.

He kept Darby to a slow pace, not wanting to jostle Valerian. He tightened his arm around her waist, and pressed his lips against her hair above her ear. She sat sideways across his lap, her head bent forward. She had one hand pressed against her forehead. He could not see her face, and she was as still as stone. Protectiveness washed through his blood like an illness, making his muscles weak with concern for her now that the danger was past.

"Is this the house?" he asked as they came in front of a stone, slate-roofed building that was almost indiscernible from its neighbors, except for the cobbler's sign. "Valerian?"

When she did not stir, he leant back and tried to see her face. Her eyes were closed, her face pale where it was not coated with blood. "Valerian!" She did not respond, did not even seem to hear him.

"Mrs. Storrow!" he called to the house. "Mrs. Storrow, come quickly!"

He dared not try to dismount with her like this. He was on the verge of calling out again when the door opened. Theresa came out, as imposing as ever despite the haggard cast to her complexion. Her daughter followed close behind, a thin-lipped, sour-faced shadow of her mother.

"Valerian has been injured," he explained. "The miller's daughter attacked her."

Theresa stepped around the horse to where she could look up at Valerian. Her face held the calm, intense focus of a woman who had spent her life dealing with crises, and she knew that the gathering of information was the first necessity. "The wound, is it under her hand?"

"Yes, a gash about an inch long."

The information seemed to relieve her somewhat. She looked up at him as if weighing a choice. "Would you mind holding her there until she comes out of this? It should only be a few minutes more."

"Certainly."

The simple request begged a dozen questions, but he was not about to pry for information in these circumstances. If Mrs. Storrow thought the best course for her niece was to sit on his lap in a trance and bleed for another ten minutes, well, he supposed she knew what she was doing. Her daughter had retreated to the doorway of her house, where she watched with eyes that showed her ill ease.

They stood in a silence as still as Valerian's. He wondered that neither of them asked about the circumstances of the attack. Had this type of thing happened before? While they waited, Paul came riding up, Valerian's basket in front of him. He handed it down to Mrs. Storrow as Nathaniel introduced them.

Valerian's hand dropped away from her wound, and Nathaniel felt her muscles relax. She drew in a ragged breath and raised her head. Before she could say anything, Mrs. Storrow reached up and helped slide her from his lap to the ground, where she stood weakly, swaying on unsure legs. He quickly dismounted, and moved to lift her into his arms.

"No, she will be all right now," Theresa said, placing a hand briefly on his chest to keep him back. "Thank you for all your help. I am sure the wound looked worse than it was. Scalp wounds always bleed so much, you would think the person was surely about to expire."

Valerian blinked up at him. "I will be fine. I am tired, is all. Please, go now, and let Aunt Theresa care for me."

There was something strange going on, something they were not telling him, some reason they wanted to be rid of him. He could feel it in his bones. The social training ingrained in him since birth strongly urged him to leave at their request. It was what any gentleman would do.

"Paul, you go ahead," he said. "I am going to stay." Since when had he been a gentleman?

Paul shrugged and reined his horse around, the shod hooves of his mount clip-clopping on the cobbles as he left. However much Paul aggravated him, Nathaniel spared a moment of gratitude to have such a friend.

He turned back to the women in time to catch the end of a silent communion between Valerian and her aunt. Valerian gave the slightest nod of her chin, and the fractional raising of Mrs. Storrow's eyebrows suggested a shrug.

Nathaniel narrowed his eyes. He would discover what these women were hiding, or know the reason why.

Chapter Thirteen

Nathaniel could not help but notice that Theresa's daughter, introduced as Charmaine, was considerably less serene than her kin as she led the way into her home. She looked like she wanted to be a thousand miles away from the situation, and she kept casting worried looks at him, as if he were a strange dog she thought might bite.

The front room of the house was the cobbler's shop, complete with work benches, piles of leather scraps, and tools. Charmaine led them through to the kitchen in back, a small room with a flagstone floor and a scarred table. Narrow stairs beside the fireplace led to the living quarters above. Nathaniel felt the bulk of his size in the small room with the three women, and tried to keep himself out of their way.

Valerian seemed to gain strength with each passing minute, sorting through her basket, checking for broken glass with Theresa as Charmaine poured heated water into a basin on the table, her hands shaking slightly. They all three seemed in no hurry to tend to Valerian's gash, and Nathaniel found himself growing anxious at their delay.

Finally, Valerian herself dipped a rag in the water and wrung it out. She looked up at Nathaniel, the wet cloth dripping in her hand. "You are here because I trust you," she said. "And I do not believe you will be frightened by what you are about to see."

He held her eyes, and without knowing to what he agreed, he nodded in acceptance of her faith in him.

He watched as she scrubbed away the blood from her chin, her cheeks, her nose. She rinsed the rag in the basin and started in on her forehead. He flinched at the vigor with which she attacked her skin with the cloth. He had looked into that wound. Surely such rough treatment was not beneficial. His faith in the healing skills of Valerian and her aunt began to falter.

And then, she removed the cloth. His lips parted in wonder, and his eyes scanned the flesh above her brow, clean and pale but for a few transparent smudges of blood. He stepped closer to her, examining the healthy skin, his fingertips brushing her damp brow. He could just make out a pale pink line where the gash had been.

He fumbled behind him for the bench, and sat with a creak of wood. He had seen that gash with his own eyes, and had enough experience from the army to know that it had not been faked, that it had been deep enough to need stitches. And yet, Valerian stood there now with hardly any hint of injury, the skin of her brow smooth.

He barely noticed Theresa taking Charmaine's arm and leading her up the stairs, leaving him and Valerian alone in the small kitchen. The first thought that came to his mind was *witchcraft,* but he quickly pushed the thought away. To believe that would be to believe the world was nothing like he thought it. Tales of magic were for the ignorant, for those who had no other way to make sense of the world.

She was watching him, wary and expectant, waiting for his response. It occurred to him, in light of what had occurred today in Greyfriars, how big a risk she was taking in revealing this to him. Rejecting hearsay was one thing. Physical evidence was another.

"Explain," he said at last.

She gave him a small smile. She dipped the rag back into the bowl and wiped the last smudges of blood off her skin, then pulled a stool up to the end of the table and sat. "You are not frightened?" she asked.

"I do not know that I would completely deny that reaction. I assume, however, that you are shortly to give me an explanation that will remove any such trepidations from my mind."

She shrugged. "Perhaps."

"An encouraging beginning."

She smiled, and rubbed the pink line on her forehead. "Neither Aunt Theresa nor I are witches in the biblical sense of the word. In the Bible it is poisoners that are being spoken of. A woman who can heal with herbs must also know which herbs and plants can kill, and I would not disagree with anyone who sought to punish a person who sold poisons to murderers, or poisoned people for her own benefit. We also do not conjure spirits or cavort with demons, we do not worship Satan, we do not shape-change or cast spells."

Nathaniel nodded. "I never thought you did."

"Sometimes we do dowse for water, when a farmer needs a new well."

"As do many men, who have never been called witch."

"Yes. And on very rare occasions, when someone's property has gone missing or there is dispute over ownership of a sheep or goose, Aunt Theresa will play the role of thief-catcher. Invariably, the guilty party confesses before she is required to do anything. People are afraid of her, and would rather face an angry neighbor than the eye of a witch."

"Very sensible," he agreed.

"That fear also has other uses. People believe us to be so much more than we are, our words and actions are given more strength than they warrant. No matter what I say to the contrary, if I give a woman a decoction of peppermint leaves to ease her digestion, she will believe there is a bit of magic in it that makes it effective, and she will claim relief far greater than it is possible for peppermint to give. Her own beliefs do half the work for me."

"I have always thought that those claiming to be bewitched were under the influence of their own imaginations," Nathaniel said.

"Yes, I believe that to be largely so, or perhaps they are deranged. It is often useful, though, this belief people have that we are witches. Thieves are caught, advice is taken seriously, and our medicines do more healing than they would otherwise. Aunt Theresa thinks that people need to believe in witches, because we are so much more accessible than a distant god. If they know witches exist and have supernatural powers, it is evidence of a sort that God exists. You cannot have evil without also having good."

"That puts you in a dangerous position, does it not?" Nathaniel asked. "You foster the illusion of being a witch for a variety of reasons, but in so doing you give the town an easy target, one they can turn against at a moment's notice. You cannot pretend to be the enemy of God with impunity."

"No. Obviously not." She brushed her fingers against her brow once more, and Nathaniel noticed that the pink line had all but vanished.

"What has all this to do with the healing of your wound? You know that I will not think you a witch, whatever the explanation may be."

Valerian gave a hopeless laugh. "But that is just it. I am not a witch in the way the townspeople see me, and I am innocent of any accusations they may lodge against me. But I am, in the end, what they fear me to be: someone with access to a mysterious power. I healed the gash on my forehead with my hand. With my *hand,* Nathaniel. Every female in my family has had a gift of some manner. Some have seen the future, some spoke with spirits, some have moved objects with their minds."

"And you can heal?"

"Yes."

He did not quite believe it, despite what he had seen. "Then why do you not do that all the time, instead of wasting your energy digging up plants and grinding roots?"

"Part of the answer should be obvious. Aunt Theresa and I would have been hung or burned by now if I did something so blatant. People do not want their mysteries so shockingly displayed. And the other part of the answer—well, you saw some of it. It is tiring. I would not have the energy to do this for everyone who needed it. And if I know of a plant that can do the work for me, why not let it?"

"So you never use this ability for the benefit of others?"

"I do use it for others, of course I do, but as an aid to my medicines, and only when I can do so without being detected. Or if a life is in danger, I will do what I can, without much mind to the consequences, although that has only happened once or twice in all my time here, and there was so much chaos that no one noticed."

"So Theresa is a healer, as well?"

"Well, with herbs. But that is not her gift. She has a different ability. I do not think it is my place to say what."

"But what of your cousin, Charmaine? She lives in town, and I have heard nothing about her."

"Charmaine's gift, whatever it is, is hidden from us and

from her. She wants nothing to do with any of this. She wants a normal life."

That explained the woman's reluctance to have him here, witnessing the family secret. "Assuming these powers do exist, an assumption of which I am not yet convinced, whence do they come?"

Valerian shrugged. "God only knows. Where does red hair come from? It runs in families, and who is to say why it runs in this family and not that? It does not seem to come from either God or the devil. I sometimes think it is more a product of nature than anything else. Just as some people are gifted in conversation or in working with their hands, I am gifted in healing."

"Have you had it since a child, this gift?"

"I do not know. It was Oscar who showed it to me."

"Come now, I cannot credit the bird with that much intelligence."

She smiled. "He did not *tell* me about it. It was when I rescued him from the cliff, I held him in my hands and cried over his injuries, stroking his feathers, begging him to wake. And he did. I remembered my parents telling me that I had a gift to share with the world, although I did not understand what they meant at the time. With Oscar fluttering in my hands, I finally knew."

"You make it sound no more startling than discovering a talent for watercolors," he said, aware that he was in a slight state of shock over this information. He could understand it intellectually, but it was not sinking in that his Valerian could cure by the touch of her hands.

"If it were a more common gift, would you find it so remarkable? I believe it is only the rarity of this gift that makes it worth comment."

He stood and walked slowly round the kitchen, stopping when he saw a knife lying amongst recently cleaned cutlery. He picked it up and turned to face her. "No matter that

I saw with my own eyes your wound, you must know that I will doubt that I was not fooled in some manner. I did not see it inflicted. I know how easy it is to believe one sees what one thinks is there. One need only listen to a troop of soldiers describing a battle to hear how the truth is easily twisted beyond recognition."

He folded back the lace at his wrist, and shoved up the sleeve of his jacket, examining the flesh exposed. "So you will understand if I wish to perform one small test to check the veracity of what I saw."

"Do not!"

He nicked the skin on the back of his forearm. Not a deep cut, nothing that would not heal easily on its own, but deeper than a scratch. He poked lightly at it with the tip of the knife, frowning, confirming that his skin had been opened. It felt none too pleasant, and for a moment he wondered at his own idiocy.

"Can you heal it?" he asked her.

"Was this really necessary?"

"I do not accept the fantastic so easily as yon gullible villagers."

"You could not have taken my word for it?" She sounded hurt.

He sighed, holding a finger over the seeping wound. "It is not a matter of trust, Valerian, but of the nature of the world. If I am going to believe anyone can heal with their hands, then I need to experience it myself. Come, I am in danger of staining my shirt."

She stood and came to him, lifting away his finger and laying her palm over his cut. "This will not hurt, but you will feel my hand grow warm."

"It is already warm."

"You will see." She closed her eyes, and he watched her face grow placid and still. The hand on his arm slowly grew warmer, until it was almost hot against his skin. He looked down at it, and almost thought he saw a white smudging of light spilling from beneath her palm. Whatever pain had been there began to fade, until all he could feel was the heat of her hand, which seemed to reach up through his arm, tracing a trail through his blood to his very heart. A calm acceptance came over him, a sense of soothing, internal warmth, and then she pulled her hand away.

He caught her as she swayed, and helped her to sit down, the warmth still filling his senses like a drug. It was an echo of that sated feeling a man had after sex. "Valerian? Are you all right?"

"Give me a moment," she said, and bending forward rested her head in her hands. Her shoulders were quivering.

He felt a twinge of guilt and went to wash off his arm with the rag she had used earlier. He should not have asked this of her, so soon after her earlier exertion. Whatever she was doing, it clearly drained her. He looked down at his clean arm.

There was not a mark on it.

He rubbed at the skin, examined it closely, and held it to the light from the window, but no mark showed itself. He viewed the skin with the fascination he would give a new invention, or a work of art. At last he rolled down his sleeve and straightened the cuff of his jacket over his wrist. He went to sit near Valerian and rubbed the back of her neck as she sat hunched over.

At last she straightened up, rolling her head to further loosen the neck muscles he had been massaging. "Thank you," she said. "That felt wonderful."

"Not half so wonderful, I am certain, as what you did to me."

"There is no doubt in your mind now, is there?"

"Doubt that you can heal with your hands? No. But I have no idea how you do it. I refuse to believe that you call upon magical or demonic powers, as the villagers would think."

"How would you explain what I just did?" She sounded genuinely curious, as if despite her matter-of-fact explanations earlier, she herself wondered from whence her ability came.

"I will admit a passing thought of witchcraft. I have heard so much of witches since I arrived here, I could hardly be faulted if I blamed the next thunderstorm on them." He smiled his reassurance at her. "Being possessed of a reasonable intelligence and solid education, however, I hope I am not so witless as to succumb to such a simple and tempting explanation. The ignorant create superstitions to explain that which they do not understand. In this instance, I am ignorant. I would prefer, however, to conclude that there is an explanation of which I am unaware, and indeed may forever be unaware, than to believe that you have had congress with demons or are some manner of unnatural creature."

To his consternation, tears pooled in her eyes and overflowed down her cheeks. "What have I said?" he asked.

She sniffed once, pressing the back of her hand against her nose, and gave a wet laugh. "You are the first person, outside my family, who has treated me like a completely normal human being—and this when you know the strangest part of me. I am so happy." She collapsed into sobs.

He did not know of any man who would not rather suffer a gunshot wound than be alone in a room with a weeping female. He lifted Valerian onto his lap and put his arms around her, stroking her hair and saying nothing. Thank God for sisters. Margaret, his junior by two years, had once viciously punched him in the shoulder in the midst of one of her weeping fits. *"Stupid man! When a woman cries, she wants a warm chest against which to do so. Stop offering me brandy!"*

As Valerian soothed herself against his chest, his thoughts roamed to less mysterious matters than healing hands and the workings of the female mind. He caressed her hip and thigh, pressing his face into her hair to inhale the scent of her. He worked her skirt up her leg until he reached the bare skin above her garter, and felt himself go hard at the smooth softness of her flesh under his fingertips.

He hardly noticed as Valerian's sobs dried up. "Nathaniel, what are you doing?"

"Hmm?" He shifted her position on his lap, and slid his hand up to the juncture of her thighs, lightly brushing the damp curls of her womanhood.

"Ohh," she sighed, as he found the nub of her desire, and gently teased it with the tips of his fingers, then cupped the whole of her mons within the palm of his hand, pressing in gentle circles.

"Why did you leave my bed last night?" he whispered into her ear, following the words with a tracing of his tongue.

"You fell asleep," she said, and arched her head back onto his shoulder.

He slid one finger deeply within her, pressing in light circles against the roof of the slick passage. "You could have woken me. You deserved more attention, especially for your first time. I want memories of pleasure in your mind: Memories strong enough to lure you back to my bed every night."

The thump and creak of footsteps overhead reminded them both of where they were. Valerian stiffened, then pushed his hand away. She scrambled off his lap, pulling down her skirt.

"You will come to me tonight?" he asked, standing up

and stroking the hair away from her face, trying to ignore the throbbing desire in his loins. He wanted her more than he had last night.

"I do not know. If I can." She cast a nervous glance at the stairway.

"Or perhaps I should take you home with me right now. For your own protection, of course." He bent and kissed the side of her neck, tracing his lips down to her collar bone. He could not resist bringing up one hand to caress her breast through the heavy material of her bodice.

"There will not be trouble now, not after what you ordered for Gwen," she said.

"Say you will come tonight," he murmured into her neck, feeling her pulse against his lips.

"If I can, I will."

He captured her mouth with his own, his arms coming around her, pulling her against the hardness of his arousal. He squeezed her buttocks, then released her. "See that you can, and do."

He bowed to her, then left. He was afraid if he stayed any longer, the thought of having her on top of Charmaine's kitchen table might have started looking less and less inappropriate.

She might not be in league with the devil, but she had certainly bewitched him.

Chapter Fourteen

"Are you certain you do not want to accept Charmaine's offer?" Valerian asked her aunt.

"Heavens, yes. Can you honestly see me living with her and Howard? We would all kill each other inside of a week. She knows that as well as I do." Theresa sat in the chair by the fire, propping her feet up on a stool. "Would you make me a cup of tea, dear?"

"Of course. Would not you like something to eat? I have not seen you down a bite all day."

"I had a bit of soup with Charmaine."

"It is not enough."

Theresa shrugged.

Valerian put down the mugs in her hands, exasperated. "I will not try to heal you, if that is the way you want it, but please do not hide things from me. Do not make me scrounge for hints to how you are faring. I will worry more in ignorance than I ever will in knowledge."

Theresa sighed. "I know. It is the habit of a lifetime, and hard to break."

"Well?"

"It hurts me more to eat than to go without. I do not seem able to digest anything."

Valerian bit the inside of her lip to keep herself from showing concern that would only disturb her aunt. "Then we will have to make sure those liquids you do consume do you a bit of good." She took out the hard cylinder that was what remained of their sugar, and with the tongs clipped off a chunk.

Theresa groaned. "You know I hate sugar in my tea."

Valerian ignored her, and ground the sugar in the pestle, then dumped the lot into the analgesic tea she had steeping. "It should not upset your stomach, and your intestines will absorb it. You are wasting away as it is."

"And I will not be around long enough for my teeth to rot from that cup of syrup you are about to force on me."

"There is that."

Theresa accepted the cup of tea with a sour expression that was not sweetened any by her first sip. "Is there someplace else you should be tonight?"

"*Should* be?"

"Want to be. Were invited to be. He sounded rather insistent. Or do you not want to go, and discover what pleasures await those who have abandoned their virtue?"

"Aunt Theresa!"

"Well?"

"You were eavesdropping!"

"I was looking out for your welfare. And if I had not, you would have skulked around here until I had gone to sleep, fretting over whether or not you could slip away."

"Maybe I am not as eager as you to see me spend all my nights in his bed."

"Why ever not?"

"I do have more on my mind than sex."

"Which is as good a reason as any to indulge. It will be good for you, to be distracted from thoughts of me, and Charmaine, and that witless Gwen. There is nothing like the release of a good tussle in bed to relax a woman after being chased down the street by a murderous mob of witch hunters."

Valerian stared at her aunt.

"You have got to have a sense of humor about these things, dear," Theresa said. "He rescued you—riding in on his mighty steed, as it were, his henchman with sword at the ready, all quite dramatic and satisfying to the female vanity—and he made it quite clear that harming you was forbidden, punishable by all manner of unpleasantness. That is, after all, what we wanted: his protection. No harm done, in the end, and much gained."

"I would we could have gained it without the attack on my forehead."

"It will make an entertaining story for your grandchildren."

"Do you think it is truly over then, any threat from Gwen or the town?"

"It may be. Or it may not. In any case, his lordship has made a public stand now, and is not likely to go back on it, for his pride if nothing else."

"Then it does not matter if I do or do not return to his bed."

"As if that were the reason you went in the first place! You are such a serious young woman, Valerian. Even when the opportunity for fun presents itself, you need to find a practical reason for taking it. I regret at times that I have not given you a more fashionable, light-hearted youth."

"Aunt Theresa, do not. The life you led before—I know it would not have suited me. I love the forest and the sea, and being free to roam as I will. I would have been miserable in a city, going to balls and supper parties, wearing stays and satin slippers, leading a useless, ignorant life."

"So you say. But you come from a long line of harlots. Perhaps you would enjoy such a life."

"We have had this conversation a hundred times. Why do you keep on about it?"

"I worry, is all. I have faith in you, Valerian. You are a smart girl, and will land on your feet whatever happens. I would that you tasted more of life than what you have here in Cumbria, though. It is one thing to choose this life after experiencing another, as I did. But you need to know the world before you can make a decision of where you want to be in it. And you are going to have to make that decision when I am gone."

Valerian came and sat opposite her aunt. "I have been avoiding thinking about it, what I will do after." She swallowed back the rising emotion, willing her voice to be steady. "Even the thought of it leaves me feeling lost. My anchor will be gone, and I will drift."

Theresa took her hand. "I know it feels that way. But sooner or later the currents or the wind will take you to shore, even if you have not yet found your rudder. You find yourself living, whether you wish to or not."

"Could you perhaps give me a look into what will happen?"

Her aunt took a long minute to consider, then shrugged her shoulders. "Hell, why not? At least if you know you will be miserable, it will not be such an unhappy surprise when it happens," she said, grinning. "And maybe you will see that you will be happy again, too. Fetch a pan of water. I think this calls for a scrying."

Valerian hurried to do as Theresa bid. Her aunt only rarely did a scrying, and the results were always much more vivid and precise than when she relied on the canvas of her closed eyes alone. Theresa had once admitted that it was perhaps for reason of that accuracy that she avoided it. Sometimes she preferred not to know what was to come.

Valerian extinguished the two rushlights and set the shallow pan of water on the stool in front of Theresa. The only light came from the small fire on the hearth, just enough to turn the smooth surface of the water reflective.

Valerian sat cross-legged on the floor. Oscar hopped down from his perch on the mantel and found his favorite place on Valerian's shoulder, curious to see what the women watched.

They all three sat silent, eyes on the silvered water. Valerian heard the crackle of the fire and the rain start up on the roof. Oscar shifted, rustling his feathers with a sound like rushes in the breeze. Valerian focused her attention on her own breathing, listening to it come in through her nose, out through her mouth. She lengthened each breath, as Theresa had taught her to do, holding it briefly at the end of each in—or exhalation. She never had the visions of the future that Theresa did, but she did see the chimerical visions that haunted that state between sleep and wakefulness, projected upon the mirrored surface of the water.

Colors swirled before her eyes, and then from their midst appeared a strange badger-like creature, which began eating linen sheets left out to dry. Before Valerian could discover just where this peculiar vision would lead, Theresa spoke, describing what she herself could see. Valerian let Theresa's words guide her own vision, and in the pan of water she pictured the images Theresa described.

"Water. Darkness. The wavering light thrown by flames. You are in the water, wet. Your hair spreading. The baron is there." Theresa fell silent, and Valerian waited, watching the image of herself and Nathaniel, her own imagination continuing in the scene, Nathaniel leading her naked out of the water, caressing her wet skin, her own hands skimming over the planes of his back . . .

"Candlelight. Crystal," Theresa said, and the amorous scene was replaced by the images given by her aunt. "Many people. Silks and satins, bright colors, music. I can see no faces. A man approaches. His face, I do see. Blue eyes. He is an older man." There was a long silence, and then, "He looks almost like—"

Theresa's foot jerked, kicking the stool where the pan sat. The images rippled violently, fractured. Valerian surfaced from her trance, and saw that Aunt Theresa had done the same. "Who was it?"

Theresa rubbed her eyes. "I am not certain. For a moment I thought . . . but no, it could not have been."

"Why were you startled so?"

Theresa stared into the darkness for a long moment, as if still caught in her vision, then abruptly came back to the present. "Never mind. No use chasing after phantoms. It is nothing to do with your future, in any case."

Valerian wisely chose to drop the subject. For whatever reason, Aunt Theresa apparently did not want to talk about it. It was not unusual for faces or occurrences from the past to pop up during a scrying. Not every image was a portent for the future, not even for a talented seer like Aunt Theresa.

"And the image of me in the water, what did that mean?"

"You would know better than I. Not a particularly useful scrying, I am afraid."

Valerian shrugged, her cheeks slightly pink at the meaning she herself had given to the scene in the water. "At least it gives me something to wonder about."

A gust of wind blew rain against the windows, and the flames on the hearth danced in a down draught. "It does not look like much of a night for a walk in the woods," Theresa said.

Valerian shivered. "No. Much as I would like to see Nathaniel tonight, I am not at all certain I have the energy." That was a portion of the truth. She was exhausted, yes, but she was also aware of the vulnerability Aunt Theresa was showing. Just hints of it, like her upset over the face in her vision, but even that much was unusual. She felt her aunt would prefer to have her close by tonight, even if she never said so outright. "Besides, I would not want him to start taking me for granted, would I?"

"For a woman with no experience, you are certainly quick to catch on to the games men and women play."

"What can I say? I come from a long line of harlots."

Chapter Fifteen

Eddie gave the new hinges and hasp on the stocks a final polish with his rag and stood back to admire his work in the dawn light. The twittering birds in the shadowed trees had kept him company as he worked through the early morning, tearing out the old metalwork by the light of the lantern that now sat extinguished at his feet.

He understood that repairing the stocks was a punishment for his own foolishness, and the care he took in his work was a reflection of how richly he felt he deserved the task. It was his own cock that had bewitched him, and the scent of Gwen, not witches or owls. He could see that now. The baron was an educated man, and he trusted that Valerian was nothing but an herbalist and midwife. His lordship probably thought him the dimmest of the dimwitted to have made such claims against her.

Eddie flushed, thinking of the fool he had been these past weeks. It was as if the moment a woman came by, his brain gave over all control to his crotch.

A heavy hand grasped his shoulder, and he turned to look at his father. Eddie watched as the man ran his assessing eyes over his work, then nodded in approval, giving his shoulder a brief squeeze. His father had not once reproached him for his part in this mess, for which Eddie was eternally grateful. He felt a mixture of love and shame well up inside at his father's calm acceptance of his errors and penance.

He would not fail his father so again. Until he was ready to marry, he would keep a dozen paces between himself and any woman. And as for Gwen—well, she could practice her wiles on some other cock-headed fool. He did not need one such as her controlling his life.

The sun rose above the horizon, accompanied by the beat of a rawhide drum. A procession came around the corner, led in its stately pace by Randolph Miller, Gwen's ten-year-old brother. His freckled face was grinning, his head bobbing with each beat of the drum that hung from a strap around his neck.

Several paces behind Randolph marched Gwen, eyes red-rimmed and glaring, and behind her her father and mother, looking stiff-necked and more ashamed than their daughter. Baron Ravenall and Paul Carlyle took up the rear, mounted on their fine horses, faces somber.

The drum slowly drew the villagers from their houses and shops, as if they had not been waiting behind the shutters since the crack of dawn for this very sight. The solemnity of the procession was mimicked by the villagers, although one attuned to the moods of the town could sense the pulse of their excitement underneath. Whether Gwen deserved the stocks or not, 'twould make for an entertaining day.

The procession drew to a halt, and the baron rode forward to address Gwen in tones that carried to the gathered crowd.

"Gwendolyn Miller, for the crimes of assaulting an innocent woman, accusing her of witchcraft, and inciting a riot in this peaceful town, you are sentenced to one day in the stocks. Do you accept your sentence and understand the reasons for it?"

Gwen pursed her lips in distaste, but after a glance at the angry eyes of her father responded. "Yes, my lord."

The baron nodded, then turned his attention to Eddie. "Edward O'Connor, open the stocks."

Eddie did as directed, and he helped Gwen to lay her neck and wrists into the depressions of the wood, touching her as little as possible, lifting her braid to the side with the tips of two fingers, as if the braid were a snake of the lowest order. He closed the stocks, careful not to pinch her skin where the wood met, then secured the end with a pin.

"She may be released for five minutes at noon, to attend to necessities," the baron declared, to a general sigh of approval. It took Eddie a moment to realize that without that gesture of mercy, Gwen might have had to wet herself as she stood there. "She shall then be returned to the stocks until sundown, at which time her parents may release her."

The baron then turned his horse about and set his heels to its side, Mr. Carlyle lingering for several moments more, giving Gwen a long, final look before turning to follow the baron.

Eddie looked at Gwen, her head already sagging under its own weight as she stood bent forward in the stocks, and wondered what he had ever seen in her.

Nathaniel rode at a canter down the path to Valerian's home. He was pleased with how Gwen's punishment had been implemented—there had been neither fuss nor protestation, and even Paul had expressed his satisfaction before riding off to Yarborough on an errand. Nathaniel was confident that the townsfolk would not act against either

Valerian or her aunt now that he had shown that he strongly disapproved of such actions, and of superstitious beliefs.

Still, he mused, it was well-thought of Valerian to keep the full extent of her healing talents hidden. The villagers would not evaluate such information with a logical mind, and could be tempted to behave even more foolishly than they had already. But as things were, he was certain that the threat of his displeasure would keep them in line.

He emerged from the woods into the meadow and spotted Valerian drawing water from the well. He dismounted, tying Darby to a tree, and proceeded on foot to where she cranked the handle of the winch. She did not hear him approach, his footsteps obscured by the grass and the creak of metal.

Her hair hung over one shoulder, and he could not resist creeping forward and pressing his mouth against the bare skin of her neck, gleaming pale and tender in the soft light of the morning.

His reward was a shriek and an elbow in the jaw, accompanied by the wild ratcheting of winch gears let loose as the bucket dropped back to the bottom of the well.

"Nathaniel! My God, you scared me."

He rubbed his jaw and grimaced. "That is a sharp elbow you have on your arm, Mademoiselle."

She briefly touched his chin. "Sorry. I did not know it was you."

"Were you expecting someone else to come kiss your neck?"

"Of course not. But you should know better than to sneak up on a lone woman, whatever your intentions."

He doffed his hat and bowed low to her. "You have my apologies. You are correct. My only defense is that I was overwhelmed by the vision of your loveliness, and was unable to control my lascivious tendencies."

"Satyr."

"Seductress."

He saw the smile pulling at the corners of her mouth, and he waggled his eyebrows suggestively.

"Did you come from town?"

He straightened, and after a brief search for the devil bird, put his hat back on his head. "I did. I do not think you have anything further to worry about."

"Mmm."

She did not sound convinced, but he would let time prove him right. He put his hand to the crank and began to draw up the bucket. Valerian leant on the edge of the well, watching.

"You did not come to see me the night before last, nor yesterday," he said as he worked.

"You did not come to see me, either."

"True. I waited for you, though. Have you changed your mind about this arrangement?"

She cocked her head and looked at him speculatively. "Are you worried that I might have?"

He shrugged. "It would be a disappointment." It was a gross understatement, and he saw her smile fade. "You were not expecting me to make a grand declaration of love, were you?" he teased.

"Me, expect the great Baron Ravenall to express his undying devotion to a poor country lass? No, of course not."

He pulled the bucket over the edge of the well and set it down. "Would it please you more if I said I could sleep nary a wink for listening for your tap upon my window glass, and that every footstep in the hall became yours? That I could not eat for thoughts of having you naked in my bed, your skin damp with sweat, your thighs parted in invitation, the folds of your womanhood swollen with desire, your—"

He was cut off by her fingers pressed to his mouth. "Yes, 'twould please me more," she said in a whisper.

He pulled her hand away and sank his fingers into her hair, holding her steady as his mouth came down on her own. He gently sucked her bottom lip, then traced it with his tongue, the smooth flesh feeling much as he knew those other lips between her thighs would. He pulled her head back, and slid his lips down her neck, nibbling at where it joined her shoulder. He brought one hand up to caress her breast and felt her breath quicken.

He released her, and she took a stumbling step to regain her balance. "You have not answered my question," he said.

"Question?"

"Our arrangement." He smothered a smile, watching her try to gather her thoughts. It was gratifying to know he had such an effect on her.

"Oh." She picked up the bucket of water, then set it down again. "No, I have not changed my mind."

"Then why is it that I have spent the last two nights alone?"

Her glance flicked to the cottage, then back to him. "It is nothing to do with you. With us. Truly. Things have been a bit chaotic, is all. Aunt Theresa has not been feeling well, and I did not want to leave her alone."

"I trust it is nothing serious. If there is anyone who could remedy a person's ills, it would be you."

"My powers are not so grand as you might think."

He pulled her back into his arms, gently this time, and kissed her on the forehead. Valerian's concern for her aunt roused feelings of tenderness in his own breast for this caring young woman. Tenderness, and a faint sense of yearning. He felt her arms reach around his waist and hold him tightly. "I am glad you came by," she said into his chest.

"As am I, although I do believe I hear a dismissal in that."

She leaned back until he could see her face. "Only a temporary one. Come back half an hour before sunset. I have something I would like to show you."

He kissed her again, then let her go with reluctance. "I shall be counting the hours." *And shall be at a loss for how to fill them,* he silently added as he left her there by the well.

Chapter Sixteen

Valerian scratched at the damp skin under the fake linen bandage she wore over her forehead. She had thought she would have today to spend quietly tending to Theresa, and mixing up sleeping and painkilling draughts that her aunt could use as her illness worsened. There was no reason to have her aunt spend her nights awake and in pain when there were ways to give her rest.

Theresa had pointed out that sleeping draughts of wolfsbane, belladonna, or mandrake could not be much of a danger to one who was facing her end soon anyway, although Valerian still preferred to use the safer herbs like her namesake, Valerian, and wild lettuce, and she planned to make a pillow of hops. Still, she would have the more powerful drugs ready for when her aunt wanted them. It was the least she could do.

Instead of the quiet day at the oak table crushing and mixing and distilling, contemplating her later meeting with Nathaniel, she had been plagued by visits from ill and barely ill people seeking treatment from the local witch. Apparently her newly confirmed status as a sorceress, the baron's declarations notwithstanding, had roused in the district not only feelings of dread, but utter faith in her powers and an overwhelming curiosity to see for themselves.

She had treated them all: handed out pumpkin seeds for deworming a child; Scotch broom tea to relieve a woman's water retention; nettle juice for a rash; mullein and wild cherry for a cough and sore throat; and a lotion of rue to cut down on the fleas and lice making one family's life an itching hell.

The only person she had actually allowed inside the cottage was Sally, who had come to visit her and not to gawk. For Sally she made chamomile tea, and sat with her and Theresa before the fire.

"They have taken to calling you the Raven Witch," Sally said. "On account of Oscar, I suppose."

They all three turned to Oscar, who was eyeing the plate of biscuits. "Poor hungry bird," he said.

"Yes, he is a terrifying beast," Valerian said, breaking up a biscuit and feeding him from her hand.

"You are on everyone's mind and lips," Sally continued. "You, and Gwen and Eddie. They are not speaking to one another, and Eddie is cured of whatever it was that ailed him. I do not know how to describe the mood in the air, though—tense and fearful, but excited, too, like when there is a fair at Yarborough."

"Judging from the visitors we have had today, there does not seem to be much animosity towards Valerian," Theresa said, sipping tea.

Sally shrugged a little uncomfortably. "That is there, too. All the men sit around The Drunken Raven, swilling ale and muttering darkly, and twisting everything that has happened to such a degree that you would not know you had taken any part in it. The more they drink, the more horrible and plentiful the stories become. Or so my husband tells me."

"And Mrs. Torrance no doubt presides over them all, dirty bar rag in hand," Valerian said. "She spreads more poison with that tongue of hers than any witch ever has with potions."

"As long as they stay at the inn, I do not think we need worry about them," Theresa said. "The baron's protection may well be enough to restrain them to muttering only. And as for Mrs. Torrance—I would sooner believe the sun would cease rising than that that woman would cease her gossiping."

Valerian tried to take some comfort from her aunt's words, but wondered if this time it might be different. There seemed no way to live down what had happened this past week. She would be treated as even more of a leper than she had been before.

After Sally left, Valerian went outside to clean up her impromptu infirmary. She was moving the bench back against the cottage wall when she saw yet one more woman headed towards her through the knee-high grass of the meadow. *Oh lord, who now?*she wondered.

To her surprise, it was Mrs. Torrance herself. To her recollection, the woman had only once been out to the cottage, and that shortly after Valerian and come to live with her aunt. She had never asked what the innkeeper's wife had wanted of Theresa, had been too wrapped up in her own grief over her parents to care.

Pretty pink ribbons fluttered from the straw hat Mrs. Torrance wore.

"Rrrr . . ." Oscar said from his perch on the edge of the roof.

"Oscar," Valerian warned in her sternest voice.

"Rrrr . . ."

"Oscar, no!"

"Finders keepers! Rrrraw!" Oscar cried, and launched himself into the air and across the meadow at Mrs. Torrance's hat.

"No! You bad, bad bird, come back here this minute! Mrs. Torrance, duck!" Even as she shouted it, she knew it was hopeless. She ran towards Mrs. Torrance, who stood rooted in place, her eyes wide with fearful fascination as Oscar flapped his big glossy wings towards her.

The battle was brief and bloodless. Mrs. Torrance covered her face with her hands, hunching her shoulders in terror as the black spawn of Satan landed atop her head with the weight of a thousand demons. His talons dug into the straw of the hat, scraping her scalp, and his wings beat the air about her face as he tried to lift off with his prize. A keening cry rose from Mrs. Torrance's throat, and she stumbled around in a circle, blinded and whimpering, until at last the ribbon beneath her chin gave way, and Oscar and the hat rose free.

"Finders keepers! Oscar is a superior bird! Rrrraw . . ." Oscar's voice trailed off as he flew into the woods with his prize.

"Mrs. Torrance, I am so dreadfully sorry. Are you all right?" Valerian asked, reaching her at last. She held the woman's shoulders, checking visually for any injury Oscar might have wrought in his greed. The woman's hair had been pulled loose from its pins, and stuck out from her head in ratty clumps.

The woman finally gathered her wits enough to recognize Valerian, and when she did she took a step back, her face turning angry.

"You! That bird!"

"I know, I know," Valerian interrupted before she could go any further. "He is horrible he has no manners whatsoever. He attacked Baron Ravenall in just the same way."

From the look in the woman's eyes, Valerian knew she thought Oscar had been sent purposefully to attack her. "Please, come sit down. Perhaps Oscar will bring it back and we can salvage it. I will pay for it, if he does not. Please believe me, Mrs. Torrance, I would never let Oscar do such a thing if he were within my complete control."

"I should not have come here," Mrs. Torrance said. "I was a fool to do so. A fool!"

Valerian led her to the bench and sat her down. She was intensely curious as to just why Mrs. Torrance had chosen to darken their doorstep at long last. "Let me get you some tea, something to soothe your nerves."

"No. Do not give me any of your brews." She took several more deep, ragged breaths until at last she seemed to gain some control over herself. Valerian waited, having learned that silence was the best prompt to speech. She had no reason to like this woman, but if she had a physical complaint, Valerian would not hesitate to help her.

"Is your aunt here?" Mrs. Torrance asked at last.

"She is not seeing anyone."

"Not seeing anyone. Huh. Not seeing anyone, or just not seeing me?"

"Not seeing anyone," Valerian repeated calmly.

"I have come about the warts."

She said it like Valerian should know whereof she spoke. "The warts? Yes?"

"Yes, the warts. They have been on the bottoms of my feet for ten years now, and I want to be rid of them. You tell her that. Tell her Alice Torrance is tired of those things, tired of standing on them all day, sending their pains through my feet, reminding me of what is past. If she will not take them off, then you do it. You have proven you can. You are neither of you in a position to say no to me, not when the whole town is ready to take my side, baron or no baron."

Valerian wondered if perhaps the woman had been inhaling beer fumes for a little too long. What on earth was she on about? "Will you excuse me while I consult with my aunt?"

"You tell her Alice Torrance is here."

Valerian left her glaring on the bench and slipped inside. Aunt Theresa was waiting for her, her expression halfway between exasperation and amusement.

"That woman," Theresa said in a voice low enough not to carry out the window. "She has all the sense of a particularly malicious goose."

"What is she going on about, with the warts and all? Do you know about this?"

"Ten years she has not spoken to me, and I have not missed the sound of her voice for one of them."

"What happened ten years ago?"

"It is not a pretty story."

"I do not expect it to be. This is Mrs. Torrance, after all, and apparently there are warts involved."

"Ten years ago she came to me claiming to have been raped, and she asked me to rid her of the child the man had started in her belly. She was in such distress that I agreed and prepared the juniper. She was violently ill for two days, until at last her blood came. I thought that was the end of it.

"When she had recovered, she came to see me again, weeping as much as she had the first time. After much ranting and accusation, it became clear that she had not been raped, and had in fact aborted the child of her lover. She had been afraid that her husband would know the child was not his and she'd rid herself of it for that reason. She was feeling guilty now, though, and found me a convenient scapegoat. She claimed I had forced her to do it and stolen the baby for use in spells and incantations.

"I confess I lost my temper at that, and told the woman

that until she accepted responsibility for her own actions, she would feel the pain of her guilt every day of her life. All I really meant was that she would never find a cure for the pain in her heart as long as she looked to other people instead of herself. If she would have just allowed herself to grieve for the babe, instead of blaming me, she would not have had this eating at her for ten years.

"But that is not what she heard. From what she said to you just now, she blames the warts on her feet on me."

"So what should I do?" Valerian asked.

"What would you normally do?"

"Tell her they would go away in time, although apparently these have not," Valerian said. "Or I would have her rub her feet several times a day in fresh nettles, to bring on a severe rash, and then soak her feet in very hot water. That sometimes helps, but it is not a pleasant cure."

"Or?"

"Or, if the patient seemed particularly gullible, I would prescribe a 'witchcraft' cure, and have her do something ridiculous and frightening, like catch a cat at midnight and touch its nose to each wart three times while reciting the Lord's Prayer backwards. 'Twould scare the warts off her body."

"Now," Theresa asked, "which of the above seems the most suitable to our dear innkeeper out yonder?"

"Personally, I would prefer to rub her feet with nettles." Aunt Theresa gave her a look, and Valerian pursed her lips and rolled her eyes. "But I suppose it could be just as satisfying to scare the daylights out of her. I do feel a bit sorry for anyone who has spent ten years eaten up inside over a choice she made. But why did she come now?"

"I can only guess. Whatever reasons she may say she has, perhaps she is finally ready to forgive herself. And as the guilt goes, so can the warts," Theresa said.

Valerian got up and started searching the shelves for

eerie paraphernalia to use in the cure. "Well, perhaps she will stop spreading so many lies if the warts do disappear."

"Let us not start expecting gold to shower us from heaven."

When Valerian returned outside, she was carrying an old wool blanket under one arm, in the other hand a basket with various animal bones and four stubby candles. She ignored Mrs. Torrance and spread the blanket on the ground, then set one candle at each corner and lit it. She stood in the center of the blanket in her bare feet, and with a sheep's horn in hand pointed to the north, south, east, and west, all the while lowly chanting a memorized Latin passage on digestion from one of her father's medical texts.

When she finished, she pointed the horn at Mrs. Torrance and stared for long moments, watching the color drain from the woman's face.

"Remove your shoes," Valerian ordered, keeping her voice low and flat, as she imagined a true sorceress might.

Mrs. Torrance scrambled to obey.

"Remove your stockings."

When she had obeyed, Valerian stepped off the blanket, and pointed to its center with the horn. "Sit within the square of power." Valerian could see a sheen of sweat on Mrs. Torrance's face as she came and sat in the center of the blanket.

"Do you recognize this horn?" she asked, holding it out. Mrs. Torrance shook her head mutely. "It is the horn of a three-headed goat, killed at midnight on All Hallow's Eve three centuries ago by the great druid queen Vama-wama. It has been twisted by the power of that which lies beyond sight."

In a sudden movement, Valerian clamped the horn to her own forehead, over the linen bandage. She winced, then turned the expression into a grimace of agony for Mrs. Torrance's sake. After a long moment she pulled the bandage away from her forehead, revealing the smooth white skin beneath.

Mrs. Torrance gave a little shuddering gasp of awe.

"This horn holds the power of the earth and the stars, and of the blood that flows in each creature's veins," Valerian said. "It knows what lives inside us, each and every one. It knows *you,* Alice Torrance. And it will free you."

Valerian knelt at the woman's feet and took one foot into her lap. "You will feel a freezing as of ice upon each wart." She touched the horn to one of the flat warts, and Alice whimpered, tears spilling from her eyes. "You will walk home barefoot," Valerian said as she worked, moving the horn from wart to wart. "And every morning and every evening you will scrub your feet with soap scented with roses, the scent of mercy."

"I do not have any rose-scented soap," Alice whined.

"I will give you some to start, and then your husband must find you more. You must wash your feet twice a day for each remaining day of your life. Nine days from today, Alice Torrance, you are to go to church and pray for your soul. On the morning of the tenth day, when you scrub your feet with the rose-scented soap, the warts will fall from your body. You will have been cleansed."

Valerian put the second foot back down on the blanket, and waved the horn in a complex, meaningless pattern over Alice's head. "Now stand up and say the Lord's Prayer while I go get the soap."

Aunt Theresa had the soap ready for her when she came inside. "A lifelong sentence of foot scrubbing?" Theresa asked.

Valerian shrugged, a crooked smile on her mouth. "It cannot hurt her. Her feet do not exactly smell fresh, and they are rough with dead skin. And I like the idea of unbathed Mr. Torrance going to Yarborough once a month for rose-scented soap."

She went back outside with the soap, and Oscar flew down and landed on her shoulder. Alice's mutilated hat lay upon the ground near the blanket, devoid of ribbons.

Valerian went to each candle and extinguished it, reciting body fluids in Latin as she did so. Mistress Torrance was still reciting her own prayers in the center of the blanket.

"Alice Torrance, you are free to step from the square of power," Valerian intoned.

Alice opened her eyes and cautiously stepped off the wool. Valerian handed her the soap, then picked up what was left of the hat and gave it to her. "I am sorry about your hat. That part was not necessary."

Alice clasped the crumpled straw to her chest like a talisman. "No matter."

"I am afraid I will have to burn your stockings and shoes. It is part of the ritual. They are from your old life, and you cannot walk with them into your new one."

"Yes, I understand."

"Remember now, morning and night with the scrubbing, and to church on the ninth day. The warts will fall off the morning of the tenth. You can go now."

"Rrrraw," Oscar added.

Alice lost no time in leaving them. Valerian watched her hobble off, wondering if the cure would work.

She shrugged off the thought. There was nothing she could do about it now. She had almost finished picking up her implements of sorcery when Oscar's gleeful cry of "Eee-diot!" caught her attention. She stopped mid-fold of the blanket, and turned to see Nathaniel leading his horse across the meadow from the trail that led to Raven Hall.

She waited for him, her heart beating a little more rapidly at his approach. She loved to watch him move, this masculine presence in her life. He was tall and strong and graceful, moving with an animal confidence. It seemed like a hundred years ago that he had been arrogant with her, although he certainly still showed that side to others, given his opinion of the townsfolk.

"Your servant," he said, bowing before her, then straightening with a devilish grin on his face. "That was a marvelous performance you put on for Mrs. Torrance. I believe you could make a fine living as a witch in a traveling production of MacBeth."

"You saw the whole thing?" she asked with a trace of trepidation. She still found it hard at times to remember that he accepted her as she was.

"I am thinking of building a theater box in one of the trees, so I may spy in more comfort."

"I thought you were all for the punishment of pretenders to witchcraft."

"And who said I was not going to punish you, my enchantress?" he said, and growled menacingly.

She giggled and she let him sweep her into his arms and give her a noisy kiss on the lips. He dotted a dozen more kisses all over her face, and she squirmed in his arms as he made more growling noises and lightly chewed on her neck.

Nathaniel stopped suddenly and held her away from him. "Shall I go in and greet your aunt?"

"I think she is resting. Perhaps it would be best not to." She felt a twinge of guilt for the half-lie. Aunt Theresa looked even more worn down than she had two days ago, and if he saw her, he might know that there was something seriously wrong. She did not want him to feel the burden of her grief, to have yet another unhappy piece of her life to think on. She was too cautious of his affection to risk putting another load upon it. And besides, Aunt Theresa had already said that she did not yet want outsiders to know of her illness.

"Wait here. I will be right back." Valerian went inside the cottage. Theresa was dozing by the fire, but woke at Valerian's presence.

"Not another one, surely?" she asked, straightening up in her chair.

"No, and I think I would go drown myself if it were. 'Tis Nathaniel."

"Ahh." Theresa noticed what Valerian was putting in her basket and raised her brows suggestively.

"Not one word," Valerian warned.

"But I think it is a very nice idea."

Valerian grunted.

"And I am certain the baron will find it—"

"Aunt Theresa." Valerian's tone said she had gone far enough.

"I do not know how you got to be so squeamish about these things. I thought you had been loosening up a bit of late. You will see, you will be a true Harrow wench yet."

Valerian stuck out her tongue at her aunt. "You are a dissolute woman, do you know that?"

"Thank you, my dear. Do have a nice time."

Valerian kissed her aunt on the brow. "You will be all right?"

Theresa waved her away. "Of course I will. Now go, git, before that lusty young man wanders off in search of less troublesome game."

Valerian put a cloth over the contents of the basket, and hurried out the door.

They left Darby hobbled in the meadow, grazing on the tender grasses. Nathaniel insisted on carrying the basket as Valerian led him through the woods and up the rocky trail. Oscar flew in and out of view, but his appetite for hats had been satisfied for the day, and he kept his distance from the baron.

"Where are we going for this picnic?" Nathaniel asked.

"I never said it was a picnic."

Nathaniel gestured to the basket. "What is in this, then, if not food?"

"I believe 'tis true what they say of men, that they think only of their bellies."

"Wherever did you hear such drivel?" he asked, offense in his tone. "Everyone knows that food is second in a man's mind."

"Second to what?" she asked, turning around.

His eyes traveled over her breasts, and he made exaggerated leering grimaces until comprehension dawned. She made a shocked noise. "And here I thought it was drink that had taken first place," she said.

Nathaniel started to lift the corner of the cloth in the basket.

"If you peek, I shall stop right here and not bring you any closer to the surprise."

"I do not like surprises."

"If you do not like them, then why are you following me up this trail?"

"Ah, my dear, do you truly need to ask that question?"

Valerian rolled her eyes and continued up the trail.

A few minutes later they left the path, and Valerian led him to the shadowed opening to her cave.

"A cave! You know, I once explored a cave with my sister Margaret, when we were children," Nathaniel began to babble beside her, in that excited, boyish tone he had used when she first introduced him to Oscar. She lit the lamp while he continued to talk.

"It was disappointingly shallow, but we were convinced we would find treasure or even a dragon somewhere deep within. Scared ourselves silly with our imaginings, really. When my mother found out where we had gone—my God, I had never seen her so angry. She forbid us ever to return, and had the backing of my father, sad to say. She was convinced we would fall into a crevasse and disappear."

"And did you obey?"

"Of course not. It was a cave. What child could resist?

As I said, though, it was rather shallow, and there were no treasures but some old animal bones that were almost as good. We told ourselves they were human, or at the very least left over from some troll's supper."

Valerian laughed, and led the way into the cave, cautioning him on places where the ceiling was low, or where he should be particularly careful to watch his step. She told him about how she had found and explored the cave on her own, and how she had kept it secret from all but Aunt Theresa.

"Were you not frightened, going in alone?" he asked her.

"Yes, at first. But I was not quite so creative with my imaginings as you and your sister. I eventually decided that whatever was in here could not be worse than what had already happened to me."

"You felt that way a lot after your parents died."

She paused, holding up the lamp so he could see the colored stains of minerals on the walls. "I was braver then than I have ever been since. Once I learned that life still had moments of sweetness, I wanted to be here to taste them. We all die soon enough. I would like to go on a full belly."

She glanced at him, and although he did not touch her, she felt as if he caressed her with his eyes. His pupils had dilated in the darkness, making his eyes look black, and yet there was a softness there that unnerved her. She was learning what to do with his lust and his lighthearted affection. This softness, though, that looked as if for this moment she could see into his heart, was a more private emotion and she did not know how to respond.

She lowered the lamp in confusion and continued through the passageway, explaining side passages and the sound of rushing water. He added his own information on the types of rocks and formations, adding that after that bit of cave exploration, he had had some interest in geology.

"Am I mistaken, or is it growing warmer in here? And more humid?" he asked.

"You are not mistaken," Valerian said, and she took him around the last bend to her private pool. The lamplight reflected off the uneven surface of the pool; the gurgle of water from the stone face rebounded in echoes from the curved walls. "Let me light the other lamps, so you do not fall in."

"A Roman hot spring." The boyish excitement was back, coupled with awe. "Look at that carving, think how old it is. And it is been under here, faithfully pouring water, for centuries." He knelt down and swished his hand in the water. "Hot enough for bathing."

"Of course," Valerian said. "Otherwise, why make the pool?"

"You have a smart mouth on you, wench."

"No one called me a wench until I became involved with you. You have had a most damaging effect upon my innocence."

"So I have."

Valerian took the cover off the basket, revealing the soaps and towels within. She hoped he could not see the color in her cheeks. "Do you, ah, care to do a little more damage?" She cringed inwardly even as she said it. She sounded like an idiot.

He looked at the contents of the basket, then at her, then back at the basket. He picked up a bar of lavender-scented soap, and examined it. "Just what, exactly, did you have in mind?"

"Well, I thought perhaps we could, well, we could both. . . ." She saw that he was laughing at her floundering attempt at seduction. "Cad!"

"Wanton."

"Scoundrel."

"Goddess."

She opened her mouth to respond, but then he had his arms around her legs, and had buried his face in the front of her skirts. She took his hat off and ran her fingers through his thick hair. She felt a push at the back of her knees and suddenly she was on her back, and he on top of her, kissing her soundly.

"Of course I want to bathe with you," he said when he finally let her up for air. "And I am sorry I laughed."

"No you are not."

"I would be if it meant you would not be making me such offers in the future. I wish to do nothing that would inhibit you from thinking up such unusual—and enticing—rendezvous."

She rolled her head and looked over at the basket of bathing accessories. "You do not think I am ridiculous?"

"My dear, no invitation to frolic in the water with a young, beautiful, naked woman will ever be seen as ridiculous by any man. Add in the exoticness of a secret Roman bath, and you have created an event that he will pull from his memory to relish to the end of his days. He could be moments from death, and the memory would still give life to his dying old bones."

"Well then."

"Well then, indeed."

She ducked her head shyly, and began to unfasten the laces of her bodice. She peeked up as she heard Nathaniel undressing as well. She had staged this encounter, but it was still only the second time she had been naked with a man, and as soon as the last garment was removed, she slid gratefully into the concealing water.

Nathaniel joined her a moment later, and she pushed out into the center of the pool. He followed, his head and shoulders dark shadows above the water, despite the three lamps placed about the small cavern. She felt disoriented for a moment, the situation unreal and dreamlike. Was this

the scene Aunt Theresa saw in the scrying, with the lamps and her own hair spreading in the water?

When alone here, she had fantasized about making love to a man, had brought herself pleasure with her own hands, Nathaniel's image in her mind. And now he was here. This place was hers more than anywhere else, and some primitive part of her felt that she was marking him as hers by making love to him here, under the eyes of the Roman carvings, deep in the heart of a mountain.

The dream state vanished when his hands came around her waist, sliding up over her breasts. The pressure of his touch sent her floating backwards, and he laughed and held her more firmly. She let her own hands wander down his back, to stroke gently at his buttocks. Her palms were greedy for the feel of his skin.

He kissed her, their mouths wet from the hot spring water, and Valerian pressed herself against him as well as she could. She felt his manhood hard against her belly, the sack at the base soft in the heated water. Her nipples brushed against the hair on his chest, but the lightness of her body in the water kept her from getting the strength of contact she wanted.

"Damn, you keep floating away from me," Nathaniel said.

"Perhaps the seals know what they are doing," Valerian said.

"What?"

"The seals. They mate on dry land."

He laughed, swam her to the edge of the pool, and hauled her up onto the smooth, clean rock floor. They sprawled there for a moment, feeling heavy and awkward out of the buoyancy of the water. The floor was cool on Valerian's back, but not uncomfortable. Her body had absorbed too much heat from the water to feel cold. She closed her eyes.

She heard him fumble in the basket, a splash as of a hand in the water, and a moment later felt the slick gliding of a soaped hand across her belly. She smelled lavender, and opened her eyes to him leaning over her, huge and dark in the dim light.

"I feel as if I have been captured by Hades," she said.

"Perhaps you have. And captives must always do what they are told. Raise your arms."

She obeyed, clasping her hands together above her head, her breasts arching upwards, feeling thoroughly wanton. His soaped hands massaged her breasts, sliding smoothly over the contours of her body. She half-closed her eyes in pleasure. He dipped his hands in water again and continued soaping her, his thumbs pressing lightly as his strong hands slid up her arms, then back again to her chest and belly.

He did her hips, the outside of her thighs, brushed once, lightly, over the hair that concealed her womanhood, then skimmed down over her legs. He worked for several minutes on her feet, his fingertips finding the sensitive places between her toes and digging lightly into the hollows behind her ankles. She felt a pulsing tingle of pleasure run through her.

"I never knew it could feel so good to have a man touch my feet," she whispered.

He chuckled softly in reply, and then his hands slid up her calves, over her knees, and pressed into the soft flesh of her inner thighs, urging her to open.

She obeyed, shutting her eyes in an embarrassment heavily edged with anticipation, but it was not his hand that touched her this time. She gasped and opened her eyes, seeing in astonishment the top of his head above her belly. She was about to protest, but then he moved his tongue against her and her head fell back as she writhed with pleasure.

She had never known that anything in life could feel this good. Her breath starting coming in short gasps, her mind silently pleading for him not to stop, and then he did. He gave her one long caress with his tongue, then lifted his head.

Valerian opened her eyes and stared at him.

"Patience, little wench," he said, and smiled at her. He slipped back into the pool, but was out again in a moment, the water dripping from his large body. He lay down beside her, then pulled her atop him. She almost slid off, the soap covering her body mixing with the water on his.

"Now it is your turn to wash me," he said. "Only you cannot use your hands."

Her soapy legs slid apart over his thigh, her womanhood pressing against the firm muscle, and comprehension dawned. "Whatever my master desires," she said.

He stretched his arms above his head as she had done, and she knelt and looked down on him. She knew he would protest nothing she did, would welcome whatever touch she chose. The thought sent her imagination racing.

She rested her weight on her hands on the floor, and moved her hips against the thigh tight between her legs. Her woman's flesh slid along his lightly haired skin, a gentle pleasure that it pleased her to take from him. She leaned down until her breasts were against his chest, and brushed her nipples against his skin, then pressed more firmly and slid her whole body down the length of him, until her breasts were on his thighs and his manhood was against her face.

She rubbed her cheek against the head, the skin as soft and velvety as that on her own face. Curiosity prompted her to taste the head, her tongue laving it like a piece of hard candy. He jerked in response, and she smiled despite the sting of the soap on her tongue. She slid back up his body until his manhood pressed against the jointure of her thighs, and she rubbed gently against him.

His arms came up, and he pulled her down to his chest, then rolled them both into the pool. The splash echoed weirdly with her laughter. "Little heathen," he said, and rinsed the soap from her body.

This time when he pulled her from the water, there was no waiting on the stone. He lifted her legs around his hips, and guided himself to her opening. She felt the pressure against her, and her muscles tightened in memory of the discomfort of last time.

"Relax, *mañ chère,*" he said. "You are tight, but it will not hurt if you relax."

"I . . . I do not know how," she whispered. She could still feel him pressing against her, feeling too big to ever enter that small space. She wanted him within her, yet could not release the nervousness she felt.

He gently lowered her legs, so that her feet were flat on the ground, her knees bent. He leaned down and kissed her, gently. "I will go slow. If it hurts, I will stop. Now relax yourself. Pretend you are dropping your muscles down into the stone."

She did what he said, concentrating on those tight muscles deep within her womanhood, the muscles she had had little reason to pay attention to for most of her life. She let them drop into the floor, and felt the tip of Nathaniel's manhood slide slightly within her.

"Yes, that is it," he encouraged her and moved slightly in and out, each gentle thrust bringing him a little farther inside. "Do you hurt?"

"Only a little," she managed to say, her breath forced out of her in little gasps by his movements. He stopped his thrusts, and she moved against him. "Do not stop. It is not a bad pain—it is like a mix of pain and pleasure."

"It is because you are so new to this. In time you will loosen." He was halfway within her now, and he thrust a little more deeply. "But I do not complain."

Her eyes widened as he thrust farther, feeling herself spread to accommodate him. His thrusts took on strength as she moved with him, her body finally accepting his, and although it was not the same intense pleasure that his mouth had given her, there was a different pleasure, fainter, but wrapped in her whole body's awareness of this man thrusting within her. She gave herself over to him and the strength of his body.

He froze above her, his hips pressed tightly to hers, then kissed her roughly several times, saying her name, and she felt the pulsing throb of his manhood through her woman's flesh as he reached his climax. He collapsed atop her, his face pressed into her neck. She welcomed the weight of him and the sweaty heat of his skin.

After a few moments he rolled off her and cupped her breast in his hand. He kissed her check, then spoke into her ear. "I will not leave you as I did last time."

Before she could ask what he meant, his hand moved down and his fingers began to work their magic on her. She was slick from their lovemaking, her nerves sensitive and waiting. She turned her face to his chest as he leaned against her, her lips touching his damp skin. She closed her eyes and abandoned herself to pleasure, soft sounds rising from the back of her throat.

Muscles all over her body tensed as her climax neared, as if by straining she could urge it closer. She grabbed his arm and squeezed, her fingernails digging in, a plea for him to keep going, not to stop, to keep doing the same thing. He kissed her as she reached her final shuddering release, stroking her lips with his tongue even as his fingers echoed the movement below. She quivered as it came, and felt the undulations within her, a constriction of muscles four, five, six times, each contraction further away from the last.

She clamped her thighs around his hand, stilling his

movements, and pulled him down beside her. He put his arm over her body and brushed the wet hair away from her face.

"Thank you," she whispered.

He kissed her nose. "Thank *you*. I promise you, each time it will be better than the last. Sooner or later I will learn to control myself with you, and we will have time to savor all the pleasures to be had between man and woman."

"Will you teach me exotic positions?"

"Whatever will please you."

"Will you put my legs over your shoulders? Or have me stand on my hands and knees, like an animal? Will you have me sit in a swing above your bed?"

"I beg your pardon?" He pulled back from her, to look her in the face, his expression shocked.

"There is a book in your uncle's library, with drawings. Many, many fascinating drawings."

The shock faded. "Ahh. So I recall. I discovered it myself when I visited as a boy. Those pictures played a large role in my nocturnal fantasies as I grew up."

"Mine too."

He quirked an eyebrow at her. "You fantasized about what you saw there?"

"Of course."

"But you are a woman."

She laughed. "Yes."

"But women do not—"

"Do not what? Fantasize about men, about what a man and a woman do together under the sheets? Women do not . . ." she almost could not say it, then felt the urge to shock him even as she shocked herself. "Women do not touch themselves?"

He blinked. "Women are different from men that way. I thought."

She shrugged. "I do not think so."

He looked into her eyes with interest. "Have you fantasized about me?"

She felt her cheeks heat. She had been daring enough! "I do not know that I would tell you, if I had. It might do irreparable damage to your opinion of yourself." She rolled out from under him and back into the water. She kicked her way into the middle of the pool, watching him slide in after her. "If I said no, you would be crushed. If yes, your head would bloat so large I would not be able to get you out of the cave again."

"Harlot!"

"Peacock!"

"You will pay for that," he said, and lunged through the water at her.

She spluttered water as he caught her. " 'Tis what I count upon!"

Chapter Seventeen

"A guinea for your thoughts," Nathaniel said, sitting down at the end of the sofa where she lay. They were in the drawing room of Raven Hall several days after the cave, a fire burning on the hearth, the two of them ensconced in the pocket of light thrown by the flames.

She tucked the soles of her stocking feet against his warm thigh. "That is above the usual asking price."

"The better to tempt you, m'dear. There are times I think there are depths to your thoughts that you do not share."

She wiggled her toes against him, and he picked up her feet and stroked his thumbs along her arches. "If I laid myself bare to you, where would the mystery be?" she said. "You would find some other poor country wench with whom to while away your time."

"You do not believe that," he said and massaged each individual toe.

She shrugged. "I suppose not." But part of her did. She

had been thinking about how much she had come to cherish the few hours she could snatch with Nathaniel, about how knowing she could lose herself with him for however brief a time made it easier to cope with what was happening to Aunt Theresa. And the more she cherished their time together, the more certain she became that each hour together would be their last: that he would tire of her, or that some unforeseen event would pull him from her.

His hands slid up her calves, and she let her lids droop shut. "If a guinea will not tempt you, perhaps there are other ways to lure forth your secrets."

She smiled as his palms slid over her knees and touched upon the bare flesh of her thighs.

A pounding upon the front door, audible even from the drawing room, stopped Nathaniel's progress up her skirts. They both listened as the door was answered, and a noisy tumult of voices and footsteps entered the front hall.

Valerian sat up, pulling down her skirts and slipping her feet into her shoes. It was hardly a secret any longer that she was intimate with the baron, but she knew better than to flaunt the fact. "Who do you think it is?" she asked him.

She saw his eyebrows draw together as he listened to the voices, then his face cleared in surprised recognition. "Of all the—" He broke off, and with a gesture for her to stay where she was, went out into the hall.

She sat for a moment, listening to the exclamations of greeting and delight, clearer now that Nathaniel had left the door ajar. Two voices stood out amongst the rest.

"La! We have missed you in town!" a woman trilled.

"Do not listen to her, it was the stink that drove us to your door. The Thames has flooded again, and there is not a house in the city that does not have its cesspit bubbling up through the floorboards," a man said.

"But I truly have missed you, Nathaniel. It is all so dreary without you."

"Not to mention that the season is well and truly over," the man countered.

Valerian stepped quietly to the door and peered out into the hall. A finely dressed man and woman in traveling clothes stood with Nathaniel, having the look about them of brother and sister. Four other people, in equally fine dress, were removing gloves and having their cloaks taken by servants, and as she watched yet another pair came in through the open front door.

"Since you have been so cruelly exiled from the delights of society," the woman said, "we have elected to bring society to you. Now where is that terrible Mr. Carlyle? He did say he would be here."

"Paul wrote to you?" Nathaniel asked.

The man answered. "He said you were languishing in these wilds, and verily, after this journey, I understand what he meant." The man glanced meaningfully around the hall. "A bit gloomy for what you are used to."

"It suits."

The woman looked around, then her eyes lit on Valerian. "You, girl. Stop skulking in the shadows and come and help with our things."

Nathaniel opened his mouth to speak, but then caught Valerian's eye. She shook her head at him, and slipped back into the drawing room. There was nothing he could say that would not embarrass her as much as or more than the woman's first assumption.

She gathered her own worn wool cloak over her arm. Any minute those guests could enter the drawing room, seeking a place to warm themselves while their rooms were readied. She did not want to be here when they did. She gave one last look over the room, the fire crackling in the hearth, the sofa where she had been sitting with

Nathaniel, and felt a twinge in her heart. *Do not let it be over already,* she silently prayed.

When she got back to the cottage she was damp and thoroughly chilled from the walk through the woods, the wet undergrowth crowding the path having brushed against her cloak. Aunt Theresa was asleep in her bed, her snores reassuringly heavy. She had taken to dosing herself before bed to insure that she got the rest she needed. Valerian checked on her, then drew the bed draperies all the way closed and went to stir up the fire and light a candle. She doubted that she herself would find sleep for some time yet.

She busied herself making a pot of tea and cutting bread and cheese for her supper. She broke up some stale biscuits and put them in a dish of milk for Oscar, and the two of them sat at the end of the table and ate in silence. She could not finish her meal, meager as it was, and ended up breaking the cheese into pieces and rolling it into balls that she fed to Oscar from the tip of her finger, trying all the while not to think about what the arrival of Nathaniel's London friends would mean to their relationship.

A futile endeavor.

She cleared away the dishes and took down a half-finished carving, no bigger than the palm of her hand, of a bear. She settled by the fire with her tools, the thick leather apron spread across her lap, and began working. It required almost all of her concentration to make the careful grooves in the wood, and to keep from a slip that could deeply cut her hand. The bit of her mind that floated free, however, taunted her without mercy, striking at her insecurities and ignoring rational argument.

You knew it could not last, you knew Paul Carlyle was right to try to keep you apart, you knew Nathaniel only took you up because there was no one else for miles. Now that his friends are here, women of his own class, he will have no need of you. She sniffed, and a tear slid down her cheek. *He let you leave his house without a word. That should tell you what you need to know.*

She was working herself into a thick wallow of self-pity when she was distracted by the creak of the door. She looked up, sniffing, and wiped at her nose with the back of her hand.

Even before seeing his face in the darkness at the other end of the cottage she knew it was Nathaniel, and as he walked as quietly as he could across the floor and came into the light, she saw his expression turn from one of anger to one of exasperation.

She looked at him, her mouth quivering, and then he was on his knees beside her, pulling her into his arms, the wooden bear in her hand a solid lump between them.

"Foolish wench," he rumbled into her hair. "I thought you had gone 'round to my bedroom. Why did you leave?"

"You had guests," she mumbled into his shoulder. "I did not think I was wanted."

"Uninvited guests," he said, and held her away from him by the shoulders. "Look at me, Valerian." She slowly turned her eyes to his. "Paul wrote to them suggesting that they come, not I, but now that they are here, I can hardly put them out and tell them to lodge elsewhere. If I had my way they would not a one of them have set foot in Raven Hall to begin with, but they are here now and we must make the best of it."

"You will not have time for me now." It came out petulant, and she hated the weakness in her own voice. Where was the calm, confident Valerian she had once thought herself to be?

"I will not give you up simply because some friends I do not particularly care for have arrived," he said, offense in his tone.

Valerian suddenly recalled Laetitia, that other unfortunate young woman beneath his class with whom he had dallied. Despite herself, she wondered if he would eventually try to shake free of her, as well.

"I cannot come to you," Valerian said. "Not with those people at the hall. I do not want them to know about me."

"They would never know if you came to my window."

"It would be different now." There was something distasteful to the idea of sneaking into his bedroom with his noble friends in residence. She did not want to be his dirty little secret, hidden under their aristocratic noses. "Come here, to the meadow," she said, grasping him on the forearm. She was equal to him here, in her own world, and no secrets were necessary.

"If you wish. But promise me, Valerian," he said. "Promise me that you will not allow this to change anything."

She tried to smile. "How could it?" she asked lightly, her answer an evasion.

He pressed a kiss to her forehead. "I will return as soon as I can."

He stood up before the words had fully registered in her mind. "You are leaving?"

"It was bad enough of me to slip away when they have just arrived. I cannot spend the night here."

She forced another smile to her face, wondering that he could not detect the falsity of it. "Yes, I know. Go on, you cannot leave them alone at the hall."

He kissed her once more, this time hard, on the mouth, and then was gone.

She sat in the quiet several minutes, feeling cold and sick inside. Whether he thought he wanted it or not, his friends would force him to abandon her. It was only a matter of time. Even knowing that, she could not bear to end it herself, to cut short a relationship that only had a few hours left in it. Even painful hours were better than none.

She came out of her thoughts enough to realize that Aunt Theresa's snoring had stopped. She got up, walking as stiffly as an old woman, and went to check on her. She pulled the draperies open a few inches. "Are you awake?" she whispered into the warm shadows.

"Unfortunately."

Valerian pulled the draperies open wider. "I am sorry if I woke you. How are you feeling?"

Theresa grunted. "There is no topic I would not prefer to that one. Come, sit. Distract me by telling me what our baron was doing here."

Valerian pulled a stool up to the side of the bed and explained the whole sorry tale, her eyes tearing. Theresa was silent for so long when she had finished that Valerian feared she had gone back to sleep, but at last she gave a heavy sigh and spoke.

"I think you are right to worry, and right as well to keep yourself hidden from his friends. The baron is no stranger to the sin of pride, and his friends' casual ridicule of your relationship might cause him to view it with the same jaundiced eye."

"That is what I fear. Do you think he cares so little for me that he can be so easily influenced?"

"You know him better than I. I would like to think not, but you have not had so very much time together."

"I do not want to let him go," Valerian said, her voice cracking. "Oh, God, listen to me. What is happening to me?" she asked, swallowing down the incipient sobs and getting ahold of herself. "He has friends visit, and I fall apart."

Theresa gave her a knowing look, but did not answer her query. "His friends will not stay forever. See the baron only away from them, and do not press him for declarations of his feelings or of his commitment to you. Demand nothing of him, and when they have gone, he will come back to you."

"You mean I will be the only cow left in the field."

"If you want to look at it that way. It is at least realistic. Men can afford to lose themselves in romantic illusions. Women cannot. These friends will demand his attention, and if you whine to him of your own needs, he may see you as a source of distress rather than pleasure."

Valerian made a face. "I do not understand how you could ever have said that this being a mistress is either an easy or a pleasant way of life."

"Ah, well, it is all a little different when you are stuck in the country with only one available protector, and he is both handsome and of a comparable age. He takes on more significance than perhaps he is worth. And perhaps, dearest, you have let your heart become entangled in what was to be a physical pleasure."

"I sometimes think he has become my world," Valerian said sadly.

"And when was that ever good for a person?"

Valerian went to bed with Theresa's final words repeating in her mind. Of course it was not good to make a person the whole of your existence. But if she lost both her aunt and her lover, who would be left?

Chapter Eighteen

Nathaniel stood in the rain, looking across the meadow to the cottage, and felt he deserved every bit of misery the weather could deal out. In the past two weeks he had only been to see her once, when the shock of his friends' arrival had still been new, before he had been drawn into their games and way of life. He had complained to her about them, about their intrusion, their noise, their concern with a lifestyle that had suddenly felt alien to him, and he had known that she was cheered to hear that he did not prefer their company over hers.

He forced himself to come out from under the trees, to walk through the tall grass of the meadow. He had not ridden Darby, half from a desire for time to think, and half from the compulsion to punish himself with a slog through the mud. He had said he would not abandon her, but for the past week and a half she must have thought he had done just that.

It was early morning yet, his friends all sound asleep,

but there was already smoke trailing from the chimney of the cottage, and he knew that Valerian and Theresa had most likely been awake for some time. He reached the door and knocked.

"Eee-diot!" he heard from inside, muffled by the wood of the door.

It was a long minute before Valerian appeared at the door, wearing her forest green cloak, pulling its hood over her head as she stepped outside. "I would invite you in, but Aunt Theresa is not yet dressed."

She looked pale, tired in a way that he had not seen before. His gut twisted, wondering if she had been staying awake late at night in hopes that he would come to her.

"Do you mind walking a bit more?" she asked. "The cave is the only private place I can think of that is dry and warm."

"I do not mind at all. Your aunt is an admirable woman, but I confess that I would much rather see you alone." He brushed his fingers along her cheek, the skin so white and fragile in the grey morning light. She pressed his palm to her lips and kissed him, then took his hand and led him out into the rain.

They did not talk as they walked, the track in the mud requiring attention to avoid a slip, eye contact impossible. Her hood fell back in a gust of wind, and she let it lie on her shoulders, apparently not deeming the rain heavy enough to be a bother. He tried to imagine Kate or Beth, or any of the other women presently at his house, climbing with such little concern through rain and mud and wind.

His Valerian was a creature of the wilds, more at home in a cave than a ball room. Just as he could not picture Kate out here now, he could not see Valerian with her hair dressed close to her head and covered by a lace cap, her waist and ribs squeezed tight by stays, her feet bound by delicate silk shoes with soles meant only for walking indoors. Her differentness felt unbearably precious in that moment.

They did not speak more than a few words until they were deep inside the cave. Valerian tossed her cloak onto a boulder outside the hot-spring cavern, where it would not become even more wet from the steam, then slipped off her shoes and sat at the edge of the pool, pulling her skirts above her knees and dangling her feet in the heated water.

He hesitated only a moment before following suit, his cold skin burning at the touch of the water.

"I am glad you came," she said simply and smiled at him.

He felt the guilt return. "I am sorry, Valerian. I did not mean to stay away so long—and after I swore to you that they would not change anything between us. I should have come sooner."

She took his hand, and met his eyes without recrimination. "There is no need to apologize, Nathaniel. You are allowed to enjoy your friends. You have been alone amongst strangers, and it is understandable that you should wish to spend time with your friends when they come to see you."

"But to have kept you waiting—"

She put her fingers over his lips. "Hush. You have not kept me waiting. Do you imagine that I mooned by the window from dawn 'til midnight, with nothing to do but wonder where you were?"

Well, yes, he thought to himself, but was wise enough not to say it. Even he could see the arrogance in such a thought.

"I am not an idle woman. I have had my hands full with rashes and earaches and illnesses of indeterminate origin. There has been the garden to work upon, and plants to be harvested and preserved, not to mention laundry to wash, food to cook, pots to scrub—"

"All right, all right," he interrupted, and forced a laugh. "I understand. You did not perish for loss of my company."

"But that is not to say I am not happy to see you." She raised the back of his hand to her lips and gave it a kiss, her eyes sparkling at him with amusement.

Whatever guilt remained faded away under a wave of private shame. He had been a peacock indeed to think that her world revolved around him, and he had been a fool not to have remembered that her heart was larger than his, more forgiving and more generous.

"And I am happy to see you," he said at last, feeling within himself the sting of his own failings. When he was with her, he wished to be a better person. "I do wish I had come sooner, if only so that I had not gone so long without the pleasure of your company."

"Your friends have brought out the flatterer in you."

"Are you so averse to a compliment, then?" he tried to tease.

"Only if it is on such meaningless things as my stunning intellect or saint-like character. Why do you not compliment me on my elegant coiffure, or the stylish cut of my clothes?"

He smiled, relaxing, beginning at last to feel at ease with her. "Surely Mademoiselle knows she is forever at the height of fashion."

"Naturally. 'Twould shame the family name to be anything less. Now tell me, kind sir, with what low amusements do your guests entertain themselves? I take a scientific interest in the behaviors of the common rabble."

"Mademoiselle wishes to know such trifles?"

"Mademoiselle has a shameful curiosity."

He dropped out of the game. "Do you truly wish to hear about them, Valerian? They are nothing compared to you."

"They are your friends. To learn of them is to learn something of you."

"I am not entirely certain that would be in my favor."

"Come, Nathaniel. They cannot be that bad."

"Ahhhh, if you only knew," he joked, waggling his brows. Sitting here in the dark cave with Valerian, their feet dangling in the water of an ancient Roman hot spring, he felt again the gulf between her world and that of his friends, where all was artifice and true feeling something to be ridiculed. At that moment, he wished he could stay where he was forever.

"Their day starts with breakfast, of course," he said, "which is served at the early hour of eleven."

"A trying hour at which to be awake," Valerian said, and brought one leg up to where she could cross her arms across her knee, resting her chin there and smiling at him with interest.

"And the day only grows more strenuous as it progresses." He described it all for her, the card games, the riding, the walks in the garden, the drinking, and the flirtation, describing it all as if it were the odd behavior of a native people of some far-off land. He did not mean to mock his friends, and yet it was impossible not to. He no longer belonged entirely to their world, and he felt as if his eyes had been opened to the true shallowness of their pursuits.

But he did not belong to Valerian's world, either. His voice trailed off as that realization came to him.

He felt her touch upon his arm. "What is it, Nathaniel?"

He leaned over and kissed her. "Nothing but self-indulgent fancies." For the present, he would rather drift between worlds than give up hers entirely. Some half-conscious part of himself knew that she was someone he needed.

He came home to a drawing-room full of bored aristocrats. He had hardly noticed the rain on his walk back, his mind wandering in confused contemplation. It was a bit of a shock to see his friends trapped inside by that same rain that had done him no harm.

"Nathaniel! Where have you been, dear man?" Kate cried, throwing down her hand of cards. "We have been most frightfully bored without you."

There were murmurs of assent throughout the room. "I never claimed Cumbria to be filled with amusements, myself included," he said. At this moment, he rather wished the lot of them would pack up and leave. He had tired of entertaining them.

Kate noticed his damp hair. "You have been out, in this foul weather? You are becoming quite the country man!"

Paul spoke from the chair where he sat swirling brandy in a glass. "Ah, but where has he been? What could draw him out into the weather on such a day?"

Nathaniel narrowed his eyes at his friend, but Kate jumped in before he could say anything. "Indeed, there is only one thing I know of that draws a man through foul downpours and cold alike."

"A fine piece of horseflesh?" Christopher asked, to the amusement of the group.

"Hounds for sale?" another of the men asked.

Kate arched her eyebrow at the lot of them. "A woman."

"Now where would he find a woman in this godforsaken corner of the world?" Christopher asked.

"Our dear baron could find a woman anywhere," Paul said.

Nathaniel recognized the mood Paul was in, one of boredom and mischief combined. He felt himself the baited bear, but declined to amuse them. He went to the window and looked out, turning his back on his friends. He knew from experience that this sort of conversation was best left to its own course. Anything he said would only make it worse.

"We have been here a fortnight already," Beth said. "Why is this the first we have heard of her?"

There was a chorus of speculation.

"Perhaps her parents do not know."

"She may be entirely unsuitable."

"She is a hag."

"He fears I shall steal her from him."

"He intends to marry her and wants to surprise us with the announcement." A round of laughter followed that suggestion.

"You do know that our dear baron has not yet properly introduced himself to his neighbors in the district," Paul said. "Some have stopped by to pay their respects, but he has yet to be at home to a single one of them. He has made himself quite the hermit."

"For shame!" Kate said. "We must remedy the situation, if he is incapable of doing so himself. I think a party is in order. A ball, perhaps, at which his dear neighbors can at last make the acquaintance of the brooding baron of Raven Hall." She cast her eyes at Nathaniel, the question hanging there. Even Kate would not be so bold as to plan a party at his house without his assent.

He did not want to meet his neighbors, the term being loosely applied. No doubt he would have to search over many miles of countryside to find sufficient guests of a quality suitable for a ball. And yet, it was true he had been remiss in his neglect of those neighbors. He had been brought up well enough to be aware that he had offered a degree of insult to his neighbors by not so much as saying "Good day" to any who had stopped by to meet him and offer condolences on Uncle George.

He turned from his contemplation of the rain and nodded to Kate. At least it would keep the lot of them entertained, planning the party. Perhaps when it was over, they would at last feel satisfied with their visit and leave.

"We shall have to make it a masquerade," Beth said.

"What a confoundingly stupid idea," Christopher said.

"How is he to meet his neighbors if he cannot see their faces?"

"I think it a splendid idea," Kate said. "He will be the more likely to invite his lady love if she is in disguise, do you not think? And what fun, to guess who she might be!"

Nathaniel was not fooled by Kate's enthusiasm. Since long before he left London, he had been aware that her interest in him was a bit more than friendly. He did not doubt that her interest in his "lady love" was a competitive one.

And yet, even knowing that, he knew suddenly that he would ask Valerian to come to the ball. She did not speak like a country girl, and in proper disguise no one but Paul would guess who she was. For one night, he could bring her fully into his world.

For one night, he could pretend that their worlds were one.

Chapter Nineteen

There was no help for it: She was going to have to go to Raven Hall. Valerian gave herself a headache thinking about it, but she could not come up with an acceptable alternative. Daniel was a capable enough gardener, and had most likely remembered to water their plants in the greenhouse, but the various exotic plants had been too long without expert care.

And of course she could not trust Daniel to know how to harvest the resin from the opium poppies. There were plenty of poppies growing here in the meadow, but they were not yet in season. She was running low on laudanum pills and needed to make more for Aunt Theresa.

With Nathaniel's accounting of the daily schedule at the hall, she could at least reduce the risk of meeting any of his friends if she went early in the morning. Unfortunately, after scoring the seed pods, it would be several hours before she could scrape off the resin that would bead along the scratch, which meant she would still be hiding amongst the pots and withered orange trees when the household awoke.

Ah well. There was nothing for it. She would just have to hope that Paul did not see her, and that anyone else, chancing upon her in the greenhouse, would take her for a servant and ignore her.

She made it to the relative safety of the greenhouses with only a brief encounter with Daniel, pruning back a wisteria that grew wild over an arcaded walkway.

"Coming to see the baron, are you?" he asked, and she imagined there was a touch of disappointment in his tone.

"I have come to tend the plants."

"Ah. That is all right, then. Where be your aunt? I have not seen her about."

"She, er . . ." She could not come up with a lie that would suit. She should have thought of this. Daniel would not be the only one wondering why Theresa had disappeared of late.

"It is the death of old George, I imagine," Daniel filled in. "We all knew—well, we did not expect she would want to come back here much after that. It was surprised I was, that one day she did come."

"She was fond of the old baron."

"And he of her. Or so I hear, and that is just gossip." He gave her a long look, one that said as plain as spoken words that he knew she had taken over with Nathaniel the role they all thought Theresa had held with old George.

Valerian excused herself and escaped to the greenhouse, her cheeks flaming. It was obvious that Daniel did not approve of her behavior, and it surprised her. She had thought no one here cared a whit for her virtue or lack thereof, as long as she stayed away from their own sons and husbands. Daniel looked as if he cared about her behavior for her own sake.

She set to work with petty resentments churning in her

gut. *It is not his or anyone else's affair what I do,* she grouched silently, carefully scoring a seed pod. *They could have found me a husband, if it mattered so much with whom I slept.* Behind that thought, though, was the memory of her mother, who had chosen to marry and had intended that her daughter do the same. But her mother had intended her to grow up with both her parents, as well, and that had not happened.

For a moment she wanted to blame Aunt Theresa for her easy fall from virtue, and just as quickly banished the thought. Her aunt and her mother had been cut from different cloth, but both had loved her without reservation, and done their best for her. She was old enough to take responsibility for her own decisions, and to deal with the consequences.

Milky resin was already beginning to bead along the scores on the poppy pods, and Valerian moved on to tend to other flora. The sun slipped from behind a cloud, heating the room, creating a steamy warmth rich with the scent of earth and greenery. Valerian hummed softly under her breath as she worked, loving the feel of dirt in her hands, and imagined herself on some far away isle in the Indies, tending tropical flowers in her plantation garden.

Her reverie was gradually interrupted by the sound of female voices approaching. She looked up in time to see two women go past outside the glass wall in front of her, their bright dresses turned to shimmering watercolor by the sunlight and waved panes. They settled on a bench near the garden entrance to the greenhouse, and even as she told herself she should not, Valerian found herself moving slowly to that end of the building, where she might be able to listen in on their conversation.

"I cannot imagine that he will remain here past the summer," one of the women said, her voice high and cultured and, Valerian thought, quite smug.

"But his family, the scandal—"

"Pish, Beth. What scandal? A trollop drowns herself, and it is a scandal? No, they will have him back, and be glad of it, too. And they will most especially welcome a wife."

"Kate! Has he—" Beth seemed unable to voice the stunning thought, but at last managed. "Has he spoken to you?"

Valerian hung on the answer as much as Beth.

"La, well, not precisely," Kate said.

Valerian gave a fierce nod of her head. Of course he had not!

"But I have a strong sense it is in his mind," Kate continued. "And would we not make a fine match?"

Valerian shook her head in denial.

"Certainly my own parents would approve, for all that they think him a bit too fast."

"I can only pray they never learn you are here now," Beth said. "Christopher is not the most scrupulous of chaperones nor protective of brothers."

"He is a gift," Kate said, laughing, then turned her head and caught a glimpse of Valerian through the glass. "I say, Beth! We have a little spy upon us!"

Valerian winced in dismay at being caught, and tried to slink away back down the aisle.

Kate moved more quickly than Valerian would have thought a woman in such a voluminous gown could, coming around to the entrance to the greenhouse, Beth stumbling after.

Valerian ducked her head and dipped a curtsy. Perhaps if she put on an adequate display of servitude, they would the more quickly abandon her. "Mistress," she said to her muddy shoes, "I was tending to the plants. I was not eavesdropping."

"Look at me, girl."

Valerian raised her face and met the full force of a slap. She gasped, her hand going to her cheek.

" 'Tis bad enough to spy, but you lie as well."

Valerian barely heard the words. Rage such as she had never known boiled up within her. She dropped her hand and met Kate's eyes straight on, putting the full force of her anger in her gaze. She bared her teeth, only vaguely aware that a purely animal growl rumbled from her throat.

Beth grabbed Kate's arm, trying to pull her away, but Kate stood frozen, her face draining of color at the ferocity of Valerian's response, so unexpected from a servant. Very faintly, she began to shake.

Valerian wanted to slap her, to spit on her, to drag her dirty hands down her face and over her pristine bodice, and knew even as she wished it, even as her eyes told Kate that she would tear her to shreds, that she would not. She was better than that.

Like a dog who is not willing to make good on his threat, she was now stuck wondering how to end the confrontation. She stepped forward, purposefully increasing the volume of her growls, and Kate showed her first hint of good sense and stepped back. Step by step Valerian intimidated her out of the greenhouse, helped along by Beth's hand on Kate's arm.

She was about to slam shut the door when the worst happened. Both Paul and Nathaniel appeared behind the two women.

"Thank heavens!" Beth cried, dropping Kate's arm and grasping now onto the baron's. "This horrid creature, stop her, she is completely mad—"

Valerian dropped her growl and turned her narrowed eyes on Nathaniel.

Nathaniel patted Beth's hand where it clung to his jacket and interrupted her hysterical babble. "She looks to be completely in control of herself. I am certain you were in no danger."

Kate turned to him at that, regaining her boldness at the

arrival of a champion. "She is a lying little sneak, and dared to threaten me when I caught her at it. You must dismiss her immediately."

"That would be a trifle difficult, as she is not a member of my staff."

Valerian glared at him. Why did he not go along with the assumption that she was a servant? She had told him that she did not want to meet his friends! He could not mean to reveal their relationship, especially not here, not like this.

"You have had the good fortune, Kate," Nathaniel continued, "of making the acquaintance of the local healer."

Valerian exhaled in relief, although the feeling vanished when Paul added his own comments.

"And the resident witch," Paul said. "You should count yourself lucky if all she did was threaten you. She could have done much worse, you may rely upon it."

Both women immediately crossed themselves and then made the hand symbol for defense against the evil eye. Valerian rolled her eyes, stepped back, and shut the greenhouse door in their faces.

There was an immediate babble of female voices, overlaid with the deep, patronizing tones of men trying to soothe and calm. She stomped down the greenhouse to the hand pump and washed her hands, then set to work scraping the now-black resin from the poppy pods.

Moments later Valerian heard Nathaniel not so gently direct Paul to return the ladies to the house. The door opened, and his measured footsteps approached where she worked, her back to him. She scraped the knife-load of resin off into a vial. "You could have gone along with what she first thought," she said without turning.

"And that would have been better?"

He put his hand on the small of her back, the heavy, comforting weight of it going straight to her gut. She turned, breaking the contact.

"Why did you come here and risk a confrontation?" he asked. "You said you would not."

She made a gesture towards the plants, not meeting his eyes. "I had to."

His hand nudged her chin up so she had to look at him, then his fingers brushed lightly over her cheek where Kate had slapped her. She was undone by the compassion she saw there.

"I did lie to her, you know," she said. "I was eavesdropping, and quite intentionally."

"And I suppose you threatened her, too."

"I wanted to rip her eyes out even before she caught me spying."

"Why?"

A simple question, and such an ugly answer. "Because! Because I was jealous."

That drew a laugh from him, but her glare quickly stopped it. Or at least stopped any audible chuckles. His eyes danced most suspiciously.

"I am not as good-natured about your guests as I led you to believe," she said. "I am not just jealous of her, scrawny little Kate in her garish dresses. I am jealous of the lot of them, of the time you spend in their company. I wish none of them had ever come!" There. Now she had done it. Aunt Theresa's good advice all thrown to the devil.

"All this time you have claimed to have spent deworming children and dosing coughs, you truly were mooning over my absence, then?"

"Well, not precisely. Worms must be dealt with, but it was you I thought of while I did it."

His kiss was as sudden as the slap, but a hundred times more gentle. One moment she was debasing herself with a display of neediness and jealousy, and the next she was being held tight in his arms.

Just as suddenly he pushed her away, although holding her steady by her shoulders. "We cannot do this here."

Valerian blinked around her at the glass walls. No, not the best of locations for a tryst. "I did not want to make you feel guilty for spending time with your friends," she said, back on what had become a safer topic.

He looked at her quizzically. "My guilt or lack thereof is my own responsibility. You cannot make me feel it if I do not agree it is warranted."

She thought a moment, thinking it sounded like something Aunt Theresa would say. "I believe that makes a certain sense," she admitted, then moved forward in his arms until she could lean her cheek against his chest and hear his heart beating beneath her ear. "You know, I thought this would all be much easier than it is," she said.

"All what?" he asked into her hair.

"Having a lover. I want you to see the best of me, and yet somehow it is the petty and insecure part that comes out. I grow selfish of you. I want more of you than you can give. I have all the generosity and reason of a two-year-old where you are concerned."

"Perhaps it would have been better if I had never noticed you, and left you to your worms and boils, if this is causing you such misery."

She shook her head in fierce denial. She could not explain to him the importance of this joyful torture. It was life to her, when all else was turning to death. "I would not trade this for the world." Aunt Theresa's cautions not to press him for commitments or declarations came back to her at that admission, which she knew to be too much, too soon. "It is a marvelous chance to learn about men, after all," she said to cover herself.

"I hope I do not discover you poised with dissecting knife in hand above my helpless body some night."

"Rest assured, I would drug you first. You would not feel a thing."

"All in the name of science," he said, and did not resist when she pulled away.

"Of course. And now, dear sir, I truly must finish my work here. I have no desire to stay and risk another meeting with the charming Kate." Which was only partly the truth. She had been away from Aunt Theresa all morning, and it was time she got back, much as she wanted to stay in his arms come Kate or Paul or Hades himself.

"Would you like a chance to meet her on equal ground?"

"A duel? Nathaniel, how delightful of you to suggest it! Do you think I would do better with swords or pistols?"

He smiled. "We are to have a masked ball. The gentry of the entire district is to be invited. I thought you might enjoy attending, as a pirate with both sword and pistols if you wish." He raised a brow at her. "You could tell yourself it was purely an educational experience. I know you are above such motives as revenge, curiosity, or hedonistic pleasure. Not that I believe there is much pleasure to be found at a ball, but it has been my experience that women feel differently."

"I truly do not want another confrontation with her," Valerian said more seriously.

"Your face will be concealed, my dear. No one will know who you are. You can disappear before the unmasking."

Her instincts told her it was a bad idea. She would be stepping quite beyond her station to attend and opening herself to all manner of ridicule if discovered.

But if she went, she could show Kate that Nathaniel preferred another's company, could drive out any illusions the woman had that he could want to marry her.

And perhaps there would never be another chance to attend such a party. For all that she had always claimed to have no desire to live that sort of life, honesty compelled her to admit she was curious. For a moment, her head was filled with candles and music and swirling colors. She saw herself with her hair piled high, a black mask concealing her features, moving amongst the lot of them as if she belonged. And perhaps she could, for one night.

She smiled up at him. "It sounds splendid."

"I do not know what he was thinking," Valerian said, and dropped heavily into the chair by the fire. "I do not know what *I* was thinking, to have agreed to go."

"I am not entirely certain that this is a good idea," Theresa said from the opposite chair, a blanket up over her legs. Her stout health had deteriorated to gauntness, and her skin was taking on a yellow tone, but she seemed happiest trying to take part in day-to-day life, so Valerian had ceased encouraging her to stay in bed.

"You are the one who kept saying I should have the chance to go to balls and parties. I had thought you would take his side in this."

"I did not mean for you to sneak in by disguise, as if you were a secret to be hidden."

"It is a fancy-dress ball."

Theresa snorted. "You know what I mean."

Valerian picked at the end of her braid. "I confess, though, I am a bit curious. I have after all never been to a ball before." She looked up at her aunt, and saw her wry smile. "You are not going to say 'I told you so!' are you? I could not stand it if you did."

"Certainly not. I have more restraint than that."

Valerian narrowed her eyes at her aunt, hearing the faint whisper of smothered laughter. "But perhaps I will not go. I have nothing to wear."

"That, at least, I may be able to help you with. Go pull the chest from beneath my bed."

"Your special box?"

"Yes, that one."

Valerian went to the bed and knelt on the hard floor, peering under the bed at the shadows and dark shapes. At last she located the long, low wooden chest, and dragged it forth by the tarnished brass handle on the end. Theresa got up and slowly made her way over to the bed, sitting down on its edge with an audible sigh.

"There now, open it up," she said. "There are other things in there you should see as well."

Valerian lifted the lid, and was overwhelmed by the scent of the herbs used to keep moths away. She had only seen Theresa open the box a few times before, to place inside keepsakes that might perish if kept loose in the cottage. A few of Charmaine's baby clothes were inside, as well as a drawing of Valerian's mother, Emmeline.

At Theresa's instruction she lifted these out, as well as a small bundle of letters, one of Valerian's first carved animals, and several other items. It was soon apparent that the chest had two compartments, and Valerian lifted out the wooden tray to reveal what lay beneath.

"Good lord!" Valerian swore, gazing at what was revealed.

"You would make a fine forest maiden in that. Or perhaps a druidic priestess or elven queen."

Valerian reached out a hand to gently touch the emerald silk gown folded and half-crushed from its long stay in the bottom of the chest. Jet beads picked out a pattern of trailing ivy across the bodice, narrowing down to the waist. She lifted the gown from the box and saw that one tendril of ivy continued down the front of the gown, then widened like spilled water to splash around the hem.

"It was the dress I wore the night your mother and I fled London, the night our own mother was killed," Theresa explained. "I was never certain why I kept it." She took one of the creases of silk between her fingers. "It will need a good airing, that is for certain. And the attentions of an iron."

"Are you certain you want me to wear this?"

Theresa raised an expressive eyebrow at her. "Do you think I am saving it for a party invitation myself? Now, being a masquerade, we might baste a bit of real ivy over the hem—"

"Gracious, no! I can hardly see fit to wear the gown, much less destroy it with sewn-on vines."

Theresa shrugged. "Then I suppose we could twine the ivy in your hair. And a mask, we will have to make a mask. . . . But that can wait for the moment. Here now, lay the gown over the table. There is something more I need to show you."

Valerian did as bid, and returned to the trunk. Two velvet pouches sat in bottom corners of the trunk. She knelt down and lifted the nearest, feeling the unmistakable clink of coins. Her eyes were wide as she handed the bag up to Theresa.

"This is what is left of the gold your mother and I took that night, from the hiding place at our home." She opened the drawstring and poured the coins into her lap, one coin sliding off to thunk on the floor. "There is enough here for you to establish yourself in another town, if the need ever arises. You can disappear as thoroughly as your mother and I did."

"It has lasted all these years?"

"Well, the bag was considerably fuller when I started. I purchased the cottage and furnishings, and when times have been hard I have dipped into it. But beyond that, there has not been much in Greyfriars worth spending it upon, compared to saving it to save our lives, if necessary."

Valerian helped her scoop the coins back into the pouch and replaced it in the trunk.

"Now, that other bag."

This one was lighter, but by its feel Valerian suspected she knew what it held: jewelry.

"When your mother was born, your grandfather gave your grandmother a gift. He gave her one when I was born as well—I long ago passed it on to Charmaine, who sold it so that she could marry Howard and set up a shop and home with him. You will not want to wear this to the ball, but it is time that you knew it was here, and knew it was yours."

Valerian bit her lips as Theresa drew the sparkling sapphire and diamond necklace out of the bag. "Oh my," she said on an indrawn breath. Valerian took the necklace, draping it across her fingers, the facets of the gems catching the light.

"And let us not forget the earbobs."

Valerian spared only a glance for the matching earrings, astounded still by the jewels she held in her hand. For the first time, she caught a glimpse of the life her aunt spoke of when she talked of her youth. "I did not quite imagine. . . ."

"Your grandmother had chests filled with such baubles. As I have said, mistressing can be a lucrative way of life."

"Not that it did her much good in the end."

Theresa shrugged. "No, I suppose not."

Valerian wrapped the necklace around her wrist, admiring it, then let it slide off into a pile in her hand, and gave it back to Theresa to return to the pouch. "Perhaps it will not be so bad, masquerading as one of the nobility, if only for a night."

Theresa smiled and patted Valerian on the hand. "There, I knew you were a Harrow at heart."

Chapter Twenty

"Oscar! You are not helping."

Oscar continued to cry like a baby and tucked his head yet further into her hair.

She tried once more to remove him from the crook of her neck, and got her hair pulled as a reward for her efforts. It felt very much as if there was a raven claw entangled in one of her braids, and lord knew he had already yanked several tendrils free of their mooring in his efforts to remain close to her, under the protection of her hood.

"I told you to stay at home, if you will recall."

A gust of wind drove rain onto her already-wet face, and she held tight to the hood of her cloak. It was little wonder Oscar preferred to hide in her hair than ride on her shoulder in this weather. She herself had given more than one thought to staying home, safe and dry and warm, but recognized her reluctance for a failing of courage, and so forced herself to follow through on what had been planned for over two weeks. Tonight was the night of the masked ball.

The cloud-darkened twilight was settling into full night when the lights of Raven Hall at last came into view. Her dress and accessories were carefully packed in the basket over her arm, waiting to be donned in the dry privacy of James and Judith's quarters off the kitchen. They were the only people she would trust with the knowledge that she would be attending tonight's festivities, and she had rejected all of Nathaniel's offers of assistance in preparation.

These past two weeks, Nathaniel had not let more than two days go by without seeing her, however brief the visit. With the cottage off-limits because of Theresa's illness, they had often walked together to the cliff and sat watching the ravens and the water, sometimes talking, but many times sitting silent, side by side, sharing warmth and what Valerian wanted to think of as a companionship of the spirit.

A companionship of the spirit only, for certainly they had not been sharing a companionship of the body. She could feel his desire for her, could see it in his eyes, yet he did no more than kiss her, always breaking off when the heat of passion began to rise.

His reasons were a mystery, and one that she did not care to solve. If she asked why, he might tell her, and she did not think she could stand it if he said he had thought better of their arrangement. She did not want to hear that he was considering marrying Kate, or that he had realized that he belonged with his friends and family and not with someone like her.

The Raven Hall kitchens were a mad flurry of activity. The moment she stepped inside and pulled off her hood, Oscar released his hold on her and flew a ragged course over the heads of screeching kitchen workers, their hands flapping to keep him away, cries of "Bat! Bat!" sending scullery maids into yowls of terror.

Oscar landed on a convenient perch in front of Hairy the dog's wheel. "Eee-diot! Eee-diot!" he cawed, and Hairy set up a wild series of howling barks, his measured lope becoming a mad dash within the turning wheel. The boy basting the meat on the spit cried out as he was sprayed with hot drippings, the large roast spinning madly.

"Silence!" James roared, and banged a rolling pin against the central work table. "Oscar! Hairy! Quiet, both of you!"

Hairy snarled and snapped in answer. Valerian made haste to recover Oscar. "You are a very naughty bird, Oscar. There will be no biscuits for you," she scolded.

Into the newly fallen silence of the kitchen Oscar sent up a loud wail of distress. "Pooooor hungry bird," he cried.

The tension in the room dissolved into laughter. Most of the staff were at least passingly familiar with Oscar. It had been his sudden and unexpected arrival amidst stressful preparations that had set them off.

"There now," Judith said, brushing her hands off on her apron and coming towards Valerian. "No need to berate the poor creature." She took a scrap of dough off one of the tables and held it out to Oscar.

"He is a shameless fake, and well you know it," Valerian said, watching Oscar gulp down the treat. Around them the sounds of a kitchen at work gradually built up again, and Judith led her out the door to their cozy quarters.

"I will come back in a few minutes to help you with your lacing," Judith said. "Will you need anything else?"

"Perhaps a bottle of whiskey."

Judith raised her eyebrows in question.

"I would have to be drunk to think any of this a good idea."

Judith gave her a knowing smile. "Sometimes the human spirit cries out to do stupid things, especially when there is a man involved."

Valerian made a face. "How reassuring. Go on, get back out there before James clobbers someone with that rolling pin."

Judith ducked out the door, and Valerian gave an exaggerated sigh and sat on a stool. This was a monstrous mistake. She should be back at the cottage, reading by the fire, watching over Theresa. A week ago Valerian had more or less decided that she would not attend the ball, for Theresa had seemed to have grown so weak as to be approaching death.

Then, for no reason she could tell, her aunt had rallied, and appeared to be doing better than she had for a month. Yesterday Theresa had wound all of Valerian's freshly washed hair onto scraps of cloth, tying them off at her scalp. She had put the finishing touches on the black mask that sat now in the basket, covered in iridescent black and green bird feathers. She had even arranged for Charmaine's husband to make Valerian a new pair of black shoes, without letting disapproving Charmaine know the exact purpose of the footwear.

That last had not been too difficult. Charmaine was seven months pregnant now, and her mind was almost wholly occupied with the child growing within her. What little attention she had left for others was occupied with convincing herself that her mother would be there to see the birth. Charmaine visited the cottage to be examined by her mother, and to discuss the signs and symptoms of her pregnancy, but would not allow Valerian to touch her. She had let it be known that she trusted only her mother to see her through this.

For her own part, Valerian was just as happy with that. If she did touch Charmaine, she might confirm what she had dimly suspected the day they were told of the pregnancy: that all was not well with the babe. It was her own exercise in denial not to confirm that, but she had hopes that whatever was wrong had righted itself. She feared even her abilities to heal were not strong enough to save a baby that grew wrong in the womb. She would deal with the birth, and with Charmaine's preference for her mother, when the time came.

She stood and went to look at herself in the small mirror on the wall, surveying the damage done by wind, rain, and raven. Unwound from its rags this afternoon, her hair had become a nest of snaky black ringlets. She had then made the mistake of running her comb through them, with the result that the compact curls became a wild froth of hair that dwarfed her in its immensity. She had gazed upon herself in horror.

"Sit down and let me handle this," Theresa had said.

"You are not strong enough. No one is strong enough. You will be devoured," Valerian had moaned, feeling hot and cold flushes of panicked vanity. It was a new sensation, and not welcome.

"Nonsense. Sit."

And bit by bit, Theresa had shaped the wild shrubbery of her hair into a complex work of art, composed of braids and knots and trailing ringlets. Much of the coiffure was still in place, but there was a disheveled look to it now. She tried to tuck escaping wisps back into place, but they refused to be captured.

She shrugged at herself in the mirror. It was a masquerade, after all. No one would know that this was not quite her intended appearance. In her basket along with the dress and shoes were several vines of ivy that she had thought to wrap neatly round her head in a coronet of sorts. Perhaps an effect a little closer to nature would better suit her costume. With Oscar watching and vines in hand, she set to work.

* * *

Nathaniel greeted guests in the grey robes of an abbot, the design stolen from a portrait of one of the long-dead abbots who had once been head of Grey Friars Abbey, now Raven Hall. He could not fault the robes for their comfort, but he still felt half a fool for wearing them.

His older guests seemed no happier than he to be playing fancy dress, and several of those more advanced in years had done no more than add last-century details to their clothes, and call themselves images from Rubens or Van Dyck. Or perhaps the clothes *were* from the last century—Nathaniel got the distinct feeling that times did not change quickly in Cumbria.

The younger guests were a different matter entirely. Persian princesses, shepherds and shepherdesses, pilgrims and Gothic abbesses, and more nymphs than could fill an Arcadian forest swarmed happily through his home. His own house guests had decked themselves out as a troupe of wandering gypsies.

A quartet of fifth-rate musicians scraped out what passed for music in the great hall, the only room large enough for dancing. Other rooms had been opened for card playing, sitting and chatting, and for the buffet. He had no doubt that his house would be crowded well past midnight. Old Uncle George had been more likely to entertain men his own age than to invite their wives and daughters for an evening of dancing and flirting, and so this novel invitation to the hall to meet the new baron had been met with enthusiasm in the district. His neighbors were starved for a good look at both the hall and himself.

Coaches were still arriving, a short line of them waiting to let their passengers off in front of the door. He stood in the open doorway, watching torches flicker in the wind and rain, and began to wonder if Valerian had changed her mind and stayed home.

"Warrington! Or I suppose it is Ravenall now," a man said, clasping his hand. "I almost did not recognize you."

Nathaniel drew his attention back from the dark night. "Good lord! Lord Carlyle, this is an unexpected pleasure." Nathaniel vigorously shook the man's hand. "Paul did not tell me that you were expected."

"That could be because I was not. Expected, that is. My son did not see fit to tell me where he had disappeared to." Lord Carlyle gave a smile that promised a dressing-down for Paul, for all that he was a grown man now. "And I see that I have surprised you in the midst of an entertainment."

Nathaniel waved away the festive scene. "It is my introduction to the neighbors, and not entirely my idea."

"Becoming fond of banishment and isolation, were you?"

"It has its advantages," he said, and then in a lighter tone, "You are welcome to join the party, if you wish. There are extra masks. But let me have a room prepared for you, so you may refresh yourself after your journey."

Lord Carlyle waved off the offer. "Your staff has enough to contend with. I will share with Paul for the moment."

"As you wish. And may I say, it truly is good to see you, sir."

Nathaniel sent Lord Carlyle off with a footman. Paul would faint when he saw his father. Nathaniel had always liked Lord Carlyle, for while the man had stringent rules of conduct, they were based on his own sense of human decency rather than the teachings of the church or the appearances of society. He was an exacting man, but fair. Unfortunately, Paul saw rather more of the exacting side of the man than the other.

It was another half hour before the last of the carriages deposited its occupants at the front steps, and then at last he was free to roam the crowd and seek out Valerian. He was hoping that she had sought out her own surreptitious entrance, since he had not seen her at the door.

It was getting so that even a day without her company was unbearable to him, the time he spent with his friends resented as it took him away from her. Each time he saw her he longed to take her back to his bed and make love to her. If his bed were not possible, the cave would do, or the bushes, maybe an open field—even the cliff top was beginning to seem feasible.

And yet, as much as he wanted to hike her skirts and take her the moment he lay eyes on her, something held him back. It had been one thing to spend a whole day with her and have making love be a part of it. But now, when they only had a few hours at a time, there was something distasteful to the idea. He did not want her to feel that he came to her only for sex, when she meant so much more to him than that.

He kept searching for her in the crowded rooms. She had not told him what she would be wearing, but she should be easy to spot. Her costume would undoubtedly be one of the more simple ones, likely a milkmaid or some such as would be within her means to create. Whatever it was, he knew he would be proud to have her on his arm.

Valerian peered through the crack of the door at the room where the buffet had been set up. Guests had already devoured a considerable portion of the spread, and servants would be coming soon to replace empty platters with fresh delicacies. Judith had taken her from her quarters in a roundabout fashion, to avoid going back through the kitchen and being seen by staff.

"You had best go now," Judith said from behind her.

"I do not belong out there. What if one of the staff recognizes me?"

Judith nudged her aside and peered out the crack herself,

then eyed Valerian. "First off, you are dressed as fine, or finer, than most of that lot. Half of them are pretending to be farm folk to begin with. And second, none of the staff here will recognize you, or give away the secret if they did. I myself would not know it was you if I had not laced you into that gown myself."

Valerian lightly touched the mask on her face. It covered her from her forehead to the end of her nose, and feathers swept down to cover her cheeks almost to her jaw. All that was visible was her eyes, darkened by the shadows cast by the mask, and her mouth, which she had stained red.

Footsteps and voices approached from behind them. "Go, now!" Judith hissed, and opening the door gave Valerian a push out into the room and directly into the path of a gypsy.

"Your pardon, miss!" the man said, as he fumbled the plate of food in his hand, reaching with the other to steady her.

" 'Twas my fault, sir."

"Nonsense. Accidents are never the fault of a beautiful woman."

Valerian glanced up at him, frowning for a moment until she placed the voice. Christopher, Kate's brother. She had heard his voice on the night they arrived, when Kate had thought her a servant. "That is most kind of you, sir," she murmured, looking down and pulling from his grasp. She started to move away.

"Did your curiosity get the better of you?" he asked.

She stopped, fear of discovery quivering in her belly. "I beg your pardon?"

He gestured with his head towards the door. "Taking an unescorted tour of the hall, doing a little snooping? Not that I blame you." He came up beside her and took her elbow, leading her out to another room where people milled about, chatting. She could hear the strains of tortured music from the great hall.

" 'Tis not every day one gets invited to Raven Hall," she said.

"My own curiosity has been eating at me. Do you suppose we might be wicked, and explore together?" he asked, leaning close.

She looked at him in puzzlement until it dawned on her that he assumed she did not know he was staying at the hall. Why, the lying lecher! "Ah, but the great fun of wickedness is that it can only be indulged in small doses," she said, giving him a flirtatious smile. "Give it free rein, and it becomes rather a bore, do you not think? Now please excuse me, but I truly must speak with my . . . cousin." She turned her back on him and walked away towards a pair of dowdy nymphs, her shaking hands belying her calm and confident front.

The nymphs watched her approach with a wariness apparent even through their masks, but with Christopher watching she had no choice but to join them and continue the charade. "I wanted to come tell you both that you look lovely in those costumes," she said when she reached them. *Pretend that you belong here*, she told herself. *No one will know you do not unless you tell them. And stop shaking! Breathe!*

The two young women flushed, their hands fluttered, and at last one of them spoke. "You are too kind."

"Indeed," the other said. " 'Tis plain that yours is the most striking figure in the room." She paused, and glanced at her companion, who gave an infinitesimal shrug. "I am afraid that we neither can guess your identity, although you seem acquainted with ours. Do you care to give us a hint?"

"And spoil the purpose of the masquerade? No, you will have to wait until the unmasking," she said, and smiled sincerely at the two. *They are as nervous as I!* She saw that Christopher was deep in conversation with another man, and for the moment at least paying her no attention. "Now do excuse me, I must find my . . . brother."

She slipped out of the room and into the great hall, a smile playing on her lips. She was still nervous, but she was beginning to think that this evening might not turn out so badly after all. Tonight she was not Valerian Bright, healer cum witch, pariah of Greyfriars, forever cautious of her words and actions. Tonight she was the Lady in Green, mysterious and "striking."

A familiar titter of nearby laughter drew her gaze. Standing a few feet away, yet another masked male gypsy had his head bent down towards a curvaceous country girl, who was giggling at whatever words he whispered close to her ear. Even from behind Valerian knew that giggle, and knew as well that the clothes the girl wore were her best. Her eyes widened at the realization that she was not the only changeling in the house tonight, nor perhaps the only woman sleeping with her betters. The giggle belonged to Gwendolyn Miller.

The gypsy was known to her as well, and seemed to feel her eyes on him, for he turned and looked directly at her, his gaze sweeping over her hair and mask, taking in her dress, then her ivy-tangled hair again. He tilted his head slightly in consideration, and to help him decide just who it was who saw him dallying with a village lass, she gave him her wolf's grin. She saw his eyes widen behind his mask.

She turned her back on him and surveyed the hall for a glimpse of Nathaniel. She did not know what mischief Paul was up to with Gwen, and truly did not care except to take pleasure in the knowledge that he was a hypocrite for decrying Nathaniel's involvement with her.

She moved through the people gathered round the dancers, beginning to notice the way the eyes of the men skimmed over her half-exposed breasts. It was a new experience, to be seen by strangers as desirable, but at the same time that it pleased her it made her vaguely uncomfortable. She caught several pairs of male eyes assessing her, young, old, half in the grave, it made no difference. It was starting to set her nerves on edge. She wished her gown covered her breasts completely, a way that she never felt with Nathaniel.

The sense of being watched intensified, and began to send her hair crawling up the back of her neck. She looked around, her vision hampered by the mask, but could see no specific person watching her. She moved further through the crowd, and then all but bumped into Kate talking to Nathaniel, her hand on his forearm.

She immediately made an about-face and hurried back in the direction of the sitting room, her heart thumping in her chest, mentally berating herself for her lack of courage on all fronts. *Damn, damn, damn!* she swore to herself. She should have spoken to Kate, should have taken Nathaniel away from her, but all she had been able to think was that Kate would know who she was and expose her.

She passed a man who stood staring at her with only a plain silk mask upon his face. She gave him a long, level stare as she went by, warning him off.

She looked about for someplace inconspicuous where she could wait, feeling nervous as a rabbit. Seeking safety in the shadows, she went to the far corner of the room and placed herself in front of a tall alcoved window, half-hidden by the curtains, and pretended to stare out into the night as she watched the reflections in the glass of the guests milling behind her.

Several minutes went by, and then the plain-masked face appeared above her shoulder. Her whole body went tense as her eyes met his in the glass. She saw his hand rise up and reach out, as if to touch her.

She could not bear him to do so. She turned suddenly,

and met his gaze. He looked into her eyes for a long moment, standing barely a foot away, and then it was as if something within him collapsed, visible in the pain that filled his eyes.

"Your pardon, miss," he said, and with a short nod of apology, he disappeared back into the crowd.

That was enough. Kate or no Kate, she was not going to do this alone any longer. She marched back toward the great hall just as Nathaniel and Kate came through the doorway.

"Baron Ravenall, do forgive me," she said in her most aristocratic tone. "But my grandmother has insisted that I find you and fetch you back to her side. She has several tales to share with you of her childhood here in the district. Why, her memory goes back nearly a century! Would you mind terribly? She has been so looking forward to talking to you."

She watched as recognition came to him, and his eyes flicked in amazement over her beaded gown. "I would be delighted," he said, and then spoke to Kate, "You will excuse me?"

Kate's head jerked once as she realized she was being abandoned. "Certainly," she said, smiling stiffly. "But will you not introduce me to your charming friend before you go?"

"Kate, darling," Valerian chided, "You know the rules of the masquerade. What would be the point if we went about introducing one another? But I do thank you for releasing his lordship. Kindness is obviously a trait you share with your chivalrous brother."

Kate's eyebrows rose above her mask, but she was too surprised to speak.

Valerian took Nathaniel's arm and led him away, through the buffet room, and out the door that the servants used to reach the kitchens. "Grandmother grew weary of the noise," she explained, and dragged him through another door into an empty room where they would not be interrupted by either guests or servants, and then she dropped down onto a settee, removed her mask, and released an enormous sigh.

Nathaniel remained standing, looking down at her. "It truly is you under there. I half-wondered if it might not be someone else."

"Surely a dress cannot make such a difference. I have recognized any number of your guests, and I think I would know you even with a hangman's hood over your head."

"I do hope that is not a prediction."

"Merely an expression of my sentiments towards you at the moment."

He removed his mask and sat down beside her, stretching out his long legs and crossing them at the ankle, his thigh pressed against her own. "Whatever have I done?" he asked, lifting a hand to play with a strand of ivy that trailed over her shoulder.

"Left me to defend myself against that mob while you cavorted with that horrid Kate."

She watched him look over her costume once again. "You cannot tell me that you honestly think I enjoyed her company," he said, sounding distracted, his eyes lingering on the low neckline of the dress. "I have been looking everywhere for you, and trying to shake her at every opportunity. Where did you find such a gown?"

She smoothed the silk over her thighs, enjoying the feel of it beneath her palms, and feeling slightly mollified by his apparent inability to keep Kate present in his mind. "It was Aunt Theresa's."

"So your aunt has not always been a healer in the woods."

"No."

She felt his fingertips along her cheek and turned her face into his hand.

"I am sorry I could not find you sooner," he said softly. "I had feared you might have changed your mind and not come."

"Promise you will not leave me alone out there."

"Everyone will wonder who you are, if you remain at my side," he teased, his lips brushing her cheek.

"Let them wonder."

He kissed her softly on the lips, then looked into her eyes, his hazel ones gentle. "I would not be angry with you if you chose to leave. It is clear enough that you have not been enjoying yourself."

A twist of returning jealousy went through her. Perhaps he wanted to be left alone to pursue Kate. "And forgo my one chance to play at being a lady?" she said lightly. "I think not."

He stood then, and grasped her hands, pulling her quickly up from her seat. "I was hoping you would say that. Even the inanity of a masquerade ball will be bearable, knowing I have you hidden by my side."

She turned away to take up her mask once again, and the better to hide her thoughts. He made it sound as if it was the amusement of playing a trick on his guests that pleased him more than her company. She tied the mask into place and tried to push the thought from her mind, detesting this suspicion and doubt that had her reading a dozen meanings into the simplest of sentences. It was simply not rational, and surely not fair.

He escorted her back to the party, and she soon discovered that the ball was much more pleasurable at Nathaniel's side than when she had braved it alone. She did not wonder where to put her hands, for she held his arm, and she did not have to avoid over-forward males, for she was clearly taken. She no longer wondered where to place herself in the room, for Nathaniel led their movements from guest to guest, starting and ending conversations, and keeping them to topics that she could comment upon if she chose.

Once she relaxed, she found that she was not having such an awful time, after all. The costumes were entertaining, the food delicious, the music enthusiastic if occasionally out of tune even to her untrained ears, and the guests from the local area were not truly so different from the folk of Greyfriars. Or perhaps it was simply easier to see them as people no different from herself when they wore masks and silly costumes, and displayed some of the same social awkwardness that she herself felt.

It was a quarter of twelve, quickly approaching the hour of the unmasking, when Valerian spied Judith, poking her head from behind a door, beckoning frantically with one hand. She excused herself from Nathaniel and the middle-aged couple with whom they were talking, Nathaniel giving her a questioning look which she answered with a glance at the clock on the mantel. He nodded at her silent excuse, knowing she meant to avoid the unmasking, and knowing that she had agreed to meet him later in his rooms.

When she got to the door, Judith all but yanked her behind it. "I have been trying to catch your attention for the past five minutes!"

"There is still a quarter of an hour until midnight. I was in no danger of being discovered."

Judith shook her head in vehement denial. "It was not that I came for. It is Charmaine, she is in labor."

"Now? It is too soon!" Her heart thumped. She followed Judith down to her quarters.

"Howard!" Valerian called upon seeing Charmaine's

husband, pacing the floor in front of the hearth. "Tell me what has happened."

He stared at her uncomprehendingly, and she realized she still wore the feathered mask. She tore it impatiently from her face. "Yes, it is I."

He seemed to gather his wits. "The cramps came upon her suddenly, waking her. She sent me for her mother, but . . ."

"I know. She could not come."

"Mrs. Storrow had me take your basket of herbs and sent me here to fetch you. I have a horse."

Valerian spared a look for her workaday clothes on the back of the chair where they lay, but there was no time to don them. She gave a silent apology to the lovely green silk she wore, and followed Howard out the side door to the waiting horse. There was no time to waste if Charmaine had gone into labor two months early.

Chapter Twenty-one

Whatever magic the masquerade held for Nathaniel left with Valerian. From the moment he had seen her green-gowned figure sweeping toward him, she had caught his senses in an enchantment. The candles had glowed brighter, the atrocious music had sounded sweeter, the wine had been more intoxicating—and all because she was there with him.

Valerian in country rags was lovely as the twilight.

Valerian in silk was an eclipse, beautiful and alien at once. Until, that is, she had dragged him away, pulled off her mask, and plopped herself onto the settee with that familiar enthusiasm she had for a soft cushion. Then the strangeness of her dress had passed, and he could be easy with her and touch her without fear that she would slap him for his effrontery.

He had made it his quest to entertain her as they moved through the crowd. Knowing her own curiosity about these people that she only ever saw from afar, he had taken pleasure in asking them questions and listening to their answers, trying to draw from them hints of who they were—not their names or positions, but their characters. He knew instinctively that that was what would most interest Valerian, and much to his surprise he found that his guests were not entirely the boring lot of self-satisfied, bird-chasing country squires that he had expected.

True, they were not London sophisticates, but they expressed a sincere pleasure at this chance to meet him and spoke warmly of his uncle. It was easy to see that they were flattered by the questions he asked, and surprised by the interest he showed in them. They were a kinder, less polished version of London society, a version he found he could bear with greater grace than that in the city.

Valerian, though quiet, had seemed happy to be there with him. When she did speak, he would watch the faces of his guests, and see how they softened or warmed at her words. She had a way of setting people at their ease, when she chose.

But now she had left, and he waited with growing impatience for the evening to end so that he could join her. The unmasking came and went with laughter and drinks, and then at last the first few older couples left, then a few others followed, and Nathaniel quietly directed the servants to begin a surreptitious cleanup as the quartet called a final dance.

At two in the morning, the last group departed, and Nathaniel went quickly to his rooms. To his dismay, although not completely to his surprise, she was not there waiting as they had agreed. Of late she had seemed more cautious than he of the hours they stole to be together.

Disappointed, and unwilling yet to face his empty room, he headed to the library for a brandy. A healthy fire burned in the grate, inviting him to one of the chairs pulled close, but the brandy decanter was not on the tray with the others.

"Are you looking for this?" a weary voice asked from the shadows of one of the chairs by the fire, a hand out to the side dangling the crystal decanter by its neck, firelight glinting through the cut surfaces.

His empty glass in hand, Nathaniel came around to see who had spoken. "Sir!" he said in surprise. Lord Carlyle was the last person he would have expected. "I had thought you retired long ago."

Lord Carlyle lifted the decanter, and filled Nathaniel's glass before refilling his own. "I do not think that sleep will be coming easily to me this night."

"Is there something amiss?" Nathaniel asked, feeling a stirring of anxiety, and belatedly wondering what had drawn the man so far to visit his son. He sat down in the opposite chair. "I do not wish to intrude, but is there some bad news that you have brought to share with Paul?"

Lord Carlyle lifted his eyebrows and gave a laugh that was little more than an exhalation of air. "No, all is well at home, although Paul took my arrival rather poorly all the same."

Nathaniel waited. He could not recall ever seeing Lord Carlyle in this mood, and certainly never half-drunk.

"I could not find him in the crowd, and upon returning to his chamber. . . . Well, let us say that he was already entertaining company." Lord Carlyle tucked in his chin and looked at him meaningfully.

The man's meaning became clear. "Good lord."

"Yes, I believe his comment was something to that effect. I did, of course, make a hasty retreat."

Nathaniel imagined the aftermath that must have followed after Lord Carlyle left. He very much doubted that Paul had been able to finish what he had started. "You have only to ask for another room," he offered weakly.

"I did, and it awaits me even now. But for the moment, I prefer it here."

Nathaniel took a sip of his brandy, sensing that the tale was not finished. It would take more than catching Paul in flagrante delicto to send his father to the brandy and a sleepless night, he felt sure of it. Several minutes passed, and when Lord Carlyle spoke again, it was on such an unexpected topic that his wandering attention was caught in full.

"Who was the lady in green, the one with ivy wound through her hair?"

"Sir?"

"You could not have missed her."

"I believe she left before the unmasking," Nathaniel prevaricated.

"Damn," Lord Carlyle said under his breath, and after a long look into his glass drained what was left in the bottom. He reached again for the decanter.

"Why do you ask?"

"I do not know if I am sufficiently foxed to tell you that." He swirled the liquid in his glass, then set it on the side table with a clunk of glass on wood. "Hell, maybe I am."

Nathaniel remained silent, afraid that anything he said would stop the man from speaking. Anything that touched on Valerian, he wanted to hear.

"You will think me a damned fool, not that it matters. I mistook her for a woman I once knew, the first woman I ever loved."

Nathaniel sat forward, intrigued. "Will you tell me about that woman?"

Lord Carlyle's eyes settled on a point in time that only he could see. "She was a beautiful creature. Hair black as sin, eyes of a green to make you ache, and a bearing like she was a royal princess, which she would have been had circumstances been different." At Nathaniel's raised brow, he clarified. "She and her sister were both bastards of Charles II. Their mother was a widow, wealthy, and for a time one of his favored mistresses.

"I pursued her for months," he continued, "intending to make her my own mistress. And then, just as I won her, she was taken from me."

"How?" Nathaniel asked, caught up in the story.

"Her mother, in addition to being a former mistress to a king, was reputed to be a witch. As were her daughters. The mother made one dark prediction too many at just the wrong time, and she was killed. Her daughters fled for their lives, and that was the last I or anyone else ever saw of them."

An uncomfortable sensation was riding up Nathaniel's neck. "And the lady in green tonight, what was it that you found familiar?"

"Her hair, her chin. But most especially the dress. My Theresa wore one like it the night she fled. But it was not her, of course not—the woman tonight had blue eyes, not green, and was young enough to be Theresa's daughter."

"And what—" Nathaniel had to pause to take a swallow of brandy, for his throat had gone dry—"and what was her family name, this Theresa?"

"Harrow."

Harrow. Storrow. Not so very different. "And no one ever heard from either of the daughters?"

"Not a word. I wanted to go after Theresa, to help her to hide. To marry her, if doing so would give her protection. I thought myself in love with her, after all."

"What stopped you?"

"I thought that nothing would, but my brother more or less sat on me and talked to me of honor and the family, and my fiancée, God help her, until I relented. I think I wanted to be persuaded against it, truth be told. I was afraid of her, even as I loved her, and I was just realistic enough to wonder if giving up family and funds was worth pursuing a woman who might feel no more than amused tolerance for my sorry self. Still, I have never forgotten her. Never forgiven myself, either, for not doing more to help her."

Nathaniel considered for several minutes, but in the end knew what he had to say. "My lord, there is something I must tell you."

Lord Carlyle looked at him with barely any curiosity, still lost in his own memories, so Nathaniel spoke bluntly. "Theresa Harrow is living not two miles from this hall. It was her niece you saw in the green gown tonight."

Lord Carlyle sat up straight and turned wide eyes on Nathaniel. "She is here?"

"I have spoken with her. She goes by Storrow now, but it can only be the same woman." He looked at the stunned man, and knew that now was not the time to ask if he wished to see her. "We can talk again in the morning, after you have had time to think on this."

Lord Carlyle's attention focused inward, and Nathaniel barely heard his response, more sighed than voiced. "Aye, I shall do nothing but think on it."

Nathaniel was settling down to sleep in his own bed, longing for Valerian, when a piece of Lord Carlyle's story came back to hit him in the face. He sat up in the dark, and exclaimed aloud to the empty room. "Good God. Her grandfather was the bloody King of England!"

Chapter Twenty-two

"Keep her away from me!" Charmaine cried.

Valerian locked eyes with Howard. "Explain to her. I must be allowed to help."

Howard stood motionless, his eyes wide as he stared at his wife, writhing on the mattress, her brow being cooled by the wet rag in Alice Torrance's hand.

"Howard!" Alice commanded, evidently as frustrated as Valerian herself. "Do as Valerian says. Your wife will not listen to anyone but you."

Valerian flashed a look of gratitude to the woman. She had not expected help from that quarter.

Howard shuffled slowly over to the bed and tried to take Charmaine's hand, but she snatched it away and pointed her finger at his face. "You will not let her touch me, you know what unnatural forces are in her hands. You know, Howard!"

"Your mother cannot come, darling. She told me to fetch Valerian."

"I want my mother, not her," Charmaine cried.

"She cannot come," Howard said, his voice rising, spurred on by his fear for her.

"I want my mother! Go back and get her!"

"You cannot have her, Charmaine!" the normally gentle Howard shouted at last. "Shut up for once and listen to Valerian. She knows what to do."

All three women blinked at him, and a silence fell. Howard mumbled an apology, then beat a quick retreat from the room, the door shutting quietly behind him.

"I never knew he had it in him," Alice said. Valerian felt the woman's eyes turn to her, examining for the fourth or fifth time her bizarre outfit. Alice's voice hardened. "I do not trust you. I know the evil forces Charmaine speaks of are real, but you know the healing ways, and I cannot think that you would hurt your own kin. I will give you what help you need."

"Thank you." Even grudging assistance was more than she would have hoped for from the woman.

Valerian slowly approached the bed. "Charmaine, will you let me touch you?" she asked in her most soothing tones, the ones she used to lull people into trance.

"I wanted my mother with me," Charmaine complained, turning her face into her pillow.

"I know. I would have wanted her with me, as well. You are frightened and need comfort. You hurt and need healing."

Valerian waited while Charmaine made up her mind. Another contraction convulsed her body, making her cry out.

"Oh, go ahead," Charmaine gritted out as the pain faded. "You cannot make it any worse."

Valerian sat down on the edge of the bed and put her hand over Charmaine's belly, closing her eyes and gathering her thoughts to send her senses seeking for what was wrong, for what had caused the baby to come early.

She did not expect what she found.

The baby was not right. She caught a confused sense of two hearts, one of which did not beat, both within the same form. There were the wrong number of limbs, and yet it was just one body in Charmaine's womb, one body that even if it survived the birth, would not survive more than an hour or two in this world.

"Charmaine," Valerian said, "Listen to me. The baby must come now. You cannot keep it within you." Charmaine's body had chosen to abort the child, and it would be best to trust it. If it continued to grow, the birthing of it at full term might be fatal to Charmaine.

"It is too soon, it has not been nine months," Charmaine said, pleading in her voice. "Help me keep my baby, Valerian. Do whatever you have to, just let me keep my baby."

"I am sorry, Charmaine. It must be now."

Time moved slowly as Valerian and Alice sat with Charmaine, waiting for her body to go through the process of birth, the contractions still far apart. Dawn came, and then morning turned to afternoon, and still the baby did not come. Valerian lay her hand again on Charmaine's belly, and listened to what her cousin's body told her. The contractions were growing further apart, not closer. The labor was ending, without delivery.

Valerian went to her basket of medicines, and then to the fire where there was water heating, and mixed up a concoction of ergot. It would bring back the contractions, and help expel both the child and the placenta, and help as well to prevent hemorrhage. It was a drug she only used in the most critical of cases, for it had side effects that could be severe.

Charmaine made a face at the ugly brown liquid, but drank it. She was too tired to protest.

It was over an hour before the drug began to take effect, and the first signs of it were not good.

Charmaine's eyes darted from one side of the bed to the other. "What is that?"

"What is what?" Valerian asked.

Charmaine's eyes moved as if tracking something, over to the corner of the room where the shadows had begun to gather. "That," she whispered, staring, and then was overcome by the pain of a contraction. She shut her eyes and writhed, moaning. Alice held her hand and murmured soothing words to her.

When the contraction ended, Charmaine opened her eyes, staring again at the corner of the room. "It is still there. What is it?" Her voice rose. "It is watching me, stop it, it is watching me!"

"Charmaine, listen to me," Valerian said calmly, her voice as low and commanding as she could make it. "It is the medicine I gave you. It is making you see things that are not there. It is not real, whatever you see."

Her cousin seemed not to hear her. Her feet jerked, and then she was kicking at the empty space at the foot of the bed. "Get away! Get off me!"

"What is it?" Alice asked, eyes wide. "What do you see?"

"Do not touch my baby!"

"What is it?" Alice shouted, catching Charmaine's panic.

"Alice, it is an illusion," Valerian explained, but the woman did not hear her, her eyes focused on Charmaine.

"A demon, a black demon with yellow eyes," Charmaine cried. Another contraction hit her, and she screamed. "It claws at me! It rips my belly!"

Alice backed away from the bed, dropping Charmaine's hand and beginning to recite the Lord's Prayer, her eyes wild. "Our father, who art in Heaven, hallowed be—"

"Alice. Mrs. Torrance!" Valerian demanded, trying to pull the woman out of her terror, to no effect. *Damn. Damn, damn, and double damn,* she cursed silently.

The contraction ended, and the room fell quiet except for the soft chant of Alice's prayer, ". . . this day our daily bread, and forgive us . . ."

Charmaine's terrified gaze slowly moved from her feet, across the bed, and then over Valerian's shoulder. Despite herself, Valerian turned her head to look, so intense was Charmaine's gaze.

"You brought it," Charmaine said. "You called forth the demon."

Alice's chanting stopped as she listened.

"It is the medicine, making you see things, Charmaine. That is all. I will try to take its effects from you," Valerian said, moving towards the bed, reaching out a hand to lay on Charmaine's forehead.

Charmaine shrank from her, then rolled to her side and tried to claw her way off the bed. "No!"

"Where is it now?" Alice asked, her eyes darting about the room.

"Do you not see it?" Charmaine cried, clinging to the edge of the bed, her legs drawn up around her belly. "It crouches there upon her shoulder, its tail wrapped round her neck." The next contraction hit, and she screamed, the cry one of terror and pain. "It claws me! It chews upon my baby!"

Alice gaped in horror first at Charmaine, and then at Valerian, and then ran from the room.

Chapter Twenty-three

It was late afternoon when Nathaniel and Lord Carlyle rode into the meadow around the cottage. No smoke rose from the chimney, and all was quiet. Nathaniel dismounted, Lord Carlyle following suit, and went to go knock upon the door.

There was no answer. Nathaniel could almost feel the tension in his companion's body, waiting for some sign from within the silent cottage. To come after all these years to find no one at home seemed to Nathaniel too much for the man to bear. He sent a silent plea for forgiveness to Valerian and her aunt, and pushed open the door uninvited.

The familiar scent of herbs and wood smoke was overlain with an odor of illness. The interior of the cottage was no warmer than the outside, the fire long dead in the grate, and at first he thought that there could not possibly be anyone at home. And then, in the quiet, he heard the rasp of labored breathing.

He took the three strides that separated him from the

curtained bed, his boot heels loud on the plank flooring, and pulled back the draperies. The sight that met his eyes hit him like a punch to the gut.

"My God," Lord Carlyle swore behind him, as he too saw. "Theresa."

Nathaniel stepped away as Lord Carlyle shoved the draperies farther back and knelt beside the bed, finding one of Theresa's hands and taking it in his own. "Theresa, can you hear me?"

Nathaniel watched as her eyes slowly opened in the gaunt, yellowed face. The body that he remembered as being stout and robust now barely caused a rise in the blankets that covered her. She must have been ill for several weeks, and Valerian had never told him how bad it was. The thought that she had been living with this secret for weeks, and had not trusted him with it, made him almost dizzy with rage and hurt.

And where was she now?

"Thomas," Theresa said softly to Lord Carlyle, apparently unsurprised to see him at her bedside. "It is good to see you."

"Shall I fetch a doctor?"

Theresa smiled at him. "No. It will not be long now."

Nathaniel went and rebuilt the fire, then came back to the bedside, his agitation only growing. "Where is Valerian? She should be here, caring for you." When he thought that she had been happily accompanying him at the ball last night while her aunt lay here dying, it made him sick inside. It did not fit with what he knew of her, but the evidence before his eyes appeared irrefutable.

"She is needed elsewhere."

"By whom? Who could be more important? How could she leave you?"

"Nathaniel," Lord Carlyle said. "This is no time for arguments."

"Valerian is the one person who could save her," he bit out, then turned again to Theresa. "Why is she not here?"

"Hush," Theresa ordered him, a hint of her old authority in her rasping voice. "She has followed my wishes in all things. She does not know how close my time is, and you will not tell her."

"Like hell—"

"No!" Theresa ordered, and Nathaniel snapped his mouth shut. "There is nothing she could do for me," Theresa explained more quietly. "And there is much she can do for Charmaine. She has been brought to childbed too soon, and Valerian labors to save both her and the child. Would you have me give up my daughter and grandchild for an hour more of my own life? I will not have her distracted by worry over me."

"And how will she feel when she finally returns and finds you dead?" Nathaniel asked.

"That will not happen. You will see to it that she is not alone when she hears of my death."

He looked into her eyes for a long moment, and then could only nod in silent assent, feeling some of the anger drain out of him. He did not have it in him to argue with the wishes of a dying woman. If Valerian had indeed followed Theresa's wishes in all things, then it could have been Theresa's idea to keep her illness a secret. His anger would do nothing to help Valerian when she learned she had lost her aunt. "What can we do for you?"

"Stay with me."

Nathaniel almost smiled at that, suspecting she did not trust him not to fetch Valerian. He dragged two chairs over to the bed. Lord Carlyle did not release Theresa's hand as he rose from his knees to sit in the chair.

Theresa's eyes closed and she seemed to drift off to sleep. Neither of them spoke, watching, listening to each of Theresa's labored breaths. The shadows grew deeper, and Nathaniel rose to light candles and add more wood to the fire.

Nathaniel did not know how much time had passed when Theresa opened her eyes again, but it felt like hours.

"Still here, are you?" she asked Lord Carlyle.

"It was wrong of me to abandon you the first time. I would not do it again."

"Oh, Thomas," she said on a sigh. "Have you been feeling guilty all these years?"

"I could have done more for you."

"You gave me more than you will ever know."

"I loved you. I love you still."

"No, Thomas, you do not."

"You cannot know what is in my heart," he protested.

"Can I not? Do not confuse guilt with love. Do not confuse decades of regret with decades of pining for a woman. You do not love me, Thomas, except as a reminder of the pain shame can bring."

"You are wrong," he said, and even Nathaniel could hear the thin thread of doubt in the words.

"I never thought ill of you, Thomas. And it was a very fine horse you gave us upon which to escape."

Lord Carlyle's lips quirked at that, and Nathaniel saw their eyes meet in silent communion as understanding and forgiveness passed between them.

Theresa's eyes closed again, her breathing slowed, and then stopped. Lord Carlyle released her hand, and lay it gently on the counterpane.

Theresa Harrow was dead.

Chapter Twenty-four

Valerian felt tears of frustration start in her eyes, and sniffed them back with determination. Aunt Theresa would not cry. Aunt Theresa would not let the situation get the best of her. She would do something about it.

She stood still and blocked out the sounds of Charmaine's howls of pain and terror. She summoned all her reserves, drawing from deep within herself the love she felt for her parents, her aunt, and the people of Greyfriars, her love of mountains and ocean and green growing things, her love of Oscar and the animals of the forest and the meadow. She drew on the tenuous bond she held with Nathaniel. She drew on it all, to a depth she had never before attempted, and let it fill her body, then flow down through her hands.

She approached the bed, and Charmaine huddled away from her, her eyes glassy, her limbs too weak for her to escape. Valerian lifted her hands and placed them both over Charmaine's eyes. She saw light glowing around her hands, then spreading over Charmaine's face and down her body.

Valerian could sense her cousin's dark illusions, and feel them slowly giving way under her touch. The ergot was still active, but under the influence of her healing touch the images metamorphosed into sunlight and heavenly creatures, there to help and not to harm.

She lifted her hands away, and saw that the terror had left her cousin. Her eyes were still lost, but in a place of light rather than darkness.

Another contraction came and Charmaine whimpered, her jaw clenching, but she did not fight it. Valerian knew the time had at last come, and she helped her cousin out of the bed and to the low, crescent-shaped birthing stool that stood beside it.

The birth itself did not take long, and Valerian helped ease from Charmaine's straining passage the small, misshapen body of her children.

For it was not one child, she saw now, but two, twins who had not separated in the womb as they should have, and were forever melded into one form. She felt the life ebbing from the surviving child, and with the touch of her hand sent love and quiet peace to its fragile consciousness as it slipped away.

She wrapped the children in a blanket and set them gently aside, returning the focus of her concentration to Charmaine. Once the placenta was delivered, she helped her cousin back to the bed, washing her, and changing her sleeping chemise.

"My baby?" Charmaine asked on a whisper, her eyes heavy with weariness.

"They sleep with God," Valerian said softly. She kissed her cousin on the forehead, sending her into a deep sleep of her own where she could begin to heal, and where she could avoid for at least a time the loss of her babies.

Valerian's own strength began to fade, now that the crisis was finished. She cleaned up the floor as best she could, and washed her hands and forearms, bloody from the delivery. She looked at the small bundle lying on the floor, then went and picked it up, sitting down in a chair.

She pulled back the cover of the blanket, looking at the two small faces, touching one downy cheek with the tip of her finger. They were so small, so fragile. Their life had been taken before it could even begin. Tears slipped from her eyes and rolled down her cheeks, dripping onto the blanket, and she covered the children once more. She would have to tell Howard.

But first, for a moment, she would rest. She was so tired. Her eyelids drooped shut, and she let her head fall forward, resting her chin on her chest. Just a moment of rest, just a moment . . .

The pounding of many footsteps rushing up the stairs woke her with a start. For a minute she was disoriented, blinking at the dim room, then at the bundle on her lap, held there by the weight of her arm.

The door flew open, banging against the wall, and a group of villagers piled in, led by Alice and a confused Howard. The quiet in the room brought them to a halt, and for a long second they were frozen there, taking in Charmaine's quiet sleep, and then the bundle on Valerian's lap.

"Hush," Valerian said softly, and gently shooed the crowd back. Bewildered by the peaceful scene, they obeyed, murmuring lowly, and Valerian followed them out of the room, for the moment her only concern that Charmaine not be disturbed.

Once down below in the kitchen, voices rose in volume, arguing over the peaceful scene above. Obviously, there were no demons tearing at Charmaine now.

Valerian held the bundle close to her chest, and as she

felt the unnatural form through the blanket it dawned on her what danger she might be in if these villagers asked to see the baby. Eddie's imagined groin ailment was as nothing compared to concrete proof that evil was at work.

She wanted to believe that here in her cousin's house, she was safe. And she could be, if she handled this well with Howard.

There was no space to speak privately with him in the kitchen, so she led him into the shop in front while the others continued their debate. Alice made as if to follow, but Howard, perhaps having had enough of her, asked her to wait. He looked nervous, although whether of the group in his kitchen or of Valerian herself, she could not be sure. She had known him as a gentle man, but never known him well. She did not know how thoroughly he might share Charmaine's dislike of anything bordering on the supernatural.

"Charmaine?" he asked.

"She sleeps. She is well," Valerian said. She saw some of the tension leave his eyes. A good sign.

"The child. It was too soon," he said, looking at the silent, motionless bundle she held, the light from the open kitchen door catching in the folds of the small blanket. He blinked several times, as if clearing tears from his eyes.

"They did not survive," Valerian said. "I am sorry." It would be easier for her if she did not tell him the whole truth, if she offered to take the babies away unseen. It might even be easier for Howard and Charmaine.

"They?" he asked, surprised for a moment out of his grief.

She swallowed against the tightness of her throat. "Yes, they. Girls. Twin girls." She took a deep breath. It was only right that she tell him the full truth. "They could not have survived, even if brought to term."

Howard looked at the bundle, and she almost felt as if

she could hear his thoughts. Infant death was no rarity, the causes often unknown and unknowable, and it was almost unheard of for twins to be born healthy. He nodded his head in understanding, and Valerian gave a mental sigh of relief. He would not ask to see their little body while the villagers were here. There would be time enough in private.

"I will prepare them," Valerian said, referring to the children and their burial.

They went back into the kitchen, the milling group waiting expectantly. "Frank," Howard said to the carpenter. "We will be needing two small caskets."

Valerian opened her mouth to protest they only needed one, but shut it before the words came. A rustle of discomfort went through the gathering at the news. No one seemed inclined to press the issue of Alice's demon, not when Howard stood before them, his grief in his eyes. If he of all people was not going to accuse Valerian, then they had no right to do so.

A few made their apologies and left through the back door, but Alice stood staring at the blanket-wrapped children in Valerian's arms. Valerian tucked the bundle more closely to her chest.

"Where is the other child?" Alice asked, as more people left behind her.

Valerian watched the others go, silently urging them out. "They are both here."

"In one blanket?" Those remaining in the room turned their heads, their interest stirring. Howard sat at the kitchen table, his head in his hands, oblivious. "They are very small," Alice said and came up to her, reaching out a hand to lift the blanket. "Let me see them."

It was on Valerian's lips to deny the request, and she looked to Howard, but he was lost in his own world. If she said no, Alice's curiosity would only be the stronger for it. She turned slightly away from the group and lifted the edge of the blanket, arranging it so that only the two small faces were showing. It looked like they were snuggled against each other.

She turned back, and watched Alice's face as she examined the babies. A mix of emotions played there: disappointment, pity, and the faintest hint of tenderness. She touched one of the little faces with a fingertip as Valerian herself had done, and then there was a growing hint of suspicion in her expression. Before Valerian could discern her purpose and stop her, she grasped the blanket and jerked it down, revealing the body that the twins shared.

Her horrified gasp drew the attention of those left in the kitchen, and before Valerian could cover the twins again, they had seen.

" 'Tis the seed of Satan!" Alice proclaimed.

"No!" Valerian protested, already knowing it would do no good. She saw the kindling light of fanaticism in Alice's eyes, and saw the fire spread to the others in the room. It was the confrontation at the smithy again, only she knew it would be worse this time. Much worse.

With a horrid sense of déjà vu, she turned and stumbled through the kitchen doorway to the shop, and then to the front door. She struggled for long moments with the lock, the children clasped in her other arm making her clumsy. She whimpered with frustration, and then with a quick apology to the souls of the twins, set the bundle on a nearby work table.

"The devil himself was at the birth," Alice was saying in the kitchen to her followers, her voice rising. "Sitting upon her shoulder, then clawing to get at his child through the very womb of their innocent mother. If 'twere not for my reciting of the Lord's Prayer, the demon child may have lived. What further proof do we need of the witch's evil? We must stop her, before she finds another in whom to implant the devil's spawn!"

The door came open under Valerian's hands as she heard a rising murmur of agreement from the kitchen. She ran out into the darkness, her long heavy skirts and the unfamiliar tight stays of the silk dress hampering her movements.

Despair pulled at her, weakening her even more. There would never be a place she could live in peace as another face in the crowd. There was no place she could live without fear of discovery and hate. Not here, in Greyfriars. Not with Nathaniel, where to meet his friends she had to don a mask. There was nowhere for her.

She tried to push the thought from her mind, feeling how it slowed her steps. Better to think of survival, first. She was exhausted from a day and a half without sleep and the healing she had done, and the only place of safety was Raven Hall, but the road that led there was at the opposite end of town. She would never make it.

She turned instead down the road that led to the mill, and the bridge that led across the small river and on to the road to Yarborough. With luck, she could leave the road somewhere and disappear into the forest. With luck.

She heard shouts behind her, and knew that the entire town would soon know of Charmaine's poor children, and the demon sitting on Valerian's shoulder.

Nathaniel, she called out silently. *Help me. Please help me.*

Chapter Twenty-five

Nathaniel rode slowly into town, his mind on Valerian. He had never had to break the news of a death to a family member, and he did not know how best to do so. At least it would not come as a total surprise, given how ill Theresa had been.

Lord Carlyle was still with the body, waiting for the women that Nathaniel had sent for from Raven Hall to take care of Theresa. If neither Valerian nor Charmaine had any objection, Nathaniel would have her buried in the cemetery at the hall.

He imagined that Valerian would want to stay on in the cottage, but he could not let her do that. It was no place for a young woman, alone. She would have to move in with her cousin, unless she had other relatives he did not know about. If this were London, he could set her up in a townhouse of her own, and no one would so much as blink an eye at the arrangement. But this was not London.

Which left Raven Hall, only she could not live there as a

servant, as she was not one. And living there openly as his mistress would, he knew, be unacceptable to both her and the village.

Not that he would mind having her there. He liked the few quiet evenings they had shared on the couch before the fire, and he enjoyed talking with her. In fact, all questions of lust put aside, he rather liked her as a person.

He reined Darby to a halt, surprised by the idea. He had plenty of friends he found somewhat entertaining, but did not find commendable as people. He examined the strange, unfamiliar sensation he felt when he thought of Valerian, the one other than lust and pleasure. It felt, rather remarkably, like respect.

He nudged Darby and resumed his slow ride into town, examining this revelation. He had never before combined respect with feelings of desire for a woman. It was a novel experience. It occurred to him that she deserved more than what he had been giving her.

A shout in the distance brought him back to the present, and to the purpose of this journey. A quiver of self-reproach went through him, as he realized his thoughts had been on his own emotions, when he should have been thinking about how to soften the blow his news would bring to Valerian.

The village felt both alive and empty at once, and he began to pay a little more attention as he rode through. Here and there a door hung open, or a child peered out a window, although as far as he could tell there was nothing to see.

He dismounted in front of the cobbler's shop, intending to wait downstairs until Valerian had finished with Charmaine. The front door here, as well, hung open, the shop dark, but there was light coming from the kitchen in back. He rapped on the open door frame. "Hello?" he called inside. "Is there anyone here?"

There was no answer, but perhaps everyone was upstairs. He was hesitant to enter his second house today uninvited, but then mentally shrugged and went ahead. After all, the door was hanging wide open.

In the kitchen he stopped short when he saw the back of the man sitting at the table, his head down on his crossed arms. "Your pardon, sir! I did not believe anyone to be about." Which made him sound, he realized, rather like a housebreaker.

The man stirred at his voice, raising his head and turning, then staring blankly at him. "Pardon?"

"Forgive me, I did not mean to intrude. I came to speak with Miss Bright. You are her cousin?"

He did not answer, only continued to stare.

"Miss Bright is here, is she not?" He was beginning to wonder if he had stumbled into the wrong house. They did all look alike.

"No."

Nathaniel turned about, looking at the kitchen. Did the houses all look the same inside, as well? He could swear this was the same kitchen he had been in before. Then the man spoke again. "She has gone."

Nathaniel felt his heart trip. She could not have gone home, he could not have missed her. He had promised Theresa. "When?"

"Five minutes past? Ten? Maybe longer." The man resumed staring at nothing.

What was wrong with the man? Nathaniel gave up trying to gain any more definite information from him. He was already on his way out when the man spoke once more.

"I know she is not a witch, whatever they may say. She did all she could for my Charmaine and the babes."

The words brought Nathaniel up short. "What do you mean?"

"I have no wish to see her harmed. It was not her fault."

Nathaniel came back into the room, and lay his hand on the man's shoulder, mustering all the patience he possessed. "What is not her fault?" Did he have to drag every word out of the man?

But the man would tell him nothing more, and pulled away from his hand, dropping his head back onto his arms. His shoulders shook, and Nathaniel knew he was weeping.

He ran back outside and mounted, the empty village and open doors now taking on an ominous cast. He rode back to where he recalled a child's face at the window. She—or he, it was not clear which—was still there.

"Where have your parents gone?" Nathaniel demanded.

The child stared.

"Answer me!" Could no one in this damned village speak?

Another head came up beside the first, slightly older, hair in braids. She looked him over for a long minute, then pointed a pudgy finger down the street. "Mam and Pap went down there, with everybody else."

"My thanks!" Nathaniel shouted as he wheeled Darby about and dug in his heels, urging the beast to a gallop, his own heart beating in his chest with a growing fear for Valerian.

A short distance past the edge of town the road led by the mill, and Nathaniel saw the lantern and torch light even before he heard the voices, raised suddenly in a cheer. He bent low over Darby's neck, urging the horse to run as it never had before.

Whatever it was that made that mob cheer, he knew it could not be good for Valerian.

"She should be burnt!" Alice Torrance declared, backed by several assents.

"Hang her!" someone else opined.

Valerian cringed on the ground at the center of the group, listening to the low hatred that murmured from their throats. She was bruised but otherwise unharmed.

Jeremiah O'Connor, the smith, pushed through to the front of the group, meeting several gazes before speaking. "I am not convinced she is a witch."

"Nor I," said Mr. Miller, Gwendolyn's father, as he came forward.

"What more proof do you need?" Alice shouted, and grasping Charmaine's melded children by the feet, held up their naked body in the torch light as if they were trussed fowl.

"No!" Valerian cried, and rising tried to snatch the children from Alice. She could not bear to see them displayed so, these innocent children. At that moment, she thought she could see the true face of evil, and it belonged to Alice Torrance.

Alice jerked the body out of her reach, as someone else knocked Valerian back to the ground. "See how she craves to have it, as if it were her own child. Hers and Satan's!"

"I do not believe she is a witch," Sally said and pushed forward to stand beside the two men. "She has never harmed me or my children, has only used her gifts to help us."

Valerian turned a grateful look at the threesome, and became aware of a shift in the crowd. A small, ever so small faction seemed to be growing behind the lead of these three. The majority, however, still had bloodlust in their eyes.

Alice lowered the body, letting the children dangle by her side as she held them by one foot. "If we are not certain, then we should try her in the old way." The crowd waited, expectant. "By water!"

A moment of silence was followed by a murmur of assent, rising, growing in strength as the group considered and found the idea acceptable. Even a few of those who seemed to support her were nodding their heads. Then Gwendolyn offered to get rope from the stables, and new energy ran through the mob.

Aunt Theresa's vision in the scrying came back to her, that she would be in the water with the light of flames about her. She had thought she had made it come true herself, when she took Nathaniel to the cave. She should have known better. Nothing ever came true as one expected.

Then, the final words of Theresa's vision came back to her. *The baron is there.* She tried to see past the crowd, tried to find some hint of his presence, but there was none. Not yet. But he would come. He had to. She had to hold tight to that hope, even as she felt a shudder of fear run through her.

She tried to fight the fear by focusing on her breathing, on the beat of her heart, trying to find the calm that Theresa had taught her. She had to hang on to her reason, lest she panic and somehow bring about her own demise. The baron would come. He would come. The crowd and their intentions faded slightly from her awareness as she focused on that thought.

Gwen returned with the rope, and it was decided Valerian should be stripped down to her chemise, as the weight of the green gown might give her unfair advantage and help her sink. If she floated, however, it would prove that God's water had rejected her and she was indeed a witch.

Sally stepped forward to tend to the task of undressing her, taking the opportunity to speak for Valerian's ears alone. "We will pull you up as soon as we can. Hold your breath. We cannot stop the dunking, but perhaps we can make it shorter."

"The baron will help," Valerian said under her breath, her voice flat as she sought to deepen her trance. "He will come."

Sally nodded, but Valerian knew she doubted her words.

Someone pulled Sally away, and then rough hands shoved Valerian to the ground and pulled her hands forward to tie them to her feet. A rope was wrapped around her waist, with which they would haul her out when they were through. The fear she had been holding in firm check fought to break through, and she trembled, but then forced her muscles to go slack. Her only chance of survival was in submission.

Your hair spreading in the water. The baron is there. She clung to the words. He would come when she was in the water. He would come.

She shut her eyes as hands lifted her and carried her to the edge of the millpond, swinging her to build momentum. "One . . . Two . . ." the voices said in unison, "Three! . . . Heave!"

She was in the air, free for a moment, sung to by the cheer of the mob. She took a deep breath and hit the hard, cold water, a sudden smack against her body, and then was swallowed by the cold dark mouth of it.

Swallowed for long seconds, and she held herself from struggling, counting slowly in her head. She could last half a minute, she was certain, and perhaps a full minute or two if she had to, if she kept control of herself.

She reached eleven in her counting when she felt her back break the surface of the water. It was a moment before the significance came through to her. *I float.* They would drag her out and burn her, baron or no baron. Why did she float? Why?

The answer came to her as clearly as a diagram in an anatomy book. Her lungs were full of air, keeping her buoyed at the surface, her arms and legs beneath her.

Nathaniel, come soon, she silently pleaded, and released her breath in soft bubbles. She twisted to the side, bringing the weight of her legs and arms over her body, and slowly sank to the bottom of the pond.

Chapter Twenty-six

Darby suddenly shied, a shadow dashing at horse and rider out of the darkness. Nathaniel struggled to bring the horse under control, finally succeeding despite the continued presence of the fluttering shadow.

"Baron Ravenall, is that you?" the shadow asked in a woman's voice.

"Aye. Step aside there." Impatient to get to Valerian, he would not be delayed.

"Wait! Miss Bright needs your help."

"Tell me what is happening," he demanded, his urgency matching her own.

"They have thrown her in the millpond. It has been too long already, we have not been able to get them to pull her up. You must help her!"

A witch dunking. Good God. His heart beat a wild rhythm in his chest as he spurred Darby to cover the remaining distance to the torchlight. No one noticed his approach, everyone's attention on a brawl along the edge of the water. Two large men were struggling against at least four others, with much cursing and grunting, and bloodied faces on several. Beyond the onlookers, the smooth surface of the millpond threw back only the wind-rippled reflections of the torches. The lack of waves or splashing chilled him to his very soul.

"Cease!" he roared into the crowd, surprising the watchers, but doing nothing to break up the brawl. He had no time for that. He recognized the innkeeper's wife at the edge of the water, and pinned her with his gaze. "Where is she?"

She looked quickly to the mob, then down at her hands. Nathaniel followed her gaze to the rope she held, the other end of which disappeared into the water. In the next moment she was sprawled in the mud, and he was hauling on the rope, barely aware that a few other hands had joined in, while the men continued their battle.

How long had she been under? Long enough for a fight to break out, long enough for a woman to run for help. Long enough for the last of her breath to break the surface and vanish, the water absorbing the last trace of ripples.

Her chest and every muscle ached with the need to take a breath. She had lost count of how long she had been under, her mind filled with the pain and the utter necessity of not breathing. A small part of her knew she rested on the bottom of the pond, in the cold silt, and could feel the pressure against her ears, the aching pain of the frigid water that was nothing compared to the pain of her body's cry for air.

Her control was slipping, her concentration fading. She would breathe against her will, she felt it coming, she was losing the battle. . . .

And then she was in a sun-filled meadow, in summer. The pain was gone, and the cold, and all was quiet except for the sound of summer insects. Two black-haired toddlers came and took her hands, giggling, leading her through the wildflowers and grasses.

In the center of the field a group of people sat around a table having dinner. As she approached they turned and looked at her, then one by one stood and came forward. The little girls dropped her hands and went to play together in the grass. Valerian stood still, knowing this place although she had not seen it like this, and knowing the people who came toward her.

"Mother? Father?" They looked as they had when she was twelve. "Aunt Theresa?"

Her mother touched her face, and then took her hand and led her to the table. "Your grandmother," she said, gesturing to an older, graceful woman, who smiled warmly. "Charmaine's daughters," she said, inclining her head toward the little girls rolling about in the grass.

"Yes, I know," she said, for she did know. And she understood as well that Theresa had died, and felt around her in the air the souls of countless kin she had never met, as well as the souls of people she had known in her life and who had passed on, even those who had been but an acquaintance. Yet, at this moment, she knew them all, and felt the warmth of their souls moving in the air about her.

"I could not hold my breath any longer," she said, almost an apology.

"You held it long enough," Theresa said. "We could not have asked more of you."

"You have a choice about remaining with us," her father said, sitting her at the table and pouring her a glass of wine. The others sat as well and resumed their meal. "Last time you did not."

"I am not dead, then?" She took a sip of the wine, sweet and fruity.

"The difference is small," her grandmother said between dainty bites of custard. "And you rest upon the division."

"So the choice is yours," her mother said. "You may remain on Earth, or move on. You have shared your gift, even in the face of distrust and threat to yourself. You have lived well. It is for you to decide if you have lived fully."

Valerian sat back, looking around the table. Everyone she loved was here. In life she had darkness and cold and people who feared her, a cousin who disliked her, a few friends who were kind to her, but could not erase from their eyes or hearts the doubt that she was one of them.

But then there was Oscar, the foolish bird. Who would care for him if she was not there? And Nathaniel. Just as she felt the bond with those around her, she could now feel the bond she shared with him, and the pull he exerted on her heart. He would suffer if he lost her like this, to a murderous mob he had thought he could control. Laetitia had drowned, and so would she. He might never recover from the guilt of it.

"I cannot leave him alone," she said.

"No one is ever truly alone," Theresa said.

"He will not know that. He will not understand. I must go back."

As soon as she said the words the field began to fade, and then she was hovering above a small crowd lit by torchlight. Her body lay in the mud, wet and pale, and Mr. O'Connor was using a knife on the ropes around her hands and feet. Nathaniel knelt with her head in his lap, his hands moving frantically over her face, pushing back her hair.

"Valerian, come back. Valerian. Wake up, wake up, please, wake up. Oh God, please," he cried over her, his body rocking.

The bonds came loose and Mr. O'Connor and Sally straightened her limbs, and she felt herself sucked down and into her body.

Her breath came in on a wrenching gasp. She was cold, so cold. She opened her eyes to a blur, feeling kisses on her forehead, and then Nathaniel lifted his head and she could see the tears in his eyes, and he was laughing, laughing and holding her cheeks and bending down to kiss her on the mouth.

"Cold," she whispered. From somewhere a blanket appeared and he wrapped her in it, lifting her in his arms. "I came back for you," she said into his chest.

"Yes, you did," he said, laughing. "And you had better stay here now that you have."

The clarity of her time with her family began to fade, but she clung tight to the sense of connectedness she had felt. She would not let that leave her, she promised herself, as she was carried away from the pond. She would not forget that no one was ever completely alone.

No matter who rejected her here, she knew a place where she belonged.

Chapter Twenty-seven

"I must ask you all to leave in the morning." A room of stunned faces turned to his voice, and Nathaniel took a step farther into the drawing room. "There have been some . . . unfortunate occurrences in Greyfriars. I will be better able to deal with them if I do not have a houseful of guests to worry about." He knew he was being astoundingly rude. One did not kick one's guests out of one's home.

He did not care.

"What has happened?" Kate asked, and then, her tone supercilious and half-mocking, "Have the peasants revolted?"

Nathaniel looked at her, formulating an answer that would suit his audience, and then abandoned the endeavor. He did not care to explain. He wanted them out of his house. He did not want them here with Valerian, did not want them asking their uncaring questions about Theresa, did not want to see them lounging on his furniture and eating his food and playing their pointless games.

"Paul," he said, turning to his friend. "I would like you to stay, with your father. At least for a time."

"Certainly." There were questions in Paul's eyes, but he did not ask them.

"You may, of course, call upon any of my staff to help you in your preparations," he said to the group. "Good evening." He gave them a stiff bow, turned on his heel, and left. He strode across the great hall and down the opposite corridor, not wanting to be anywhere near them when their shock wore off. They probably thought he had lost his mind.

On the contrary, he felt as if at long last he had found it.

Valerian sat on the edge of the chair by the fire in Nathaniel's bedroom and allowed Judith to gently rub her hair in a towel. Maids had already taken away the tub that she had bathed in with little consciousness of her own actions. Indeed, she might have sat in the tub indefinitely, staring into the fire as she was now, if Judith had not been there to help her.

Everything seemed to be happening underwater, as if she were still at the bottom of the millpond. Nothing was quite real. She knew everything that had happened today, but it was as if the connection between that knowledge and her heart had been blocked. She could summon no emotion, no thought for the future, no care for where she was or was not. She dimly recognized that she was in shock, and knew it would fade in time.

But for now, she stared into the flames, and did not notice the sound of the door opening, or the sensation of Judith draping a blanket over her shoulders, lifting her damp hair above it to keep it from soaking the clean chemise she wore.

"Valerian."

She heard her name and turned her gaze from the flames.

Nathaniel sat across from her, his muddy knees not four inches from her own. There was distress showing in his eyes, though he was trying to keep his face calm. She vaguely wondered how he could summon so much feeling.

"Your breeches are dirty. You should change them," she said.

He glanced down, then back at her, the distress in his eyes deepening, and then dissipating, his face relaxing. She could see his emotions so clearly. Perhaps he had taken on hers for the time being, and that was why she could not feel.

Nathaniel held Valerian's glazed blue eyes. *She is in shock,* he realized, and felt a breath of relief. Shock was something he had seen before, in the army. Felt it, as well. Given rest and quiet, she would come out of it.

"I need to find Oscar," she said. "He does not like to be alone."

"I will find him for you."

"Thank you."

She was silent again, her gaze returning to the fire, and he waited, not knowing what to say. She did not seem in any condition to hear that her aunt had died.

"I will need to bury Aunt Theresa," she said, still staring into the flames. "Will you help me with that? She died today, I am not certain when. She had been ill for several months."

He stared. *How could she know?* No one would have told her, he had ordered them not to. Or perhaps the question of how she knew was foolish considering the talents of her family. "I was with her when she died," he said at last, softly. "Paul's father was there as well. He knew her in her youth."

She turned back to him, a smile on her lips. "That is good. She would not have died alone, but I am glad that you were there with her."

He nodded, although he could not quite make sense of that statement. "I think it is time you got some sleep."

"If you wish."

He shook his head in mild exasperation, and scooped her up into his arms. He carried her to the bed and tucked her in. Her lids began to droop as soon as her head sank into the pillow, but she managed to hold onto his hand.

"No one is ever truly alone," she said, "but will you stay with me tonight?"

"I will not leave you."

Her grip on his hand weakened as she began to drift off to sleep. "But find Oscar first," she murmured.

Well, that put him in his place. Second to an ill-mannered bird. But Oscar could not take care of her the way that he could, and the way he was going to. When her shock faded, she would probably think there was nothing wrong with going back to the cottage or to her cousin's house, even though half the town had just tried to drown her.

For a moment the image of Laetitia's waterlogged body, pulled from the Thames, merged with that of Valerian as he dragged her from the millpond. His life was repeating itself. He had the chance this time, though, to do it right. He could keep Valerian safe, could give her a better life than she would have scraping by as a healer, alone in the woods, despised and feared and shunned.

Perhaps there was a God, and this was his God-given chance to make amends for his past.

He went into his dressing room and changed his clothes, glad to remove the damp breeches and all traces of what had almost happened. A few seconds longer, and she would have been dead, he had no doubt of it. He had thought her dead when he pulled her from the water, for there had been no breath in her, her skin cold, lips blue.

A shudder ran through him, a delayed reaction, and he sat down, his legs and hands shaking. A few seconds more, and those bright blue eyes would never again have looked into his, alive with mischief. He would never again have heard her voice explaining to him the use of a plant he had never before noticed. Would never again have followed her confident lead through the rain, or lain beside her on a cliff top, or held her naked in his arms, warm beneath the covers of his bed.

He clenched his hands tight. *He had not lost her.* And he would not, not ever.

"Pooooor hungry bird. Pooooor hungry bird. Pooooor . . ."

Valerian dragged her eyes open as the refrain continued. That pitiful plea would wake the dead.

"Pooooor hungry—"

"All right, Oscar! Enough!" She squinted against the daylight, her body heavy as she struggled to sit up in bed. She felt as if she had been asleep for days. She could feel the dampness of sweat between her breasts, the sticky taste of sleep in her mouth, and the uncomfortable pressure of a full bladder.

Oscar hopped from the headboard behind her down onto the bed, waddling awkwardly over the folds and lumps of the covers. She scratched him gently over his eye ridges. "We shall have to find you something to eat," she cooed.

"The bloody bird already had half my breakfast," Nathaniel said.

Valerian turned to his voice. "I did not see you there," she said, finding him at last in the chair by the dead fire. He looked clean but tired, a book discarded face down on the small table beside him.

Oscar hop-flapped his way to the end of the bed, then flew the short distance to the back of the chair opposite Nathaniel. "Eee-diot!"

"Oscar!" Valerian scolded.

"Ungrateful wretch," Nathaniel said, looking sourly at the raven.

"Oscar is a superior bird," Oscar said. "Biscuit."

"Biscuit, my foot. 'Tis eggs and sausages you prefer." And to Valerian, "How do you feel? Are you hungry?"

"I could eat something."

"Then I shall go find you something to eat." He rose from the chair with his customary grace, sending her a brief look that made it clear he was more concerned than he let on. She was suddenly certain that he had spent the entire night in that chair, watching over her.

"Thank you." She was not truly hungry, but knew she should eat, and that it would comfort him to see her do so. As she washed and took care of her personal needs, bits and pieces of the night before came back to her, but it was too much to consider at once. She focused her mind instead on the fragments of the vision she had had at the bottom of the millpond.

Aunt Theresa lived still, with Charmaine's daughters and her own parents. She would see her again. She was not gone forever.

But, oh, how she was going to miss her in the meantime. She felt tears sting her eyes, and the ache in her jaw as she clenched it against the grief that sought to well forth. She would not let it. Aunt Theresa still lived, beyond her death here. She was not gone. She was not.

"Valerian?" Nathaniel's voice came to her, and she felt his hand on her shoulder.

She looked up at him, confused for a moment. How had she come to be sitting on the side of the bed? "I must tend to Aunt Theresa. And tell Charmaine."

"I had your aunt brought here. She is in the chapel, and if both you and your cousin agree, then she will be buried here."

Valerian nodded. "She would have liked that."

"I have sent word to Charmaine's husband. He will tell her of her mother's passing."

Valerian nodded again. "Thank you." Her gaze drifted off into space, and she brought it back to Nathaniel with an effort. She needed something concrete to do, something to distract her mind and her hands. She was acquainted with grief, and did not want to disappear into it for months, for years even, as she had when her parents died.

"I should go to the cottage."

"You are going to stay here, at the hall. It is not safe for you to be alone."

She focused on him, frowning a bit. "I know I cannot be there alone, but you cannot keep me here, either. Your friends are here."

"They left this morning."

She raised her eyebrows at him.

"It was time for them to seek their amusements elsewhere. You will stay here."

She nodded. She did not know where else to go. Not yet, anyway. "There are things I need at the cottage, and things I do not wish to leave unattended. The books, my clothes, the medicines that have been prepared . . ."

She could see he did not want to let her go back, did not want her to so much as leave the bed if he could help it. " 'Twill be better for me if I have things to do," she explained. "And I will need your help."

Those appeared to be the magic words, for at last he nodded his assent. "We will make a brief trip today. In a few days, after the funeral, we will bring a cart and staff and do a more thorough job of it."

"Thank you," she said, and felt her mind begin to drift again.

* * *

The funeral service was short, given by a priest who had not known Theresa, but had apparently heard of her reputation. His hands shook, and his voice lacked sincerity when speaking of the good she had done for her neighbors. Valerian knew that Nathaniel had spoken with the man beforehand, making clear to him that Theresa had been a woman of God, devoting her life to easing the pains of others, and that any suggestion to the contrary would be unacceptable.

Charmaine stood silently with her husband, still pale from her ordeal, but when Valerian met her eyes, she could see no ill will there. Somehow she had erased those hellish visions of a demon from Charmaine's mind. She could only wonder at the pain her cousin must be feeling, to have lost her mother and her children at the same time.

Also present were Sally and her husband, and their boys. Jeremiah O'Connor and his family, including Eddie, were present, and Mr. Miller, as were a small handful of other villagers who had been unwilling to condemn Valerian out of hand at the millpond. They looked shame faced, as if they felt somehow responsible for Theresa's death, as well as for the misdeeds of their neighbors and their own inability to stop what had happened to Valerian.

James and Judith, Daniel the gardener, and a number of other Raven Hall staff who had long been familiar with Theresa also stood by. Lord Carlyle appeared genuinely grieved, and even Paul looked somber.

I was wrong to have thought myself completely friendless here. She did not have words with which to thank them, but when she spoke with each, she laid her hand on an arm, or clasped fingers, and tried to send through that connection a healing touch. One of Sally's boys looked curiously at his hand after she had touched it, giving her hope that she was at least partially successful.

They retired to the hall for a light meal, the townsfolk looking uncomfortable with the fine china plates in their hands, from which they ate James's creations as they stood, milling about, sharing stories of Theresa. When she had the chance, Valerian took Charmaine aside for a private word. "I will be cleaning out the cottage. Are there things there that you want?"

"The chest from under her bed, with the papers and keepsakes, that is all."

"I have it here already. You know about the gold Theresa saved?"

Charmaine nodded. "And the necklace, which is yours. I think you should keep the coins for yourself."

Valerian was surprised by the offer. "At least let us share them. They are yours more than mine."

"She saved them in case we should ever need to flee, to go into hiding. I have no need of that, but you do. I cannot think that you could want to stay here."

"The baron has offered me shelter, at least for the time."

A bit of the old Charmaine fire returned to her eyes at that. "You are not our grandmother. I do not care what Mother thought, it is a life with even less honor than playing village witch. Do you think I will be any happier with a cousin selling her body for protection than with one casting spells for her keep?"

She wanted to protest that she did neither, but it would be a game of words. Nathaniel would want her to remain his bedfellow, and no one could tell Alice Torrance that she had not removed a curse from her warty feet, for all that there had been no magic involved. "What would you have me do, Charmaine? Run away? Do you dislike me so much that you wish me gone?"

To her shock, a film of tears came to Charmaine's angry eyes. "Why could neither you nor Mother ever understand? I want an ordinary life, one that no one notices or gossips about, that is all. I never wanted either of you gone,

I never hated you—I wanted you normal, like everyone else."

"But we are not like everyone else."

"You never tried to be! Keep the gold, Valerian. If you have any love for me, leave this place, set up a new life somewhere else, where no one believes in witches. Do what your mother did, and marry. Have children. Forget your potions and your animal bones, and forget the baron."

"Am I to forget my power to heal, as well? I have often wondered what it has done to you, to stifle your gift, whatever it may be."

"I have no gift."

"All the women of our line have a gift. You have tried all your life to be ordinary, Charmaine, and I do not think it has brought you happiness. Perhaps it is time to be true to yourself." She paused, taking in her cousin's dragonlike countenance. "However out of the ordinary the result."

"Send the chest to my house," Charmaine said tightly, and walked away.

"I would not have guessed such a stern woman to be Theresa's daughter," Lord Carlyle said from behind her.

Valerian turned, a weak smile on her lips. She was still stunned by Charmaine's wish for her to leave Greyfriars. "I think my aunt on occasion was surprised as well. There is no question that Charmaine disapproved of the relationship."

"I recall meeting your own mother, Emmeline, on a few occasions. You are very much like her."

"Thank you, my lord," Valerian said, touched. "Now that Aunt Theresa is gone, you are the only person I have met who knew my mother." She lay a hand on his arm. "I have not had the chance to ask you how you met them, although I assume it was at a party or ball of some sort."

"Of some sort, yes."

"Lord Carlyle, I know the history of my family. I will

not be embarrassed if you tell me that either my mother or my aunt did not attend completely respectable gatherings."

He gave a sheepish grin. "I sometimes forget what I was like then, the crowd with whom I ran. I do not doubt but that my son would like it if I reminded myself more often." He led her to a loveseat and pulled up a small table for her to set her untouched plate upon, then sat beside her.

"Aunt Theresa has told me much about those times, but I confess it was like a fairy tale to me," Valerian said. "It is only in these past couple weeks that I have understood that it was real." The gown and the jewels, and the presence of this nobleman at Theresa's funeral made it seem that the window to the past was open more widely than it had ever been.

"You have more luck than your ancestress. Thank God Nathaniel came in time."

It took her a moment to realize what he was talking about, what he had been reminded of. "Were you in London the night my grandmother was killed?"

"Yes, actually. It was a mystery for some weeks where your mother and aunt had run to. Many said they had fled to the continent." He looked down at his hands, scraping at a hangnail with his thumb.

"Someone helped them to escape. It was one of my favorite stories, actually. Aunt Theresa groaned whenever I would ask her to tell it, but I think she enjoyed doing so. Or at least enjoyed telling the racy parts. She liked to shock me."

"Racy parts?" The words came out a croak, and his skin started turning pink.

"She could be quite explicit—" Valerian broke off, seeing his shock. "Lord Carlyle, is there something wrong?"

"No, no," he said, obviously trying to act as if nothing were amiss. "So tell me, did your aunt ever reveal the name of this man who had helped her?"

"Never, which perhaps made the story all that much more entertaining. The midnight lover of noble heritage, the Arabian horse he gave her . . ." Valerian sighed. "When she wanted to, she could make it into quite the tale of romantic adventure, but never would she tell his name."

"Ah. A woman of discretion." He visibly relaxed.

"Lord Carlyle," Valerian asked, frowning, "do you know who it was who helped Aunt Theresa and my mother?"

He raised his brows, his mouth parted as he searched for words. Comprehension came to Valerian before he found them.

"Good lord!" she said, standing up. "Do not tell me it was you! *You* were the one who was in bed with her when my mother came to find her?"

"She did not tell you all the details of *that*, I hope!"

She looked quickly around the room, aware that she had spoken too loudly. The one person she did not want to have heard her was out of earshot, or had not noticed, for she was talking with James and Judith. Valerian sat down again, smoothing her rough black skirt over her knees.

Heaven save her, she was sitting next to Charmaine's father, and he did not even know he had a full-grown daughter in the next room.

Chapter Twenty-eight

Valerian looked at the weed growing amongst the leeks, and could not decide if she should pull it. It was already several inches high, showing spiky baby thorns, and its siblings were making their presence seen amongst the neat rows and squares of the cottage garden. No more than a week had gone by since she had last been out here, yet they had grown so fast. Should she pull it?

The simple decision was beyond her. All decisions were beyond her. She did not know what to do with the knowledge of Charmaine's paternity, for after hearing again what Theresa's last hours had been, it was clear her aunt had had the opportunity to tell Lord Carlyle if she had wished. Valerian did not know if Theresa's decision was right or wrong. She did not know if either Charmaine or Lord Carlyle would welcome such information, and did not know if it was Aunt Theresa's right to decide for them. Or her own, for that matter.

Perhaps she should pull the weed. Or perhaps it made no difference.

She did not know when she would return again to the cottage, if ever. She did not know if she would remain at Raven Hall, or take the gold and the necklace and find a new life for herself where no one knew her.

She would lose Nathaniel if she did that. She had come back for him, so it made no sense to leave him. Not now, not so soon, when she could feel his need to take care of her like a palpable thing. And perhaps she needed taking care of, for this short while at least. She was not as strong as she had thought she was.

"They have loaded the last trunk and set off for the hall," he said, coming up behind her and laying his warm hands on her shoulders.

"Good."

There was silence for a moment. "What are you looking at?"

"The weed. I do not know whether or not to pull it."

He bent around her to get a better view, then reached down and yanked it out of the ground, tossing it aside, its delicate white roots torn and exposed, clinging hopelessly to crumbs of dirt. "There. One less thing to disturb your sleep."

"You are determined to slay my dragons for me," she said, feeling her own ineffectualness.

"I could have lost my finger to a vicious thorny weed, and this is the thanks I get?"

She tried to smile at his jest. "I am not used to being the princess who stands aside to watch."

"No, you are the sort of princess who would think of giving the dragon an herbal enema, and would probably ask me to hold his tail up while you administered the foul concoction."

The corner of her mouth pulled up in a lopsided smile. "I am sorry that I have made such a poor companion these last days."

"Valerian, for God's sake, you are in mourning. Throw fits, be rude, tear your hair out if you wish. No one is asking you to be entertaining."

"I could not do that in your home," she protested.

"Why ever not?"

"I would not be comfortable. I am your guest."

She saw the exasperation on his face, and then he sighed and gently pulled her into his arms, his lips pressed to the top of her head. She closed her eyes, for a moment feeling safe and warm and not alone, his brocade vest both smooth and rough beneath her cheek, the scent of him coming through his clothing.

"You and I need to talk," he said into her hair.

She tightened her arms around him. Talking meant thinking, and thinking meant reality. She wanted to bury herself in him, to disappear, but the moment was already gone. She loosened her hold on him. "Yes, I suppose so."

"Not here."

They rode up to the cliffs where Valerian had found Oscar, leaving Darby free to graze on the coarse grasses. It was Nathaniel who led the way to the cliffs this time, although not all the way to the edge. He chose a spot several yards back, and sat, his legs stretched out before him.

Valerian remained standing, closing her eyes and feeling the wind against her face and billowing in her skirt. He must have remembered this was one of the places she came to deal with her grief as a child. She opened her eyes, squinting against the glare of sunlight, making out the humped shape of the Isle of Man set upon the grey sea.

Her awareness of herself flickered within her, for seconds at a time disappearing and leaving her blissfully free.

She had trained her mind to lose itself in her environment, to be the sky and the waves and the sloping ground, the circling ravens and the scent of the sea. She could make herself vanish, becoming transparent, part of the wind, without thought or emotion.

For a time, at least. She knew Nathaniel waited for her, and she came back to earth, taking the last few steps towards him and sitting near him in the grass. She took off her shoes and stockings, and brought her knees up, tucking her bare feet under the hem of her skirt, her gaze still toward the sea.

"I cannot stay in your house much longer, at least not in your bedroom," Valerian said. "Everyone knows I am your mistress, but I do not wish to flaunt it. It pains Charmaine."

"Does it pain you?"

She turned her head to meet his eyes. "No. Except that it will grow awkward with many of your staff. It is not bad right now because they are understanding of what has happened, and they know you have not been sharing my bed. But that will change."

"Do you want to stay with me, Valerian?"

She looked back at the sea. "Until we can work something else out."

"I was not referring only to whose roof is above your head." He took her hand in his, his thumb rubbing gently over her knuckles, drawing her eyes back to him. "I want you to marry me, Valerian."

Her lips parted, and she stared at him, all thought flown from her mind. "I beg your pardon?"

He smiled at her. "You heard me. Marry me. It will solve everything. You will be safe and protected, your cousin cannot possibly object, you will have a place in society, and we can be together. Openly."

She tried to tug her hand loose from his, but he would not let her. "Your family, Nathaniel. They would never approve. Your friends would not approve. Putting me in a silk gown will not make me one of them."

"You are the granddaughter of King Charles II. You already *are* one of them."

"The illegitimate, impoverished granddaughter with no family, descendent of a long line of mistresses and witches. They will have every reason to object."

"My family will be glad to see me married."

"Nathaniel, you are deluding yourself," she tried to explain, as if speaking to a misguided child. "You feel sorry for me, and responsible for my well-being. You do not want to spend the rest of your life with me. I am completely unsuitable to be the wife of a baron."

"Would it be better for me to marry someone my parents chose, based upon her family and the dowry that would come with her? Do you think I would live a better life that way?"

"You might. *She* might. Can you see me dressed in stays and hoops, my hair done up, spending all day indoors sipping tea?"

"I have seen you in silk, with your hair done up. You are ravishing. As ravishing as you are in the clothes you wear now, your feet bare, hair coming free of its braid. You could move easily into my family's world, if you wished."

"My place is not there," she begged him to understand. "I would be even more of an outsider than I am here in Greyfriars. I am not a child of the city, or of grand houses. I would not know how to live in either."

"We will spend at least half the year in the country, at one of my family's estates, or even here, at Raven Hall, if you wish."

"Nathaniel, no. It would be a mistake."

He looked at her intently. "Tell me. If we were of an equal station, would you marry me?"

She considered for a long moment, trying to find an honest answer. "I cannot say. I am happy when I am with you, and you know more about me than anyone else, but still we have not known each other for so very long. I have never spent more than half a day in your company. How do we know that we would be so intrigued by each other if we lived together day in and day out?" And how would she be able to stand it if he married her, and found a year from now that he regretted the decision? If he found that he had married her out of a feeling a responsibility rather than love?

"At least you admit to being intrigued by me. I suppose I should be happy for that."

"Nathaniel . . ."

"No couple knows how they will fare alone together until they try it, Valerian. I sometimes suspect that is the purpose of chaperonage: to keep the pair from choosing a celibate life over the aggravation of their companion's exclusive company."

"I am not jesting," she said.

"Neither am I. At least tell me you will think about it. There can be no harm in that."

"Then will you think about it as well, and consider that you may be mistaken to ask this of me and of yourself?"

"Fair is fair."

She shook her head in a frustration as deep as his own. She did not believe he would reconsider, at least not as long as she was the pathetic creature that she was now, alone and miserable in this world. She could not fool herself—she needed him right now, his comfort and his protection, but she cared too much for him to take advantage of him by making their relationship permanent, and live to see his regret. She would not do it, even though had the circumstances been different she could have found great joy in being his wife.

"Then, if you will not yet agree to marry me," he continued, "I think it only fair that you grant me a lesser favor."

"I am afraid to ask."

"Come to London with me."

"London?" The suggestion took her by surprise. "I thought you had to stay here. I thought your family had banished you."

"Well, yes, but there was never a specific time frame."

"A few months could not have been what they had in mind."

"You have said it yourself, you cannot remain here much longer."

"I never meant to go to London," she protested feebly, but the idea was not unappealing. It was, indeed, growing upon her with each mention of the name. In London she would be anonymous, allowed to go her way without question by strangers on the street. "Where would I stay? Not in your house, surely."

"I will set you up in your own rooms. I am not filthy rich, but I can at least afford that."

Valerian wondered if Theresa was watching from above, laughing. And what would her parents think? But the idea had its appeal. She could spend a few weeks in London, and then when Nathaniel saw that she was able to take care of herself again, and saw as well how poorly she fit in London, he would forget this notion of wanting to wed her, and she could go on her way, however painful that might be for herself.

"I would like to see London, if only once," she finally said.

He kissed her hand and looked at her with an intensity that made her wonder if she had seriously misjudged his determination to see them wed.

Chapter Twenty-nine

"No more than three," Valerian insisted.

Nathaniel gave a beleaguered sigh. "Three, plus the one that you will leave here wearing."

Valerian tightened her lips, her eyes narrowing. "Only if I make all the choices in material and style."

"You can choose colors and styles, but the material must be of silk."

They locked eyes, judging each other for weakness. "You will wait in the corner; you will not sit here and argue with me as I choose?"

"I will leave the premises entirely if you wish," he finally gave in, his voice turning soft. "I never meant outfitting you with suitable clothing to be a source of contention between us."

Valerian was not so quick to be wooed. "But you do understand how I feel about this?" she asked in the low, intense tones she had been using throughout, aware of the seamstress waiting several feet away, face turned away but ears listening. The dress shop had only one other patron, paging through designs, and doubtless not nearly so interesting a focus of attention as this little disagreement.

"I suppose I do, although I do think that you are being entirely unreasonable."

Valerian just stared at him until he gave a shrug of his shoulders and went to go sit down in the chairs provided for long-suffering males accompanying their women on shopping expeditions.

She could understand a bit of his confusion. After all, he was paying for her room and board, the wages of the two servants he had hired to tend her, and would be paying as well for any entertainment or transportation. So why quibble at a new wardrobe?

The answer was clear enough to her: because it made her a completely kept woman, and because she would be leaving him. It bothered her to accept tangible things from him, in a way that accepting the room and board did not.

Valerian let herself be led by the seamstress into a more private area, to be shown drawings and fabrics. "A relative has recently died," Valerian told the woman. "So I will be wanting dark colors, and simple dresses devoid of decoration. Can you do that?"

Nathaniel sat and mulled over the past couple of weeks, resigned to several hours in the dress shop. He had shopped with his sister Margaret on more than one occasion, and knew that even the purchase of a single item could take well over an hour. It was beyond him how a simple task could be turned into such a torturous endeavor.

But it did give one time to think, provided one had a quiet corner in which to do so, as he did now.

Valerian was holding up much better than he had expected, but there was a distance between them now that he did not know how to bridge. He had not slept with her since before the night at the millpond, the night that her aunt had died. It did not seem right, somehow, to ask that of her now, when she was mourning. And then there was also the issue of this newly recognized respect he had for her.

He wanted to give her everything, to see her living in beautiful surroundings, with clothes made of silk. He wanted her never to have to worry about money, or about who might try next to attack her. He wanted as well to have her in his bed every night, and see her face across from him at the breakfast table each morning. And he could do all of that, it was true, with her as his mistress.

She could be his mistress, and all that he gave her would be seen as an exchange for her sexual favors. He would make of her a high-class whore—but that he could not do. His own feelings for her demanded he do better for her than that.

The only solution was to marry her, only now she seemed further away from him than she ever had. She was quiet much of the time, her thoughts turned inward. She had hardly spoken during the entire journey to London, except to ask a question about a passing sight or to talk to Oscar in his cage.

She felt so distant, it had been a relief to have her argue with him about the dresses. There had been a spark of fire in her eyes during that exchange, and a connection with him, even if of anger. He almost wished she had tried to limit him to one mud-brown wool dress.

He would not have let her win that argument. There were reasons he wanted her clad in silk, and they were not solely to increase her beauty or appease her long-ignored vanity.

His thoughts went to his family. He had been in town for nearly a week now, and he would soon have to call on them. He had, in fact, chosen rooms for Valerian directly across the wooded park from his parents' house, to make it easier to visit them.

He loved his family, and had no wish to hurt or upset them, but he would not allow them to dictate his actions, either. When it came down to it, his "banishment" to Raven Hall had been voluntary, and the choices he made now would be his own, as well. It was his hope, however, to accomplish his ends gracefully, with the minimum of familial pain and disappointment. He knew that in this world appearance did matter, and his family would more easily accept Valerian as a lady if she dressed as one.

His thoughts were interrupted by the rustle of silk, and he raised his eyes to see Valerian approaching, sheathed collar-bone to floor in a dark royal blue gown without so much as in inch of lace. No ribbon, no trim, not a single contrasting border or falling ruffle. The tight, narrow sleeves reached all the way to her wrist, the outside edges of the cuffs slightly elongated, concealing part of her hand and making her white fingers appear all the longer and more delicate. The smooth bodice ended in a sharp point, the material of the skirts falling in neat pleats over her hips.

"The woman who originally ordered the gown decided she did not care for it before the trim and decorations were added," Valerian said with a touch of defiance. "But I find it suits me."

Even he could see that it was not a fashionable gown, and the only hint of expense was in the dull sheen of the silk. A careless glance might mark her as no one of import, but Nathaniel doubted that anyone seeing her would find it possible not to stare.

The very simplicity of the dress made it striking at a time when even the common city folk embellished their clothing with designs of flowers, and collars and ruffles of lace. The dark color set off her pale skin and blue-black hair, and intensified, if that were possible, the blue of her wolfish eyes. If she had looked like a country witch before, with her rough purple skirts and black bodices, she looked like a sorceress now, fit to cast fortunes for the king.

She looked elegant, and intimidating. And completely Valerian. He felt a slow smile spread across his face, and he rose, taking her hands in his and holding her arms wide so he could better see the gown. "Stunning. Simply, elegantly, stunning."

The questioning, uncertain wrinkle of her brow amused him. "If you had let me interfere," he said, "I doubtless would have chosen something brighter, with embroidery and lace, and a neckline that showed at least a hint of what lay beneath. And I would have ruined the gown entirely."

"I am glad you like it," she said uncertainly.

"If I did not know better, I would think you were lying."

She gave him a crooked smile, and shrugged one shoulder. "I had expected another argument, or at least displeasure."

"Perhaps if we put our minds to it, we can find something else to fight about." He waggled his eyebrows at her suggestively, and felt his heart trip when a true smile came to her lips. She tugged one of her hands free to push him playfully on his arm.

"Rake," she said.

"Prude."

"I take offense at that."

"As well you should, you heartless wench."

She laughed at that, and he wanted nothing so much as to seize the moment and hold it tight, and forever keep the shadows from returning to her eyes.

If he could not do that, he could at least hold her safe from the world.

"I hear there is a wonderful production of *Volpone* at the Athenaeum. Would you like to go?" Nathaniel asked, as their carriage rumbled by the theater in question.

Valerian yawned behind her hand. The fittings at the dressmaker's had been more tiring than she had expected, and truth be told she had about had enough of the sights of London. Nathaniel had delighted in showing her the palaces, cathedrals, shops, galleries, and entertainments of his city, but it was all beginning to wear on her. "Would you mind terribly if we stayed in tonight? I do not feel quite up to another evening out."

"No. No, of course I would not mind," he said.

"Unless you are eager to see it yourself," she offered, thinking she had sensed a trace of disappointment in his answer.

"We can see it another night."

Valerian smiled and took his arm, leaning into his side, feeling closer to him than she had for weeks. "Good. I find I miss quiet evenings at home. We have not had many chances to talk since coming to London. We are always racing about from one place to another, or you are out running errands, or whatever it is you do. You do not have another mistress stashed someplace in town, do you?" she teased, hiding the suspicion that he kept her busy with public amusements because he no longer enjoyed her solitary, depressing company.

"I beg your pardon?" he asked, his tone telling her he did not take it as a joke. "Of course not. Whatever made you suggest such a thing?"

Valerian frowned up at him. "It was but a jest, Nathaniel."

"And not a very good one."

She pushed back from him, sitting up straight so she could see him better. "Nathaniel, has something been bothering you lately? You do not seem like yourself, and not once have you . . . well, you know."

"I have not what?"

"At night. You know." She rolled her eyes, then looked at him expectantly. He met her gaze only briefly, then looked away. She sighed, and made herself say it. "You have not slept with me."

"I spend every night in your bed."

"You know what I mean," she complained. She screwed up her courage for the next question she knew she had to ask. It was what she had planned for, but still she had delayed seeking confirmation. "Have you lost your desire for me? You can tell me if 'tis so."

He finally met her eyes, gazing at her for a long moment, and she could see that the fires of desire still burned in their depths. She felt her own body's answer, and the yearning of her skin for his touch. She slowly leant forward, brushing her lips softly against his. He sat still, motionless as a stone as her lips played gently upon his, and then his arms came around her and he dragged her onto his lap, his lips taking charge of hers, then moving to caress her cheeks, her jaw, her ears.

He sucked at the bend between shoulder and neck, making her arch towards him, her breasts aching, her limbs weak with growing desire, and then he suddenly stopped. She felt him press his face into her neck, his arms still hard around her.

"Nathaniel?"

He raised his head, his face close to hers. "I will not do this to you. I will not!"

"Do what?"

"Keep you as my whore," he rasped.

"Since when has making love to me been equated with whoredom?" she asked, anger and hurt flaring in her voice. "Do you think I care about money?"

"I know you do not."

"Then what, Nathaniel? Why has what we do together suddenly made me a whore in your eyes?"

"You are not a whore!"

"Thank you for that, *my lord.*" She tried to shove her way off his lap, but he would not release her.

"I know you are not a whore, but I would make one of you if I continued this liaison as it is. You deserve better. A husband, a name for your children when they come."

"You still want me to marry you," she said, stunned. With the careful way he had been treating her, she had thought his determination had been tempered by sense. Had thought, in fact, that he had wanted to rescind the offer, and had been at a loss for how to do so.

"Have you considered it, Valerian? I want you as my wife. You deserve more than to be a man's plaything."

"Thank you very much again, for telling me how you have thought of me all this time," she snapped. All this time, lying beside him at night, enjoying the comfort of his arms but briefly until he would roll away, his back to her. All the little hurts she felt, all the small rejections, had been because he was saving her from his desires in the perverted name of honor? Because he wanted to marry her?

"Do not pretend to misunderstand me," he said. "The truth is subjective, it always has been. You know I could never think of you as a whore, but neither do I want others to think of you that way. You deserve a place in society. You deserve respectability, and it is my duty to give that to you."

"So it is guilt that prompts this," she said. Just as she had always thought!

"I have made mistakes in the past," he said, his voice low. "I have caused harm to many people, not only Laetitia and her family, but my own family as well. I want to do this right. I do not want to see either you or my family hurt."

"Not making love to me now does not change what has been."

"Perhaps not to the outside world."

Despite herself, she felt the sting of tears in her eyes. "When I ask you to make love to me, you *do* see a whore now. Everything you have said confirms it."

He grasped her face tight between his hands, forcing her to meet his eyes. "I see the woman I want to be my wife."

She sniffed back tears, and pulled her head free of his hands, sliding off his lap and back onto the carriage seat beside him. She wanted nothing more than to have him hold her, to feel him wrap his arms around her and soothe the hurt of his words away, but she could not. He did not want her as his mistress, and she could not be his wife.

As she had known but had chosen to briefly forget, there was no future in this world for two such as them.

Chapter Thirty

"Oscar, I want you to pay attention to where we are. I do not want you getting lost. Someone might mistake you for a real raven and force you to live in the Tower with the others. You would not like that, I promise you. The food would not be half so good, for starters."

Oscar ignored her, his talons sharp on her shoulder as he shifted about. She was frightened that he would lose track of her if she let him fly free here in London, but the guilt of keeping him trapped indoors, and his new trick of gnawing on the furniture out of boredom, had finally outweighed her worries.

She kicked at her grey silk skirts, and swished through the gates to the park, the maid Nathaniel had hired for her following behind. The girl, Tilly, had yet to grow accustomed to Oscar, and started each time he spoke. Her skittishness was getting on Valerian's nerves, and if she could have gone to the park without Tilly, she would have. Unfortunately, Nathaniel had made her promise not to venture out unaccompanied, and as unfamiliar as she was with London and its dangers, she had thought it wise at the time to agree.

Where *he* was, she was not quite sure. He had mumbled something about business that needed attending to, and disappeared early this morning. The silences between them had been growing longer since their talk in the carriage, and her "quiet evenings" alone with him were anything but cozy.

Valerian ignored the eyes she felt on her as she walked through the park. To be sure, there were no other ladies about with ravens on their shoulders, and she supposed she made something of a novel sight. The park was surrounded by one of the better districts of town, and it served as a public garden for those who lived there.

Valerian led Tilly away from the main carriage way, where well-to-do residents rode or drove in their afternoon finery, and they wandered down a path away from all the people. The path led into a shaded, wooded area, with a small clearing dappled by sunlight. The oaks stretching their gnarled limbs overhead reminded her of the woods around the cottage, rousing a twinge of homesickness. London might be the most marvelous city in the world, but she could not imagine permanently exchanging the forest and cliffs of home for the city's man-made wonders.

"Here now, Oscar, this looks a likely spot." She transferred him from her shoulder to her hand. "You go have fun. Get some exercise for those underused wings."

Oscar cocked his head at her, and ruffled his feathers. "Go on," Valerian urged, giving him a boost with her arm.

"Rrrraaa, go for walk," he said.

"Yes, go!"

At last he extended his wings, and with one mighty beat downwards, rose off her hand. He flew up into the branches overhead, settling on one and watching as Valerian directed Tilly to spread out a blanket on the grass.

"I shall stay right here," Valerian told the bird. "You go for a nice flight, but behave yourself."

Valerian was aware of him flitting from branch to branch, watching her settle onto the dark green blanket, reassuring himself that she would not go off and leave him. At last he flew off, and Valerian sighed and tried to get comfortable, the stays of her gown stiff around her body, her mind aware of the dangers of creasing the costly gown or staining it on the grass. She wished she were in one of her country skirts, and could take off her shoes and dig her toes into the grass.

"Your book, miss?" Tilly asked, holding out the small object.

"Yes, thank you. Will you not sit here, too, Tilly?" she asked, taking the book.

"Thank you, miss, but I could not."

Valerian watched the girl spread out her own small blanket, more a towel, really, several feet away and sit down upon it. Valerian made a face behind Tilly's back. Sometimes it felt she had been less alone in Greyfriars than she was here, surrounded by thousands of people.

She had to stop thinking like that. Greyfriars was no longer home, and never would be again. Soon she would have to pick a new place to live, and leave Nathaniel, for the longer she stayed with him, the more she felt her resolve waver, and the more tempting agreeing to marriage became. She needed to leave for her own sake as well as his, before it became impossible for her to say good-bye. That is, if it were not impossible already.

She picked up her book, a romantic novel that she had found at a bookseller's stall. She blinked away her tears and began to read, trying to lose herself in the story.

She did not know how much time had passed when a God-awful screeching pulled her out of a particularly riveting scene involving villain and virgin in a haunted castle.

"Get it off me! Aieee, my hair, my head!"

Valerian lifted her head, listening, eyes going wide. "Oh, Oscar, no." She dropped the book and scrambled up just as an auburn-haired woman stumbled into the clearing, swiping her hands at Oscar, who beat his wings about her ears in an attempt to become airborne with her hat.

"Finders keepers! Finders keepers!" Oscar cawed.

"Bad bird! Release her at once, Oscar. Oscar!" Valerian ran to the woman, searching for a handhold on the madly flapping bird.

"Waaaa aa aa aa. . . ." Oscar wailed in protest as she tried to pry his talons free of the silver lace trim of the hat.

"Stop it, stop it," Valerian scolded, her cheeks red with mortification. "I do you a favor by letting you out, and look what you do! Do you want to spend our entire stay in my rooms?" At last she got him disentangled from the woman's hat and hair, and transferred to her own shoulder. "Ah, madam, I am so very sorry. He meant no harm."

The woman stood bent over, hands on her knees, body shaking, her face turned down as she caught her breath.

"Are you all right?" Valerian asked, becoming concerned.

"Mother! Mother, where are you?" a child's voice cried from down the path.

"Lady Stanford!" a woman called.

At last the woman stood straight and raised her face, and a peculiar hiccoughing gasp escaped her as her eyes moved from Valerian's face to Oscar, once quickly over Valerian's dress, then back to her face again. "He is yours?" the woman asked.

"I am afraid so, yes," Valerian admitted.

The woman stared for a moment longer, eyes wide, then dissolved into laughter. "Good lord, I have been attacked, and had my hat ravished by a lady's pet crow." She put her hand up to her coiffure, and the tatters of lace hanging from her hat.

"Raven, my lady," Valerian corrected, lips twitching. "He meant you no harm. It is just this passion he has for shiny things."

"Oh ho?" Another trill of laughter ensued, and then the owners of the calling voices stumbled into the clearing, a finely dressed woman and a little boy about six years old.

"Mother?" the little boy asked, running up to the woman, "Are you all right?"

"Lady Stanford, are you injured?" the other woman asked.

Lady Stanford wiped delicately under her eyes with the edges of her index fingers, removing the tears, chuckles still rumbling in her chest. "Good heavens, yes, Lucas, I am all right. And no, Catherine, I am not injured."

"Oscar is a superior bird," Oscar said.

The little boy's eyes widened, and he sucked in a breath, shaking with excitement. "Ohhh, he talks! Mother, did you hear him?" He tugged at her skirts.

"Yes, I heard."

Valerian lifted Oscar onto her hand, and knelt down on the grass in front of the boy, ignoring her skirts. "If you are very gentle, you can pet him," she told the boy.

Lucas looked up at his mother for permission. Lady Stanford nodded, and the boy reached out a quivering hand. Oscar tilted his head, and Lucas jerked back his hand.

"He will not hurt you," Valerian said. "He has been petted by many, many children."

Lucas reached out again, and this time stroked Oscar's back three quick times.

"Biscuit!" Oscar declared, making Lucas jump. "Poor hungry bird. Pooooor hungry bird."

The women laughed, and Valerian smiled. After an

unsure moment, Lucas smiled too, and stepped closer to get a better look at Oscar.

"Did you train him yourself?" Lady Stanford asked. "I did not know that ravens could talk."

"I have had him since he was a chick," Valerian explained, keeping her eye on Lucas and Oscar. "Ravens are intelligent birds. Smarter than parrots."

"Can we show Clary?" Lucas asked, his fear all but gone. "She would like to see him. Can we?"

"We could not impose on this lady," Lady Stanford said.

Valerian glanced up at the woman. "Who is Clary?"

"My daughter Clarissa. She is confined to the indoors, I am afraid. She is recovering from a nasty cold."

"She loves birds," Lucas said.

Valerian stood up, giving her skirts a brief shake that did nothing to remove the damp spots over the knees. "It would be no imposition to show her Oscar. I know how bored children can get, stuck indoors. I would be happy to provide her some entertainment."

"Really, I do not think I could ask such a thing. . . ." Lady Stanford said, trailing off with a hopeful look on her lovely face.

"Nonsense. It shall be my pleasure, and 'twill be little enough to amend for the fright Oscar gave you. I insist."

"Well, if you insist, then I should not be so rude as to disappoint you." Lady Stanford smiled, and Valerian found that she could not resist returning the expression.

"Have you bedded her then, and gotten her pregnant, like you did the last one?" Nathaniel's father, the earl of Roth, asked, his face red with anger as he stood stiffly in front of the fireplace.

"She is not pregnant, and she is nothing like Laetitia," Nathaniel said through his clenched jaw, hanging onto his temper by a thin thread.

"You can understand why your father might think so," his mother put in from her damask-upholstered chair. "After all, she is from no better a background, and from what you have said, has no family but a cousin who is married to a cobbler. She does not sound particularly suitable to be the next countess."

Nathaniel closed his eyes, drawing on his patience. "She is intelligent and kind, with a natural grace and beauty. She is well-educated and generous, and every inch a lady."

"It sounds to me as if you are infatuated with the girl," his father said, his tone thick with disapproval. "You are in no state to make a rational decision on the matter, if you are thinking with your breeches and not your head. This is just the situation that got you into trouble last time."

"Listen to your father," his mother said. "I do not know why you insist on choosing your women from the lower classes. Do you purposefully mean to hurt us?"

"For the last time, she is nothing like Laetitia. The situations are not in the least alike!"

"You are deluding yourself if you think not," his father said. "Perhaps you want to marry the girl because you messed things up so badly with that other chit, eh? Perhaps you think you can do it over with this one, make things right somehow, atone for what you did to Laetitia by offering to marry this girl. Have you considered that?"

"That is not true," Nathaniel protested, but even as he said it felt the subtle sting of truth. It was certainly not the whole reason he wanted to marry Valerian, but he could not deny that his guilt over his last affair had changed him, changed how he chose now to deal with Valerian. The man he had been a year ago would have thought nothing of keeping her as his mistress.

"Is it not?" his father asked. "Even though you know this Miss Bright is unsuitable, you could have married her without our permission. I think you want us to tell you you cannot, to make your choice for you, so you can absolve yourself of responsibility and tell yourself you did all you could this time around. What other reason would you have to be here, seeking our approval?"

Nathaniel looked at his father, and when he spoke his voice was flat. "Because she will not have me. She believes she is an unsuitable choice of wife for a baron, and does not even know I will inherit the earldom. She believes that my family would never accept her, nor my friends, and thus there is no future for us."

Both his parents were silent at that proclamation, and then his father grunted. "Well. It sounds as if she may be a step above that Laetitia wench, after all."

"If she will not have you," his mother asked, "then why are you here?"

His father answered for him, speaking slowly as if deciphering a mystery. " 'Twould seem he thinks that if he can get our approval, he will be able to persuade her to marry him."

"Well, he must be deluded to think we would help with that," his mother scoffed.

"I think the fool truly figures himself in love," Lord Warrington said.

Nathaniel laughed despite himself, and rubbed his face with his hands. Good lord, somewhere along the way he had lost his mind. How had he ever thought that he could enlist his parents' aid in getting Valerian to marry him? A more lamebrained scheme he had never had.

His laughter would not stop, and he stumbled over to a chair and dropped down into it, his legs sprawled out before him. He was dimly aware of his mother frowning at him.

"I do not know what has gotten into you," she scolded, then got up to leave the room. "Talk to him," she said to his father, as she paused at the door. "I begin to think he is not right in the head."

How right she was, and she did not even know the half of it. He should have carted Valerian off to Scotland the same night her aunt died, and married her before she had the sense to refuse him.

Instead, he had bungled the entire affair. Even his relationship with Valerian had suffered as a result of his efforts to be honorable. He had been keeping her at arm's length, for fear that his desire for her would overwhelm his intentions if he let her closer. And this, when she needed him most.

He had been an idiot. His parents would never see past her lack of a titled family. "I do not suppose it would make any difference to you if I said her grandfather was Charles II, would it?" he threw out.

"I do not know why it should impress me that one of her parents was a bastard."

Nathaniel nodded, aware that he must have a moronic grin on his face. "You have always been friends with Thomas Carlyle. You must have run in the same circles in your youth. You probably met her mother or aunt. They went by the name Harrow at the time, Theresa and Emmeline. Their mother was one of Charles II's mistresses at one time, although it did not stop her from later being murdered, accused of witchcraft."

Lord Warrington narrowed his eyes in concentration, then widened them suddenly.

"The very same," Nathaniel said, seeing that his father did indeed remember the sisters. "It truly would be a scandal to marry her, coming from such a family. And do you know? I do not care."

"I would have no choice but to cut you off," his father said coldly. "I would disinherit you."

"You do not have the power. The title will go to me, no matter what you do, as well as the family seat. Raven Hall is already mine, God bless Great-uncle George and his lack of heirs. I need neither your money nor your approval."

"You forget who has the upper hand here," his father said, but Nathaniel could hear the hint of desperation in his voice. "You can give up your family, but you will not get your woman without us."

"I certainly will not get her with you. It seems to me I stand a better chance alone." He felt his spirits lift giddily at the prospect. He could not please both his parents and himself in this. There was no reason to continue to try. It was his own conscience that mattered: It was his own life that had to be lived.

He stood up. "Good-bye, Father." He saw the look of disbelief in the older man's eyes, and turned away.

"Oscar is a *greedy* guts," five-year-old Clarissa said, feeding him another piece of broken biscuit. "Oscar is a *greedy* guts."

"Greedy guts," Oscar repeated, and Clarissa laughed until her laughter turned into a hacking cough.

"Perhaps that is enough excitement for one afternoon," Lady Stanford said.

They were in the nursery, Lady Stanford, Valerian, Clarissa, and Lucas. Valerian had discovered that Catherine was in fact Lady Stanford's personal maid, despite her elegant dress. She was down in the kitchen, feeding Tilly.

"No, Mother. Please, a little longer," Clarissa wheezed when she had the coughing under control.

Valerian saw the indecision on Lady Stanford's brow and added her own coaxing to Clarissa's. "A little longer will not hurt," she said. And then, after a moment, "I know something of children's ailments. Would you mind if I looked more closely at Clary?"

"The doctor has been here several times. The cough, it seems to linger no matter what medicines he brings."

"My own father was a doctor. May I check her? I will do no harm."

"Of course you would not. Yes, please, if you know anything that might help, I would be grateful to hear it."

Valerian gave her a reassuring smile and went through the motions of a brief examination, relying more on her internal senses than what she saw on the outside. Clarissa's attention stayed on Oscar, so much so that she seemed oblivious to Valerian's touch.

Valerian heard the nursery door open as if from a distance, and ignored the sound, and the soft voices that followed, focusing her thoughts deeper within herself and within Clarissa's sick body. She found the illness in the child's lungs, embedded deep within, and felt how her body fought to rid itself of the inflammation. The battle was presently a stalemate, masquerading as the relatively harmless aftereffects of a cold.

The power to heal flowed through Valerian's blood, stronger than she had ever felt it before, and she could not have restrained it if she had wished to. Her hands warmed, and she felt the force of her ability flood the girl's lungs, absorbing the inflammation and sending strength surging through the child's body.

She took her hands away and opened her eyes. Clarissa looked up at her in puzzlement, and touched the place on her arm where Valerian's hands had rested. "It tingles," she whispered to Valerian.

"I know," Valerian whispered back. She straightened, and turned to find that Lady Stanford had been joined by an older woman. They were both watching her: Lady Stanford with curiosity, the older woman with suspicion and bad humor.

"She is on the mend," Valerian said. "I would not be surprised to see her up and about within a day or so."

"Dr. Garrick said it would be at least a week yet before

she should be let out of bed," the older woman said. "I think we would do better to trust his opinion. Or are you a doctor, too?"

Valerian saw Lady Stanford tighten her lips, but she could understand the older woman's distrust, and smiled gently. "Merely a doctor's daughter, who has seen dozens of similar cases. Please do continue to have Dr. Garrick examine her. I would never expect you to take the word of a stranger."

"Grandmama, did you see Oscar? I want a raven just like him," Clarissa said, her voice clearer than it had been minutes before. "He talks." Clarissa held a piece of biscuit up, out of Oscar's reach.

"Pooor hungry bird," Oscar said.

The older woman raised her eyebrows.

"He attacked Mama's hat," Lucas added from the other side of Clarissa's bed, where he was sitting on a wooden chair, feet swinging.

"Did he indeed?"

"She screamed and screamed and ran through the park so fast that—"

"Lucas, that is enough," Lady Stanford interrupted. "I am sure that Grandmama does not wish to hear the entire story."

"On the contrary." The woman sat, a hint of a smile softening her features. She gestured to Lucas, who slid off his chair and ran to her, climbing up onto her lap. "It is a fascinating story, and it sounds like one I should very much like to hear. But first, perhaps introductions are in order?"

Lady Stanford colored. "Of course. How remiss of me. Mother, this is Valerian Bright, who is in town to visit a friend. Miss Bright, my mother, Lilith Warrington, the countess of Roth."

Valerian felt the blood slowly drain from her face. Lady

Warrington's smile disappeared, her face growing hard as she slowly stood, not even looking at Lucas as she set him on his feet.

Valerian stood as well, and lifted Oscar onto her hand, feeling her heart thumping in her chest. "Your pardon, Lady Warrington. I would not have come here if I had known whose house it was. I shall leave at once."

"Miss Bright? Mother?" Lady Stanford said. "I do not understand. Do you know each other?"

"We know *of* one another," Lady Warrington said softly. "This is the woman your brother has foolishly determined to marry. And you can see what a schemer she is, to have worked her way into your confidence so quickly."

Valerian breathed deeply through her nose, seeking calm. She liked Lady Stanford, and would not have her thinking ill of her. "Please believe me," she said to Lady Stanford. "I had no idea you were Nathaniel's sister. I could not have known. Forgive me." She moved quickly to the door, opened it, and rushed down the corridor, Oscar flapping his wings to keep his balance on her hand.

"Oh, Oscar," she whispered under her breath, as she found the stairs and fairly ran down them. "Of all the hats in all the city, why hers?"

"Rrrraww," Oscar answered.

"Foolish, foolish bird," Valerian said, her throat tightening.

"Miss Bright, wait!" Lady Stanford called from behind. Valerian did not pause, finding the next flight of stairs and hurrying down them, the heels of her new shoes clacking on the marble. She had never intended to meet his family. And doing so by accident, with her defenses down. . . .

"Eee-diot! Eee-diot!" Oscar cawed, and lifted off of her hand. "Baron Ravenall!"

"Oscar, no!" Valerian stopped, watching in horror as

Oscar took flight in the grand foyer of the house. One of the sliding wooden doors that had been closed when she arrived was open now, and framed in the opening stood a startled Nathaniel.

"Oscar? What?" was all he had the chance to say before Oscar alit on his shoulder and started pecking at the lace of his cravat. Nathaniel paid no attention, his eyes seeking her out where she stood frozen on the staircase. "Valerian? What in God's name—"

"What in—" another male voice echoed, and a man who could only be Nathaniel's father came up beside him, shoving the other sliding door wide, his dark eyes taking in the raven and then Valerian. Valerian heard the footsteps of Nathaniel's sister and mother behind her, and then they, too, halted on the stairs.

"Nathaniel, I am so sorry," Valerian said, recovering her senses. She took the last few stairs, then walked stiffly across the foyer to him. "I met Lady Stanford in the park, and her name was different, I did not know she was your sister." She reached up and took Oscar, a piece of lace cravat ripping off and dangling from his beak as she pulled him away and put him on her own shoulder.

"It is all right," Nathaniel said, taking her arm and leading her away from his family, towards the front door. "They are no longer of consequence."

Valerian looked over her shoulder at the tableaux of parents and sister. Lady Stanford stood behind her mother on the stairs, her fist at her mouth, her eyes wide and pained. Lady Warrington stood motionless, one hand clenched to the rail. Lord Warrington stepped out into the foyer as if to get a better look at her, and her gaze met his assessing one.

"Miss Bright," he said. "Before you leave, may I have a word with you?"

Nathaniel's grip dug deeper into her arm. "You are hurting me," she complained, just loud enough for him to hear.

His grip abruptly loosened. "Do not speak to him. He has nothing of importance to say."

"No, wait," she said, digging in her heels. "I think I should talk to him."

"Speaking with him will change nothing. I doubt he even possesses the flexibility to see things from another's viewpoint."

She pulled free of Nathaniel's hand and turned around. "Lord Warrington," she said, nodding an acknowledgment to him, Oscar fidgeting on her shoulder. "I would like to speak with you as well."

Lord Warrington inclined his head in acceptance. Valerian did not dare look at Nathaniel. She could feel his presence close behind her, and the tension that came off him like heat. He had obviously been speaking of her to his parents, and it had not gone well.

She took several steps towards Lord Warrington. "Please allow me to say what I feel I must. You, too, Nathaniel," she added, as he moved to stand beside her.

Oscar flew to the top of the tall clock that stood against the wall, gripping the carved tracery there with his claws, bobbing and watching the scene. Valerian took a deep breath and gathered her thoughts. She had never planned to address Nathaniel's parents, but Fate, or God—or maybe just Oscar—had given her the opportunity, and she knew that this must be done.

"Let me begin by saying that I am aware that I am an unsuitable choice for Nathaniel's wife, for reasons of family and fortune alone—"

"Your have royal blood in your veins," Nathaniel interrupted. "Which is more than any of us can say."

Valerian frowned at him, but it was Lady Warrington who chided him. "Let the girl speak, Nathaniel."

"Thank you, Lady Warrington. As I was saying, I know I am unsuitable. Perhaps that alone would not be enough to prevent a marriage, but there is more at issue here. I have no wish to be the wedge that divides Nathaniel from his family."

"You are not a wedge," Nathaniel interrupted angrily. "It is their inability to see beyond a name that is the wedge."

"Nathaniel, no," Valerian said. "They see that we are from different worlds, as I have known all along. I met your friends, however briefly. I could not be happy amongst them. I could not be happy here, in London, even for part of the year. I could not even wear these clothes, beautiful as they are," she said, touching her tight bodice. "They strangle me, confine me. I cannot be myself in them. I was not made to walk in marble halls on silken slippers."

Nathaniel grasped her by the shoulders. "We will go back to Raven Hall. You are comfortable there, you can be yourself."

"And if we had children, Nathaniel, what then? They would never know their grandparents, their aunt, their cousins. It would not be fair to them, and would not be fair to your family."

"That is their choice, not mine."

"I will not be the cause of such a division."

He looked at her intently. "There is more to it, Valerian, there has to be. You are not telling me everything. You do not want to spend your life with me, is that the truth of it? Is it that you care nothing for me? That is the only reason I know of that could justify this stubbornness on your part."

Her heart ached at the question, and it was difficult to meet his eyes. "I could not spend my life with you, not when there is another still in your heart."

"What do you mean? What other?"

"Laetitia, Nathaniel."

"Laetitia? I never loved her," he said, genuinely puzzled. "How could you think that I did?"

"She is still in your heart. Every time you look at me, part of you sees her. I know it. I feel it. It may not be love that you felt for her, but she haunts you still."

He opened his mouth as if to reply, then closed it again. She watched as he shut his eyes for a long moment. When he opened them again, there was a deep sadness there. "You and my father, you are quite the pair. Perhaps I do seek in some manner to make amends for my past, but that is not all there is." He dropped his voice to a hoarse whisper. "I care for you, Valerian. Very much."

Care. Not love. That hurt much more than the admission about Laetitia. She felt the sting of tears and willed them back. "Let me go, Nathaniel. It is the kindest thing you could do for me. Seek the forgiveness of Laetitia's father, and the forgiveness of your own heart. Rebuild the relationship with your parents."

"You need me, Valerian. You have no home, you have no place to go."

"Is that a good reason to wed?"

"Do you truly care nothing for me?"

She felt a tear spill over and trickle down her cheek. She reached out and touched her fingertips to his lips. "It is because I do care that I ask this of you. Marrying me would be a mistake, and you would come to regret it."

He released her shoulders and backed away from her, his head shaking from side to side. "You will not marry me, but would live happily as my mistress." He laughed. "The world has gone crazy. Crazy! Am I the only sane one left?"

"Eee-diot," Oscar said from atop the clock. "Ee-diot, ee-diot, ee-diot!"

Nathaniel stared at the bird, then laughed again. "You knew me the moment you first laid eyes on me, Oscar. That first day I rode into Greyfriars. I should have listened." He turned to his family where they stood, silent.

"You need not have entered the battle at all. My own queen has destroyed me."

He turned back to Valerian, and gave her a formal, mocking bow. "Your Majesty, I surrender the field to you, and wish you joy of it!" He straightened, and met her eyes with a look she knew would follow her the rest of her days, filled with the anguish of betrayal and rejection. Then he was gone, striding out the front door and slamming it behind him before she could find anything to say.

A sob erupted from her throat, and then Lady Stanford was beside her, her arm around her, helping her into the drawing room and to a chair, murmuring the wordless sounds of a mother who holds a child in pain.

Chapter Thirty-one

December 24, 1737
Goodramgate, York

Dear Charmaine,

It is Christmas Eve, and I find myself longing for the comfort of family. It has been over half a year since I left Greyfriars, and I have been remiss in not writing to you sooner to tell you of my whereabouts and well-being. I hope you will forgive me my tardiness. It has not been an easy seven months, and perhaps I thought it would go more smoothly if I did not think of home.

As you know already, I let Baron Ravenall take me to London. What you do not know is that we parted ways some few weeks later. I will not dwell here on the difficulty of that event, knowing as I do your opinions on the matter. Suffice it to say that my heart has yet to recover.

Valerian paused in her writing, examining that understatement. Her heart felt as if it had been ripped in half, and it bled with every breath. Charmaine would not want to hear of that, though, and would have no sympathy. She dipped her quill in the ink, and resumed writing.

With the assistance of the baron's sister, Lady Stanford, I took a coach to Yorkshire, and found my way to the village where I was born. I do not know what I hoped to find there—some sense of connection to my parents, perhaps, or at least the stirring of memories—but all seemed changed from when I was a child. Doubtless there were those who remembered my father and mother, and perhaps myself as well—villages do not quickly forget—but I did not linger to discover who or where they were.

It would perhaps be more honest to say that she did not dare linger, to be asked questions about what had become of her in all these years, and why she was back, unmarried, by all appearances wandering to no purpose. She did not have Aunt Theresa's gift for a plausible story, and did not wish to start her new life with lies.

I pawned the sapphire necklace in London—again, with the help of Lady Stanford—and between that and the gold coins, I have no pressing need to find work. The notion of sitting idly by, watching life through the window of rented rooms, however, does not appeal. After leaving the village of my birth, I turned my steps to York.

I do believe you would like York, Charmaine. York Minster is as impressive as any cathedral in London, the narrow streets bustle with activity from dawn to dusk and yet I do not feel as overwhelmed as I did in

London. I feel I can perhaps find a place for myself here, and hide myself in the anonymity of the crowds at the same time.

That was true enough, she supposed. She did like York, with its wall around the heart of the city, and its cozy shops that tempted her to part with her money. It felt more human than London, and it was easy to hire a mount and escape to the moors when the crowds became too much to bear.

There were many places I could have found work, paid or not (charitable institutions are forever in need of help), but in the end I could not resist the temptation of an apothecary. Mr. Jimson, the owner, had recently inherited from his father, and was (and is still) regrettably uninformed as to the proper preparation and use of the medicines in his supply. It took but little time to convince him he had need of my help, and I have all but taken over.

Poor Mr. Jimson. He could not tell the difference between belladonna and chamomile if he had a cup of each poured down his throat. He was also unmarried: That was yet another detail she would not share with Charmaine. Her cousin would think it a splendid opportunity for Valerian to settle down.

I do spend time with the sick, at the orphanage and the charity hospital, but I am discreet with my attentions. I have inexplicably grown stronger in my healing. I do not know why. Perhaps coming so close to death in the millpond unleashed some hidden reservoir of ability. I do not become as tired as I used to, and have found that I can do much to help without making a fainting spectacle of myself afterwards.

The nursing sisters publicly put improvements in their patients down to the grace of God, although I believe that privately they attribute it at least in part to their own care. Either way, I am more than content to let others take the credit.

Valerian looked up from the letter, gazing out the window above the little table where she wrote. It had started to snow, flakes like goose down sinking through the black night.

"Look Oscar, snow."

"Biscuit!"

She broke up the last of the shortbread a regular patron of the apothecary had given her for Christmas, and she fed it to him. "What is Oscar?" she asked.

"Oscar is a greedy guts."

She smiled, and thought of little Clary. She did not doubt that the girl was having a merry Christmas, with Lady Stanford for a mother, and her brother Lucas who even at age six was thoughtful of her.

She picked up the quill, nibbled at the frayed end of the feather, then dipped the nib once again.

I come now to the part of this letter that gives me the most trouble. I have thought for a long time on this, and still do not know if I am right to tell you.

The matter is thus: I have inadvertently discovered the identity of your father. He knows nothing of you, not even that Theresa ever carried a child. I am sorry to say this so bluntly. I know no other way.

I will not say here who he is. I believe him to be a good man, but I leave it for you to decide what you do or do not wish to know. No one but myself knows of this, and if it is your desire, I shall never again speak of it.

With sincerest wishes for the continued health and happiness of both you and Howard,
Your cousin,
Valerian.

"That will have to do," she said to Oscar. She blotted the paper, folded it, and sealed it with maroon wax and the old signet ring she had found for sale in a trinket shop, depicting a bird that looked much like Oscar in a bad mood.

She left the letter on the table and went to put another scoop of coal on the fire, then poured herself a mug of the cider she had left to warm. She sat in the big chair she had bought used, the velvet worn away over the arms, and tucked her feet up beneath her.

She stared into the flames and sipped her cider, the streets outside silent in the snow. As they did every evening, her thoughts went to Nathaniel, and she wondered for the thousandth time where he was and if he thought of her.

"Merry Christmas," she whispered. "Wherever you are."

She had only the rustle of Oscar's feathers in answer.

Nathaniel stood looking out the window at the soggy night, ignoring the cold that seeped through the glass, ignoring as well the sounds of his family's revelry that reached him from elsewhere in the house. He had lost the ability to don a polite mask when his mind and heart were elsewhere.

Where was she tonight? Did she think of him? Perhaps she had already found another to take his place.

That first month, he had refused to think of her and had cut himself off from his family when he learned they had helped her to leave. When Margaret would not tell him where Valerian had gone, he had for one terrible moment felt pure hatred for his sister. It was then that he had left, returning to his old haunts to lick his wounds and seek solace in the familiarity of old habits and acquaintances.

Only there was no solace to be found. The entertainments that had once filled his days proved themselves tiresome and juvenile, and even worse, incapable of performing the lowly service of distraction.

And it was then, when he was sick unto death of himself and his life, that he had let her back into his thoughts. For the first time, he examined with a clear mind what she had said to him. And for the first time, he thought he understood it.

"I have found her, God damn her," Paul said, stomping into the room behind him.

His pulse beat wildly for a moment, hope rising within him, and then logic took a cold swipe at his assumptions. He turned away from the window and looked at Paul, whose nose and cheeks were red with the damp chill of outdoors. "By 'her' I assume you to mean Gwendolyn Miller?"

"Who else? The ungrateful strumpet. I found her bedded down with Beauchamp, and she did not even have the grace to blush! Said he had more to offer, and that I was a bore, besides. Said, and I give you her very words here, 'You cannot have thought you had a claim to me.' I save her from that godforsaken ditch of a village, take her to London—which she would never have seen otherwise, you can bet your boots on that—lodge her, provide for her, buy her clothes and jewels, and the first man who comes by with a bigger diamond in his cravat, she is gone."

Nathaniel crooked a smile at his friend. "And what of Beauchamp?"

Paul blew out a breath and shrugged, a sparkle of amusement kindling in his eyes. "I thought he would have an apoplexy, lying there red in the face, sheet pulled up to his chin. Kept eyeing my sword, like I intended to use it over the likes of her. Although, I must say, there was a certain temptation to do so, if only for the novelty of playing the wronged party. I would have liked to see him climb out the window bare-assed, that is for certain. Would have made a bigger target than I ever did."

"Maybe next time you will be more fortunate."

"Next time. Now there is an unhappy thought." Paul walked over to the desk, and sprawled in the chair where Nathaniel had sat most of the day. "First I am the wronged lover, and then what next? I can almost hear the clank of ball and chain. Marriage, to some convent-bred virgin that I shall have to guard day and night from the advances of unscrupulous young men. It will be God's revenge upon me, to spend my old age a jealous miser of my wife's body."

Nathaniel crossed his arms and cocked an eyebrow. "Your disgust at that future is not entirely convincing."

"I should rather be struck dead by lightning than married! At least 'tis a quicker death." Paul's eye lit on the leather-bound diary lying on the desk, open to a page of feminine handwriting. "Here now, what is this?"

Nathaniel unfolded his arms and walked to the desk to pick it up, turning idly through the pages. "Laetitia's diary. Her father sent it to me this morning."

Paul sat back, making the chair creak. "Blow me down. Why?"

Nathaniel shrugged, uncomfortable speaking of it while the contents of the pages were still fresh in his mind. *"I locked myself in my room all Today, and with father's old razor I cut upon my arm until the self-loathing went away. I do not know why it calms me so to carve upon my flesh,"* she had written, a year before he had met her. *"Sometimes I look in the mirror and I see such an ugly, stupid, awkward girl that I wonder my own family can stand to be in my company. I am not fit to live."* The entries had gone on like that, up to and through the time that he had known her.

The entry detailing their first meeting, brief as it had

been and long forgotten by him, was unsettling to read even with the distance of time. *"He smiled at me! I do swear it, he smiled at me, and I could see he saw something he liked, however little. If only he were mine—I love him already. I love him! I shall kill myself if I cannot have him."* And then, when he had broken a date with her, *"I cannot let him undress me the next time we make love. He will see the scabs and be disgusted. I did not mean to cut so many times, so deep, but I was unable to stop. I hate him! Even as I need him, I hate him. I do not know how he stands me. I am beneath contempt."*

At last he answered Paul, "I think it is Mr. Mowbray's way of absolving me. Or forgiving me. Perhaps both. I have been writing to him for many months, trying to gain an audience with him, trying to find some means of making restitution, with never any answer. And then this morning a package arrived, containing this diary and a short letter."

"What did the letter say?"

Nathaniel walked over to the fireplace, his thumb rubbing over the smooth leather of the diary's cover. "Only that he had found the diary a short time ago, and that it had changed his perspective on his daughter, and on what had happened. He said he trusted that I would know what to do with the diary when I had read it."

He looked down at the small book in his hands. Between its covers rested a young woman's tortured world, filled with self-hatred, desperation, and death long before he himself had entered it. He had not behaved well with Laetitia, but he could no longer believe himself completely responsible for her demise. She had needed more than it was in anyone's power to give.

"And?"

"And she has suffered enough. We all have." He bent down, and gently tossed the diary into the fire. *"Requiescat in pace."*

Chapter Thirty-two

Valerian shoved the front door closed with her foot, glad to be out of the biting air, her arms sore from carrying her market basket. City living was making her soft.

"Miss Bright?" a scratchy voice called out from behind the closest door.

Valerian grimaced, then smoothed her features. "Yes, it is I."

Her landlady poked her head out of her apartment. "Thought it might be. Cold out there, eh?"

"Quite."

"Like to freeze the nipples off a—"

"Yes, I entirely agree," Valerian interrupted, stepping backwards down the hall towards the stairs. Her landlady had an unholy love of talking, and at this moment Valerian was much more intrigued by the cooling meat pie in her basket than metaphors involving frostbitten nipples.

"Now wait a moment, do not be in such a hurry to be gone—"

"My dinner, it is half-chilled already," Valerian pleaded, gesturing to her basket.

"There be a letter came for you."

Valerian stopped. "Letter?"

"Did I not just hear myself say that very word?" The woman pointed to the rickety console shoved against the wall.

Valerian dropped her basket to the floor and dashed to the table, sorting through the mail until she found it. It was Charmaine's handwriting. She had almost convinced herself that her cousin would not write back.

She slipped a finger under the flap, ready to break the seal, then remembered her landlady. She looked up. Her landlady was watching with bright eyes, looking for all the world like a hungry squirrel.

"Thank you," Valerian said. "I should not have liked to have missed this." She retrieved her basket and nodded once more to her landlady, then hurried up the stairs.

She restrained herself until she had greeted and fed Oscar, built up the fire, and set her kettle to boil, and then could resist no longer. She sat in her big chair, pulled up close to the fire, her stocking feet resting against the fender, and broke the seal.

February 10
Greyfriars

Dear Valerian,

It gave me great joy to receive your letter, however disturbing some of the contents may have been. I had feared that I would never hear from you again, and that I would have no one to blame for that but myself.

Much has happened here in the time since you left. Gwendolyn Miller ran off with that friend of the baron's, Mr. Carlyle. Eddie O'Connor ran off to sea, it is said to escape the presence of females, who have given him nothing but trouble. John Torrance injured a finger, and when all was said and done, the surgeon in Yarborough had removed his entire left hand. He blames Alice for the loss, claiming that if she had not driven you away, he would still have his hand. I do not doubt that he is correct.

The day does not pass that someone does not ask if I have heard news of you, and when you are to return. This winter has been especially hard, with many falling ill, and not a few dying. The nearest doctor is, as I have said, in Yarborough, and after John Torrance's accident, few would be willing to see him even if he came to their homes. Which, of course, he does not.

We must sound a fickle lot: We hate you one day, and love you the next. Your reputation has taken on a faint glow of sainthood in your absence. The terrors of disease are proving far stronger than those of spirits and spells. Hacking coughs and watery bowels are winning you favor where your attentions and care never did.

Since receiving your letter, I have thought long about the bonds of family. A year ago, I would have asked for the name of the man who fathered me. Today I will not. It is difficult for me to express what has changed, except to say that I see more clearly the value of those who share my life. This man, whoever he is, does not. He doubtless has his own family to care for anyway, and would not welcome a disruption of this sort. When all is said and done, family are those whom you love.

You have always been a clever girl, and I think you know what I am trying to say. The cottage has been rented out, but you could stay with Howard and me until the lease is up, and then it would be yours.

Come home, Valerian.

Your cousin,
Charmaine

Valerian dropped the letter to her lap. *Come home*. Back to Greyfriars, to Charmaine, and to the cottage. The world she thought lost to her forever was asking for her to come back. She felt a tightness in her throat, and sat staring into space as she tried to comprehend being wanted again.

And what of Nathaniel?

Charmaine had made no mention of him. But did the omission mean that he had returned to Raven Hall, or that he had not? Did Charmaine think any mention of him would frighten her, or draw her?

The very thought that she might see him again made her stomach knot. He could treat her like a mere acquaintance, or perhaps not acknowledge her at all. She knew she could not do the same, not when she still woke in the night from dreams of being held in his arms.

But to go home. . . . She looked around her rented rooms, at the touches she had added in an effort to make the place her own, to make it cozy and homey. They were comfortable rooms, but she knew they could never be home, not when friends and family were elsewhere.

Truly, it was not such a hard decision to make.

"Oscar!"

". . . is a greedy guts. Rrrawww!"

"Pack your biscuits, darling. We have traveling to do!"

Chapter Thirty-two

"Grey skies over Greyfriars, Oscar," Valerian said as she set down his cage on the muddy road. "Have you ever seen anything more lovely?"

"Biscuit!"

Valerian tucked up her old black skirts to keep them out of the mud, and squatted down to unfasten the door to the cage. She had hitched a ride with a tinker up until a mile back, and come the rest of the way from Yarborough on foot. Her silk dresses and other belongings were in her trunks at the Yarborough inn where she had stayed last night, waiting to be picked up. If, that is, she definitely decided to stay.

She lifted Oscar out on her wrist, and let him ruffle and stretch his wings. "Go on now, go see if Charmaine has laundry drying that you can pull into the mud," she said, and gave him a boost up into the air.

"Rrrawww!" he cried, and flapped his way upwards. He

circled her twice where she stood on the rutted road, then flew off towards the trailing chimney smoke of the village.

Valerian picked up the cage and continued on, then paused when she came to the millpond, grey-brown and edged with the yellow stalks of dead weeds. The millwheel turned with its regular thunk-splash sound, peaceful in the quiet of the day. She felt no lingering fear, despite what had happened here. It had all been washed away by her miraculous experience in the water's cold depths.

She walked slowly on, strangely reassured by the sight of the millpond, so placid as it powered the wheel. It was a part of her internal landscape now, forever linked to her vision of her family, and that overwhelming sense of universal connection that had led, she was certain now, to the increase in her ability to heal. It was linked as well to her awakening in Nathaniel's care.

She doubted he would ever again look at her with such caring as he had at that moment.

She pressed her lips tight together and locked away the thought. If she were to come back to Greyfriars to live, she would have to learn to think of their relationship as something in the past. Learn to think of neither it nor him at all, if she could.

Her lip trembled, and she clenched her jaw against it. She had done the right thing by refusing him, the right thing for both of them.

Charmaine's home was only a few houses from the edge of town, and Valerian made her way quickly to it, nodding a greeting to the surprised woman feeding chickens next door. She pushed open the shop door, only to have it bump against something that yelped a protest on the other side. She craned around the door to see a young boy with a broom.

"Oh!" Valerian said. "Excuse me!" And then, realizing she had never seen him before, "Who are you?"

"Bertie, miss." He looked none too pleased at her interruption of his task, a fierce little scowl on his face.

"Ah, Bertie." As if that were explanation enough.

"Valerian?" came a tentative voice, and then Charmaine appeared in the doorway at the back of the shop. "It *is* you! Why did you not tell me you were coming?" Charmaine rushed halfway across the shop, then stopped, looking suddenly self-conscious.

Valerian closed the distance between them and gave her cousin an awkward hug. It was not something she could ever remember doing, but it felt like the right thing at this moment, and after a few stiff seconds Charmaine gave her a quick hug back, then pulled away.

"Here now, let me look at you," Charmaine said, standing back and eyeing her up and down. "Why are you wearing that old thing? I thought you would have spruced up a bit, having been to London, and living in a city like York."

Valerian shrugged. "I thought I would be more comfortable in this." Thought, too, that it would be easier to slip into her old life. But perhaps wearing her old clothes had been a mistake. She was not the same person she had been when she left, and dressing as if nothing had changed could not change the fact that everything had.

"Aye, well, suit yourself. I see you have met Bertie," Charmaine said, gesturing for the boy to come closer.

Valerian raised a brow in silent inquiry.

Charmaine's narrow mouth twitched for a moment in what might have been the beginnings of a smile. "Howard's apprentice. From the orphanage in Yarborough. He has been with us for almost two months now. Right, Bertie?" Charmaine said, nudging him on the shoulder.

"Aye," the boy grunted.

"I think you have done enough in here today," Charmaine said, indulgence in her voice.

"Aye!" Bertie repeated, with considerably more enthusiasm. He needed no second hint, and was out the door like a shot.

"Be home in time for supper!" Charmaine called after him, and then to Valerian, "The boy is three parts mischief, four parts stubbornness."

"Why did you not write that you had him?"

"Why did you not write that you were coming back?" Charmaine retorted, and then relented. "We did not know if we would keep him, that is the truth of it. I was afraid that if I wrote of him, the moment I sent the letter all would go sour."

"But it has not."

"No." Charmaine's mouth twitched again in that hint of a smile. "Not that he has not been plenty of trouble, but he helps Howard and learns quickly."

Valerian followed Charmaine into the kitchen, where her cousin filled a kettle with water for tea and bent to hang it on the hook over the fire. The smells of the cobbler's shop and Charmaine's kitchen comforted her with their familiarity, even as it felt like she had been to the moon and back since last she was here and still felt the unreality of her own presence. "You have rented the cottage?"

"Yes, until summer. You are welcome to stay here with us until then, of course."

"I know. Thank you."

Charmaine turned away from the fire, giving her full attention to Valerian. "Are you home for good?"

Valerian bit her lower lip, unwilling yet to give a definite answer. She was like her cousin, afraid that if she spoke of it, it would come to naught. "I would like to be."

"Nothing has changed since my letter to you. The townsfolk still ask me when you are coming back."

Valerian could only look at Charmaine, the question that mattered most stuck in her throat.

Charmaine studied her back, then said with more softness than Valerian would ever have expected of her, "But it is not the townsfolk that worry you, is it?"

She shook her head.

"The baron is here," Charmaine said. "He has been since the first of January."

Valerian had more than half-expected it, but even so it shocked her, the news like a blow to her chest, the air forced from her lungs. "Has he. . . ." she paused before she could go on, hating herself for needing to know. "Has he asked after me?"

Pity flickered in Charmaine's eyes, and Valerian answered the question herself. "No."

She left the village behind and started down the path that led to the cottage, needing to escape from the familiar faces of Greyfriars. After her tea with Charmaine, she had gone to see Sally and discovered that the news of her return had already spread through the village.

The tentative but sincere greetings she received as she walked down the street were followed quickly by requests for treatment, either for the speaker or someone else, and Valerian realized how correct Charmaine had been in her assessment of the mood in Greyfriars. She could have horns sprouting from her head and cloven feet, and she thought they would still ask her to look at their sores and listen to their coughs. John Torrance's missing hand was a more fearful prospect than dealings with a maybe-witch.

Or perhaps she could thank Alice Torrance for her welcome. The witch-dunking test may have at long last proved her innocence to the entire village, no matter how illogical it was. Whatever the reason for the greetings and smiles of welcome, they were so numerous as to be overwhelming. She almost doubted they would let her leave, if she decided not to stay. It was an unfamiliar, but warming thought.

When she came to the fork in the path, her feet of their own volition took the path that led to the Giving Stone. She was not ready yet to see the cottage, with strangers living in it, rearranging things, doing things differently than she and Theresa had. She did not want to see the garden choked with weeds, or the walls in need of whitewashing. Better, perhaps, to wait until the cottage was hers again, and she could change everything back to how it was.

Oscar cawed and flew by overhead, and she smiled. He looked happy to be back in familiar grounds.

A gust of cold March wind struck her as she came around the final bend to the circle of stones, and she pulled her mantle more tightly about her. The Irish Sea was a grey smudge in the distance, a bank of low clouds obscuring the line between water and sky. The wind and Oscar were the only sounds, buffeting the hills and trees and twisting round the stones. She had almost forgotten how much she loved the rough beauty of this place.

She walked slowly to the Giving Stone, her skirt hem dragging in the damp grass. The stone was bare of offerings, and she sat down upon it, slipping off her muddy shoes and bringing her feet up under the warmth of her skirts, wrapping her arms around her knees. She rested her chin on her kneecaps and half-shut her eyes, listening to the wind, feeling the cold seep into her buttocks from the stone beneath her.

She was dimly aware of Oscar hopping about in the grass, but when he suddenly spoke it startled her out of her reverie.

"Finders keepers! Finders Keepers! Rrrawww!"

She opened her eyes to see him at the base of the stone where she sat, tossing his head, something silvery dangling from his beak. She dropped her legs back over the edge and bent down, reaching for him, but he hopped back, beyond her reach.

"Drop it, Oscar!" she ordered.

"Finders keepers!" He spread his wings, then flapped up into the air, carrying his treasure to the top of his favorite standing stone.

Valerian squinted up at him. She should let him have it, whatever it was, except that for a moment she had thought she recognized the thing.

She stood and went barefoot over to the menhir, and climbed atop the fallen stone beside it. If she stood on tip-toe, she could almost reach the top of Oscar's stone, but not quite. She hiked her skirts, tucking the wet hem into her waistband. She found a foothold in the rough stone and hoisted herself up.

Oscar was surprised enough by her head appearing over the edge of the stone that he fluttered backwards, leaving his treasure trove exposed. Valerian's eyes widened as she took in the trinket-filled depression atop the stone. So *this* was where all that hat trim ended up, along with pieces of glass, coins, fragments of jewelry, and nameless bits of junk. And on top of it all, the silver bracelet.

She plucked the bracelet off the pile and lowered herself down. She stood upon the fallen neighboring stone, skirts still tucked up, wind whipping her mantle, and looked at the bracelet in her hand. It was the same one Nathaniel had offered to her that day almost a year ago, in payment for her pulling the stitches from Paul Carlyle's behind. She traced her finger over one of the flowered ovals, remembering.

"Eee-diot!" Oscar cried. "Eee-diot!"

Valerian sucked in her breath, fist closing over the bracelet as she looked up. Nathaniel stood watching her from the other side of the circle. Her heart beat a rapid tat-too, stars sparkling in her vision as a momentary dizziness swept over her. He was as handsome as ever—more so, even, for there was a quiet certainty in his stance that had not been there before.

Her muscles quivering, it was all she could do to untuck her skirts and let them drop over her legs. To climb down from the rock was beyond her. She stood, swaying slightly in a gust of wind, unable to speak.

"Valerian," he said at last.

"Nathaniel," she whispered back, the sound carried away in the wind.

"You found the bracelet."

She looked down at the links in her hand, then up at him again. "Oscar did, in the grass."

His eyebrows rose, and he smiled slightly, walking forward. "Then he has for once done me a favor. I left it on the stone for you. The last storm must have washed it off."

"You left it for me?" she repeated stupidly, her thoughts frozen in her mind.

He gave a self-conscious shrug, showing his first sign of uncertainty. "Perhaps I am not completely immune to superstition. I thought that if I left it, someday you might come back for it."

Her mouth was dry, hope kindling to life in her breast.

He closed the remaining distance between them, looking up at her where she stood on the stone. "You see, it took me a long time to realize that you did not leave because you cared nothing for me."

"No, it was never that. It was your family, Laetitia. . . ."

"It was more than any of that. Do you not even know yourself?"

She looked down at him, confused, unable to form a coherent thought with him standing beneath her, so close, after all this time and so many hours spent dreaming of him. Why else would she have left him, when it hurt her so badly, if not for Laetitia and his family?

He told her. "You never believed I could love you. You thought that someday I would come to my senses and see what a mistake I had made, and seek to be rid of you. You could not believe I wanted you, just as you are."

"But you did not, not completely," she protested. "You admitted as much."

"I know I did. Like you, and like my family, I could not be sure that Laetitia was not an influence." He wrapped his warm hands around her ankles, then smoothed his hands up her calves. "I know better now. The past is finished, Valerian. Laetitia is dead and buried, as is my part in that affair. It is you I am asking for, not a salve for a guilty conscience. We can be husband and wife, or we can be distant acquaintances, but nothing in between."

"And your family?" she could not help but ask, remembering the bitter, angry face of his mother.

"This is our choice to make. Raven Hall is my home now. Make it yours."

His hazel eyes were deep with emotion, unclouded by doubt or the shadows from his past. He was right, she knew: She had thought he could never truly love her. Had thought that no one could, beyond her parents and Aunt Theresa. She felt the cold shield she had worn around her heart split asunder, the broken halves melting in the heat of the emotion that welled forth.

"I do love you," she said at last. "I always have." She held out the bracelet that she had once so angrily rejected. "Will you help me with the clasp?"

She smiled as comprehension lit his eyes, and then she yelped as he pulled her down off the rock and into his arms, spinning with her in mad circles within the circle of stones. At last he stopped, and she tucked her face against his chest, her arms around his neck, feeling her world complete within this warm embrace.

"Ah, Lady Ravenall," he said into her hair. "I love you, too."